THE OLD BATTL

It all starts with a lie. M___ _____ sister Madge has come back from Europe for a visit, but is found dead on the sidewalk outside the gate the next morning. Mrs. Herriott is only trying to protect her sister's reputation when she tells the police that she has no idea who the dead woman is. But one lie leads to another. Silas, her chauffeur, aids her in the lie. Her niece Carla even dresses up like her sister to continue the deception. But why is everyone trying to keep Madge's death such a secret? Before long Mrs. Herriott is caught up in a web of deception that seems to have no end. In this world of lies, is there anyone who can be trusted? And more importantly, is there anyone who *should* be trusted?

DARK POWER

Diana Leonard comes to the Chalet at the invitation of her long-lost uncle, but soon finds that her visions of a family reunion are shattered by feelings of dread and suspicion. Her Aunt Emma is a stern, domineering woman, a professor of psychology who conducts experiments on two cretin children who live with her. Uncle Peter himself is either a fool or a sadist, and Di can't figure out which. Their son, her cousin Miles, is a guilt-ridden alcoholic, his confidence long ago destroyed by his manipulating mother. And then there's her grandfather Rufus, a rich eccentric who comes to stay but who spends every moment in fear for his life from the rest of the family. It will take every ounce of Diana's courage to survive her stay in the Chalet—and an even greater act of will to survive her family.

ELISABETH SANXAY HOLDING BIBLIOGRAPY

Invincible Minnie (1920)

Rosaleen Among the Artists (1921)

Angelica (1921)

The Unlit Lamp (1922)

The Shoals of Honour (1926)

The Silk Purse (1928)

Miasma (1929)

Dark Power (1930)

The Death Wish (1934)

The Unfinished Crime (1935)

The Strange Crime in Bermuda (1937)

The Obstinate Murderer [aka No Harm Intended] (1938)

Who's Afraid [aka Trial by Murder] (1940)

The Girl Who Had to Die (1940)

Speak of the Devil [aka Hostess to Murder] (1941)

Killjoy [aka Murder is a Kill-Joy] (1941)

Lady Killer (1942)

The Old Battle-Ax (1943)

Net of Cobwebs (1945)

The Innocent Mrs. Duff (1946)

The Blank Wall (1947)

Miss Kelly (1947)

Too Many Bottles [aka The Party Was the Pay-Off] (1950)

The Virgin Huntress (1951)

Widow's Mite (1952)

THE OLD BATTLE-AX

+++

DARK POWER

TWO COMPLETE
MYSTERY NOVELS BY
ELISABETH
SANXAY
HOLDING

**STARK
HOUSE**

Stark House Press • Eureka California
www.StarkHousePress.com

THE OLD BATTLE-AX / DARK POWER

Published by Stark House Press
1315 H Street
Eureka, CA 95501
griffinskye3@sbcglobal.net
www.starkhousepress.com

Cover design & book layout by Mark Shepard, www.shepgraphics.com
Proofreading by Rick Ollerman

First Stark House Press Edition: November 2008

Reprint Edition

INTRODUCTION

We have the Depression to thank for Elisabeth Sanxay Holding's career as a mystery author. Until 1929, she had been writing serious, mainstream novels like *Rosaleen Among the Artists*, *Angelica*, *The Unlit Lamp* and *The Shoals of Honour*. She published six novels before the Depression, starting with *Invincible Minnie* in 1920, and ending with *The Silk Purse* in 1928. Early critics noted her expert characterization, and in the *New York Times* review of *The Silk Purse*, the reviewer said: "They are as real a collection of peoples as ever said yes when they wished to heaven they could say no."

So when the Depression hit in 1929 and she was no longer able to sell her leisurely character novels, Holding turned to writing mysteries. Or, more properly, suspense novels. Because, simply put, Elisabeth Sanxay Holding is the precursor to the entire women's psychological suspense genre, and authors like Patricia Highsmith and Ruth Rendell owe her a very large debt of gratitude.

Holding was one of the first to write mystery novels that didn't so much ask whodunit, but whydunit? In fact, we know whodunit because it's quite often the main character. It's the "why" that is always the most important part of her books. The psychological underpinnings of her novels form the basis of the mystery. Her characters always act from a very determined point of view. Whether from guilt, discontent, deception, misconception, or even pure altruism, they act out their dramas with very little consideration for other points of view. And therein lies the conflict. They have all got blinders on, seeing just what they want to see, each with their own misguided agenda. They lie when it will get them in the most trouble and tell the truth when it's in their own worst interest. In other words, her characters feel very real to us—we believe in them.

A rich, alcoholic husband grows tired of his well-meaning but lower-class wife. Everything she does irritates him. He decides he must get rid of her but his drinking is making him delusional and easily annoyed. Who can he trust? As he rushes from one hidden bottle, one seedy bar to another, the answer is clearly "no one." When his chauffeur comes to him with a plan to catch his wife with another man, he jumps at it. After all, sooner or later you've got to trust somebody.

This is the basic plot of *The Innocent Mrs. Duff*. What makes the book so compelling is the degree to which Holding gets under the skin of this self-deluded man. She wrote the story in a crisp, staccato style and makes the reader feel every bit of the scheming husband's mounting alcoholic mania.

Though casual drinking was more a part of the daily lifestyle in Holding's day, she wasn't afraid to shed some light on its darker aspects. In fact, she had previously explored the theme of the alcoholic male in the The Obstinate Murderer—albeit more sympathetically—and clearly knew this personality well.

The Innocent Mrs. Duff and The Blank Wall (filmed twice, as The Reckless Moment in 1949 and The Deep End in 2001) are arguably two of her best works and the only two novels of Holding's that remain in print, thanks to Academy Chicago. Dell published several of her novels in paperback in the 50's, and Mercury published a few in digest form as well. And back in the 1960's, Ace Books published twelve of her books as Ace Doubles. But since then she has almost entirely gone out of print. A sad state of affairs for an author whom Raymond Chandler called "the top suspense writer of them all" in a letter to his British publisher.

All in all, Holding published eighteen suspense novels in her lifetime, beginning with Miasma in 1929, and ending with Widow's Mite in 1952. Many of these novels were also serialized in national magazines, and almost all were published in paperback and foreign editions, as well as by mystery book clubs. She also published quite a few short stories in magazines ranging from McCall's, American Magazine and Ladies' Home Journal to Alfred Hitchcock's Mystery Magazine, The Saint, Ellery Queen's Mystery Magazine and The Magazine of Fantasy and Science Fiction. She even wrote a children's story, Miss Kelly, the story of a cat who could understand and speak human, and who comes to the aid of a terrified tiger.

Elisabeth Sanxay was born in Brooklyn in 1889, the descendant of an upper middle class family, and was educated in a series of private schools, specifically Whitcombe's School, The Packer Institute, Miss Botsford's School and the Staten Island Academy. She married a British diplomat named George E. Holding in 1913 and together they traveled widely in South America and the Caribbean, settling in Bermuda for awhile where her husband was a government officer. She also raised two daughters, Skeffington and Antonia, the latter of whom married Peter Schwed (until his recent death the executor of Holding's estate and a retired author and publisher with Simon and Schuster).

Holding was thirty-one when her first book was published. Right from the beginning she introduced the theme of discontent that she was to use so often in her mystery books. Invincible Minnie starts off slowly—telling at first when it should be showing—but evolves into a fairly lurid tale, the compelling story of a headstrong woman who uses sex to control men and get her way. There's no pat, happy ending either. Minnie runs roughshod over everyone, including her sister and children, and prevails through sheer determination. Holding's lean 40's style was only seen in glimpses in this first effort, but her characterizations were already taking shape in the relentless actions of Minnie and the various people she controlled.

With her second novel, Holding lets the story tell itself, vastly improving over the style of her first book. *Rosaleen Among the Artists,* a bit less melodramatic than *Invincible Minnie,* tells the story of a self-sacrificing young woman struggling to survive and find love in New York City. Though polished off with a sweeter ending, there is much travail as Rosaleen hits rock bottom before finally being united with her soul mate, Mr. Landry. In fact, the two are so matched in the stubbornness with which they hold onto their ideals—tenaciously sacrificing their own happiness at every turn— that they almost wear each other out by the end of the book. Ironically, it is their own principles that almost kill their only chance at love.

In 1929, when the Depression killed her mainstream career, Holding had to do something to help support her two daughters. She could have started writing nice, cozy romantic mysteries. But she just didn't have it in her. The characters she was creating were too contrary, too impulsive—too flawed—and not particularly romantic. They didn't act in their own best interests, holding onto ideals that invariably precipitated trouble. It's as if they felt compelled to do the very thing that caused the most havoc, even if for all the best reasons.

As a consequence, the mystery novels Holding began to write were dark affairs, having more in common with noir than standard detective fiction. It's easy to understand why she was such a favorite of Chandler's. Murder and mania are always lurking in the wings—and the menace doesn't always exist from the outside, but is quite often found from within. These are characters with something to hide. Sometimes there is a happy ending, sometimes not. Sometimes there is a detective, but he's usually as clueless as everyone else. You might say that Holding's characters are quite often lucky if they can make it to the last page with their health, if not their sanity, intact.

In *The Virgin Huntress* we follow young Monty on V-Day as he meets an older woman, Dona Luisa, and is brought into a world of class and culture he had always dreamed of. He is a charming if somewhat insecure young man, somewhat expedient—perhaps too expedient—in his past dealings with women. In fact, he is constantly nagged by secrets from his past, secrets that begin to fracture him as Dona Luisa's niece Rose begins to pry into his past life. By the end of the short novel, Monty has become completely unraveled, the victim of his own expediency. It's not a pretty portrait.

Another of Holding's favorite themes involves fractious family relationships and domestic disputes. *Dark Power* is a perfect example. In the first chapter we meet a young lady, Diana, who discovers that she is quite penniless and soon to be out on the street. Before this happens, however, she is suddenly rescued by an eccentric uncle she didn't know she had. He happily escorts her back to the family home, where she meets such a thoroughly dysfunctional collection of relatives that by the end of the book she barely makes it out alive.

Holding also loved to examine the way stress works on characters, particularly middle-aged men, and would combine this with her theme of domestic disharmony. *The Innocent Mrs. Duff* is an obvious example, but *The Death Wish* is another in which a man, Mr. Delancey, who had always thought himself happily married, comes to a moment of crisis in which he discovers that he actually hates his wife. She has slowly been emasculating him by controlling his purse strings, but when his best friend reveals a similar domestic situation and announces his plans to kill his own wife, Delancey is plunged into a world of self-doubt. At first he is shocked by his friend's confession, and when the wife is found drowned, he hopes that it is the accident that it seems to be. But a seed has been planted, and nothing in his formerly phlegmatic life will ever be the same.

Holding's deft hand at characterization makes all these situations ring true, giving them a psychological perspective that not only presents all her characters' foibles sympathetically, but creates the tension that propels her story along as well. Their actions are understandable, given the circumstances, and all the more frustrating because they are so identifiable. In *The Death Wish*, we watch Delancey try to convince himself at first that his wife is simply moody and a bit insecure. He wants to think the best of her. But the reader knows that his wife's insecure nagging is stifling him, her words little barbs that sink in and latch Delancey to her side, subtly but firmly controlling him. We feel his weakness and frustration, his mounting domestic horror, and nothing that proceeds from this realization seems anything less than inevitable. Not even murder.

This is Holding's true forte, that she can make the commonplace, the ordinary, so horrific and so suspenseful. But make no mistake, whether writing about dysfunctional families or failed marriages, her books are full of mystery. In *Lady Killer*, a young recently-wedded ex-model named Honey is on a cruise ship in the Caribbean with her older husband, who is turning out to be a fussy, fault-finding old crab. At the same time that she begins to realize that a life with this man will be completely intolerable, she also becomes aware that the man in the next cabin might possibly be trying to kill his wife. She begins to set about a campaign to protect this poor, plain and unfortunate woman, who doesn't really seem to want her help. In fact, no one on board seems to feel that Honey has any business stirring up trouble.

But the more Honey finds out, the more mysterious her fellow passengers begin to seem to her. Even her own husband begins to seem alien to her. And when she finds a body, even that isn't quite what it seems. But still the little mysteries pile up, and we are swept up in Honey's suspicions and doubts until even we begin to believe, like her, that *no one* is to be trusted.

Miasma presents us with another set of mysteries. A young doctor named Dennison has just about reached the end of his financial resources when he is contacted by a wealthy older doctor in town who wants him to take up residency in his house and assume the care of his patients. All well and good, except that the doctor's young nurse immediately warns Dennison to leave, mysterious patients come and go in the middle of the night, and his predecessor has gone missing. And then there is the weird drug that the older doctor prescribes to certain of his patients, one of whom is now dead from an apparent heart attack. Holding keeps the mysteries coming until both we and Dennison are wondering what the hell is going on here; daring us to put the book down no matter how late it is and how early we have to get up the next morning.

And then there is her rarest mystery, *Strange Crime in Bermuda,* a peculiar tale of a missing person on an enclosed island community. Young Hamish is asked to journey to Bermuda at the request of his old friend Malloy, but when he arrives, Malloy sets an appointment to meet him and then fails to show up for their meeting. It soon turns out that no one has seen the man that day, but everyone has a different idea of what has happened to him. A sense of confusion and dread sets in as we experience the unfolding events from Hamish's stubborn, narrow point of view. Hamish is continually misled by his various misguided allegiances, until he himself becomes the prime suspect. The resolution is both obvious and unexpected.

There is a reason that Dorothy B. Hughes said that "connoisseurs will continue their rush when each new Holding reaches publication." Her books are first and foremost very readable. Not only are they excellent examples of psychological suspense and first rate character studies, they move along at a nice, brisk pace. Holding was never one for overwriting. Her dialog always sounds just right, all the doubtful pauses and self-serving/self-deceptive lies in place. We may not always like these characters, but Holding makes us feel compelled to keep reading about them.

Elisabeth Sanxay Holding's mystery novels have been out of print far too long. Until her death in 1955, she was one of the best, and it is a pleasure to be able to bring her books back into print again, many of which have been unavailable in any edition for well over sixty years. It's time to rediscover Elisabeth Sanxay Holding. Her books may have gone out of print, but they have never gone out of fashion.

Gregory Shepard
Publisher, Stark House Press
September, 2003

The Old Battle-Ax
By Elisabeth Sanxay Holding

To Bertha March
who laughed when she heard this title

CHAPTER ONE

Mrs. Herriott stood behind the barrier among a little crowd of people, all facing toward the pier that stretched before them vast and dim and strangely quiet. For some time the passengers had been coming down the gangway, but they stayed there, far away; there was no bustle, no stir.

But it's not really—queer, Mrs. Herriott told herself. Naturally, with that horrible war in Europe, there must be all sorts of new rules and regulations. She herself had had some experience with that; she was not allowed a dock pass, no one would even tell her when the ship was expected. It was Silas who had found that out, in some way of his own, and he had driven her in to New York, just in time. If it hadn't been for Silas, she thought, there'd have been no one here to meet Madge. Think of coming home after twenty-five years and finding no one....

She had taken pains with her appearance today; a tall, slight woman, drooping forward a little from the waist, with fine gray eyes, dark-lashed, and abundant dark hair threaded with gray; there was an absent-minded jauntiness about her in her belted blue suit and her new three-cornered hat. I don't want Madge to be disappointed in me, she thought, Only, naturally I've changed a great deal.

But she had no picture in her mind of how she had looked twenty-five years ago, and she did not really know quite how she looked now, at fifty. She was simply Mrs. Herriott, and nobody looked at her particularly. Madge must have changed, too, she thought. She's forty-eight. It's hard to realize that.

The last time she had seen her sister had been on another pier, but in an atmosphere so different it was like a memory from the Golden Age. Madge had been a bride then, sailing off to France, where her new husband had a very good position in the Paris branch of his uncle's business. All the wedding party had gone on board; they had had champagne in the young couple's suite, and to this day Mrs. Herriott could remember how Madge had looked then, in a fawn-colored suit and a wide pale-blue hat turned up behind her soft pompadour; how lovely she had looked and how happy, in her sweet, shy way.

Her longing to see Madge rose in a wave; her throat contracted. *It's almost too good to be true,* she thought, and not for the first time. Fragments of her childhood's training came back to her. Don't set your heart on a thing too much, Miss Sharley.... We must be prepared for disappointments in this world, dear.... She had been told, by her parents, by nurses, by teachers, that life was a sorry affair, once you were grown up and it really began. And she had found it so. Maybe Madge hasn't come, she thought.

I wanted this too much, she thought. Ever since she had got Madge's letter with the news that she was coming home, she had been too happy. You must be prepared for the worst.

Two men were coming down the gangway, carrying a stretcher, and followed by a trained nurse. That's Madge, Mrs. Herriott told herself with a sickening pang. I know it. You *feel* those things. As soon as I got here, I had a feeling that something was wrong. That's Madge.

They were coming toward the barrier, and she had to be ready. It may be some quite minor accident, she thought. Madge may have slipped on the deck and sprained her ankle. That often happens on ships. Or perhaps it's just weakness, exhaustion, after all she's been through in Europe. But now that she's home, where I can look after her....

The stretcher was coming nearer. Her gloved hands tightened on the rail of the barrier, her breath came fast. It was here. She leaned forward and looked down into the stern and noble face of a man with a black beard and a skullcap. His black eyes looked straight into hers, and she moved back, abashed.

The other passengers were coming now: two men, carrying their own bags, walking in a quick, preoccupied, businesslike way; a stout woman all in black, wandering about, carrying a big oilskin valise.

"Mama!" shouted a man's voice behind Mrs. Herriott, and someone tried to push forward.

"Step back to the waiting room to meet passengers," said a pale steward.

The stout woman had stopped at the sound of that cry, and stood there, dazed; the steward took her by the elbow and edged her forward.

"Sharley?" said another voice.

Mrs. Herriott turned her head; her gray eyes narrowed, her lips parted. Then she straightened her shoulders.

"Madge..." she said. "We'll have to meet in the waiting room, Madge. Go straight ahead and I'll meet you there."

Turning, she began to make her way politely through the crowd. Excuse me.... Excuse me.... Madge was there before her; she threw her arms around her sister and a cloud of musky perfume enveloped Mrs. Herriott. Then they stood back and looked at each other.

A woman, childishly thin and flat, in a scanty black suit, a little yellow hat, a glow of rouge on her hollow cheeks, long bright-gold hair almost to her shoulders, tired eyes beneath purple lids; that was Madge.

"Madge.... How are you?"

"Oh, I don't know... it's been such a nightmare." She paused. "Sharley," she said, with a giggle, "you look like George Washington!"

"Do I?" said Mrs. Herriott, with a hasty smile. "I'll get Silas now, Madge, and he'll look after your baggage."

"I haven't anything but these two bags. Who's Silas?"

"I've written you about him, Madge. You remember the Polks, in Carbury—"

"Sharley, for God's sake! I haven't been in Carbury or even given it a thought for a million years. I don't remember anything."

"Well, Silas Polk drives my car for me."

"Oh, your chauffeur."

"Silas is a great deal more than a chauffeur—" Mrs. Herriott began.

"Sharley, what goes on?" cried Madge, with a laugh.

"Oh..." Mrs. Herriott said, aghast. Then she recovered herself. "Let's go down now, Madge. I'll take your bags."

"You take one. I'll keep this one."

They got into the elevator and descended; they went out into the street in the dusty spring sunshine. Silas got out of the car and came toward them, lean and haughty in his tan uniform, his chin up, his neck rigid.

"Madge," said Mrs. Herriott, "this is Silas Polk. Silas, here's Miss Madge— Mrs. de Belleforte now."

He touched his visored cap and said nothing; Madge looked at him and said nothing either. He took the bags and put them into the front of the car, and Mrs. Herriott and her sister got into the back.

"Where are we going, Sharley?" asked Madge.

"Why, home, Madge. To Carbury."

"Sharley! You're *not* trying to whisk me out there, the moment I land!"

"But that's where I live now, Madge. I wrote you long ago—and you've written to me there."

"I know. But I don't want to go there *now*. I want to stay in New York and look up people. Jeff Quillen, and dozens and dozens of people. I want to go shopping."

"Yes, of course," said Mrs. Herriott. "But I thought you'd like a little rest first, Madge. A nice little quiet time...."

"That's the last thing I want," said Madge. "I want to go to one of the good hotels, Sharley, and I want to have a hell of a time."

Oh, not now, Madge, my poor Madge, thought Mrs. Herriott. Her sister's nails were rimmed with black, her neck was grimy, her shoes were broken. But it wasn't only that; that could have been overlooked in someone just arriving from the war zone. There was something rakish and tawdry about Madge, something almost incredible in a Pendleton. She mustn't burst upon people—like this, Mrs. Herriott thought. It would give such a completely false impression.

For the greater part of her life she had been obliged to manage people. It did not come easy to her; she did not have a managing nature, but she had learned from necessity a few little arts.

"Of course you can come back to New York the moment you want," she said. "But I thought a good night's sleep in the country air—and my hairdresser could come in tomorrow morning—"

Madge shrugged her shoulders.

"All right," she said. "I dare say I'll look better after a good night's sleep.

But for God's sake, stop somewhere and let me have a drink."

"You mean—water, Madge?" Mrs. Herriott asked anxiously.

"Water?" Madge repeated, and laughed. "No. I want a nice cold American cocktail and I want it quick."

"Silas," said Mrs. Herriott, "do you know any place near here where we can get cocktails?"

"No, I don't know this part of the town, Mrs. Herriott."

"Oh, a bar, a hotel, the first halfway decent place you see," said Madge impatiently, and leaning forward she closed the glass partition behind him. "I never saw such an uncouth chauffeur."

"Madge, you must remember the Polks—when we used to go to Carbury to visit Grandfather Pendleton. Old Mr. Polk bad a boat yard, don't you remember? They're one of the oldest families in Carbury."

"This must be one of the oldest cars in the United States."

"Well, it's not new," said Mrs. Herriott, "but it's a very good car, Madge. The only drawback is, it does use a great deal of gasoline."

"You're lucky to have any," said Madge. "Before I left France—"

She lit a cigarette and began to smoke in quick puffs; a nervous way, Mrs. Herriott thought. If this reunion was—not very satisfactory, that was the reason. Madge was nervous and tired, worn out.

"How did you leave Pascal, Madge?" she asked.

Her sister glanced quickly at her.

"Didn't you get my letter? About Pascal?"

"Why no."

"He got pneumonia and died, poor soul," said Madge.

"But Madge, how dreadful!"

"Everything's dreadful," said Madge.

And now Madge was a widow—for the second time. Mrs. Herriott had never seen even a snapshot of Pascal de Belleforte, the second husband, but Madge had written about him often and affectionately. She had mentioned him in her last letter, written not three months ago. But the Pendletons never show their feelings much, Mrs. Herriott said to herself. Later on, Madge will want to talk about Pascal.

The car stopped and Silas slid back the glass.

"Here's a bar," he said. "This do?"

Mrs. Herriott looked out and saw a dingy little place on the corner of a street unfamiliar to her.

"But it's just a saloon," she said. "We'd better go uptown, Silas—"

"This is good enough," said Madge and opened the door and got out. Mrs. Herriott followed her across the pavement and through the swing door. She had been in cocktail lounges, but never before in a place like this. There were no other women in here, only men, rough-looking men, wearing their hats and caps; there was one standing at the bar in his shirt sleeves and suspenders.

"Oh, don't go to the bar, Madge!" she said. "Look! There are some little tables."

"All right," said Madge and sat down at a table. "I can't imagine what you'd take to drink, Sharley. A strawberry soda?"

"I think I'll have a Martini, Madge."

"Bring two double Martinis," Madge said to the waiter. "Extra-dry and no olives.

"I don't really want a double, Madge—"

"Then don't drink it."

"But there's no use paying—"

"I'll pay for it," said Madge. "I'm not poor, Sharley. That's one thing you needn't worry about. I won't be a burden on you."

"I never thought that," Mrs. Herriott said, as evenly as she could. "I thought you'd come and stay with me and share what I had."

"Thanks," said Madge, and was silent for a moment. "You know, Sharley," she said, "you haven't changed much. Except in looks. You've let your looks go, terribly."

"Do you think so?" said Mrs. Herriott. "Well, after all, Madge, I'm fifty years old. I can't expect—"

"You never did expect anything much," said Madge. "That's just the trouble. You married a perfect stuffed shirt—"

"Please, Madge...! James was a very fine man, and we were very happy."

"You never were in love with him," said Madge. "I knew that, even before you married him. I don't believe you've *ever* been in love, Sharley."

"Please, Madge...! I'd rather not discuss that."

Madge shrugged her shoulders, and then the drinks came, those big unseemly drinks. And at the same moment there was a burst of music, astonishingly loud, with a rollicking thumping rhythm. That must be one of those juke boxes, Mrs. Herriott thought. It's horrible. It makes your head ache.

It was necessary to talk.

"Carla is looking forward so much to seeing you, Madge," she said.

"Carla?"

"You can't have forgotten your own brother's child, Madge!"

"My dear Sharley, I never saw Ed's child. I've had two husbands in Europe, and Pascal had brothers and sisters and God knows how many cousins and so on. Anyhow, I thought Ed's daughter was called Charlotte, after you."

"She likes to be called Carla."

"Is she pretty?"

"She's quite a beautiful girl," said Mrs. Herriott.

"Well, that's something," said Madge. "Ed was good-looking—in a pompous sort of way. How long ago was it that he came to Paris? Ten years ago—twelve—I don't know. He disapproved of Europe and he disap-

proved of my taking a Frenchman *en secondes noces*. But when they met, he
and Pascal got on beautifully. Because Pascal disapproved of even more
things than Ed did."

She slipped off her jacket and spread it over the back of the chair; she
was wearing a transparent yellow blouse through which was very visible
some undergarment of black satin and lace. It looked appalling to Mrs.
Herriott.

"Ah!" said Madge, finishing her drink. "I feel better now."

"That's good," said Mrs. Herriott. "You look rather delicate, Madge."

"Strong as an ox," said Madge, and leaned back, looking at her sister.
"After I've rested up a bit, you'll be surprised to see how young I look." She
paused a moment. "I'm going to marry again, Sharley," she said.

She said it with defiance, but Mrs. Herriott refused to accept the challenge.

"I see," she murmured.

"I want to see Jeff Quillen as soon as I can," Madge went on, in the same
defiant tone. "I made a will when I was in Lisbon, waiting, you know, and
I sent it to him air mail. I hope he got it."

"I hope so," said Mrs. Herriott.

"Pascal left me quite well off," said Madge. "He was very clever about
financial things. Long before the war, he started investing money over
here, and now there's something like two hundred thousand dollars waiting for me."

"That's a very nice sum," said Mrs. Herriott. She *would not* criticize
Madge, even in her own mind, and that meant that she had, in a way, to
stop thinking and simply listen.

"I'm leaving it all to Ramon," said Madge, looking straight at her sister.
But Mrs. Herriott never turned a hair.

"Waiter!" said Madge. "Another double Martini."

"Madge!" said Mrs. Herriott, in spite of herself.

"La-la-la!" said Madge, laughing. She pushed back her chair and sat side-
ways, crossing her legs that were thin as matchsticks in black stockings full
of runs and dreadful wornout sandals. "You needn't worry about me,
Sharley. I know how much I can take."

The juke box began another tune, loud and slow and lumbering.

"A tango," said Madge, dreamily. "Ramon's the most divine dancer.... He's
so sweet to me.... But you won't like him... you'll simply loathe him."

"I hope I shan't. I don't see why I should."

"Because you're so painfully American, darling."

"Madge, you're an American yourself—"

"No, I'm not. I've been away too long. I don't like American ways. I'm not
democratic."

"Madge, this is your own country, where you were born and brought up,
and your ancestors—"

"I said you looked like George Washington," said Madge, with a laugh, "and now you're talking like him. Please don't! It's bad enough to be here, without *that*."

"All right," said Mrs. Herriott, after a moment. "I won't."

CHAPTER TWO

It was dusk when they turned into Chestnut Street, in the little Long Island town, a shabby street of small wooden houses. Mrs. Herriott's house on the corner rose high above all the rest, narrow and ugly, in a garden surrounded by a picket fence. A warm glow shone through the fanlight, and on the top floor there was one bleak and twinkling light. That meant that Josie was up there, dressing.

"Here we are, Madge," said Mrs. Herriott. "Madge, dear, wake up."

But Madge leaned back in a corner and did not open her eyes.

"Madge, you must wake up now."

"Won't," said Madge, thickly. "Let me alone."

The car stopped, and Silas got out and opened the door.

"Miss Madge is exhausted," said Mrs. Herriott. "Here's my key, Silas. We needn't disturb Josie if you'll help me to get her in."

They pushed and pulled Madge, but she resisted them, stubbornly pretending to be asleep. If only none of the neighbors are looking out of their windows, thought Mrs. Herriott. She went ahead and unlocked the door, and Silas, with his arm around Madge's waist, got her into the hall.

"We'll help Miss Madge up to her room, Silas," Mrs. Herriott said, very low.

"No!" said Madge, and sat down on the bottom step.

Silas stooped and lifted her, over his shoulder, and she began to giggle. He carried her up the stairs and into the room that was all ready for her, and Mrs. Herriott turned on the top light. Silas laid Madge down on the bed, and she sat up at once and clasped his arm with both hands, looking up into his face and giggling again. She said something to him in French that Mrs. Herriott did not understand; whether Silas understood it or not she did not know. He made no answer.

"Madge," said Mrs. Herriott, "take a little nap before dinner—"

Madge spoke to her in French, still holding Silas' arm.

"Silas has work to do now, Madge," she said.

But Madge, still held his arm and kept on talking to him in French. Mrs. Herriott turned to him, and it gave her a shock to see that he was smiling. She took her sister's hands and unloosed them.

"Close the door after you, please, Silas," she said.

When Silas had gone, Mrs. Herriott lit a lamp and turned off the top light and drew down the shades.

"Now! That's cozier, isn't it, Madge?"

Madge would not speak a word of English. Mrs. Herriott sat down on the bed and took off her sister's shoes, so shapeless, so worn, and her stockings full of holes and runs. Think what Madge has been through, she said to herself. Who could blame her for being a little—trying?

But I'll get her well, she thought, with a sort of passion. I'll see that she's not bothered by anything or anybody until she's rested. I'll see that she gets the best of food and care. She's my own sister; I'm the one who ought to understand her best and help her. She has every right to expect that of me. I don't *care* if she's a little trying, just now. She's so tired.

"Have you a dressing gown, Madge?" she asked.

She heard the word *oui* in the answer, so she opened one of her sister's bags. There was a black chiffon nightgown in it and a black chiffon negligee, very sheer, with a bow of magenta velvet hanging to the front by a thread—a crumpled and disreputable garment.

"I'll find you something more comfortable, Madge," she said, and went out, closing the door behind her.

Josie was coming down the stairs, a pretty, rosy, dark-haired little things in spectacles.

"Oh, is Mme de Belleforte here, Mrs. Herriott?" she asked, eagerly.

"Yes. But she's exhausted, Josie. She wants to rest."

"May I just stop in and say a word to her, Mrs. Herriott?"

"Well, not just now, Josie," said Mrs. Herriott. She was sorry to see the disappointment in Josie's face. No wonder she's disappointed, she thought. She's heard so much about Madge. And, of course, she's like one of the family.

Poor Josie... she came from a small town in Rhode Island, from a family of French stock, thrifty and respectable people, but without her ambition. She had got a scholarship at Barnard and had worked in a bookshop; she had worked as a waitress in the summer; she had meant to go on until she got her M.A.

In her third year at college she had met Silas, and they had got married after a very brief courtship. Silas had been a junior at Columbia; their families had very much disapproved of the marriage. But James had been willing to help them: James had believed in people marrying young. Silas and Josie had taken a little apartment near the University; they had been living such a pleasant cheerful life, with plenty of friends, going to concerts and lectures and dances. Then that summer Silas had had his dreadful accident. He had broken his neck, diving. Poor Silas. Poor Josie.

"I thought Mme de Belleforte might like it if I spoke a few words to her in French," said Josie, still hurt. "I thought it might make her feel more at home."

"I'm sure it would, Josie," said Mrs. Herriott. "When she's a little bit rested."

She went into her own room and from a closet there took a handsome gray crepe kimono with a silver dragon embroidered on it—a present from James, long ago. She took this in to her sister and helped her off with her

dress. The black underwear was even worse than she had expected: a little black satin brassiere, and then nothing at all until the waistband of a
horrid black satin petticoat with bright-pink satin hearts bordering a lace
ruffle; pink garters, no girdle.

"Would you like a cup of tea, Madge?"

"God, no" said Madge.

Well, it was something to hear her speak English again, anyhow.

"There's plenty of nice hot water, Madge. Shall I start a bath for you?"

"No. I'm too tired."

"You'll just want to wash your hands and face—"

"No, I don't."

"Madge, I'd advise you to. On account of germs, you know."

"Oh, let me alone!" cried Madge. "I want to go to sleep."

Mrs. Herriott went into her own room and shutting the door sat down
on the edge of the bed. All this doesn't amount to anything at all, she told
herself. I'm a little tired myself, I dare say, and that's apt to make you
depressed. But by tomorrow, after we've both had a good night's sleep,
everything will be very different. *Very* different. We'll have a good old-
fashioned talk tomorrow. And later we'll go shopping together, and see our
old friends.... I really understand how Madge feels. I want to be let alone
myself—for a little while.

But in less than a little while there was a knock at the door, sharp and
startling. Poor Josie always knocked like that.

"Come in!" said Mrs. Herriott, and Josie entered, full of anxiety.

"Oh, Mrs. Herriott! Ferdy's just come. I'd better send him away, hadn't
I?"

"Why, no, Josie, of course not."

"But with Mme de Belleforte here...?"

"That won't make any difference, Josie."

"I wouldn't want to think that Ferdy was a nuisance to anyone, Mrs.
Herriott."

"Oh, but he isn't, Josie!" said Mrs. Herriott.

Only he was. He always had been and he was never likely to be anything
else. It was wrong to feel like that about the boy; he could not help it if he
was not very bright. Certainly he tried; every now and then, before an
examination, he would come out to Carbury with his schoolbooks, and his
devoted sister Josie would sit up half the night, helping him with unfail-
ing patience. Then she would get up an hour earlier to wash a shirt for
him, to press his suit, to darn his socks. I won't take *your* time, Mrs. Herriott, she said.

It seemed that Ferdy, youngest of Josie's large family, had by his far from
brilliant progress in school displeased the severe and autocratic father who
had repudiated Josie when she married. Ferdy had been sent to live with
an aunt in New York, and she was none too fond of him.

"It's very nice to have Ferdy here, Josie," said Mrs. Herriott. "Maybe he'll mend the gate for me."

"He'd be *glad* to, Mrs. Herriott."

Whenever Ferdy came, Mrs. Herriott tried to find some little job for him to do, as a pretext for giving him a dollar. She knew he needed pocket money.

"I'll come down and speak to Ferdy," she said.

It's only decent to do that, she thought, while she took off her shoes and put on purple felt slippers. He hasn't any real home, poor child.

Ferdy was sitting at the kitchen table eating an apple while he bent over an open book. As Mrs. Herriott entered he pushed back his chair slowly and rose, a short and stocky boy in a white shirt strained too tight across his thick chest and baggy knickerbockers halfway down his stumpy legs. Quite a good-looking boy, in a way, but his black hair was too long and too oily-looking. And he was always so gloomy.

"How are you getting on in school, Ferdy?" asked Mrs. Herriott.

"Why, I'd have been all right, Mrs. Herriott," he answered, grieved and affronted, "only they're not *fair.* The teachers don't mark the papers in a fair way. If they get a down on you, why, they'll pick on the littlest tiniest thing and call it a mistake and take maybe ten off for a thing that if they liked you they wouldn't even *notice.*"

"Well, if you keep on working hard, I'm sure..." said Mrs. Herriott, with vague benevolence.

"I do work hard, Mrs. Herriott, only there's two teachers that have a down on me."

"Well, maybe they'll change," said Mrs. Herriott. "Maybe they'll realize how hard you try, Ferdy."

"But even the teacher who's so unfair to him had to praise his recitation," said Josie, proudly. "Ferdy, recite that speech for Mrs. Herriott."

"Oh, she doesn't want to hear that," said Ferdy, giving her a sidelong glance.

"Indeed I do!" said Mrs. Herriott.

For many years she had been hearing Ferdy recite; she had heard him play selections from Italian operas—good long ones—on the harmonica. He could be very dramatic.

He looked up at the ceiling; he moistened his lips and began:
Friends, Romans, countrymen, lend me your ears;
I come to bury Caesar, not to praise him.
The evil that men do lives after them;
The good—

The doorbell rang and he stopped; Josie went out into the hall and Mrs. Herriott felt that she was justified in looking after Josie. In a moment Carla came into the kitchen.

"Aunt Sharley," she said, "I'm so excited about seeing Aunt Madge...."

She did not look excited; she was pale as usual, blonde, delicate, aloof;

there was no expression on her lovely face except that her arched brows gave her a faintly disdainful look. She was weaving a pale-blue rayon suit, a little fancy, and a wide pale-blue felt hat: cheap clothes, poor child.

"And here's Ferdy," said Mrs. Herriott.

"Oh, hello," said Carla, without enthusiasm. "Can I run up and see Aunt Madge now, Aunt Sharley?"

"She's resting now, Carla. She said she wanted to sleep."

It was going to be very difficult to explain Madge's tiredness to Carla; it was never easy to explain anything to Carla. She was twenty-three, but she seemed much younger, perhaps because of her angel blondness, perhaps because of her shy, stiff manner. That manner, Mrs. Herriott thought, had come from the girl's unhappy life. Her mother had died when she was ten, and a year later her father had married again, a nice woman, a Bleecker. But Carla had shrunk away from her stepmother; she had used to come and stay with her Aunt Sharley for weeks at a time.

When she was eighteen her father had died, and he had left everything to his second wife except a trust fund for Carla that gave her some fifteen dollars a week. Her stepmother offered Carla a home with her, offered to send her to college, but Carla would take nothing from her. She let Mrs. Herriott pay for a business course; she found a job and took a little furnished one-room apartment in New York. But she was very unlucky with her jobs; she had a distressingly drab life.

"Come into the sitting room, Carla," said Mrs. Herriott, "and maybe Josie'll be kind enough to bring us some tea."

"Thank you, Aunt Sharley," said Carla. "How does Aunt Madge look? Is she pretty?"

"She's very tired now. She's been through a dreadful time in Europe, you know. Her husband died only a little while ago, and she's in a very nervous, upset state."

They sat down together in the little sitting room, and Mrs. Herriott *wanted* to talk to Carla. But she felt very dull and stupid.

"How do you like your new position, Carla?"

"I left it last Friday," said Carla.

"But, my dear, how have you been managing? Why didn't you tell me?"

"I thought you'd be too busy getting ready for Aunt Madge."

"I could never be too busy to think of you, Carla."

"Thank you, Aunt Sharley," said Carla.

There was a long silence. The twilight had deepened; Mrs. Herriott rose and turned on a lamp to make it cozier, but it wasn't cozy. Presently in came Josie with tea on a tray and thin bread and butter and a piece of that cake she made so often, a nice plain cake with currants in it. Josie is wonderful about keeping down expenses, Mrs. Herriott thought.

They drank their tea, but still it was not cozy. Carla ate some bread and butter, but she did not touch the cake.

"Do you mind if I go upstairs now, Aunt Sharley? Dinner at seven?"

"Yes. Your Aunt Madge is resting; you'll he careful, won't you, not to disturb her?"

"I don't think I'm so very noisy, as a rule," said Carla briefly.

Mrs. Herriott remained at the tea table and cut herself a slice of cake. *Some*body has to eat *some* of it, when Josie's takèn the trouble to make it, she thought. But today it seemed dry as dust. The house was silent. There were five other people in it, Madge and Carla and Silas and Josie and Ferdy, and not a footstep, not a voice to be heard.

Then Josie came to take away the tea things and she was surprisingly noisy for such a neat, brisk little thing. She rattled the dishes, she went along the hall with her heels pounding on the bare floor; the swing door closed after her; the house was silent again.

Tomorrow will be different, Mrs. Herriott told herself. Tomorrow we'll all be cheerful and cozy and happy. Perhaps even this evening, after a good dinner....

She thought she would go up now and take a bath, put on her nice gray dress and her black sandals. She was tired; she started up the stairs slowly, one hand on the banister rail, and smelt the very familiar aroma of Josie's meat loaf. Oh, I told her to get a nice capon! she cried to herself. I did want a nice dinner, this first night—

She stopped, surprised to hear Madge's voice.

"I don't see how I'm going to stand it. This hideous house—and a hideous way of living. I can't stand it! I need something a little bit gay and civilized."

"I'm sure Aunt Sharley wants to do everything she can for you," said Carla's clear even voice.

"I don't believe she cares about anyone," said Madge.

"Aunt Sharley's been very kind to me," said Carla. "It's just that she's rather self-sufficing."

Mrs. Herriott went on up the stairs. The door of Madge's room was open; there was no light in there. They were talking in the dark.

"She's so grim and disapproving," Madge went on. "She's a perfect old battle-ax."

Mrs. Herriott went past the dark room, noiseless in her felt slippers. She shut herself into her own room and sat down in the dusk by the window. Something fluttered so in her heart, something beat in her temples. Is that how I seem? she thought. Is that what I'm like?

CHAPTER THREE

Josie came along the hall with her brisk loud tread and knocked at the door.

"Dinner is ready, Mrs. Herriott."

"Oh, thank you, Josie," answered Mrs. Herriott and rose at once.

"Shall I take a tray to Mme de Belleforte?"

"I'll see," said Mrs. Herriott.

It seemed to her that she had been sitting in the dark for a very long time; when she turned on the light her eyes felt queer. When she looked in the mirror she thought that she looked queer. Pale, grim, a perfect old—

No. It's better not to think about that. Madge was tired and overwrought. And Carla? Carla didn't say anything unkind, really. It doesn't do to be hypersensitive. There was no time to put on her gray dress; she changed her felt slippers for the black sandals and went to knock at Madge's door.

There was no answer for a moment; then the key turned in the lock, and the door was opened by Silas.

"Mrs. de Belleforte wanted to give me some instructions," he said.

"I see," said Mrs. Herriott.

She was relieved to see that Madge was dressed and sitting in a chair. But she was a sorry sight, with her bright-yellow hair fluffed out and fresh rouge and lipstick lavishly applied.

"What is it, Sharley?" she asked briefly.

"Would you rather have your dinner up here, Madge?"

"I don't want any dinner," said Madge. "Have you any barbital?"

"No, I haven't."

"Well, you have aspirin, haven't you?"

"Oh, yes. But I do think sonic food—"

"Sharley, for God's sake, let me alone!"

"Yes, of course," said Mrs. Herriott politely. "You want to rest. Naturally. Perhaps before you go to bed.... If you want anything, Madge, just knock on the floor. Silas...?"

"I want to talk to Silas," said Madge.

"Yes, of course," said Mrs. Herriott "But later, if you don't mind, Madge. Just now.... Silas?"

"No!" said Madge. "Now."

"Silas?" said Mrs. Herriott, still with the inflection of a question.

Silas looked squarely at her, and then he came. She swallowed something like a sob, she was so glad.

"Silas," said Madge, and said something to him in French. He answered her in the same tongue, with a fluency that surprised Mrs. Herriott; then he held the door open and followed Mrs. Herriott out into the hall and down the stairs.

Carla was waiting for her in the dining room; they sat down at the table together as they had so many times before, and Mrs. Herriott tried to eat, so that Josie's feelings should not be hurt. Poor Josie was always so anxious, took so much trouble. But she found it difficult to swallow anything.

Dust and ashes... she thought. That's a curious expression, but it's really like that. Fatigue, I suppose. Tomorrow everything will seem *entirely* different.

"Have you found another position yet, Carla?" she asked.

"Well, I've been offered a position in a doctor's office," said Carla.

"I should think that might be interesting."

"There's no future in it," said Carla. "And I hate doctors."

There was an old-fashioned droplight with a shade of pleated maroon silk. It's really very shabby, Mrs. Herriott thought. This really is a hideous house. If I could rent it, If I could do something about things... I told Madge how highly I thought of Silas. It's quite natural for her to consult Silas. Some business matter, probably. Or some errand. It's quite natural.

The doorbell rang, and she started.

"Now, who could that be?" she said.

"Somebody collecting for something," said Carla.

Josie went along the hall, brisk and loud, and Mrs. Herriott heard a familiar voice, deep and grave and friendly. "Good evening, Josie! If Mrs. Herriott's at dinner, don't disturb her."

"Dr. Filson!" said Mrs. Herriott, pushing back her chair. "I must see...."

Dr. Filson was standing in the hall, in a dark suit and clerical collar, a short neat man with a pointed nose, with a soldierly look about him, so alert and erect was he.

"Mrs. Herriott, I'm afraid I'm disturbing your dinner...?"

"Oh no, Dr. Filson!"

"I was passing by, so I thought I'd stop in to ask about Mrs. de Belleforte."

"She's very tired," said Mrs. Herriott. "She's resting. It's all been such an ordeal."

"Oh, naturally."

"Won't you come in and have a cup of coffee with Carla and me?" she asked.

He protested a little, but Mrs. Herriott persuaded him, and in he came. She liked Dr. Filson; she admired his energetic and resolute character and his kindliness and found it so easy to talk to him. This was the way she had been brought up to talk, in a pleasant and effortless fashion. It was something Carla never could do.

They sat at the table under the maroon-shaded droplight, and Mrs. Herriott felt soothed by his presence and his conversation. Even Josie looked pleased.

"Sugar, Dr. Filson?"

"Thank you. And if I might have a little milk?"

"Oh, then you must have a large cup!" said Mrs. Herriott. "It's—"

She stopped, because she had heard the stairs creak. Someone going up? It's Ferdy, she told herself. Going up to his room. Or coming down perhaps. She cold not see the stairs from this room and she could not listen any more, because Dr. Filson was talking. Never mind, she told herself. It wasn't anything. It doesn't matter.

Dr. Filson finished his coffee and rose.

"I hope I shall have the pleasure of seeing Mrs. de Belleforte very soon."

I don't know, she thought. He mustn't see her until she's rested. Perhaps we could go away for a few days—to Atlantic City, some place like that.

"I hear glowing accounts of Mrs. de Belleforte," he said, "from some of the old residents of Carbury who knew her as a young girl."

She was lovely, Mrs. Herriott thought. She was shy, but very friendly. We used to go down to the beach and sit there and talk and talk—about how we thought our lives were going to be. It came back to her with heartbreaking vividness, just how Madge had looked, in a middy blouse, her light hair blowing in the sea wind. He *shan't* see her yet! she thought.

"You'll let me know when it's convenient for me to pay my respects?"

"Oh, yes!" said Mrs. Herriott, and rose to go to the door with him. He opened the door, and she went out with him into the sweet cool air. Everything was stirring here, insects were chirping, the bushes rattled like paper, the trees rustled. She wished that she could stay out here, out of the house, for a long time. But that would look very odd.

"I'll go to the gate with you," she said, and they went along the path together, Mrs. Herriott tall and drooping, Dr. Filson somewhat shorter and straight as a soldier.

"I'm very glad, Mrs. Herriott, that you're to have this companionship," he said. "I've thought, more than once, that you were somewhat lonely in Carbury."

His deep and pleasant voice sounded so kindly in the dark; she wanted to say something appreciative.

"Of course, I was born and brought up in New York," she said, in her vague, polite way. "It's very different...."

He pushed open the gate and stopped suddenly; he stepped back so quickly that he jostled her.

"Mrs. Herriott.... Don't come any farther. There's been—some sort of accident."

But she had seen what was there. It was Madge, lying sprawled on the pavement like a tawdry doll; the street light shone on her dry bright-gold hair; her short tight skirt was pulled up above her knees, showing the pink garters on her matchstick legs.

"Mrs. Herriott, go back to the house, please—"

"No!" she said, and tried to push past him. But he closed the gate behind him and knelt down beside Madge.

"But this is most distressing!" he said, holding Madge's wrist.

"She's fainted," said Mrs. Herriott. "Please—help me—and we'll bring her into the house."

"That wouldn't be advisable, Mrs. Herriott. If you'll go back to the house and call the police—"

"Police?"

"I'm afraid it's necessary."

"No! We must bring her into the house first. We can't leave her here—like this."

"Mrs. Herriott, I'm afraid the unfortunate woman is dead."

Unfortunate woman? That's my sister. That's Madge Pendleton. Mme de Belleforte. That's my sister lying there.

"We really shouldn't delay, Mrs. Herriott. If you'll call the police, I'll remain here."

"No! We can't leave her here—"

"I'll remain here, Mrs. Herriott, to see that she's not disturbed. It's very shocking and distressing, but we must comply with the law."

"Your coat, please, Dr. Filson!"

"I beg your pardon?"

"Please let me have your *coat,* Dr. Filson!"

"I'm afraid I don't—"

"I want to cover her up. Please give me your coat."

"Oh, I see!" he said, and took off his neat dark jacket and laid it respectfully over Madge's face. Mrs. Herriott opened the gate and came out; she moved the coat to cover Madge's knees.

"The police must bring her in," she said. "Please see to that, Dr. Filson. They must bring her into the house at once."

That was all she could think of, to get Madge into the house, to protect her, to hide her from curious eyes. She went into the house; Josie was in the hall.

"Mrs. Herriott, shall I cook prunes for?—"

"There's been an accident," said Mrs. Herriott. "Please telephone for the police."

"Oh, Mrs. Herriott! Who?—"

"Outside the house. Hurry up, Josie, please."

"What kind of accident, Aunt Sharley?" asked Carla from the doorway of the sitting room.

"Hush!" said Mrs. Herriott.

"Oh, I forgot that Aunt Madge was resting," said Carla.

Mrs. Herriott looked at her blankly; as she moved her head she saw Ferdy peering through the half-open door to the pantry. It was atrocious, unbearable to see them all so eager and interested.

"The police, please," she said, and went up the stairs.

She had to get Madge's room ready for her. She locked herself in there and turned on the light. She wanted to sit down for a moment but she felt that she would not be able to get up again. It was better to lean against the wall. Madge is dead, she said to herself. But no grief stirred in her; she felt nothing but that great urgency to prepare for Madge.

With an effort she moved away from the wall. She smoothed the rumpled bed, she picked up little things here and there; she closed the suitcase; then she remembered to pull down the shades. Now everything's ready for her, she thought.

She stood waiting, resting one hand on the chest of drawers. Madge is dead, she thought. Madge had a heart attack. Like Aunt Anna. She went out into the street—to get fresh air. That's how people feel, with a heart attack. My sister was exhausted—after the trip.

There was a very gentle knock at the door. She crossed the room and opened it, and Dr. Filson was standing there.

"Will you step out for a moment, Mrs. Herriott?" he asked, in a whisper, and she came, closing the door behind her.

He moved along the hall and she followed him.

"There's no need to disturb Mrs. de Belleforte," he said again, firm and patient. "She can rest quietly in her room—"

"What?" said Mrs. Herriott. How could he talk like that, as if Madge were there behind that closed door?

"I'm very sorry that you have to be disturbed," he said. "But Sergeant Tucker says it's unavoidable."

"I see!" she said, seeing nothing, understanding nothing, feeling nothing but that longing to get Madge safely home. "Are they bringing her up now?"

"Let me help you, Mrs. Herriott," he said, and taking her arm he started her toward the stairs. "It's only a matter of a few questions, and then you can rest."

There was a man in a dark suit standing in the hall below, a stout young man, remarkably sloppy-looking, she thought, for any sort of policeman, with pale yellow hair in little curls all over his head and pale-blue eyes, heavy-lidded. He stood with his stomach out and his shoulders bunched; he looked weary and very watchful.

"Mrs. Herriott, this is Sergeant Tucker, of the Carbury detective force."

"Oh.... How do you do?" said Mrs. Herriott. He did not reply to that.

"You were present, Mrs. Herriott, when Dr. Filson here found the deceased?"

"Yes. Yes, I was."

"Did you get a chance for a good look at the body?"

"Yes. Yes, I did."

"Are you able to identify this woman, Mrs. Herriott?"

"Why, no," said Mrs. Herriott, "no."

CHAPTER FOUR

Nothing happened. She told that monstrous lie and nothing happened.

"Did you touch or disturb the body in any way, Mrs. Herriott?" asked the sergeant.

"No," she answered. "I put a coat over her, that's all."

He asked her a few more questions, and she answered slowly, but without a tremor. It helped her to speak of 'the body' and 'the deceased.' Not Madge. Once I've got Madge safely in her own room they can know, she thought. But not now.

"Now," said Sergeant Tucker, "I'd like to see Mrs. de Belleforte for a moment."

"I'm sorry," said Mrs. Herriott quickly, "but she's asleep."

"Y'see," said Tucker, "the body must be visible from the front windows upstairs, and Mrs. de Belleforte might have heard something, seen something."

"I'm sure she didn't. She was in bed and asleep. She's still asleep."

This is impossible, said something in her mind. You can't do this. It's impossible. It's insane.

But something else in her mind, or her heart, maintained a stubborn and reckless defiance. She was going to go on saying that her sister, Mrs. de Belleforte, was shut up in her room, safe, inviolable, respected. Mrs. de Belleforte had nothing to do with the poor limp doll, the 'unfortunate woman' outside in the street. When I've got Madge in here, in her own bed, in a nice clean nightgown—when she looks like herself—then I'll tell them. And not *before*. I don't care what they do to me.

"Just a brief statement from Mrs. de Belleforte—" said the Sergeant.

"She can't be waked now," said Mrs. Herriott. "I gave her some sleeping medicine. She's not well."

"Might get the medical officer to take a look at her and see if she's able—"

"No!" cried Mrs. Herriott. "Please—!"

"Don't you think that tomorrow morning would do, Sergeant?" asked Dr. Filson.

"I'll ask Captain King," said Tucker. "But I'm naturally expected to get all the information I can, and without any delay, either."

"Yes, we understand that, Sergeant, but in the circumstances—"

"I'll ask Captain King," he said again. "Now I want to see Miss Pendleton."

"She doesn't know anything," said Mrs. Herriott.

"Have to ask her if she can identify the body," said the Sergeant.

All right, thought Mrs. Herriott. This is the end. Carla will tell them, of course. All right. I'll say that Madge was ill, very ill. Delirious.

"I'll go with Miss Carla," said Dr. Filson. "It's a distressing ordeal for a young girl."

"Maybe so," said the sergeant, with a slow and drowsy smile. "Will you send for her, please?"

"Yes, I'll go," said Mrs. Herriott, and went along the hall to the kitchen.

Silas sat at the table in his shirt sleeves, reading a newspaper; Josie stood at the sink, looking like a laboratory assistant in her clean white smock and with her tidy dark hair, her rosy face intent upon her work; Ferdy stood by her, drying a cup very slowly, wiping it round and round and round, in a sulky dream. Silas rose, and Mrs. Herriott looked at him blankly.

"Josie," she said, "will, you find Miss Carla, please? The policeman wants her to—look at the—person outside."

Josie's eyes widened behind her spectacles. "Oh, but, Mrs. Herriott!—"

"They'll ask all of us if we can identify her," said Silas. "You too."

It will all be over in a moment now, thought Mrs. Herriott. The dining room was dark, and she went in there and stood by the window. There were people in the street; she could hear low voices; she saw the headlights of a car that stood there and a flashlight moving. Carla will scream, she thought, and she waited for that. She heard footsteps on the gravel path. I don't know what they'll do to me, she thought. I suppose it was a shocking thing to do. But I can't really care.

The front door opened. She went into the hall and saw Dr. Filson leading Carla by the arm into the sitting room. She sat down on the sofa, very white, her eyes lowered. Perhaps she can't bear to look at me, after what I've done, Mrs. Herriott thought. Carla's so very truthful.

"An appalling sight!" Carla said, in her clear even voice.

Mrs. Herriott glanced at her, startled.

"A human wreck," said Carla. "So tawdry—"

"Carla!"

"I'm sorry," said Carla, "but I can't be sentimental about some stranger...."

Mrs. Herriott sat down in an armchair. Carla *doesn't know*, she thought. I hadn't realized that she never saw Madge, only talked to her in the dark. She doesn't know.

There were more footsteps going by along the gravel path. Josie and Silas, she thought. I'll be glad when it's ended. Will they arrest me, I wonder? I don't think so—but I don't care. It will be in the newspapers. Mrs. de Belleforte, formerly Miss Madge Pendleton. She saw Silas and Josie go by along the hall, toward the kitchen. No, she thought. Now that policeman will come. I don't care....

"Mrs. Herriott," said Dr. Filson, "you must rest. You look exhausted."

"I'm quite all right, thank you," she said. "I'd rather wait here."

"There is nothing to wait for, Mrs. Herriott. There is no reason why you shouldn't go upstairs and rest."

"I'll wait here, thank you."

"Suppose I ask the sergeant if there is anything further you can do?" he suggested.

"Thank you," she said, and he went away.

I don't know what *he'll* think about this, she said to herself. I dare say he knows a great deal about human nature, but still I think he'll be shocked. I wish that policeman would come back and be done with it.

She waited and waited for him, but he did not come. Dr. Filson returned.

"The sergeant says he won't need to trouble you again tonight, Mrs. Herriott," he said.

"Then will they bring her in please."

"That's a very kindly thought, Mrs. Herriott, but—"

"Now!" she said. "Please! Please tell them to bring—to bring her in here at once!"

"I'm afraid that—"

"Dr. Filson!"

"Mrs. Herriott, please...! Things of this sort are very distressing and painful, but we have to face them. There's a regular procedure that has to be followed. Do, please, sit down again, Mrs. Herriott."

"Do you mean—they're taking her away?"

She stood before him, her gray eyes narrowed.

"Do you mean...?"

"In the first place, Mrs. Herriott," he said, gently, "the Police want to do everything possible to have the poor woman identified."

"But—she hasn't been? You mean nobody—?"

"Not so far," he answered. "Nobody in this house or in the house next door has been able to identify her."

"Not Silas—and Josie?"

"No. Please, Mrs. Herriott, at least sit down. There's nothing you can do for the poor woman—"

"Has she gone?"

"Not yet. But—"

"I want to see her again!"

She started toward the door, but he caught her arm in a firm grasp.

"No!" he said, quietly. "You must go upstairs and rest, Mrs. Herriott. You're only doing yourself harm by this agitation. That poor woman has gone now to face her Maker. What lies outside your house is a mere—"

She drew her breath in through her nose with a queer sound. Yes, she told herself. Yes, that's true. That's not Madge out there. Madge has gone.

"I should like to ask Dr. Saylor to stop in, Mrs. Herriott," said Doctor Filson.

"No," she said, absently.

"He could give you a mild sedative—"

"No, thank you, I never take things like that."

"And at the same time he might just look in on Mrs. de Belleforte. I think that would be a sensible precaution, Mrs. Herriott."

Do keep quiet! she thought. Do let me alone for a little while. I've got to think things out. Go away, do go away.

"I really feel, Mrs. Herriott, that you ought to allow Dr. Saylor to see Mrs. de Belleforte, if you've given her some soporific."

"Wait!" she said, looking at him with frowning concentration.

He'll be the best one for me to tell, she thought. I'll have to tell the truth now. This can't go on. I dare say I've done something illegal, but I don't really care. But Silas has too, and that's my fault. He did it to help me. I'm responsible. I'll see to it that he doesn't get into any trouble.

But I need time to—arrange my thoughts. I'm going to tell Dr. Filson the truth. But I'm not going to blurt out, here and now, that that—was Madge. I'm going to explain that she was ill. I'm going to say that she had to borrow those clothes from someone on the ship. There are so many things.... I must have a little time....

"Mrs. Herriott," said Dr. Filson's grave deep voice, "I wish I could persuade you to see Dr. Saylor—"

"There's nothing the matter with me," she said. "I don't want him."

She realized that she was being very brusque, even rude, to Dr. Filson, and she was sorry.

"Dr. Filson," she said, "I appreciate all you've done. You've been most kind and helpful. And I'd like—" She paused. "If you can spare the time, I'd like to see you tomorrow morning."

"With pleasure, Mrs. Herriott. I'll come at any time—"

"Oh, no! I'll come to the rectory, thank you."

"I shall be at home all the morning, Mrs. Herriott. And if you feel, later on, that you'd like me to return this evening, a telephone call will bring me."

He seemed unusually grave; he seemed pale. Maybe he knows, she thought. I hope he does. It's going to be very difficult, explaining all this.

"Is there anything further I can do for you, Mrs. Herriott?"

"No, thank you, Dr. Filson. Thank you very much."

"Then good night, Mrs. Herriott. Good night, Miss Carla."

He smiled at them then, but it was a grave smile.

"Aunt Sharley," said Carla, "let's go upstairs."

"We might as well," said Mrs. Herriott, and started up the stairs.

"Aren't you going to stop in and see Aunt Madge?"

"Not now," said Mrs. Herriott.

"But she hasn't had any dinner! She hasn't had a thing—"

"She needs rest and quiet more than anything," Mrs. Herriott said.

And then she wanted to cry for her poor Madge. For the first time the sheer sadness of this came over her. Madge was dead, and strangers had taken her away. She had come home; she had had plans to go shopping, to see her friends, to have a gay time. And what had happened to her?

She closed her door and sat down in a chair, to cry. But no tears came. It was as if she had forgotten how to weep, as well as to laugh. She had been looking forward to Madge's coming with a tense and passionate concentration; her whole life had been centered upon that; she had thought of it as being the beginning of a perfect companionship, a perfect happiness. And in the first hour it was ended, there was nothing left. Nothing but her gay, anxious daily life, with the responsibilities she could never quite manage, the people she could not manage.

Perhaps if I'd been different with Madge, she thought, this wouldn't have happened. Perhaps she wouldn't have run out into the street. She wondered for a moment about that, but she could imagine no cause or reason, and it did not matter. I only want to get her back, she thought. That was all she wanted in the world now, only to know that Madge was lying in her own room, in dignity and quiet.

There was a knock at the door. She sighed, but she was resigned to that; no matter if she were ill, no matter how much she wanted to be alone, people came knocking at the door to ask questions, about the grocer's bill, about the laundry, about the car, about Ferdy, about the plumber who was always so rude to Josie.

"Come in!" she said.

It was Josie. "Mrs. Herriott, there's a man here to see Mme de Belleforte."

"Oh.... What man? Who is he?"

"He says his name is Honess, and she's expecting him."

"Oh," Mrs. Herriott said again, and rose. "I'll speak to him," she said.

She powdered her nose and patted the thick rolls of hair over her temples; she looked absently in the mirror at her pallid face, and then she went down stairs. Josie had left this visitor in the hall. He was standing there, hat in hand, slender and strikingly handsome in a dark and foreign way, with a scornful, outthrust underlip and fine dark brows and smooth black hair.

"Mrs. Herriott?" he said. "I am Ramon Honess."

You're Ramon? she thought. You're that one? The dancer, the gigolo, the one Madge was going to leave all her money to? So this is how a gigolo looks—a man who makes it his business to flatter women, rich middle-aged women....

"I'm sorry to trouble you," he said, "but I'm very anxious to see Mme de Belleforte."

I can't tell *him,* she thought. I can't tell him that the police have taken Madge away. He'll find it out later, but not now.

"My sister's sleeping," she said, with a vague little smile. "She's very tired."

"Then may I wait a while in case she wakes up?"

"Well, I gave her a little sedative," said Mrs. Herriott. "I don't think—I'm quite sure that she won't wake up till morning."

"I don't want to be a nuisance," he said, "but there's a little package for me.... Mme de Belleforte was to leave it at my hotel as soon as she landed, but—" He paused, and smiled. "She didn't."

"Mme de Belleforte was *very* tired," said Mrs. Herriott.

"Oh, naturally," he said.

He was everything she most distrusted, a gigolo, a fortune-hunter, a dancer, a foreigner of some sort, yet she could see, she thought, what it was that had disarmed her poor Madge. It was his grace, his gentle and almost caressing deference, his faintly ironic decorum. He was completely sure of himself and at ease.

"I'm very sorry to trouble you," he said, "but I think Mme de Belleforte would excuse it if you disturbed her."

"I'll try, later on."

"If you could possibly ask her now...? Perhaps if you could find my package without disturbing her, Mrs. Herriott? You see, I'd like to take it back to New York tonight."

A sort of despair came over her. She was so weary and dazed; she wanted so much to be left alone, and he was so persistent.

"Is it something that belongs to you, Mr. Honess?" she asked.

"Something Mme de Belleforte was bringing for me," he answered.

Madge has promised him a present, she thought, and he won't go away until he's got it.

"I'll look," she said, "I'll see if I can find any package without disturbing my sister."

"I'm afraid Mme de Belleforte would have put it in some safe place, Mrs. Herriott. You see, it's rather valuable."

Mrs. Herriott had never yet said to herself that anything was too much to bear. She had endured grief and loss and loneliness and years and years of grinding financial worry without rebellion or resentment. But now, at the end of this most terrible day in her life, she came suddenly to the end of her endurance. She had to get rid of Ramon Honess at any cost.

"If it's a question of money," she said unsteadily, "I've got some money in my purse."

To her shame and dismay she felt a flood of tears rising; she squeezed her eyes shut and opening them saw him in a blur.

"Thank you," he said, "but it's not quite like that. I'll go now, Mrs. Herriott. I'll wait to hear from Mme de Belleforte in the morning. She has my address. Please don't worry."

She was not able to answer. He moved forward a little and took her hand; bending his dark head, he raised it to his lips.

"Don't worry, please," he said, "I hope to have the pleasure of seeing you soon again."

She stood where she was until the door closed after him, and then she hurried up the stairs, stumbling a little. She undressed, and all the while tears ran down her face. She got into bed and turned out the light, and the tears still came. But she was not thinking of anything at all; she was just crying. The fresh cool air blew in, and she fell asleep almost at once.

A knock at the door roused her; she opened her eyes and sat up. The sun was coming in at the window; she felt a dim formless alarm, as if she had overslept and missed something of urgent importance.

"Who is it?" she asked.

"Its me, Mrs. Herriott. Josie."

"Oh, come in, Josie," she said, as she had answered so many times before. Josie represented all the worrying wearisome things in her life, the bills, the disputes, the crowding duties. There's something... she thought. Something I've forgotten....

Josie entered, rosy and clean in a blue cotton dress, her eyes bright behind her spectacles.

"I thought you'd want to get up, Mrs. Herriott," she said. "The policeman is here, and he's brought a doctor."

That... she thought. All that... the weight of it came down upon her, and it was difficult to breathe; she put her hand to her throat.

"Mrs. Herriott, they're very impatient. They say they've got to see Mme de Belleforte."

"Hand me my dressing gown, Josie. Thank you."

She sat on the edge of the bed and put on her purple felt slippers; she pinned up her thick braids of hair. Here's the end of it, she thought. There's no time now to ask Dr. Filson's advice or to think things over. I've got to face it, that's all. But I wish I could have had a cup of coffee.

She went out into the hall, with Josie following; from the top of the stairs she looked down to see Sergeant Tucker in the hall with a gray-mustached man who carried a little black bag.

"I've brought Dr. Crowley, Mrs. Herriott," said Sergeant Tucker.

"Why?" she asked, with great calm, looking down at them.

"Because I want to ask Mrs. de Belleforte some questions," said Tucker, "and the doctor here will be able to tell me if she's fit to answer 'em."

"You can't see her," said Mrs. Herriott.

"Why not?" he asked, and when she did not answer, the two men started up the stairs, Tucker last, with an indolent and rolling gait.

"No use delaying this, Mrs. Herriott," he said. "Only makes it harder all round. The body was found where it could be seen from Mrs. de Belleforte's windows—and I want to hear what she's got to say."

"She's—not here," said Mrs. Herriott, with a dreadful effort.

"All right. Where is she then?"

"Which is her room?" asked the doctor sharply.

"There," said Mrs. Herriott. "But you can't go in—"

"This door?" asked the doctor, frowning.

"Yes. But she's not there."

He rapped briskly on the door. "Doctor!" he announced.
"Come in!" said a voice.
He turned the knob and entered, closing the door after him.

CHAPTER FIVE

Mrs. Herriott leaned back against the wall. She felt calm, quite calm, and strong, ready to deal with anything that might happen. Simply, it seemed better to use this interval for not—thinking. Sergeant Tucker stood facing her, but he was not looking at her; his heavy lids were down—he had an aloof and sulky air.

Nobody inside that room could have said come in. The room was empty. So there was really nothing to think about.

The door opened, and the doctor came out.

"All right, Sergeant," he said. "Mrs. de Belleforte is ready to see you." He turned to Mrs. Herriott. "Nothing much wrong there," he said crossly. "But I'd advise you, madam, not to go around administering sedatives without consulting a physician."

She did not answer. The bedroom door was a little open, and she could hear Tucker's voice in there, and a woman's voice, talking in quiet tones. The doctor gave her a curt nod and went down the stairs; she heard the door close.

This is too farfetched entirely, she said to herself. After all, I'm a mature, sensible woman, and this... I'm not going to think about this. I will not.

Sergeant Tucker came out of that room and closed the door. They looked at each other.

"I'd like a little more information," he said, "in regard to last night."

"What sort of 'information'?"

"I'd like to know did you see or hear anything unusual-like?"

"You know what I saw," said Mrs. Herriott.

They were still looking at each other; they were hostile, yet in a way they had respect for each other.

"This is a peculiar kind of a case," he said. "Of course, the doctor hasn't finished the checkup for poison."

"Poison?"

"Why couldn't it be?" he said.

"I don't know," said Mrs. Herriott.

She was perfectly sure that he was trying to trap her, and she was determined not to be trapped. But she was completely in the dark. She could not even imagine what was going on around her. Why did the doctor pretend that Madge was there in her own room, and why did the sergeant stand here, talking about her being poisoned? It was a trap, a very strange and elaborate trap, designed to betray Madge in some way.

"A peculiar feature in this case," said Tucker, "deceased didn't have any hat. Well, that's not so strange these days. But she didn't have any kind of a purse or handbag. Now, you practically never find a woman that hasn't got some kind of a purse along with her. That's definitely a peculiar feature."

"It might have been stolen," said Mrs. Herriott.

"Could've been. Somebody could've come along the street and snatched her bag. All right. That's your theory?"

"I haven't any theory," said Mrs. Herriott.

"Oh, you haven't?"

"No, I haven't."

"Very good," he said, "you haven't any theory. All right. Later on, when deceased has been identified, we'll have something to work on."

"Yes, I suppose you will. Now if you will excuse me, please, I want to get dressed."

"All right," he said, to her surprise and great relief. She had not expected to be freed. She went into her room and stood listening behind the closed door until she heard him go all the way down the stairs. Then she began to dress in great haste, pinning up her thick hair, slipping on a gray print dress. There's somebody in Madge's room, she told herself. They've put somebody in there, to trap me. That's a horrible thing to do, cruel and horrible. But I'm not going to be—silly about it. I'm going in there. I'm going to see for myself.

She crossed the hall and opened that door without knocking. The dark shades were drawn down, and in the dusky light she saw somebody sitting up in the bed, someone with light hair loose about her shoulders.

"Who are you?" she asked.

"Close the door, Aunt Sharley," said a voice in a whisper. She closed the door and went over to the bed.

"Carla?" she said. "Carla, why...?"

"Silas told me what you'd done," said Carla. "He said you'd get into very serious trouble if I didn't help you out."

"He shouldn't have told you that," said Mrs. Herriott.

"I think it's the only thing possible," said Carla coldly. "When you refused to identify poor Aunt Madge.... Of course, I didn't know who it was, lying out there. I'd never seen her."

"Yes," said Mrs. Herriott, and sat down in the chair, looking anxiously into the girl's face. "Who fixed you up like this?"

"Silas got me the make-up from the drugstore. I know how to use it; we learned that in the Dramatics Club."

"The doctor...? Was the doctor satisfied?"

"He seemed to be."

"And the detective—policeman—that sergeant—didn't he ask you questions?"

"Only about whether I'd heard or noticed anything last night."

"This can't go on, you know," said Mrs. Herriott.

"Naturally," said Carla. "It's simply horrible, shut up here in the dark with absolutely nothing to do. But Silas thinks we might be able to get away before very long."

"Who might get away?"

"He thought you might tell people you were taking Aunt Madge to New York for a while."

"No," said Mrs. Herriott. "This can't go on. I shall see Dr. Filson and tell him—"

"Aunt Sharley, you can't possibly do that without consulting Silas and me," said Carla, sitting up straight. "You've got us both involved, seriously involved."

"I didn't ask anyone to do anything."

"What else could Silas do, when he found out you hadn't identified poor Aunt Madge? He *had* to say he didn't know who it was."

"No, he didn't," said Mrs. Herriott.

"You'll have to talk things over with Silas before you do anything, Aunt Sharley. It's only fair."

"Yes," said Mrs. Herriott, after a moment. She rose. "Yes, I will."

"And could I possibly have some breakfast, please? I haven't had *anything.*"

"I'll bring you a tray," said Mrs. Herriott.

She was in a hurry to see Silas. It was an immeasurable relief to think that he knew everything, all that she had done. Of course he had stood by her, had helped her, had never yet failed her. Ten years ago, when she and James had driven out to Carbury, to see about disposing of some of Grandfather Pendleton's houses, Silas had been sent by the real-estate agent to show them around, and James had taken a fancy to the boy. Eighteen, Silas had been then, cool, easygoing, obliging. He had passed his entrance examinations for Columbia; he was going to be a mining engineer; he was going to see the world. His parents were dead, but his grandfather was doing well enough with his boat yard to give the boy a good start, and James had given him a job in his office for the summer.

When James had died Silas had been of inestimable help to Mrs. Herriott. He had looked after the details, about which she was so helpless, he had run errands, he had been at her side whenever she needed him.

That summer he had met with his dreadful accident; he had broken his neck diving. James' estate was, Jeff Quillen told her, not what it should have been; some of his investments had not been sound, but she had been able to help poor Silas through his months and months in the hospital and to keep Josie, too. And when he had come out, she had taken him on as her chauffeur. He hadn't wanted to go back to college; he had not seemed ambitious any more; he was still nonchalant and obliging, but he was curiously, distressingly aimless.

Mrs. Herriott had been growing poorer and poorer. She had given up trying to understand what was happening, only that Jeff Quillen was battling mightily to save what he could for her. She had moved to a small hotel, she had gone out less and less, she had seen fewer and fewer people. A chauf - feur and car were out of the question, and Silas had found a position for himself. But he still stood by, still did errands for her, still helped her in all her plans. The house in Carbury was his idea, and he had offered to come for nothing but food and shelter for Josie and himself. Mrs. Herriott would not agree to that; they got a salary every month, a very small one, but they seemed entirely satisfied. It was a wrong sort of life, Mrs. Herriott thought, for two young people, but they seemed to feel at home here.

Silas and Ferdy were sitting at the kitchen table, and Josie was serving their breakfast.

"Josie, if you'll get a tray ready," she said, "I'll take it upstairs."

"I'll take it, Mrs. Herriott! I'd love to."

"Well, no—thanks, Josie. I think I'd rather."

Ferdy had risen at once; he stood behind his chair looking greatly aggrieved, his long black hair plastered back from his forehead, and a blue-and-green bandanna around his neck. "Go on with your breakfast, Ferdy," Mrs. Herriott said, and he sat down again. Silas finished his cup of coffee and pushed back his chair.

"When you finish, Silas, I'd like to speak to you for a few moments," she said.

"Finished now," said Silas, and followed her into the sitting room; he closed the door.

"Silas, it was very good of you to try to help me this way. But you see, of course, that it can't go on. I'll tell the police, Silas. I'll take the whole responsibility."

"I'm afraid you haven't thought this out," he said.

"What do you mean, Silas? You must see for yourself that we can't keep this up."

He stood before her with his eyes lowered, and because of the stiff car-riage of his head, it gave him a very haughty look.

"You might be able to explain yourself out of it," he said, "you might say you were so shocked, so much ashamed of your sister—"

"Silas! It wasn't that! She was ill—exhausted—"

"Yes," he said. "You might get away with it. But you couldn't explain me."

"Yes, I could, Silas. I'd say you'd acted out of loyalty to me."

"Nobody'd believe it," he said. "I'd have to be the biggest fool that ever lived to get you—and myself—and Carla—into a spot like this, just to save you a few moments' embarrassment."

"But, Silas, then why did you say you didn't know her?"

"I'd rather not tell you just now. Will you leave it to me, and just carry on for a while?"

"Silas, I can't! Not possibly."

"When I found out that you hadn't identified her," he said, "I thought you knew—or suspected, anyhow."

"Knew *what*? Suspected what?"

"I'd rather not tell you just now. If you'll have a little confidence in me—"

"I can't," she said flatly. "I've got to know."

"All right," he said. "That wasn't your sister."

She looked at him, her brows drawn together, her lips parted, as if she were making an extreme effort to hear. "Excuse me," she said politely, "but that was my sister."

"No," he said. "She told me herself. She'd got hold of your sister's papers and came here in a hurry to get hold of your sister's money before Mrs. de Belleforte could get here."

"Oh, did she?" said Mrs. Herriott, with the same politeness.

"She told me, because she thought she could bribe me to help her. It was me she went out into the street to meet."

"Oh, was it?"

"I wanted to hear all she had to say. I wanted to find out all I could. But I missed it."

"I see!"

"Mrs. Herriott," he said, "you understand what I'm saying, don't you? You're listening, aren't you?"

"Oh, *yes!*" she said.

"There were other people in it with this woman," he said. "She had friends here. If we want to get them, if we want to trace Mrs. de Belleforte, this is the only way we can do it. If these other people think she's alive, they'll try to get in touch with her, and then we'll get them. But if they know she's dead, they'll never show up, and we'll never find out what's happened to your sister."

"Yes, I see!"

"If we tell the police, the whole story will come out. They'll make their own investigation. And maybe that wouldn't be too good for Mrs. de Belleforte."

"I see!"

He sighed and leaned his broad shoulders against the door. "Will you let me handle this thing for a while?" he asked.

"I'd like to think it over, Silas."

"But you won't do anything, won't tell anyone anything, without letting me know first?"

"No, I won't, Silas."

She managed a vague little smile and came nearer to the door; he stood aside and opened it for her.

"It's hard to understand how you feel about things sometimes," he said.

"I know," she said, smiling again, and went off along the hall to the kitchen.

I don't believe a word of all that, she said to herself. It's a lie.

CHAPTER SIX

Mrs. Herriott got the tray from Josie and started up the stairs with it; she went slowly, in a sort of daze. Carla had pulled up the shades and lay back on the pillows, reading a magazine. Her pale, soft hair glittered in the sun, and in the full light of day the make-up on her face was shocking to Mrs. Herriott. With rouge high on her cheekbones, purple eye shadow, and dark, moist lipstick, she was a caricature, a travesty of Madge.

"Oh, thank you, Aunt Sharley," she said. "Have you spoken to Silas?"

"Yes," Mrs. Herriott answered.

"Didn't he tell you that you mustn't do anything or say anything to anyone just now?"

"*Tell* me...?" Mrs. Herriott repeated mildly.

"Well, he's thinking of you," Carla said. "He's trying to protect you."

It was a curious thing to hear Carla defending Silas. Ever since she was a child of fourteen, she had disliked and resented him; she had called him 'disrespectful'; in her own arrogant fashion she had called Silas arrogant.

"He's absolutely devoted to you, Aunt Sharley," she said, as if in reproach.

"I know," said Mrs. Herriott.

For ten years Silas had been her faithful friend and ally; he had never disappointed her, never failed her. I'm not going to forget that, she said to herself, standing beside Carla, her gray eyes fixed upon nothing. The least I can do is to give Silas the benefit of the doubt.

Of every doubt that she could imagine. Perhaps he believes that story, she thought. But that was very difficult to accept. That implied that Madge had told him she was someone else and that he had instantly and unquestioningly believed it. And he's not like that, she thought. He's not at all credulous; in fact, he's quite skeptical.

"Aunt Sharley!" said Carla. "I wish you'd say something. You're the most aloof person... it's just impossible to get anywhere near you."

"I can't help it," said Mrs. Herriott. "Now eat your breakfast, Carla, and I'll come back for the tray later."

If Silas told me a lie, she thought, he had some reason, some good reason. I can't suddenly turn against him. But this horrible masquerade can't go on. He must realize that. It will come to an end any moment. Someone will recognize Carla, or someone will find out who my poor Madge really is. And then we'll be in a dreadful situation, all three of us, Carla and Silas and myself.

I don't care, she thought, starting down the stairs again. It's really all my fault. I started the whole thing by not identifying Madge. I'm responsible, and when the police find out, I'll tell them so. I really don't care. I think perhaps I'm rather tired.

The doorbell rang, and Josie went to open the door for Captain King, of the Carbury police. Mrs. Herriott had met him before, a tall heavy man with dark pouches under his sad eyes. He was courteous, in a subdued and toneless way.

"Sorry to disturb you, Mrs. Herriott," he said. "But we're having quite a lot of difficulty, and it occurred to me that possibly you could help us."

They sat down together in the sitting room, Mrs. Herriott still in her condition of dazed and almost numb calmness.

"It's a peculiar case," he went on. "Absolutely no clue to this woman's identity. Carbury's a small place, nothing here to bring strangers, no defense work to speak of. Nobody in our two or three industrial plants is able to identify her. We've been around to most of the boarding houses, rooming houses, hotels; nobody missing. Unless something turns up, we've got to assume that she came here by bus or train or car. In that case, we can pretty well take it for granted that she had some kind of purse or handbag. And, nothing of that sort being found on or near her, we can pretty well assume that she was robbed."

Mrs. Herriott found it difficult to keep her mind on this; it seemed to her so repetitious, so boring. But she realized that she must appear interested and helpful and she kept her eyes upon Captain King's face with an expression of earnest attention.

"If this woman was robbed," he said, "it will be reasonable to consider it a death by violence."

"Oh, violence...?" Mrs. Herriott said.

"The medical officer isn't prepared to state definitely the cause of death, except a blow on the head. This blow could have been the result of a fall, or it could have been caused by a blow with some instrument."

"Perhaps she was ill."

"So far, the medical officer hasn't found any signs of illness. She'd been drinking, it seems—"

"But not much!"

"What?" he said.

"She didn't look—as if she'd been drinking."

"You can't tell by a casual glance, Mrs. Herriott. Anyhow, the first step, for us, is to find out, if possible, what she was doing on this quiet street. It's not a thoroughfare, particularly. It's occurred to me, Mrs. Herriott, that possibly this woman was coming to see you."

"Me?"

"You've done a good deal of charitable work here in Carbury. It occurred to me that maybe this woman was coming to you for some sort of help."

She found nothing to say to that.

"Or there are other possibilities. I know it's not a pleasant topic, Mrs. Herriott, but you realize, I'm sure, that we can't overlook anything. Now, when you saw this woman outside your gate, did she, however remotely, remind you of anyone else you have ever seen? I mean, the general type. For instance, did you, while living in New York, ever have a servant, or a dressmaker, or anyone like that, who was the same general type as the deceased?"

"No," she said.

Her indifference had gone now; this was dreadful. "No," she said again. "I didn't think she was—that type."

"When you think it over, Mrs. Herriott, you don't have any association in your mind with anyone of that type? Say in a beauty parlor, for instance?"

"I—can't think of anyone," she said.

"No delinquent girl you helped some time in the past, for instance?"

"No," she said, "I didn't think that poor woman—looked like that."

"I understand that you wanted her brought into the house, Mrs. Herriott?"

"Naturally."

"You didn't think, at that time, that possibly the deceased was someone you knew or had known?"

I'll be glad when they find out the truth, she thought. It'll be bad, but not so bad as this.

"It seemed to me natural," she said.

"Well, we all know your kindness, Mrs. Herriott," he said. "I'm sorry to bother you—not a pleasant topic, I realize. But if anything comes into your head—if you can think of anyone you formerly knew who was the same general type, you'll let me know."

"I'll try to think," she said.

"One more matter," he said. "I hear that Miss Pendleton went back to New York last night. Will you give me her address, please?"

"Why, yes," said Mrs. Herriott. "But I'm afraid you won't find her there just now. She's going to visit a friend for a while."

"Then if you'll give me this friend's address...?"

"I'm sorry but I don't know it. I don't even know the friend's name."

"You don't know any way to get in touch with your niece?" he asked.

That must seem—queer, Mrs. Herriott thought. "She'll write to me," she said, with composure.

"If you'll let me have Miss Pendleton's address, please," said Captain King, "we'll find her."

"Certainly," said Mrs. Herriott.

"When your niece comes out here, she usually stays for some time, doesn't she?"

"Well, usually," said Mrs. Herriott.

"Did she bring any baggage with her, Mrs. Herriott? A suitcase, for instance?"

"Let me see—" said Mrs. Herriott, with a thoughtful frown.

"What I'm trying to get at," he said, "is whether anything happened to upset Miss Pendleton—make her change her plans. She may have seen something—may have been looking out a window and seen something that upset her."

"I don't think so," said Mrs. Herriott.

"Young ladies get upset about things," he said. "And then, of course, a lot of people have the idea that they don't want to get involved in a police case. They have the idea that they'll avoid trouble by withholding information. Biggest mistake they could make. The police never make any unnecessary trouble for any reputable citizen provided—" he paused, "provided they co-operate," he said. "The one rule to follow is, tell the police frankly and fully all you know, and you'll have nothing to worry about."

"Oh, certainly!" said Mrs. Herriott.

All she wanted was to be done with this. For the sake of Silas and Carla she had to do the best she could, but it was repulsive and horrible to her. No one had ever sat down and asked her questions before; no one had ever before assailed her vague reticence. And now she must not only answer questions but answer with lies. I'm doing so badly, she thought. Captain King can't believe me.

And in her heart she hoped, she wished he would not believe her.

He rose. "Sorry I had to trouble you, Mrs. Herriott," he said.

"Have you finished?"

"Well, I wish I could say yes to that," he answered, "but I'm afraid we're just starting in this case. I won't need to bother you any more just now, though. I'll get in touch with Miss Pendleton."

She rose too and went to the door with him. This will finish it, she thought. He'll find out that Carla isn't in New York and he'll trace her here. I'm sure they can do that. And then it will be over. It's my fault. I started the whole thing. I'll willingly, gladly take the whole responsibility. It will be over, and my poor Madge can be left in peace.

She went out on to the little porch with Captain King. A shabby sedan was coming down the street; it stopped before the house as Captain King opened the gate, and Silas got out, followed by a dusty broad-shouldered man in a rumpled brown suit and wide-brimmed brown hat, worn with a swagger.

"I hoped I'd catch you here, Captain King," said Silas. "I've got someone here who's got some information for you. This is Peters... Willie Peters from Freeport."

Willie Peters took off his hat.

"I called up Peters this morning," said Silas. "I asked him to run over and take a look at the body."

"Why?" asked Captain King.

"I wasn't sure enough myself to say anything," said Silas, "but if Willie has the same idea as I have, it'll be something."

What can this be? thought Mrs. Herriott, astonished and frightened. She watched Silas and Willie Peters get back into the sedan, and Captain King set off ahead of them in his car. Where were they going? What were they going to do?

And now what shall I do? she thought. The day stretched before her, strangely empty. There were plenty of things she ought to do, but they seemed all of them futile and tedious. Even the thought of making her bed and tidying her room, which she did every day to help out poor Josie, seemed now an unbearable task. It is a hideous house, she thought. It's a dull narrow sort of life.

She turned at last and re-entered the house. She could not escape talking over the market list with Josie; if she did not go to Josie, Josie would come after her. She went along the hall to the kitchen and found Josie standing on the back steps outside the screen door, just standing there, looking at something. Mrs. Herriott, being much taller, could see over Josie's shoulder, and she found that the object of interest was Ferdy.

In his khaki shirt and shorts he was standing in the yard where the clothes were dried, whirling a lariat around him, sometimes jumping over it; he whirled it faster and cried, "Yipee!" His black hair flopped over his forehead, his dark face glistened with sweat; he looked unusually alive and pleased with himself.

And Josie looked so pleased with him. It was odd to see the busy little thing standing idle; it was touching to see her so indulgent and interested in her brother's skill. For he was skillful. "Yipee!" he shouted, spinning the lariat up in a spiral and neatly looping it over the top of a clothes pole.

"That's very good, Ferdy," said Mrs. Herriott.

He grew sulky at once. He got the rope off the pole and stood, clumsy and heavy again, looking down at the ground.

"I've got the list all ready, Mrs. Herriott," said Josie, "but I don't know where Silas has got to. I wanted him to drive me to the fruit man early so that there'd be a good choice, but he's gone off somewhere, without a word."

"I'll go to the village, Josie. I'd like the walk," said Mrs. Herriott.

She did this every now and then. She was nothing like so good a marketer and bargainer as Josie, but she enjoyed going. She liked to talk to the butcher and grocer, she liked the cozy neighborliness of it. And today she had a purpose, something to do for Madge. It was part of the purpose that had taken possession of her when she had met Madge at the pier, only now it was crystallized into something definite.

She did the marketing faithfully; the tradespeople were civil and obliging as usual, and she felt the better for this interlude of ordinary daily life. She saw people she knew in the main street of the village; she bowed politely to them and went on her way, thinking of nothing but her purpose. It was Madge's funeral she was thinking of; she was going to see to it that everything was done with decency and dignity and that Madge should rest in peace in Carbury cemetery.

"Mrs. Herriott," cried an excited voice, "I was going to come and see you, Mrs. Herriott."

It was Miss Lizzie Bascom, who did sewing, a big ungainly woman of forty or so, in a brown print dress and purple felt hat on her auburn hair and wearing pince-nez that always quivered a little as she talked.

"I haven't anything at the moment, Miss Bascom," said Mrs. Herriott courteously. "Later on, the curtains—"

"Oh, I wasn't thinking of work, Mrs. Herriott," said Miss Bascom. "I was just thinking of the *shock*. When I heard about the dreadful thing that happened right in front of your house...why, when I saw you come marching down the street, I couldn't believe my eyes! But then, goodness knows there's nobody has more will power than you. Why, everybody'll be flabbergasted to see you walking around as cool as a cucumber."

"Well, thank you," said Mrs. Herriott, wanting to get away. But Miss Bascom stood before her.

"I've been wondering," she said, "if that had anything to do with sabotage."

"I don't think so," said Mrs. Herriott, startled.

"Mr. Santi—that has the fruit store—he said the woman looked like a Nazi!"

"Oh, no!" said Mrs. Herriott.

"Flaxen hair, Mr. Santi said, and foreign shoes—"

"No!" said Mrs. Herriott sharply.

"And with all that happening right in front of your house and you finding the body," said Miss Bascom, "and the police coming and all, you go right ahead, without turning a hair, like a steam roller."

This was meant as a compliment; Mrs. Herriott realized that.

"Thank you," she said, and escaped.

It was stupid of me not to realize, she thought. But it really had not come into her head that everyone in Carbury must know what had happened; it had seemed a thing entirely private, even secret. Only now, as she turned into Doctor Filson's superior street, she knew better. Everyone was looking at her, everyone was talking about her, and how she shrank from that!

Tall and slight and stooping a little, she went on, feeling herself utterly unprotected and vulnerable. She was out in the world now, and she longed, almost in a panic, to turn and hurry back to the shelter of her house.

But she went on. Like a steam roller.

CHAPTER SEVEN

Dr. Filson's praise was immeasurably painful to her.

"I quite understand," he said, as they sat in his pleasant orderly study. "I quite understand, Mrs. Herriott."

No, you don't, she thought.

"It's a most humane and generous thought," he said. "I'll arrange all the details, Mrs. Herriott, as soon as the medical officer will issue a permit."

"I see!" she said.

"The police are hoping from hour to hour that someone will come forward to identify the poor woman," he went on. "I've discussed the case at considerable length with Captain King, and, as he says, it's the simplicity of the case that makes it so baffling."

He looked so upright and earnest that she was stricken with remorse. And, at the same time, a shocking irritation stirred in her: she felt that he ought to be more suspicious.

"A premeditated crime, as Captain King explained, is easier to solve, as a rule, because premeditation involves planning. But the captain doesn't think this crime was premeditated. It scarcely seems likely—"

"But it wasn't a crime!" she interrupted.

"The signs point that way, I'm afraid. Captain King himself is disposed to think it a case of homicide and robbery."

"No," said Mrs. Herriott.

"I understand, Mrs. Herriott, that it's a very unpleasant topic, but life has a way of intruding upon all of us, roughly at times, forcing upon us a fuller realization of what lies just beyond our gates."

"Yes, indeed," said Mrs. Herriott warmly, for she was ashamed of her impatience. "Then you'll let me know, Dr. Filson, when we can have the funeral? Thank you very much."

She went home in a roundabout way, to avoid the main streets. But she felt that everyone she passed stared at her and wondered, and all she wanted was to get into her own house and shut the door. When she turned the corner of her street, she saw a police car standing there.

Isn't there any end to this? she cried to herself. Can't they let me alone even for a few hours? She mounted the steps, and Josie opened the door.

"Captain King and Sergeant Tucker are here, Mrs. Herriott," she said almost in a whisper. "They've been talking to Miss Carla."

"Miss Carla?"

"She just came back. They've been asking me questions, too, Mrs. Herriott. Was it all right to tell them about that Mr. Honess who came last night?"

"Why, yes," said Mrs. Herriott, and as she was hanging up her coat in the hall closet the dining-room door opened, and Captain King came out.

"I'd like a word with you, Mrs. Herriott," he said, "if you'll step in here."

When she went into the dining room, Sergeant Tucker was there, in the chair tilted back against the wall; he rose indolently.

"This visitor you had last night, Mrs. Herriott," said Captain King. "This Honess? I understand he insisted upon seeing Mrs. de Belleforte."

"He asked to see her, and I said she was resting, and then he went away."

"What can you tell me about this man, Mrs. Herriott?"

"Why, nothing," she said.

"He was a foreigner, wasn't he?"

"He didn't speak like a foreigner."

"I'd like to know just what this man said to you, Mrs. Herriott."

"He said he wanted to see Mrs. de Belleforte, and I told him it wasn't possible, and then he went away."

She was not going to say a word to help the police in this. No matter what he's done, she thought, I hope they'll *never* find out. That would be worse than anything else—for there to be any sort of gossip, any scandal about Madge and that man.

"I'll have to see Mrs. de Belleforte now," said Captain King.

"I'll see if she's awake," said Mrs. Herriott.

She started up the stairs, and Captain King stood in the hall, looking after her. Where is Carla? she thought. If I can find her in time and she can get ready.... I can't put Captain King off any more. He'll insist upon coming up, and if Madge's room is empty—well, that'll be the end. She found Carla in her own room.

"Captain King is coming up at once to see your Aunt Madge—" she began.

"Then I'll get ready," said Carla, without any objections or even any questions. She took off her dress and got out her little make-up boxes from a bureau drawer.

"He wants to ask questions about that Mr. Honess," said Mrs. Herriott "Perhaps you'd better say he's someone you met quite casually in Paris."

"Yes," said Carla absently, intent upon her make-up.

"Carla, I don't *like* you to do this."

"I don't mind, particularly," said Carla.

She was very quick and oddly businesslike about the whole thing. When she was ready she crossed the hall to Madge's room and put on the kimono. With the shades drawn down she looked, Mrs. Herriott thought, quite horribly like Madge.

The Pendleton girls had been brought up to consider calling up and down the stairs a major offense, but Mrs. Herriott did it now. She leaned over the rail and called to Captain King in the hall below.

"You may come up now."

He came, but when he went into Madge's room, she followed him. He didn't seem to mind.

"Good morning, Mrs. de Bellaforte," he said.

"Good morning," Carla answered him. "Do you mind if I smoke? This is all so ghastly."

She looked up at him, fluttering her purple lids.

"Not at all!" he said. "Go right ahead."

She brought out a pack of cigarettes from under the pillow—and where in the world had she ever got them from? Never had Mrs. Herriott seen her smoke.

"Have you a match?" she asked, giving him a sidelong look that astounded Mrs. Herriott. Overdoing it, she thought.

Captain King struck a match and held it for her; then he sat down in a chair.

"Mrs. Herriott told you, of course, about this Mr. Honess who came to see you?"

"Oh, yes!" she answered. "How he ever found me here I can't imagine."

"Then you didn't expect to see him?"

"Well, no, not exactly. But it's not *too* surprising."

"I'd like to know a little about Mr. Honess, Mrs. de Belleforte."

"I'm so sorry, Captain King, but I really can't tell you much. He's just one of those good-looking boys one meets here and there in hotels and so on. I never took enough interest to ask him any personal questions."

She lay back against the pillows, looking at him in *that way*. Overdoing it, Mrs. Herriott thought again, alarmed and disturbed.

"What do you think was the purpose of his visit, Mrs. de Belleforte?"

"He's such a silly boy...."

He went on asking her questions; he wanted to know where she had first met Honess, but she didn't remember; he wanted to know where Honess had lived, what friends he had had, but he got nothing for his trouble. With that incredible, that gruesome coquetry, Carla insisted that she had no idea why he had come here and that she knew him only in the most casual way.

"It's just one of those things," she said. "Nobody could possibly take that boy seriously."

"I'm very anxious to get in touch with him," said Captain King. "If you can give me any idea—the name of any friend he's ever mentioned—anything of that sort."

"I couldn't," she said, with a laugh. "And the last thing in the world I want is to get in touch with him."

"Well," said Captain King, "it's too bad you can't give me anything more definite to go on, Mrs. de Belleforte."

"I'm sorry," said Carla, and as he rose she held out her hand, smiling and imperious.

He coughed and then advanced and took the out-stretched hand.

"Au revoir, mon capitaine!" she said.

"Er—good morning, Mrs. de Belleforte."

Mrs. Herriott went down to the door with him, and she found him very different from his former self, with an air of absentminded aloofness. He saw through that, she thought. He's a trained observer. He'd never take a girl of twenty-three for a woman of nearly fifty. No. He knows. And now he'll—do something. Bring back a policeman and arrest us, perhaps.

She felt curiously indifferent about it. Carla's masquerade, the light laugh, the fluttering lids, the sidelong glances, had shocked and wounded her. It was like the cruelest mockery of her poor sister.

"Lunch is ready, Mrs. Herriott," said Josie.

Mrs. Herriott turned.

"Mrs. Herriott," said Josie, "that bread we're getting isn't good. It isn't really whole wheat."

"Well..." said Mrs. Herriott.

This was a familiar theme. Josie had taken a course in nutrition at college and was very serious about food values. She was quite right, of course, but Mrs. Herriott liked that baker very much; she had been dealing with him for a long time and did not want to change.

"We can see, later on," she said.

But Josie had a one-track mind.

"Bread is really important, Mrs. Herriott," she said. "If you'll let me get Hygeno bread—"

"Let's discuss it later, Josie," said Mrs. Herriott.

"Very well," said Josie, offended. Mrs. Herriott noticed that, with a stifled sigh. It could not be denied that Josie was a little touchy, and as a rule Mrs. Herriott tried to appease her. Only today she could not.

"Miss Carla?" she asked.

"Miss Carla is coming down in a moment," said Josie, offended again. She had no great liking for Carla, and small wonder. The two girls were of almost same age, and Josie was really better-educated than Carla, more serious, more ambitious. Yet Carla felt herself superior, and showed it. The 'miss' had been a mistake.

Oh, how wearisome all this is! Mrs. Herriott cried to herself. When I have this dreadful other thing to think about... Carla was coming down the stairs now, and Mrs. Herriott stopped in the hall to wait for her. And looking at the girl, blond and cool and handsome in her dark-blue dress, a feeling of bleak isolation seized upon her. I don't understand Carla, she thought. How could she have impersonated Madge so cleverly, so horribly? And why?

She had begun it—so she said—to help her aunt, because Silas had told her it was necessary. But when had Carla ever before listened to Silas? Then, having begun, she had to keep on for her own sake, to keep clear of trouble with the police—so she said. But didn't she realize how great a risk she was taking?

She showed no sign of nervousness; she and her aunt sat down to lunch together, in an ordinary and matter-of-fact way. But Mrs. Herriott had no appetite for the cold meat loaf, the creamed carrots, the apple tapioca. They were dishes she never had liked, and today she could not force herself to swallow them, although she knew this would still further hurt Josie's feelings.

I must have a talk with Silas, she thought. A frank talk.

"Josie," she said, "is Silas at home?"

"Yes, Mrs. Herriott, he's eating his lunch."

"Ask him to come up to my room when he's finished, please, Josie. If you'll excuse me, Carla... I'm a little tired."

She pushed back her chair and rose, and Carla and Josie watched her with an air of cold surprise. She went up the stairs to her own room. She was impatient to see Silas, she was really longing to see him. He was her ally, her trusted friend, he was the one person with whom she would talk freely.

In a few minutes he came knocking at the door, and she let him in.

"We must have a talk, Silas," she said. "A serious talk. This won't do at all, Silas. Carla is getting dangerously involved—"

"Her troubles are nearly over," he said, standing before her, with that faint smile that made vertical lines in his lean cheeks. "There's been an identification."

"Silas, what do you mean?"

"Well, Peters has identified her."

"Silas, do you mean that you've dragged someone else into this? Silas, what have you done?"

"Don't worry," he said. "Peters is doing it voluntarily."

"But why? Why should that man do such a thing?"

"Oh, he believes what he's saying. He getting a big kick out of it, too."

"Explain!"

"I suddenly thought of Willie Peters," said Silas, "and I called him up. I told him that the woman found in the street here looked sort of familiar to me, but that I wasn't sure enough to say anything about it, and I'd like his opinion. He was pleased as punch, just as I expected. As soon as he saw her, he wagged his head. 'Oh, yes,' he said. 'Sure. She's the one.'"

"Who did he say she was?"

Silas turned his shoulders in his wooden way, to look at her.

"He says she's a waitress he used to see at the Boulevard Barbecue a couple of years ago."

"Silas, why is he saying such a thing?"

"He believes it. And every time he says it, he believes it more. He likes to believe it; it makes him feel important, gives him something to talk about."

"You put it into his head, you must have."

"Me?"

"You must have. You must have suggested to him that she was—this waitress."

"Well, maybe she is."

She looked at him, and he looked at her as steadily as ever he had in his life.

"Silas," she said, "it's so very strange to think of you doing things like this."

"I always was resourceful," he said.

She was silent for a time. "Silas," she said with heavy reluctance, "I *know* that was my sister."

"You can't know," he said. "Not after all these years. You say it was, and I say it wasn't."

"Silas, you only have to look at Carla, the likeness—"

"All blondes look more or less alike," he said with astonishing levity. "Only two kinds of blondes," he said, "fat ones and thin ones."

She was silent again. "A thing like this, Silas," she said finally, "can't possibly succeed."

"Truth always conquers?"

"I hope so. I think so. Anyhow, I can't go on with it—living a lie. And Carla can't go on—with this masquerade."

"We'll all get away for a while and give Tucker a chance to find out more—maybe."

She stood with one hand resting on the chest of drawers, her eyes downcast.

"It's a dreadful thing," she said. "It's a wicked thing. And it's my fault, I started it. I'm responsible."

"No," he said. "You're not responsible for anything anyone else does. You acted on impulse, and it wasn't a bad impulse. You didn't know there'd been any crime committed. We'll get away, and the thing will blow over and you'll forget it."

"Forget it...?" she repeated, half to herself. "Silas, as soon as you and Carla are out of danger of any serious trouble, I shall tell the truth. I couldn't go on *living* if I didn't."

"You'd be surprised..." he murmured.

"What do you mean by that, Silas?"

"I mean," he said, "it's a lot easier than you think, to live a lie. Gets to be second nature."

He went out, closing the door behind him. But what does he mean? she thought. That *he's* living a lie? Or was he thinking of Carla? Or does he think that everyone does? That's a cynical, horrible idea, and what's more it's not true. I know people who are as honest as daylight. Dr. Filson, for instance. And many, many others.

She was sure of that; she clung to that. Yet, in the background of her mind was that chilly feeling that she was surrounded by strangers. Standing there where Silas had left her, she remembered Carla's face, like a painted mask of dead Madge's face. And Silas, too, with his shadow of a smile. And Josie's bright dark eyes behind her spectacles. All masks...?

CHAPTER EIGHT

She waked in the night from some unremembered dream and at once began to think of Sergeant Tucker.

That's one person Silas didn't take into account, she thought. He may be able to deceive Captain King, because he wouldn't be likely to suspect a Pendleton of being mixed up in anything—wrong. But he won't fool Sergeant Tucker with this Frieda Hoff, not for a moment.

This gave her a feeling of satisfaction that was almost triumphant. She would not take any action or say any word that would betray Silas or Carla, but she longed for this thing, this lie, to end. At any cost. It seemed to her that it must inevitably end with violence, but even that would be a relief. I *do* believe that truth always conquers, she thought.

She went to sleep again and dreamed of Sergeant Tucker. He was riding a white horse, looking around him with his drowsy and secret smile, and as he came riding down the street, a crowd of people scattered before him, screaming and struggling in a panic. Don't! she tried to call out to him, but he went clattering past the house....

And it was Josie coming along the hall to knock at her door.

"Come in!" she said.

"I hate to disturb you, Mrs. Herriott, but it's nearly eight o'clock, and I know you never like to sleep late."

"No. I'm glad you called me, Josie."

Lying in her bed, Mrs. Herriott was assailed by temptation. Josie stood there with a look of miserable anxiety; obviously she was waiting to be asked what was wrong. And Mrs. Herriott was tempted *not* to ask her. After I've had my coffee, she thought...

Josie gave a little sigh and pushed her hair back from her forehead, and Mrs. Herriott was ashamed.

"Is anything wrong, Josie?" she asked.

"It's Ferdy, Mrs. Herriott. He's been having such terrible indigestion—and Silas says he's got to go home, no matter *how* he feels."

"Silas must have some good reason for that, Josie."

"He *says* it's because Ferdy shouldn't miss any more school. But it's really because he just doesn't like Ferdy around. I've noticed that, and so has Ferdy, and it makes him just wretched. He's such a high-strung little fellow."

High-strung? thought Mrs. Herriott. He's the stodgiest child I ever saw.

"He's so unhappy in that school, Mrs. Herriott, with those teachers, and our aunt is as mean as can be to him. And Father won't let him go back home. It's a terrible thing, Mrs. Herriott, for a child of that age to feel he's not wanted anywhere."

It is a terrible thing, thought Mrs. Herriott. I ought to do something about it. Perhaps I could go out to Rhode Island and talk to his father. But not now. I can't do anything about Ferdy just now.

"Ferdy clings so to me," Josie went on. "I'm all he's got, poor little fellow. I don't think it matters if he misses a day or two of school, when he's got such indigestion. And he *doesn't* bother you, does he, Mrs. Herriott?"

"Of course not, Josie."

"Silas says he does. Silas says that with Madame de Belleforte here, and that accident happening right outside the house, you don't want Ferdy around."

"I'll talk to Silas about it, Josie."

"I *wish* you would, Mrs. Herriott. He'll listen to *you*. Mrs. Herriott, I'll bring your breakfast up on a tray. You look tired."

"Oh, no!" said Mrs. Herriott. "I'll come down, Josie. But thank you just the same."

The moment the door closed she forgot Josie and Ferdy and began to think again about Sergeant Tucker. He'll be here any minute now, she thought, and that made her dress in haste. Carla was still asleep. The house was very quiet; the dining room looked shabby and a little dusty, but the morning sun was shining in, and Mrs. Herriott decided to enjoy a brief moment of tranquility. She did what she had done on other occasions: from her desk in the sitting room she got out her big checkbook, four checks to the page; she laid this thing open beside her on the breakfast table, with a pencil on it, and whenever she heard Josie coming she looked at it with a faint frown.

She was finishing her second cup of coffee when the doorbell rang. Josie went to answer it, and came back along the hall.

"It's that Sergeant Tucker, Mrs. Herriott. I told him you were just having breakfast—"

"No, I'll see him now, Josie," Mrs. Herriott said, rising.

Impossible to explain to herself the feeling she had about this man. Toward everyone else she was polite, conscientious, even a little apologetic, but for Sergeant Tucker she had a feeling that almost resembled belligerency.

"Good morning!" she said. "Come in here, please. Sit down, Sergeant."

"Thanks," he said, and sat down facing her, with a sort of slovenly impressiveness about his portly form, his curly fair head resting against the back of the chair, his heavy lids lowered, as he watched her.

"Now, about this Frieda Hoff," he said. "What can you tell me about her, Mrs. Herriott?"

"Nothing at all, Sergeant," she said. "I never heard of her before."

"Ever have a cook or a maid by the name of Frieda?"

But what a strange thing it was, thought Mrs. Herriott, that Sergeant Tucker, and Captain King, and Lizzy Bascom, and that fruit man, should think that Madge was a Nazi, or a servant, or a waitress? Wasn't there anything about a Pendleton that people could recognize unlabeled...?

"Not that I can remember," she answered.

"Have you ever been tied up with Germans, Mrs. Herriott?"

"Tied up...?"

"Ever known any Germans?"

"Certainly," she said. "Plenty of them. My father had German business friends. In the decalcomania business and china importing, and so on."

"Ever employ any Germans?"

"We had a *Fräulein* when we were children."

"What's a froyline?"

"A sort of nursery governess, ours was."

"Have you contacted this—froyline lately?"

"No, I haven't Sergeant. If she's alive," said Mrs. Herriott, "she must be at least eighty."

"Reason I asked you," he said, after a moment, "was that I understand the Hoff woman was friendly with those New Jersey Bundists three or four years ago."

"I don't see why you should think that poor woman was a German."

"Well, I happen to know she was," he said.

"'Know'?" Mrs. Herriott repeated. "Have you found out anything definite about Frieda Hoff?"

"A little," he said. "She was born over in Hoboken in eighteen-ninety-five, both parents German. She left home when she was sixteen-seventeen years old and went to New York. Haven't got any line on her in New York. No police record. Nothing more till she turns up in East Carbury, around four years ago."

There's a real Frieda Hoff, thought Mrs. Herriott. A real person. And when she reads all this in the papers, she'll come forward. Unless she's dead, too.

"She got this job at the Barbecue," Sergeant Tucker went on, "and she took a furnished room with a Polish family."

"What have they got to say about her?" Mrs. Herriott asked.

"Just about nothing," he said. "She paid her rent regular, and that was all they cared about. They didn't see much of her. She came in late at nights, on account of her job. She didn't have any friends come to see her there. When she got her day off, she stayed in bed, mostly."

"What a miserable sort of life!" said Mrs. Herriott.

"Waitresses generally have trouble with their feet," said the Sergeant. "And the Hoff woman drank. They's why she got fired from the Barbecue. She was a good waitress, they say, and the guests liked her, except when she had a couple too many, and then she got fresh. So they fired her, and we haven't got any line yet on where she went."

"Haven't you found any relations or friends?"

"Not yet."

"But you will, of course."

"Maybe. Maybe not."

"But everybody must have *someone*...."

"You'd be surprised," he said. "There's more people than you'd ever imagine that haven't got a soul that's interested in them. Look at the morgues in New York, Chicago, San Francisco. Plenty of the bodies are never identified. Nobody ever misses 'em."

He was presenting to her a dreadful, an intolerable world. "But in this case," she said, "when she's been identified... someone who knows her will surely come forward. Someone will read about her in the papers."

"Maybe. Maybe not. She's not going to get much notice in any papers, outside the local ones. And there's a lot of people that don't read papers."

"Well, in a case like this, I suppose you'll broadcast it over the radio, won't you? I mean, ask for information?"

"Why?"

"Don't you want to find her relations, her friends?"

"It's not keeping us awake nights," he said.

"But you want to—solve it," she said.

"Well, the medical officer's satisfied, and Captain King's satisfied. Accidental death."

She was silent for a moment. "Are you satisfied?" she asked.

"Oh, I'm a funny kind of a fellow," he said jocularly. "You never can tell about me."

He rose.

"And how about you, Mrs. Herriott?" he asked. "*You* satisfied?"

"I don't quite know what you mean, Sergeant."

"You got any ideas—any little theories about why this woman fell down right outside your house and cracked her skull?"

"No," she said.

"The thing is," he said, "the medical officer and Captain King and just about everybody else concerned are all local people. Now me, I came here from New York, and I've got a different way of looking at things—and people."

She understood him very well. He was telling her that to Captain King and the others she was Mrs. Herriott. But not to him.

"I hear you're paying for the funeral," he said. "That's a mighty kind-hearted thing for you to be doing, Mrs. Herriott."

She remained standing in the middle of the room after he had gone, filled with dismay and the curious anger that he alone aroused in her. If he suspects anything, she thought, why doesn't he *say* so? Why doesn't he do something? He's simply making a horrible sort of game out of this.

Hearing Josie's brisk loud step in the hall, she hastily sat down at the desk and pretended to be writing.

"Are you very busy, Mrs. Herriott?" Josie asked.

"Well, I am, just at the moment, Josie. Is it anything important?"

"I guess it doesn't matter," Josie answered unsteadily.

It isn't right to treat poor Josie like this, Mrs. Herriott thought. But I must have time to think. Suppose the real Frieda Hoff suddenly appears? Or someone who knew her well, and will say that this is—someone else.

That would be sheer disaster. It would be disgrace for all of them, shame and misery, and nothing else. There would be no benefit, even to the memory of Madge. It would not be the truth revealed in private to Dr. Filson and other grave, high-principled persons in Carbury. It would be a truth printed in the tabloids, brought out bit by bit in open court. A truth that would be a triumph for Sergeant Tucker and nobody else.

It would come to that in the end; she was certain of it. Yet she cherished that strange delusion that she could 'gain time,' that the blow could be better endured tomorrow than today.

She was still sitting at the desk when the doorbell rang again, and again Josie went by along the hall. There isn't *anyone* I want to see! Mrs. Herriott cried to herself. I want to be let alone, that's all. And, of course, I *can't* be. I've got to take the consequences....

"It's Sergeant Tucker again, Mrs. Herriott," said Josie from the doorway. "He says he wants to see Mme de Belleforte."

He's trying to trap me, coming back like this, she thought. He'll expect me to be frightened and flustered. Very well, he'll see....

She went out into the hall, smiling as if faintly amused. "Back again?" she said. "Is it really necessary for you to see Mrs. de Belleforte? She's very tired and not very well."

"No, ma'am," said he. "If you don't care to have me see Mrs. de Belleforte just now, all right. I can wait."

Everything he said was given a sinister implication by his indolent and heavy-lidded glance.

"It's not a question of my not caring to have you see her," she said. "It depends upon how she's feeling."

"All right," he said blandly. "Maybe you'll be kind enough to ask her how she's feeling."

Mrs. Herriott started up the stairs in a leisurely way. Only, her heart was beating fast. Carla can never manage this, she thought. But if I say she can't see him, he'll come back, again and again, forever and ever....

Carla was in her own room, mending a slip.

"Carla," said Mrs. Herriott, closing the door. "Sergeant Tucker is here to see—your aunt."

"Oh, I'll get ready," said Carla, rising.

"Carla, this is *very serious.*"

"Don't worry, Aunt Sharley," said Carla. "I'll manage him."

This confidence frightened Mrs. Herriott more than anything else could have done. "Sergeant Tucker is a very observant man," she said. "He's very different from Captain King."

"I know," said Carla.

Mrs. Herriott followed her across the hall to Madge's room, and Carla opened the suitcase that stood on a chair and took out that pitiable black negligee with the magenta bow hanging by a thread.

"Oh, don't wear that, Carla!" cried Mrs. Herriott.

"I'll *feel* more like Aunt Madge if I wear this. I can do much better."

"But Carla, it's—very sheer. And you've always been so particular about things like that."

"I don't want to feel like *me,* Aunt Sharley. I want to feel that I really am Aunt Madge," said Carla, getting out the make-up box.

"That's impossible, my dear," said Mrs. Herriott. "You didn't really know her at all."

"I talked to her," said Carla. "And I'm very intuitive about people. I can feel what they're like."

Mrs. Herriott did not share in this happy assurance.

"Carla," she said, "this is very serious. Don't try to talk to Sergeant Tucker. We'll pull the dark shades down, and you can lie there and—and murmur."

"I won't talk any more than I have to," said Carla. "And I was thinking, Aunt Sharley. I'm going to say that the reason I have the dark shades down is because the lack of vitamins in the food I got in Europe has affected my eyes. Vitamin A, isn't it? Or is it D?"

"I don't know," said Mrs. Herriott. "Carla, he's certain to ask you all sorts of questions—"

"I wish you'd have a little faith in me, Aunt Sharley," said Carla, offended. "It's enough to undermine all my self-confidence for you to go on like this."

That would be disastrous, and Mrs. Herriott said no more. She went halfway down the stairs to summon Sergeant Tucker, and when he went into that darkened room, she stood outside in the hall, shaken with miserable anxiety.

It was a very long time, she thought, before he came out; he glanced at her with a sleepy smile and said not a word, and she did not dare to ask a question.

When the door closed after him, she went in to Carla and found her lying back on the pillows, smoking a cigarette.

"It wasn't bad at all," she observed, nonchalantly.

"What did he ask you, Carla?"

"Oh, he asked about the Nazis, mostly," Carla answered. "I think he's rather stupid."

"Well, he's not," said Mrs. Herriott. "Now you'd better take that thing off, my dear. It's getting on to lunchtime."

She went out of the room, closing the door after her, and met Josie just coming up the stairs.

"Lunch is ready, Mrs. Herriott," she said.

Mrs. Herriott was stricken with remorse at the sight of her woebegone face.

"I'll speak to Silas at once, Josie," she said. "I'll have a talk with him about Ferdy—"

"It's too late, Mrs. Herriott. Ferdy's gone. Silas just drove him down to the station and put him on the train."

"We'll get him back next Saturday, Josie. I'm very sorry, Josie."

"Thank you, Mrs. Herriott," said Josie forlornly.

Mrs. Herriott had to wait until Carla had taken off that make-up and put on a dress of her own, and Carla did not hurry herself. That meant that lunch was nearly three-quarters of an hour late—a fresh trial for Josie. They were still at the table when Dr. Filson telephoned.

"Mrs. Herriott? I've just been in communication with Captain King, and he's given permission for the ceremony to be held tomorrow. There are one or two little details I'd like to discuss with you. Suppose I drop in this afternoon, about four?"

"I'd *rather* discuss them now, if you don't mind," she said. "I have quite a bad headache, and I thought I'd lie down after lunch."

Because she could not endure the thought of facing Doctor Filson, the man she so greatly respected and liked, and whom she was so shamefully deceiving.

"I'm extremely sorry to hear that you have a headache, Mrs. Herriott," he said, so nicely. "I'm afraid the whole thing has been too much for you, coming on top of all the excitement of Mrs. de Belleforte's arrival. Perhaps you'd rather leave it to me to arrange about the ceremony to the best of my ability?"

"Oh, yes, I should!" she said fervently.

"And I strongly advise you, Mrs. Herriott," he said, "not to attend the ceremony—"

"I want to," she said, and he accepted that as if it were a perfectly reasonable and valid desire.

"I'm sorry you have a headache, Aunt Sharley," said Carla, when she returned to the dining room. "Why didn't you tell me?"

"It will be better, as soon as I've rested," said Mrs. Herriott.

She had no trace of a headache, but she took advantage of the established fiction and went up to her room after lunch; she turned the key in the lock and lay down on the bed. She meant to use this precious time for thinking, but no thoughts came, and no emotions; she felt blank and empty. She picked up the book she had got from the lending library, and it was very interesting.

When Carla came knocking very softly at the door, to ask if she felt like coming down to dinner, she answered that she would like just a little something on a tray up here. It was wrong to make Carla eat alone, to cause this extra trouble for poor Josie. But I've done so many horrible, deceitful things, she thought, I might just as well do one more. I want, I need a little rest before tomorrow.

She was certain that the crisis would come tomorrow. Something would happen, something must happen to stop this shocking funeral.

CHAPTER NINE

It was raining the next morning. This is the day of my sister's funeral, Mrs. Herriott said to herself, and she was trembling.

She had gone to James' funeral, to her brother's, her father's, her mother's and she had gone with fortitude, with sorrowful willingness to pay her last respects to these beloved people. But this was a very different matter; this was atrocious.

She dressed herself all in black. People might well think this was an affectation, for the funeral of Frieda Hoff, but that did not trouble her. As she came out of her room, Carla met her in the hall.

"I'll go with you, Aunt Sharley," she said.

"Thank you, Carla, but I'd really rather you didn't."

"I think I ought to," said Carla. "After all, she was my aunt."

"I'd *rather* you didn't," said Mrs. Herriott.

They went downstairs together, and Josie was waiting in the hall.

"Doesn't Mme de Belleforte want any breakfast, Mrs. Herriott?" she asked.

"She had a bad night," said Carla. "She'll be sleeping late. If she wants anything, Josie, she'll call you. But don't disturb her unless she does."

She spoke with authority and none too pleasantly, and Mrs. Herriott was troubled. She opened the front door, and she and Carla stepped out on to the little porch.

"I think," she said, "that you might be a little more tactful with Josie, Carla."

"I can't stand her," said Carla.

"She's in a very difficult position," said Mrs. Herriott. "There she was, a brilliant scholar, with such a promising future—"

"I simply don't believe she ever was a brilliant scholar," said Carla. "She's as stupid as an owl."

"No," said Mrs. Herriott. "She was offered a scholarship at Barnard. But she gave up everything to help Silas."

"She doesn't help him," said Carla. "She nags and nags at him."

"I don't agree with you, Carla."

"You don't notice anything, Aunt Sharley. You've got such an exaggerated opinion of Josie. She's a nasty little thing with a martyr complex."

"She's a very loyal, hard-working girl."

"She's the world's worst cook," said Carla.

"She tries to economize," said Mrs. Herriott. "I wish you wouldn't talk this way about Josie, Carla. She's been so devoted, for such a long time—"

"She's not a bit devoted to you," said Carla. "She thinks she's a martyr and that you don't appreciate her."

"You're mistaken, Carla."

"I happen to know. I've overheard her say things."

"It's not very nice to repeat things you've overheard," said Mrs. Herriott.

"I'm simply trying to warn you, Aunt Sharley."

"I don't need to be warned against Josie," said Mrs. Herriott. "She's a fine, honest, conscientious girl, and I think *very* highly of her."

"More highly than you do of me," said Carla. "You've always been kind to me, but you've thought I was a sort of nonentity. Just as my stepmother did. Colorless, I heard her call me."

Mrs. Herriott felt it necessary to say something kind and reassuring, but a mortal weariness assailed her, and she was silent. Then Silas came driving up in the big car; he got out and stood in the rain, holding open the door.

"You're my own niece, Carla..." said Mrs. Herriott.

All this is extremely bad for Carla, she thought. Certainly I have no right to blame her for being—rather trying. I've led her into this.

They drove sedately in the heavy old car through the streets of Carbury to Bowers' Funeral Home. Mrs. Herriott was dismayed to see a policeman standing in the street outside the building, and a little crowd of people, mostly women.

"Who are those people, Silas?" she asked.

"Just here out of curiosity," he answered. "Don't bother about them."

He parked the car and helped Mrs. Herriott out; the policeman recognized her and saluted, and they went inside. Mr. Bowers received her with decorum, but without the air of sympathy he had for genuine family mourners. He was a tall bald Irishman, in a dark suit and a black tie.

"I trust you'll find everything satisfactory, Mrs. Herriott," he said. "We've received a good many flowers."

"But whoever from?" she asked, surprised.

"From the public," he said. "People take an interest, you know, in a case like this. We received a handsome wreath for Miss Hoff from the waitresses at Paul's. And Mr. Peters sent white carnations and smilax." He lowered his voice. "Would you care to see Miss Hoff?"

"Yes," said Mrs. Herriott.

She was glad to feel Silas' hand close over her arm. For this was the supreme ordeal, to look once more, and for the last time, upon her poor Madge in her sorry decline.

What she saw almost stunned her. She saw a lovely and tranquil Madge, ethereal, with delicate brows and a sweet mouth, the bright-gold hair smooth. She could have stood there forever. She did not know that tears were running down her cheeks; she forgot everyone and everything else in the immense solace that flooded her heart. Madge is at peace, she was saying to herself. Her troubles are over.

"Better come," said Silas very low, but she did not stir until his fingers tightened on her arm and drew her away. Then, glancing back, she saw Willie Peters standing by the casket, hat in hand, his head bent respectfully, a look of satisfaction on his foolish face.

She and Silas sat down side by side in the front row of chairs in the chapel, and Dr. Filson, in his vestments, came in through a door behind the altar. Oh! she thought, looking at his grave face. This is really shameful, to treat him like this.

Someone came quietly in and sat down behind her, but she tried not to look or even feel any curiosity. She tried to keep all her attention upon Doctor Filson reading the burial service for Frieda Hoff. It's probably Mr. Bowers sitting there, she thought. Or Mr. Peters.

But she did want to know. She stirred a little in her chair and turned her head, and met the black eyes of Ramon Honess.

It's happened, she thought. The crisis she had so feared had come, and in a form she had not envisaged.

If Ramon Honess had looked into the casket—and surely he had—then he must know the truth. And if he knew it, she thought, surely he would make use of it.

He'll either tell the police at once, she thought, or he'll try to blackmail me. Well, I haven't enough money to pay blackmail—unless he'd be satisfied with small payments. I could pay *something* the fifteenth of every month, when Jeff Quillen sends my cheque. I dare say it's a very wrong thing, a criminal thing, to pay blackmail. But I'd do it, willingly, rather than have any gossip about Madge.

She thought of this as they drove to the Carbury cemetery, where she had bought a plot for Frieda Hoff as near as possible to Uncle Louis Pendleton. I'm not going to tell even Silas about that Mr. Honess, she thought. About Madge taking such an interest in him. I'm not going to tell anyone.

She stood beside the grave with her eyes lowered; she heard Dr. Filson's fine deep voice speaking those austere and noble words. There were seven Pendletons lying here under the old trees; it was a right and good place for Madge to be, and everything was being done with dignity and decency.

And it's going to stay like this, she thought. I won't have her whole history dragged out for people to gossip about. I don't really want to tell anyone, ever, not even Doctor Filson. Much better for Madge to be here, with Frieda Hoff's name on the headstone. Much better to pay blackmail all the rest of my days than have my poor sister humiliated.

Dr. Filson offered his arm, and they walked along the gravel path.

"I'll go back to the house with you, Mrs. Herriott," he said.

"Oh, thank you, Dr. Filson, but there's really no need."

"Mrs. Herriott," he said, "is there anything you'd like to talk over with me?"

"No," she said. She turned to look at him, and he was so very grave. "No, thank you," she said.

"I'm not only your pastor, Mrs. Herriott, but I am—I hope—numbered among your friends."

"Oh, yes!"

"If anything is troubling you, Mrs. Herriott—?"

"Nothing is, thank you," she said, and he fell silent.

How glad she was to get back to her own house! Josie opened the door.

"Mme de Belleforte didn't call for me," she said. "I went up, three or four times, and stood outside the door, but I didn't hear a sound. She hasn't had a thing to eat, Mrs. Herriott, ever since—"

"Oh, shut up!" said Silas.

"Silas!" said Mrs. Herriott, shocked.

Josie's rosy little face grew scarlet; she turned away.

"If you'll fix up a tray, Josie," said Mrs. Herriott. "I'll take it up. It's very kind of you, Josie, to take such an interest." She went into the sitting room, and Silas followed her. "I'm sorry to hear you speak to Josie like that," she said.

"I'm sorry, too," said Silas. "Mrs. Herriott, we'd better leave tonight."

She was silent, trying to think, but conscious of nothing but a great longing to get away from here.

"Silas, if we did go—what about Carla?" she asked.

"We'll say she's gone back to New York. We'll have to manage so that nobody sees us start."

"But if anyone asks questions...? If anyone—that Sergeant Tucker, for instance—if he wants to see Carla?"

"He won't. Why should he?"

"They asked her questions before."

"It's finished now," he said. "And, anyhow, we have to take a certain amount of risk. Whatever it is, it will be better than staying here any longer. What's Honess doing around here?"

"He wanted to see Mrs. de Belleforte."

"Any particular reason?"

"They'd met in Paris," said Mrs. Herriott.

For she would not tell even her faithful Silas about that.

"We might have trouble with him," said Silas thoughtfully. "Well, we'll handle things as they come. Now you'd better call up Dr. Filson. Look queer if you leave without a word to him. Tell him you and Mme de Belleforte are leaving."

"But what about Josie?"

"She'd better stay here for the time being. After you've found a house for the summer she can come along."

"We can't take a house for the summer, Silas. And I don't think it's right to leave Josie here all alone."

"She'll be all right."

"Silas," she said, "you mustn't forget, ever, what Josie has done for you, how devoted she's been—"

"I won't," he said.

She was distressed by his tone, his attitude.

"We're deceiving Josie, Silas," she said. "When she finds out, she'll be bitterly hurt that we didn't trust her."

"All for her own good," said Silas. "You'd better call up Captain King, too, Mrs. Herriott. Tell him you're thinking of getting away for a little change."

"Yes... Silas, I don't want to be meddlesome, but can't you try to be a little nicer to Josie about Ferdy? Remember that Josie's young—"

"I'm not an old man myself," said Silas, and she said no more.

She was very anxious now to get away from here, away from Honess and Sergeant Tucker. She called up Captain King and spoke to him with fine aplomb.

"We'd like to get away tonight for a little change, if there's no objection."

"Why, no," he said. "No. But I'd like you to keep in touch with us, Mrs. Herriott."

She had more trouble with Dr. Filson.

"I called up to say au revoir," she said. "We're leaving Carbury this evening, for a little change of scene."

"I'd like very much to see you, Mrs. Herriott," he said. "I can be there within half an hour."

"That's very kind of you, Dr. Filson, but there's so much to be done, packing, and so on...."

"Mrs. Herriott," he said, "I wish, I wish very much that you would spare me just a few minutes."

I don't want to see you, she thought. I won't see you.

"We're only going to New York, Dr. Filson," she said winningly. "I'll let you know as soon as we're settled. But, we're in such a turmoil now...."

"Very well, Mrs. Herriott," he said, quietly.

Now he's hurt, she thought. I'm afraid he feels there's something wrong, too. Well, it can't be helped.

She went upstairs to pack, and Josie came after her.

"May I help you, Mrs. Herriott?"

"No, thank you Josie."

"May I help Mme de Belleforte?"

"No, thank you, Josie. I'll see to that."

"Maybe I'd better tidy up Carla's room."

"Oh, she'll do that, Josie."

"But she's gone, Mrs. Herriott!" said Josie, surprised. "Silas just drove her to the station."

"Oh, yes! I'd forgotten," said Mrs. Herriott hastily.

Of course, Carla had to be out of the way before Mme de Belleforte left the house. So complicated, all of this so dangerous, so wearisome. Poor little Josie was lingering.

"Silas says you want me to stay here and keep things going, Mrs. Herriott.

I'm sorry to bother you, but if you'll leave me some money, please—?"

"Yes, of course!" she said. "Will you ask Silas to come up, please, Josie?"

For she began to think now, with consternation, of the financial aspect of the affair.

"We can't go tearing off like this," she said to Silas, when he came into her room. "I'll have to leave money here as well as paying for us in New York, and there's nothing coming in from Mr. Quillen until the fifteenth."

"I told you I could help you."

"I'm not going to borrow from you, Silas. If you've saved anything, it really belongs to Josie. She's scrimped and done without things for a long time."

"This money hasn't anything to do with Josie."

"Then what money is it?"

"It would be a damn sight better if you didn't ask me."

"I do ask you," said Mrs. Herriott.

"All right," he said. "She gave it to me."

"'She...?' What do you mean by 'gave' it to you?"

"I mean just what I said. She gave me some money."

"Why?"

"To keep for her," he answered, with a shadowy smile.

"That money doesn't belong to you, Silas. Or to me, either."

"All right," he said. "Who does it belong to?"

It belongs to that Mr. Honess, thought Mrs. Herriott. That is, if she really did make that will she told me about.

"How much is it, Silas?" she asked, after a moment.

"Couple of hundred."

She paused again. "Did she—what was the reason she gave it to you, Silas?"

"That's pretty complicated," he said. "Anyhow, you know what she was like."

No, Mrs. Herriott thought, I don't really know what Madge was like. And now I never shall.

"I've telephoned for rooms," said Silas. "All you have to do is to go there and take it easy for a while."

"I can't—" she began, when Josie came to the doorway.

"Mr. Honess is here, Mrs. Herriott."

"I'll see him for you, Mrs. Herriott," said Silas.

"No!" said Mrs. Herriott. "I'll go—"

"You'd better let me," said Silas, but she was already on her way.

This was one thing that she must manage alone, one thing Silas must know nothing about. She started down the stairs, and there he was, standing in the hall, where she had first seen him—handsome, olive-skinned, as sinister to her as a young Mephistopheles.

"Come in here, please," she said, and as he followed her into the sitting room she closed the door.

She was in great haste to face him, to meet this danger immediately and boldly.

"Please tell me," she said, "exactly what you want."

He seemed a little taken aback by this directness.

"I thought," he said, "that perhaps you'd explain—a little."

"No," she said.

"But, Mrs. Herriott, do you expect me to keep quiet about this—it's hard to find a word for it—"

"I'll make it worth your while," she said.

"You'll—*what?*" he asked.

"I wish to avoid any gossip," she said.

"'Gossip'?" he repeated. "Don't you think it might be more serious than that?"

"No!" she said, still with this new energy. "You don't understand the circumstances, and I'm not going to explain. But if you'll go away and keep quiet, I'll give you whatever I can."

"I'm not sure I understand, Mrs. Herriott...."

"I can give you something every month," she said. "I get my check on the fifteenth. It won't be much, but it will be quite regular."

"You're offering to bribe me, Mrs. Herriott? Don't you think that's rather dangerous?"

"Yes, I know that," she said.

She did know it. But she was already entirely in his power. She could not see that she had anything to lose by trying to keep him silent.

"I can promise you twenty-five dollars a month," she said.

"That isn't very much," he said, with an odd smile.

Does he know about Madge's will? she thought, suddenly. For if he did, her offer would be ludicrous. But there was a chance that he did not know and did not even hope for any benefit from Madge's death. She had nothing to lose, everything to gain.

"You don't want a lot of unpleasant gossip yourself," she said resolutely.

"No, of course not," he agreed, and her heart leaped with relief.

He's probably got plenty of unsavory things in his own life that he wouldn't like the police to find out, she thought. If I only knew something definite against him....

She decided to take an enormous chance.

"It would be very unpleasant for you if there were any gossip," she said. "I warn you, Mr. Honess, I shouldn't hesitate to tell everything I know about you."

He glanced at her sidelong and then looked down at the floor, and his dark face was a mask. Another mask.

"I'd like very much to know what your object is, Mrs. Herriott," he said.

"My object is to protect my sister's name," she said.

"You're willing to go pretty far," he said.

"Yes," she said. "I am."

He was silent again, and she waited.

"If you'll give me my little package, Mrs. Herriott—"

"I'll look for it, Mr. Honess."

"Will you look for it now, Mrs. Herriott?"

Perhaps this is another way to keep him quiet, she thought. If there really is any package, and I can make him think I'm going to find it for him, perhaps he'll wait.... And I think, I really do think I've frightened him a little.

"I can't look now," she said. "There are people around.... But I'll look tomorrow. I'll look thoroughly."

"Very well, Mrs. Herriott," he said gently. "I'll wait till tomorrow."

And by tomorrow we'll be gone, she thought. I suppose he'll be able to trace us without much difficulty. We can't all simply disappear. But it will give me more time to think and plan.

"Then I'll say au revoir, Mrs. Herriott. Until tomorrow."

When he comes tomorrow and we've gone... she thought. He'll be furious. He might go straight to Captain King. But she did not think so. Glancing covertly at him, she did not think he was at all likely to be furious. She thought that he had an infinite and dreadful patience.

He held out his hand. She did not want to take it, but she did so, to make him go away. He raised her hand to his lips, bending his dark head with that grace, that elegance he had.

This is the way he behaved to Madge, she thought. He's mocking me, just as he did Madge.

CHAPTER TEN

When she was ready and her bag packed, Mrs. Herriott went to that room she still called Madge's, and Carla opened the door.

"Good heavens!" said Mrs. Herriott.

Carla was wearing a suit of brilliant green tussore—a fitted jacket and a short narrow skirt—and a green turban; her mouth looked wide and moist, covered with dark lipstick; her lids were purple, as Madge's had been; the rouge high on her cheekbones gave her face a hollow and haggard look. The likeness to Madge was extraordinary—and profoundly disturbing.

"Where did you get those clothes, my dear?" Mrs. Herriott asked.

"They were in one of Aunt Madge's suitcases. I thought it would be better to wear her things in the circumstances."

There was a loud knock at the door.

"Silas says he's ready," said Josie, and Carla opened the door.

Josie gave a gasp and stood staring at the girl.

"Who's this?" asked Carla, in a casual and half-arrogant way.

No, Mrs. Herriott thought. This won't do. Josie knows Carla so well. Josie won't be taken in for a minute.

"I'm Josie, madam," she said, "Silas' wife."

"Take my bag down, will you please?" said Carla, with that new manner. "Are you ready, Sharley?"

No! Mrs. Herriott cried to herself. This can't work. Josie must know. Everybody will know that Carla is not a woman of nearly fifty. It's impossible. But as she followed Carla down the stairs, she was amazed to see how the girl had changed her walk, her carriage; her very figure seemed changed; her thin body sagged a little. Only instead of poor Madge's matchstick legs, Carla's were lovely.

The car stood outside the house, the headlights blurred in the faint rain. Silas took the two bags and stowed them in the front; Mrs. Herriott and Carla got in back, and off they went.

Better not to ask any questions. Better to lean back and be quiet and look out at Carbury in the rain. Grandfather Pendleton had had a fine place here, on the shore; she and Madge used to come for visits when they were little girls. They used to play on the beach, and Madge was so pretty and gay, with her long hair floating in the wind. We used to find such interesting shells, Mrs. Herriott remembered.

A desolate and crushing loneliness came upon her. I really haven't anyone left, she thought. But that seemed a form of treachery. No, she thought, there's Silas, there's Carla, there's Josie. They're *very* loyal. And there's Dr. Filson and Jeff Quillen—and other people....

They went through the main street of Carbury, the little shops warm and dim, past the railroad station, and out into the flat empty country. This is nothing but self-pity, Mrs. Herriott told herself. It's cowardly and very wrong....

"Do you mind if I smoke, Aunt Sharley?"

"Why, no, my dear."

A match struck and a little flame sprang out for an instant.

"How strange this is, isn't it," said Carla.

"It's horrible," said Mrs. Herriott. "And it's my fault entirely. I got you into this most unsavory and dangerous situation, Carla. I reproach myself—"

"Oh, don't!" said Carla. "It's an adventure, Aunt Sharley."

"That's not the way to look at it, Carla."

"I can't help it," said Carla. "It's—I mean, apart from the sadness for you, I think it's thrilling."

This was an attitude to be discouraged.

"We're involved in lies and deceit," Mrs. Herriott said.

"You know how I used to love acting when I was in boarding school," said Carla. "And now—do you know, Aunt Sharley—I feel as if I actually *was* Aunt Madge."

"Well you're not," said Mrs. Herriott, briefly.

Carla's voice sounded so young in the dark, so clear and confident. This is an unexpected development, Mrs. Herriott thought. It's altogether *wrong* for the child to be enjoying this dreadful thing. And I'm responsible. I must think of a way out.

She closed her eyes; she did not sleep, but a fatigued blankness enveloped her; thoughts flitted through her mind without direction. The lights of the city roused her; she looked out of the window at the glistening wet streets; she looked at Silas, with his square shoulders and stiffly-held head; she glanced at Carla and found her leaning back and breathing evenly and quietly. She's asleep, Mrs. Herriott thought. I've got her into this, and I shall have to get her out of it. I shall have to help her to see things differently.

The car stopped at a midtown street before a portico with the storm curtains down. A doorman hurried out with a big umbrella. It looked like a nice quiet hotel, Mrs. Herriott thought. But when they entered the lounge, she was worried. This was luxurious; this was an atmosphere once familiar to her, but almost forgotten.

There was no escape though, now. She went to the desk.

"You have a room engaged for Mrs. Herriott?" she said.

"Yes, madam," said the clerk. "Will you sign the register, please?"

He pushed it toward her, and she looked at it. I can't sign Madge's name, she thought. I really can't. It's—that really seems *criminal*. I don't see....

"I'll sign," said Carla, and taking up the pen she wrote, in her big angular writing:

Mrs. James Herriott, Carbury, Long Island.
Mme Pascal de Belleforte, Paris, France.

The clerk rang a bell.

"Front!" he said. "Show the ladies to 1804."

"I'll call up in half an hour for your instructions, madam," said Silas, and turned away.

They went up in the elevator, and the bellboy hurried ahead of them and unlocked the door. Carla opened her purse and took out some change for him; plenty, it must have been, to make him look so pleased.

"Oh this is *nice,* isn't it?" said Carla.

Far, far too nice, Mrs. Herriott thought. It was a suite; the sitting room was charmingly furnished, softly and clearly lit by white-shaded lamps; there was a turquoise carpet and white leather armchairs. It had the clean and airy smell of a well-kept place. And it had the little touches to be found only in expensive places.

Carla was moving about, looking at everything, at the tranquil blue and white bedroom and the glittering bathroom.

"It's heavenly!" she said.

What does it cost? Mrs. Herriott thought. Something fabulous.

"I'm going to take a glorious bath," said Carla. "Look at the enormous bath towels!"

There was a knock at the door, and a boy entered with a box of flowers.

"For Mrs. de Belleforte," he said; Mrs. Herriott tipped him, and he withdrew.

"For *me?*" Carla said.

"No," said Mrs. Herriott, "you're not Mrs. de Belleforte."

She opened the box and took out the card that lay on the pink rosebuds.

> *Welcome home, Madge. I'll call up tomorrow.*
> JEFF QUILLEN

"How could he possibly know we're here!" cried Mrs. Herriott.

"Oh, Aunt Madge told me she told lots of people she was going to stay at the St. Pol."

"But is this the St. Pol? I hadn't noticed. I haven't been here for so very long, and it's so much changed...." Mrs. Herriott stood still, with one hand resting on the back of the chair. "If Mr. Quillen insists upon seeing you," she said, "I don t know what we'll do."

"I can manage, Aunt Sharley."

"No. Not Jeff Quillen."

"He hasn't seen me since I was a little girl. I *know* I can manage it."

"Mr. Quillen was very devoted to your Aunt Madge," said Mrs. Herriott. "At one time we thought she might marry him."

"Oh, that's romantic! After all these years."

"No. You won't be able to deceive him, Carla. He'll know at once that you're not Madge. What's more, he'll ask you all sorts of questions you couldn't possibly answer."

"I can be just sort of gay."

"Not with a lawyer," said Mrs. Herriott.

If Jeff Quillen ever got Madge's will, she thought, he'll begin asking questions about Mr. Honess at once. If he asks me, I can put him off, one way or another. But if he should ever see Carla.... Well, he can't see her. I'll have to keep them from meeting, somehow.

Not forever; she knew that. She was faced again with the complete impossibility of going on with this fantasy much longer. Yet she clung stubbornly and desperately to the delusion that by putting off the dreadful hour she was gaining something. Gaining time. Time for what?

"You'd better take your bath now, Carla, my dear," she said, "and get to bed in good time."

She sat down in a white leather armchair to wait for Silas to telephone. It was so strange, and so sad, to be here in the St. Pol again; strange, and sad, to think of Jeff Quillen in the days when he had been so attentive to Madge. She could hear Carla singing in her bath, and that too was sad and strange.

The telephone rang and it was Silas.

"Silas," said Mrs. Herriott, "what are we paying for this suite?"

"Don't worry," he said. "Just leave it to me."

"I shall have to know."

"I'll come around tomorrow morning, and we'll talk it over."

"Where are you, Silas?"

"I've got a room in a little hotel around the corner, the Whitecliff. Don't worry, Mrs. Herriott. Don't worry about anything."

"May I speak to Silas?" asked Carla.

She was wearing a white terry robe, and her newly washed hair was soft as silk about her face, clean of all make-up now and alive with happiness. She took the telephone from Mrs. Herriott.

"Silas?" she said. "I just wanted to tell you that everything's fine.... It's a darling suite.... Yes.... What...? Yes, I will. See you tomorrow, Silas!"

"I thought you didn't care much for Silas," said Mrs. Herriott.

"Well, he is a bit of a wolf—"

"A wolf?" Mrs. Herriott repeated. "What do you mean by that, Carla?"

"Oh, it's an expression, Aunt Sharley. It means a man who sort of prowls after women."

"You think Silas is like that?"

"Well, that's what everyone in Carbury says."

"People say that *Silas* is—one of these wolves?"

"Yes. But I must say he's been wonderful about all this. So understanding—"

"I think I'll take my bath now, Carla."

"I wish I had something to read for a while. I'm not a bit sleepy."

"Telephone and ask them to send you up some magazines," said Mrs. Herriott.

She did not care now about spending a little extra. She ran a bath and got into it; she lay back in the warm water, and at last she was relaxed, as if a little stunned.

Silas? she said to herself. Silas a wolf?

CHAPTER ELEVEN

Mrs. Herriott slept poorly, waking again and again, and in her drowsiness, she thought it was James breathing in the next bed. She spoke his name, but there was no answer, and she remembered that it was Carla. A little sound made her open her eyes, and she saw Carla sitting up and turning the pages of a magazine.

"Oh, good morning, Aunt Sharley! Silas said we'd better have our breakfast sent up here and take things easy."

"Silas seems to be taking a good deal upon himself," said Mrs. Herriott.

"Oh, let's! How do we do it?"

"Take up the telephone and ask for room service."

"What shall we have?"

"Whatever you like, my dear," said Mrs. Herriott.

"When it comes, I can hide in the bathroom, can't I? I don't want to get all made up until I have to."

She ordered and then leaned back against the pillow.

"I've never stayed in a hotel," she said, "except horrible old ramshackle ones in the country. I've never traveled. I've never done anything or seen anything. The other girls I went to school with had such utterly different lives. I couldn't even talk to them."

"I don't think it's as bad as all that, Carla."

"It is, Aunt Sharley. My life's been *miserable*. I started to work when I was just eighteen—"

"You wanted to, Carla. You said you didn't want to go to college—"

The breakfast came, and Mrs. Herriott admitted the waiter; she and Carla ate, side by side in the twin beds. Carla forgot her grievance and became happy and lively.

"Aren't those roses lovely? And was Mr. Quillen really an old beau of Aunt Madge's?"

"I suppose he could be called that."

"I don't really remember him at all. It'll be fun seeing him."

"Carla," said Mrs. Herriott, "it worries me very much, very much indeed, to hear you say things like that. *Nothing* about this situation could possibly be 'fun.' It's sad and horrible and tragic, from beginning to end."

"Don't you ever want me to be a little bit happy?" cried Carla, and Mrs. Herriott said no more.

Carla took a long time to dress, but when she was done, she had achieved her usual surprising and disturbing effect. She didn't look old, Mrs. Herriott thought, but certainly she did not look young; she carried herself with a forward droop of the shoulders that made her seem hollow-chest-ed; she had a worn and reckless look.

Silas telephoned from the lobby, and Carla opened the door for him when he came up.

"Hello!" she said gaily, and he gave a casual gesture with his bony hand in response.

"Have you got a cigarette?" she asked. He lit one for her and turned to stand before Mrs. Herriott, who was sitting on the sofa.

"Carla ought to get out and buy some new clothes," he said.

"I don't see any need for it!"

"That's what Mrs. de Belleforte certainly would have done," he said. "That's what anybody would expect her to do."

"I can't afford it, Silas. The expenses here are going to be ruinous."

"I've got money."

"A couple of hundred won't go far living in this way."

"There's a little more than that," he said.

"How much more?"

"Mrs. Herriott, there's no use fighting this thing every step of the way. We're in it, and we've got to go on. Carla ought to look nice, ought to look prosperous. Don't worry about the expenses here. I'll see to it that it doesn't run to more than we can pay. Just take it easy."

"I think Silas is right," said Carla. "I think it would look queer if I'm so shabby."

"I'd like to know—I've got to know how much there is."

He was silent for a moment.

"Just leave it to me," he said, almost gently. "There isn't any other way. If you'll take Carla out to some good store and get her a decent outfit—"

The telephone rang and she answered it.

"Mrs. Herriott?" said a voice she knew very well. "Oh, Charlotte... this is Jeff Quillen. How are you, Charlotte?"

"Very well, thank you. How are *you?*"

"Oh, fair to middling. Fair to middling. I was called to Washington suddenly. That's why you didn't hear from me before. And Washington, these days...."

This had to go on; she was resigned to it. Jeff Quillen could not be hurried. They talked about the weather and the war news.

"Now tell me," he said. "How is Madge?"

"The voyage was very trying."

"Naturally. Naturally. She's resting, I hope?"

Mrs. Herriott's lips trembled. "Yes. She's resting."

"I'd like very much to see her, Charlotte, for a few moments. D'you think this afternoon, perhaps?"

I can't do this, she thought.

"At five o'clock or so? For a few moments?"

"Jeff," she said with convincing earnestness. "I really can't tell you now.

She's very tired. Suppose I let you know later?"

"Whatever you think best, Charlotte," Jeff said cheerfully.

"Good-by," she said and hung up the receiver.

"You don't have to go shopping with me, Aunt Sharley," said Carla, "Silas can let me have some money—"

But it seemed to Mrs. Herriott her duty to superintend this matter. She believed that she was utterly indifferent to all this, but no sooner had they entered the Fifth Avenue store than her old instincts awoke. For she had been a notable shopper in her time; she had been thoroughly trained by her mother, and she knew materials, she knew values. She had nothing to say against the shoes Carla chose, high-heeled black pumps, very expensive. But when it came to a suit she was definite.

"Don't get that sleazy thing," she said. "It won't keep its shape. I'll never look like anything. It's better not to get black, Carla, unless it's good."

She picked out a suit. "Try this," she said, and it was right.

"But I don't think it's typical of—you know who."

"That's something you can't know," said Mrs. Herriott. "She had to take what she could get in Europe, with this war going on. She always had excellent taste."

"Why don't you get a suit, Aunt Sharley?"

"I don't need one."

"I'll treat you to a new outfit," said Carla.

"Carla," said Mrs. Herriott, "this money doesn't belong to you."

"I've got money of my own I've saved from my job," said Carla. "I'd *like* to get you something, Aunt Sharley."

"No, thank you."

"Do you always have to say no to everything?" asked Carla. "Couldn't you, just once, say yes, and let things be pleasant?"

"Yes," said Mrs. Herriott abruptly.

She was mortally tired of resisting; it was an inexpressible relief to yield, to go with the current, just for a little time. If Carla really wants to get me a present, she thought, it wouldn't be kind to refuse.

"First," Carla said, "you need a new foundation."

"No, I don't. This one is practically new—"

"It's all wrong," said Carla. "It's old-fashioned."

What she and the fitter selected was surprising to Mrs. Herriott.

"You've got quite a small waist, comparatively," Carla said, regarding Mrs. Herriott in the garment that gave her a sort of hourglass figure.

"I thought that was out of date," Mrs. Herriott observed.

Oh, no, they told her, and she didn't care. She picked out a suit; she looked at herself in a long mirror, saw herself neat, straight, a little majestic. It doesn't matter, she thought. Nothing is real.

Nothing is real. I can't believe I'm here, in the St. Pol, with Carla. And that Madge is dead. An extraordinary weariness came over her. It was not her habit to take naps, but by half past three she could not keep her eyes open.

"I'll just lie down for half an hour," she said, and left Carla in the sitting room putting a new shade of polish on her nails. She took off her dress and her shoes and lay down on the bed, and it was heavenly. She seemed to sink, to melt into the mattress. Fresh sweet air blew in at the windows; the room was so neat and tranquil, it was heavenly.

She slept, the most refreshing sleep; she wakened easily and lay quiet, looking at the pale-blue sky outside the window. The noises from the street far below were little more than a dull hum; rather pleasant, she thought. She was city-born and bred, and this feeling of life streaming around her was familiar and soothing to her. She sighed comfortably—and then she heard a laugh.

It was Jeff Quillen's laugh; he was there in the sitting room.

She got up in haste, and terror, and washed and dressed; she opened the door and went in. The heavy blue curtains were drawn across the windows, and in that twilight Carla was lying back in a chair smoking.

"Charlotte!" said Jeff Quillen, rising. "*You're* looking very well. Younger than ever."

He was a tall man, lean, his shoulders a little bent, with dark hair worn rather long; in the wing collar he affected he had somewhat the look of an old-fashioned diplomat; he was courtly in manner, in an absent-minded way. Of course, he knew all the things a lawyer had to know; he had a large practice; he was a man of distinction; he must, Mrs. Herriott thought, be very intelligent.

"I thought I'd stop in on the chance of seeing Madge..." he said. "We've been having a chat about old times."

And could he be deluded by a girl of twenty-three? Deluded about someone he had known as well as he had known Madge, someone he had so profoundly admired?

They sat there for a time, all three, carrying on a pointless conversation.

"Have you seen Maitland lately, Charlotte? He's very anxious to see Madge.... The Poindexter boy is in the Navy now...."

"Oh, is he? Dr. Filson's two nephews are both in the Navy."

After a little of this, he rose.

"I'm sorry to hurry away," he said, "but I have a longstanding engagement."

He stood before Carla, and she held out her hand to him, with what seemed to Mrs. Herriott a ridiculous affectation of imperious charm. She smiled up at him, and he smiled too.

"I'll see you very soon again," he said. "I suppose you'll be very busy for a time—seeing old friends, shopping, and so on."

"I want to rest before I do anything much," Carla said. "I'm thinking of going out to the country for a few weeks before I pick up the threads."

"Very sound idea," he said. "Very sound. I'll call you up tomorrow, to see if I can be of any service. Then—au revoir, for the present."

"Au revoir—Jeff," Carla said, fluttering her lids.

"I'll go out to the elevator with you," said Mrs. Herriott; he took up his hat, and they went out into the warm, quiet, thickly-carpeted corridor.

"I suppose," he said, "that you and Madge have had a fine time, talking over old days, and so on?"

"Why, yes," she said. "Yes."

"She's been away so long," he said. "I suppose she's forgotten a good deal?"

"Oh, no," said Mrs. Herriott easily.

But she was frightened, very much frightened.

"I found her—a little vague, now and then," he said. "But later, no doubt... Did she mention a will to you, Charlotte?"

"I—think so," said Mrs. Herriott.

"Naturally I was anxious to know something about this—this young protégé of hers...."

They were both silent for a time, and in spite of her great dread and fear, a queer little spark of comfort glowed in her heart. 'Protégé' was so exactly the right word; Jeff's attitude would always be so right.

"She was extraordinarily offhand about the whole matter," he said. "I asked her if she was serious about this will, and she answered no, not very. I felt obligated, Charlotte, to impress upon her the extreme seriousness of a will. I pointed out to her that if anything had happened to her during the voyage over, for instance, this will would have been valid."

"Yes..." said Mrs. Herriott.

"I took it upon myself, Charlotte, to suggest to her that she had acted very hastily and thoughtlessly, and with a great lack of consideration toward you. I told her a little, Charlotte, of what you've been through and of your magnificent courage and unselfishness."

"Oh!" said Mrs. Herriott, surprised and greatly touched.

"In our young days, Charlotte," he said, "I'll admit that I didn't fully appreciate you. But lately, within the last few years..." He rang for the elevator. "I believe that will is nothing more or less than a whim," he said, "and I believe she's quite ready to alter it."

She can't! She can't! thought Mrs. Herriott.

"In the meantime," he said, "if there's anything that troubles or disturbs you, Charlotte, let me know. Call me at my office or my hotel at any time."

"Well, for instance, Jeff...?"

"Anything. Anything at all." He held out his hand. "Remember," he said, "if you're perplexed or anxious about anything, Charlotte, I'm at your service. At all times."

The elevator door opened.

The door rattled shut, and she stood there, cold with dismay. He knows there's something wrong, she thought. I can't tell how much he knows— but nothing will stop Jeff Quillen. He'll go on and on. This really is the end.

CHAPTER TWELVE

She found Carla in the bedroom, standing before the mirror combing her hair. She turned, and under the disfiguring make-up her face was alight and young.

"I ought to get a prize for *that!*" she said. "I only wish you could have heard me talking to Mr. Quillen."

"Carla, did he ask you many questions?"

"No, very few. Anyhow, I could have answered anything. It's—I must say it's fascinating."

"Carla—" Mrs. Herriott began, and checked herself.

There's no use warning her now, she thought. There's nothing she could do about it. It would only make her wretched.

"Aunt Sharley, let's have cocktails before dinner."

"I thought you didn't approve of them, Carla."

"Oh, I don't mind once in a while. I'd like to, today."

"Very well. Telephone down for them."

"No, let's go down to the cocktail lounge. There's music there, and it's lively."

In a public place? Mrs. Herriott thought. Suppose there's someone who knows me?

"I think it would be cozier up here," she said.

"Oh, please let's go down," said Carla.

"I don't think it would be advisable, my dear."

"If you don't feel like coming," said Carla, "I'll go by myself."

"Carla, it would *not* be advisable. I have friends who come to this hotel, and it's quite possible one of them might be here now."

"Well, I'll have to meet people sooner or later. You couldn't keep Aunt Madge hidden."

"Carla, my dear, people who knew Madge at all well in the past can't be—taken in by this."

"Yes, they can! Look at Mr. Quillen!"

"I'm afraid Mr. Quillen was not quite satisfied...."

"But I *know* he was. I could tell."

"Carla," Mrs. Herriott said with reluctance, "I'm afraid he's suspicious."

"You're mistaken, Aunt Sharley. After all, I'm really the one to know. I talked to him while you were taking a nap, and I'd have seen at once if he'd been suspicious. He wasn't. He was really rather sweet, so gallant and old-fashioned."

She's like a little girl dressing up and playing lady, Mrs. Herriott thought. Poor child, I don't know what the consequences of this will be but she can't be blamed. It's simply a game for her. She's actually enjoying it.

"Don't you worry, Aunt Sharley," said Carla. "I managed Mr. Quillen and I can manage any friends of yours who might come along. Do let's go down to the cocktail lounge."

"I don't *want* to, Carla."

"I think that's very unreasonable, Aunt Sharley. I mean, after all, I'm young, and I've had such a dull narrow life. As long as we're here in a really nice hotel, I'd like to see something of it."

"I know, Carla. I'm sorry. But the risk—"

"I don't consider it any risk. I can't stand being shut up all the time with nobody to talk to, nothing to do. I've never even been to the St. Pol before.... I'm sorry, but if you won't come—"

"I'll come," said Mrs. Herriott.

As they left the suite Mrs. Herriott turned back to try the door, a habit of hers. Carla was going down the corridor, thin and supple in her new suit, too supple, Mrs. Herriott thought; the girl was walking in a new way, and not a very *nice* way. This is so bad for her, she thought. And how could it be otherwise than bad, this course of deceit and lies?

They got into the elevator, and Carla leaned back against the wall; almost flaunting she was, with her long light hair and that ghastly make-up; so sure of herself, poor child. If there was anyone here who had ever known the Pendleton sisters...

But Captain King had seemed satisfied, and the police doctor, and even Sergeant Tucker, and maybe after all it could be done. Perhaps Jeff Quillen himself could be deluded. Perhaps the evil day could be postponed.

The cocktail lounge was surprisingly attractive to Mrs. Herriott. It had been a long time since she had been in a place like this, and it recalled to her the days, almost like a dream now, when she and James used to go out together, handsomely dressed, important people. She sat down with Carla at a small table in a corner, with a good-shaded lamp on it; Musak was giving them *The Skaters' Waltz*.

"What shall I get?" Carla asked.

"Sherry is very nice," Mrs. Herriott said.

"Are other people drinking sherry?"

"Oh, yes. It's quite a popular thing before dinner."

"Will you order it, Aunt Sharley?"

"Two dry sherrys, please," Mrs. Herriott said benignly to the water.

She relaxed a little then and leaned back in her chair, enjoying *The Skaters' Waltz* and the atmosphere of subdued cheerfulness. The St. Pol was really a very good hotel; there were some nice-looking people here.

"Aunt Madge must have had a wonderful life," said Carla.

"Not so loud, my dear. No, I don't think she did. To lose two husbands... and then the war—"

"Well, anyhow she *lived*," said Carla.

"Well, who doesn't?" said Mrs. Herriott mildly.

The sherry was set before them, and Carla took up the little glass with a certain eagerness that troubled Mrs. Herriott. How strange it was, how sad, to sit here with Carla, as reluctant as she had been to sit in that dreadful bar with Madge, so short a time ago....

"Good evening," said a voice behind her, and turning, she looked up at Ramon Honess.

She looked and looked at him, dazed, in despair.

"May I join you?" he asked.

She did not answer; he waited a moment and then drew up a chair from another table. Carla was looking at him with surprise and curiosity, and he smiled at her, his ironic smile.

"This is Mr. Honess," Mrs. Herriott explained, in a low unsteady voice. And it was vitally important to warn the girl. "He knows," she whispered.

Carla's face grew white as paper, so that the rouge on her cheekbones stood out vividly.

Honess made a gesture to a waiter, who brought him a tall drink from another table. He took out a cigarette case and offered it to Mrs. Herriott. "No, thank you," she said, and he held it out to Carla, who took a cigarette. She dropped it on the table, and it rolled to the floor.

"Oh, take another, please," he said politely.

Her thin fingers scratched at the cigarettes, and after a moment he took one out for her and lit it. Her lip trembled, she was breathing quickly, it was dreadful to see her so, her pitiable pretenses all abandoned. For this was not someone who might suspect her or doubt her; this man knew. He knew she was a fraud, an impostor.

They sat there in silence. Then Mrs. Herriott's years of training, of social discipline, began to gather force. A situation like this was impossible, intolerable; it was catastrophe, and heaven only knew what would come of it, but it was her present duty to make it more civilized.

"That's a pretty tune," she observed.

"Very pretty," said Honess. "Do you know what it is, Mrs. Herriott?"

"It's the *Sylvia* ballet," said Mrs. Herriott.

"Are you fond of music, Mrs. Herriott?"

"Oh, very! I used to be very fond of the opera."

There was another silence and she made another effort.

"This is quite a pretty room," she said.

"Yes," he said. "I like the St. Pol."

"Do you come here often?"

"I'm stopping here now for a while."

"Oh, are you? Of course, it's a little old-fashioned...."

"But a good tone," he said.

She glanced at him, to see if he were mocking her, but she could read nothing in his handsome olive-skinned face.

"Yes, that's what I like about it," she said.

Carla got up, knocking against the table so that her glass fell over.

"I'm going," she said.

Honess rose and remained standing while she hurried across the lounge; then he sat down again.

"It's very close in here," Mrs. Herriott said. "Airless."

"It is," he agreed, and drew on his cigarette. "Mrs. Herriott," he said, "I don't want to worry you.... If I could get my little package—"

"I haven't come across it yet, Mr. Honess," she said.

"If you'd be kind enough to look for it...?"

"I—yes I will," she said. "Perhaps if you'd tell me what's in it—?"

"Some emeralds, for one thing," he said.

"Emeralds?" she repeated.

"Yes. One or two rings—things like that. If you'll find it for me, Mrs. Herriott, I'll be very much obliged. And I shan't trouble you any more."

"Were they—these rings—these emeralds—are they valuable?"

"Well, yes, they are," he said.

Is it true? she thought. Did Madge really have this package of his? Or is it a blackmail scheme? I can't tell. I don't know.

"You're not drinking your sherry, Mrs. Herriott," he said. "If you'll allow me, I'll order you something else."

"No, thank you," she said, and raised the glass and sipped it.

"If you'll find that package for me," he said, "you can count on me not to bother you again, Mrs. Herriott. About anything."

She went on sipping the sherry. She thought it helped her, steadied her.

"I'll see what I can do," she said.

He rose.

"When you find it, will you call my room?" he said. "Or leave a message in my box? I'm sorry to cause you any trouble. I have a great regard for you, Mrs. Herriott."

He went away and left her with the empty glass in her hand.

CHAPTER THIRTEEN

Is this blackmail or what? she thought. I don't know what's going to happen to us now. I don't know what's best to do.

"The check, please," she said to the waiter.

"The gentleman paid it," said he.

She went toward the elevator with an air of leisurely composure. I don't know what we'd better do, she thought.

What she had been trained to do was to ask advice from some properly authorized male—a father, a husband, a brother, a lawyer. She had two such men available now, Jeff Quillen and Dr. Filson; they were unquestionably the proper ones for her to consult.

But somehow she turned away from them, almost against them. She felt that in neither of them would she find understanding or the flexibility that she needed now. She got out of the elevator and went along the corridor to the suite, still lost in her most urgent concern; she unlocked the door and heard Carla sobbing.

The girl was lying face down on the bed in her new suit.

"But, my dear," Mrs. Herriott said, "Carla, my dear...."

"It was so awful... that man.... *Think* how I felt."

"I know, my dear. Now you must stop crying, and we'll see what's best to be done."

"Done? Nothing can be done!" Carla cried, with a sort of flounce. "I'll be sent to jail—"

"No, you won't," said Mrs. Herriott. "I'll see to that. Now, come, my dear, sit up and dry your eyes, and we'll talk."

She gave a gasp at the sight of Carla's face—the lipstick smeared, the rouge streaked with mascara, the purple eye shadow like bruises on her temple. She went into the bathroom and brought back a towel wrung out in warm water; carefully and patiently she cleaned Carla's face, while the tears still ran down the poor child's cheeks.

"Carla, you brought your aunt's bag. What was in it?"

"Clothes... and a paper book and some medicine."

"Was there any sort of little package?"

"No, there wasn't."

"I'll just look," said Mrs. Herriott. "Don't cry any more, my dear. You'll give yourself a headache. I'll get you a glass of water, and presently we'll have a nice little dinner sent up."

"I couldn't tell you—how I felt. How cheap and—ridiculous.... And he's a horrible man. Sneering.... How does he know...?"

"Never mind that now. Drink this water, child. Take off your nice suit,

Carla, and put on your dressing gown."

She telephoned for a dinner menu, and then she took out of the closet the second bag that Madge had brought from Europe. The other one she had looked through only casually; this one she examined with the greatest of care. She found some foreign pills, a little flask of something colorless, wrinkled scarves, carelessly folded clothes, but she found no little package. She had not expected to find one. It's a blackmail scheme, she thought.

The telephone rang, and she went to answer it.

"Mrs. Herriott?"

"Oh, Josie," she answered, instantly alarmed.

"Mrs. Herriott, it's too miserable and dreadful here... Mrs. Herriott, they made me go down to the police station."

"I'm very sorry, Josie—"

"And Sergeant Tucker's been here again and again, asking me questions. Mrs. Herriott, I don't think it's *fair,* to leave me here all alone in this house. I feel so nervous. I feel *frightened* all by myself."

"Josie, get Mrs. Ryan's daughter to come and stay with you."

"She's a horrid little thing. And she's no company, either. Mrs. Herriott, I want to get away from here. It's dreadful. I keep thinking about—*you* know.... Every time I'm alone in the kitchen, I think there's someone else lying out there in the street."

"Josie, you mustn't let yourself—"

"But why do I have to stay here all by myself? You and Carla and Silas have got away from all this miserableness, and I'm left here. Mrs. Herriott, why can't I come to New York?"

"I'll talk to Silas, Josie."

"Well, *why?* Why is he the one to decide about me? Mrs. Herriott, really I can't stay here any longer. Not even one more night. I'm going to lock the house up and go."

"Go where?"

"I don't know. I don't care. I'll just get on a train and go somewhere."

"You can't do that, child. Josie, try to be reasonable and wait just a little longer."

"No, I can't!" cried Josie, and her faraway little voice sounded like a scream. "I can't stand it here all alone."

"Then come here," said Mrs. Herriott, "and we'll see...."

It seemed to her that there was considerable justification in Josie's frantic complaints. She should not have been left there alone. But she was going to cause further complications. She didn't know there was no Madame de Belleforte, and it would be awkward—a good deal more than awkward—to have her here at such close quarters.

Well, it can't be helped, she thought with a sigh. She put back the bag and was glad to see that Carla was quiet now, sitting up and reading a magazine. She ordered a nice little dinner sent up for them, but she could not eat. It was a curious thing, but ever since that dreadful discovery of Madge, she had eaten next to nothing, and yet she felt great energy.

Back in Carbury there had been an immutable routine that had held her steady; after dinner, if nobody dropped in, she read a book from the lending library and went gladly to bed at an early hour. But she was surprisingly restless this evening; she could not read, she could not sit still. There's absolutely nothing to do, she thought.

She called up Silas three times, but he was not home. How strange it is, she thought. Here we are, Carla and I, in the St. Pol, where I've stayed with James.... It seemed, then, like the safest place in the world. But it isn't now, not with that Honess man here. Madge said she'd left him all her money. She must have imagined she was in love with him. And what is love?

Sitting in an armchair, Mrs. Herriott asked herself that curious question. What is love? Madge said I never was in love with James, but loving and being in love are different things. I realize I never was swept off my feet....

The doorbell rang softly, and she opened the door to admit Silas. He looked pale, and he looked happy.

"I've found a house for you," he said. "Just what you want."

"I'll go and look at it sometime. But—"

"We'll have to leave here tomorrow morning," he said. "This house is all ready for you to walk into, all furnished. We'd better leave early, right after breakfast."

"I don't want to take a house like that, Silas, without even seeing it."

"I've paid a month in advance."

"Silas, I must know what my sister gave you."

"It was a present," he said, gay as a lark. "Now, you just start off tomorrow morning for this little house, and then we'll relax for a while."

"Silas, I don't think I'll go."

"All right," he said, after a moment. "Carla and I'll go then."

"I can't allow that, Silas."

"I'm afraid it's got to be like that," he said. "The main thing is, to get Carla away for a while. Away from Quillen and from your friend Honess. Good-looking lad he is, but I shouldn't trust him too far if I were you."

Silas, talking to her like this, with this gay raillery?

"What's come over you, Silas?" she asked.

"It's getting away from Carbury, I guess."

"Josie telephoned," she said, suddenly remembering that.

"Did she? What about?"

"She's very nervous and upset, left there alone in the house. She says Sergeant Tucker's been bothering her—they made her go to the police station. It wasn't right to leave her there alone."

"Oh, she'll be all right," he said.

"I don't agree with you. Anyhow, she's coming here."

"Here? When?"

"Tonight. She—"

"She can't," he said flatly. "She's got to be stopped."

"It's too late. And I wouldn't stop her if I could."

"You've made a mistake," said Silas. "A bad one."

"Why?" she asked, and when he did not answer: "Why?" she asked again. "Why shouldn't Josie come here?"

He was silent for a moment.

"Will you be ready to start by ten, Mrs. Herriott," he asked with a sort of formality.

"I must know more about this, Silas. I must know how much we are paying for this house."

"I've got enough to pay for the whole summer."

"Silas, it's not your money!" she said. "We can't use it. It's dishonest."

"Mrs. Herriott, I told you she gave me the money. It was meant for a bribe, so that I'd help her in her little scheme. Now that she's gone, why isn't it mine?"

"Silas," she said, with a great effort, "I don't believe you. I don't believe any of that."

His face whitened; he lowered his eyes in that way of his, and now he looked not only haughty but hurt, suffering.

"I cannot go on with this," she said. "I'm sorry, but I can't."

"Will you go on for one month?" he asked.

"What good would that do, Silas?"

"I think you'll hear from Mrs. de Belleforte," he said. "If you don't, all right. We'll go back to Carbury and the good old ways." He paused. "But just take this month," he said with a subdued urgency. "Just one month in a decent place. Just try to enjoy it. You're not robbing anyone or injuring anyone. Even if you don't believe me, you couldn't feel very guilty, could you, about using some of your sister's money? She'd have left you that much, if not more."

She left it all to Ramon Honess, Mrs. Herriott thought. I suppose legally it's his money we're using.

"You'll be doing a fine thing for Carla, too," he said.

"No," she said. "This is a dreadful thing for Carla, this deceit."

"It's doing her good. She'll never be such a damned little prig again."

"Silas!"

"That's what she was," he said. "A damned self-righteous prig."

"That's a cruel way to talk, Silas."

"She needs a jolt," he said.

"That's not for you to say," Mrs. Herriott told him with spirit. "We don't know what other people need. You're talking in a very self-righteous way yourself."

"You're right," he said, looking up. "I'm sorry."

She was touched by his quick contrition; she smiled a little, and he smiled at her.

"Just one month, then?" he asked. "When we've gone this far.... Just give me this chance. If you don't hear from Mrs. de Belleforte—"

"Please...!"

"But if you get a letter," he said, "will you be happy?"

"Why should I get one in a month?"

"Frieda Hoff thought there ought to be one in about that time."

"You don't believe in Frieda Hoff," she said.

"Give me a month," he said.

And because of her affection for him, because they had, as he said, already gone so far, because she could think of no way out of this situation without the most serious consequences to them all, she said yes.

His gaiety came back then, that queer half-grim gaiety.

"Ten tomorrow morning then?" he said.

"Yes. And, Silas, will you stop at the desk and engage a room for Josie?"

"No. She can stay where I'm staying. I'll leave word at the desk for her to come over there."

"It will be late when she gets here, Silas. It doesn't seem a very considerate way to treat her. Let her stay here tonight."

"It won't do," he said. "Not with Carla."

"She'll have to see Carla."

"Yes, but we'll have to prepare Carla for that. She'll need coaching, and plenty of it. Good night!"

"Good night, Silas," she said. And after he had gone she sat for a long time by the window in the sitting room, looking out at the lights of the city where she had been born, in a mood of melancholy wonder. How very little I understand about the people nearest to me! she thought. Perhaps I'd never have been able really to understand my poor Madge. That was what she meant, I suppose, when she said—that.

Stupid, narrow, uncomprehending, she thought. Old battle-ax....

CHAPTER FOURTEEN

"I'm very sorry Josie's here," Carla said, eating her breakfast in bed. "I don't like her, and she hates me."

"Let's try to make it different," said Mrs. Herriott. "Try to see her good points."

"Oh, all right!" said Carla impatiently. "I'm going to do a little more shopping this morning, Aunt Sharley."

"Carla, don't spend any more money."

"I've got some money of my own. I told you."

"We're leaving here at ten-thirty."

"I'll be back," said Carla.

But when Silas telephoned up, sharp at ten-thirty, Carla had not come back. A boy took down the bags, and Mrs. Herriott herself descended to the lobby, where she found Josie sitting on a sofa, rosy and pretty in a clean white dress and a nice little straw hat. She rose.

"Silas says he can't wait in here in his uniform, Mrs. Herriott, but I just wanted to see what it was like in a place like this."

"I see!" said Mrs. Herriott, and sat down on the sofa.

"I've never been in a place like this before."

Mrs. Herriott realized that this was a reproach, and she tried appeasement.

"It's quite old-fashioned," she said.

"It doesn't seem so to *me*," said Josie.

There they sat side by side.

"I'm *sorry* I called you up like that last night, Mrs. Herriott. But—I don't know—everything just got on my nerves so."

"That's quite all right, Josie. I don't blame you."

"I'd never been alone in a house before. We were such a big family—such a happy family until I broke it up."

"You can't say that, Josie. It was your father's decision—"

"I thought I was doing a good thing—to marry Silas."

"I think your father was very unreasonable," said Mrs. Herriott, and there was a brief silence.

"Oh, here's Mme de Belleforte!" cried Josie, jumping up again. "Oh, doesn't she look wonderful!"

Carla was wearing a new costume, and Mrs. Herriott did not admire it; a black satin suit with short sleeves and a wide black hat lined with scarlet that gave her face a glow. With her flamboyant make-up she did not look like a young girl, but certainly she did not look like a woman of Madge's age.

"Ready, Sharley?" she asked, ignoring Josie.

The car was full of things she had bought, boxes and packages. Josie got in front with Silas with the glass slide shutting them off, and Carla, sitting beside Mrs. Herriott, took off the big hat and leaned back with a sigh.

"This is rather fun, isn't it?" she said.

"It isn't for me," said Mrs. Herriott with unusual curtness.

"I'm sorry," Carla said, and took her aunt's hand. "I keep forgetting what it means to you, Aunt Sharley, dear."

She had never spoken so warmly and kindly before; the clasp of her hand sent a little wave of comfort to Mrs. Herriott's leaden heart.

"I got some little presents for you, Aunt Sharley," she went on. "I used my own money, so you needn't mind."

"That was sweet of you, Carla, but—"

"Aunt Sharley, let's start a new life. An entirely new way of living."

Mrs. Herriott looked at her in surprise, in distress.

"But, Carla, my dear—" she said, "this can't go on. This is so wrong in every way."

"Let's get something out of it! Aunt Sharley, I was looking at you in the cocktail lounge yesterday. You're much more a woman of the world than I realized."

"Well... thank you," said Mrs. Herriott.

"Aunt Sharley, I've *never* lived!" Carla said with vehemence.

Mrs. Herriott in her day had heard other women say that, and it alarmed her: it always, she thought, led to trouble. And it always seemed to involve some man. Does Carla know any men? she wondered. I've never heard her talk about any except now and then someone in some office where she's worked.

There was one man Carla knew.

No! she thought, and tried, as was her habit, to shy away from that, from any criticism, or even appraisal of the people near her. So had she done with her husband, with all her relations, her friends. But she had come to the end of that road. She had gone forward blindly, in darkness, and now she must stop, must try to see where she was and what these people were beside her.

There was Carla, still holding her hand, but how remote... 'I've never lived....' and why hadn't she? She was beautiful, well bred, certainly what people call privileged. Then what was it in her that had kept her shut away from her fellow creatures, that had made her days dull and futile? A damned self-righteous prig, Silas called her.

Silas. There he sat, with his stiff neck and his lean broad shoulders, beside Josie his wife. Poor Josie, Mrs. Herriott thought, automatically. A pretty little thing, and so intelligent... Pretty, but how countrified. Intelligent—but how very uninteresting. Yes... Mrs. Herriott said to herself. I'll admit it. Josie's rather a bore.

And Silas was not. Carla said Silas was a wolf. A wolf... that's a rather horrible name for anyone. A lone wolf...? Silas had lied to her, boldly, even gaily. He was certainly using money that didn't belong to him, and using it lavishly. I don't believe *anything* he's told me, she thought, and I don't believe in this letter I'm supposed to get. If I do get one, it will be a forgery.

Yet, with all this against Silas, she trusted him. Trusted him more than anyone. What a strange thing that was! It's not reasonable, she told herself. It's not right, either. I ought to feel very differently about Silas after all this.

She remembered something that James used to say. Once a person lies to me or deceives me, very well. I'm finished. I can forgive him, yes. But I never trust him again. That surely was reasonable...?

No, she said to herself. No... when we were little Ed and Madge and I used to tell fibs sometimes, to our nurse, or even to Mother. But Mother kept on trusting us. I don't feel differently about Silas. I never shall. I never can.

It was a long drive. I don't know where I'm going, Mrs. Herriott thought, and a shiver ran along her spine, a horrible thought came into her head. Here they were, all four of them, leaving everything familiar behind them, and suppose they could not get back?

She faced the idea resolutely. It's possible, she thought. Quite possible. We've broken the law, Silas and Carla and I. The consequences may be very serious. We may all be disgraced. We may go to jail. Certainly something will happen. It's very likely we may never get back to the old life.

Silas stopped the car before a roadhouse. "This is a good place for lunch," he said.

They went into a big airy dining room where one other party of people was sitting. "Here's a table by the window, Mrs. Herriott," he said.

"But it's too small for us, Silas," she said.

"Josie and I will sit by ourselves," he said.

Their eyes met.

"I see!" she said.

"I think that's silly," Carla said, "we can—"

"Mrs. Herriott can't sit down to lunch with a chauffeur in uniform," said Silas. "*Ça ne se fait pas.* Come on, Josie."

He and Josie sat at a table in the corner across the long room, and Mrs. Herriott did not like to see them there, both very straight in their chairs, talking very little, in subdued voices. They looked like servants. She and Carla sat by the window, and they too had little to say. Again and again she saw Carla glance at that other table.

They had a good lunch, eaten in a leisurely way in this quiet room. But the tension was unmistakable. The lull before the storm, Mrs. Herriott said to herself, and the trite little phrase was the perfect expression of her thoughts.

The sun was hotter when they started out again. The heavy old-fashioned car ran smoothly along the roads, past farms, through suburban towns; they came presently to a road along the shore where the sea glittered in the sun. They went up a hill, and there was the house—the gracious, lovely little house, white, with a green roof, in a plantation of birches.

"Here we are," said Silas. "How's this?"

"It's a dream house!" cried Carla.

But Mrs. Herriott and Josie said nothing.

CHAPTER FIFTEEN

The front door opened into a little vestibule with a side door into a patio paved in red brick, with a fountain in the center, dry now. The sitting room and the dining room opened out of this; Silas displayed them with watchful sidelong glances at Mrs. Herriott. Charmingly furnished rooms they were, complete in every detail.

"And here's the kitchen," he said.

It was all white and red and marvelously up to date, with an electric range, a dishwasher, a mixer, and a red enamel electric clock in the tiled wall.

"How do you like this, Josie?" he asked.

"I hate it," she said briefly.

There was a moment's silence.

"It's the most convenient attractive little kitchen I've ever seen in my life," said Carla.

"*Madame est trop aimable,*" said Josie.

There was another little silence; then Josie spoke to Carla in French. The color rose in Carla's rouged cheeks.

"*Très bien...*" she said, and shrugged her shoulders.

She doesn't understand much French, Mrs. Herriott thought. Josie will see that.

"This way!" said Silas.

At the end of the vestibule rose a spiral stairway, with a delicate iron handrail, leading to the gallery that ran around the patio.

"Four bedrooms," he said, "and three baths."

"Where are the servants' quarters?" asked Josie a little loudly.

"Over the garage," Silas answered.

Mrs. Herriott drew a deep breath and made the effort she thought was her duty.

"You and Silas will stay here, of course, Josie," she said. "We'll pick out our rooms—"

"Thank you, Mrs. Herriott, but I'd *rather* be in the garage," said Josie.

"Well, *I'd* rather you stayed here," Mrs. Herriott said, trying to speak playfully. "We must have a man in the house, Josie."

"Silas can stay here, Mrs. Herriott," said Josie.

A sorry beginning for life in the dream house.

"If you'll bring in the bags, Silas," said Mrs. Herriott, "we can get ourselves settled a little and then, we can go out somewhere to dinner—some restaurant."

"I'll cook dinner here, Mrs. Herriott," said Josie. "Silas can drive me to the village, and I'll get whatever we need."

"We could start in tomorrow, Josie. But we're all tired today."

"I'm not tired, Mrs. Herriott. I'd really much rather cook the dinner here."

"I'd rather go out to eat," said Carla.

There had to be a decision, and a decision of the sort most difficult and distasteful to Mrs. Herriott. Here were these two girls, Carla in her fine new clothes—Carla to whom this was an exciting adventure—and Josie, in her countrified white dress, come here to work.

"If Josie's kind enough to cook us a nice dinner," she said, "we'll all appreciate it very much."

She did not like to use that tone, that mild and queenly authority. But she took it for granted that it would work. Even James had been amenable to that. She was not surprised to see Josie mollified, Silas relieved, Carla a little contrite. She went on.

"You can move over to the garage later, if you think you'd like it better there, Josie," she said. "But we'd better all stay here together tonight."

"Yes, Mrs. Herriott," said Josie.

The mutiny was quelled: Carla was interested in picking out a room, Josie was busy helping Silas in with the bags and packages. But it was only a truce. The situation was menacing and dangerous, and she must just do what she could.

When Carla had settled upon a room and went into it to unpack, Mrs. Herriott followed her and closed the door. "Carla," she said, "can't you be more tactful with Josie?"

"If you'll notice," said Carla, "*she* starts all these things. She's spiteful and—"

"Carla," Mrs. Herriott interrupted, "you ought to make all the concessions."

"I?" Carla asked, surprised. "And why?"

"Because you have all the advantages," Mrs. Herriott said.

Carla, kneeling before a bureau drawer, looked up into her face.

"Well, that's rather a nice point of view," she said.

"It's nothing new," said Mrs. Herriott. "My mother and my grandmother used to tell us that."

Carla, still on her knees, still looked up at Mrs. Herriott, with a sort of innocent wonder in her clear blue eyes.

"Sort of *noblesse oblige*," she said. "It's rather sweet. I'll try, Aunt Sharley."

Mrs. Herriott wanted to touch that fair head, she wanted to say something affectionate. But she could not; she could not even put any expression into her face or into her voice.

"Thank you, my dear," she said. And she felt helpless, as if imprisoned by that training that made her aware of all sorts of responsibilities, that *noblesse oblige* which had taught her to keep her troubles, her irritations, her griefs to herself—and her tenderness.

"The only thing is," said Carla, "if Josie ever finds out the truth about Aunt Madge, you know—she'll make trouble."

"Oh, I don't think so, Carla. She's very loyal. If Silas asks her not to say anything—"

"She's jealous of me," Carla said.

"Try not to let her be," said Mrs. Herriott, and went off to her own room. From her window she had a view of the sea, running in calmly over a strip of sand at the foot of a little cliff. It was a lovely thing to look out at blue water and sky, to feel the salt breeze in her face; she drew up a chintz-covered chair and sat down, not interested in unpacking. This won't last, she thought. Something will happen. I might as well rest while I can.

She heard Silas and Josie go off in the car, and then there was a heavenly quiet, nothing but the gentle rush of the sea over the sand. The tide was coming in; the sun was going down the sky; she faced the east, where little clouds sailed along, bright with gold from the glory in the west. Carla began to sing in the next room, some popular song, about love. This won't last, Mrs. Herriott thought. Something is going to happen.

A car was coming; Silas and Josie, she thought, and sighed to think of the brisk bustle and noise Josie would make. The doorbell rang. Carla's singing stopped; they were both as still as if frozen. The bell rang again, and Mrs. Herriott rose. As she opened her door, Carla came out of her room.

"Who could it be?" she whispered.

"I'll see," said Mrs. Herriott, and went down the spiral stairway. She opened the door, and it was Ramon Honess standing there.

"Mrs. Herriott," he said with deference. "I'm sorry to trouble you, but—" He shrugged his shoulders. "What can I do?" and then he said, "I have to ask you again for my little package."

"I haven't found it yet," said Mrs. Herriott.

"Mrs. Herriott," he said, "please believe me. I wouldn't trouble you this way, I wouldn't follow you around—if it wasn't a serious matter. But I'm getting into trouble now about that little package."

"I haven't come across it," said Mrs. Herriott.

"Perhaps somebody else?" he suggested. "Someone, of course, who doesn't know it belongs to me? That's really just the trouble. It doesn't belong to me."

"I'll look again," she said, with polite earnestness.

He was very polite, too—very. "You see, the emeralds are rather valuable," he said, "and if they've been mislaid, I'd like to get on the track of them as soon as possible."

"Oh, yes! Naturally. I'll take a *thorough* look, Mr. Honess."

He stood before her, with his handsome head bent; very elegant he looked, in gray flannels and a blue shirt and a dark jacket, something so neat, so finely finished in his features, his narrow hands and feet, his lean shoulders. A divine dancer, Madge had called him.

Had Madge used to dance with him in Paris? What had it been like? Had they danced in hotels, in night clubs? Had they been gay, romantic, drinking champagne? Trying to imagine her sister's life, she pictured a sort of fantasia, made up from plays and books and movies. She pictured Madge in a black evening dress, her shoulders bare, and Ramon in tails and white tie, dancing in an enormous ballroom.... Madge had wanted to be gay. She hadn't wanted to grow old and dull. You could see how that might be.

"Mrs. Herriott," he said, looking up. "I can't tell you how much I dislike worrying you this way. But, you see, those emeralds belong to my mother."

"Oh... do they?"

"They do. And she's—" he paused, "very resolute. She wants to go home, to Cuba, and she wants to take the emeralds with her. She's not easy to put off."

"I'll ask—I'll ask people about your package, Mr. Honess. I'll see what can be done."

"The whole thing was a mistake, I think," he said. "It was my mother's idea. She met Mme de Belleforte in Paris some months ago, and they arranged this thing. My mother was traveling with such a large party, my three sisters, two maids, and an English governess. She thought she'd be more suspect, with the unbelievable amount of luggage they had, and because she's not a United States citizen. So she asked Mme de Belleforte to bring the emeralds."

"You mean smuggle them...?"

"I'm afraid so. My mother's a very ethical woman," he said, with his gentle ironic smile, "extremely truthful and honest. But smuggling simply seems like a game to her. No scruples at all about it. And no doubt Mme de Belleforte felt the same way."

"Perhaps she didn't bring them after all. She may have felt that there was too much risk."

"It's the most extraordinary thing," he said, "the risks women will take. Women of reputation, and social standing, and so on. They'll risk all that for what seems to a man no reason at all."

You mean me? she thought.

"I can't put my mother off much longer," he said. "She knows Mme de Belleforte is in this country; there was someone she knew on the same ship. Mrs. Herriott, can't we talk this over a little? Perhaps we can work something out."

"I'll have another look..."

"There's one thing I'm afraid we'll have to consider, Mrs. Herriott. Maybe the jewels weren't mislaid. Maybe they were stolen."

"Oh, no. I don't think so," she said, with a wretched feeling of being lost in a fog... not knowing quite how much he knew, not knowing what he felt or intended.

"You have servants, haven't you, Mrs. Herriott?" he said.

"They're not servants," she said. "It's a young couple. They're *not* servants. They're friends. They're completely to be trusted."

"I see! I'm sorry.... But there was a boy around?"

"Oh, that's Ferdy. He's Josie's brother—just a schoolboy. He's gone home now."

"Then there's only yourself and this couple?" he asked gently. "And Mme de Belleforte?"

She drew a quick short breath. He spoke that name without emphasis; there was nothing to read in his dark face but an anxious deference. Yet he knew. Was this a trap?

"Yes..." she answered.

"Do you think anyone could have got into Mme de Belleforte's room?"

"No," she interrupted. "No, I'm quite sure. I'll look again for your package. I'll try. I'll—if you'll wait—a little longer...."

Her voice was unsteady; she felt half sick with dread and utterly confused.

"Mrs. Herriott," he said, "please believe me, if those emeralds were mine, I'd rather lose them than trouble you like this. Things are bad enough for you, without this worry."

A trap?

"Oh, things aren't bad, thank you," she said. "Things are quite all right."

He waited a moment. "I'll try to pacify my mother a little longer," he said. "I'll do my best."

He held out his hand, and when she extended her own, he raised it to his lips.

"*Dear* Mrs. Herriott," he said. "I'm so sorry."

Her gray eyes narrowed and, to her horror, filled with tears. Stop! Stop! she said to herself. You can't—

"Aunt Sharley?" called Carla's voice, clear and excited. This was the end. The play was finished. If he confronted Carla now, asked her about the emeralds, there could be no explanation, no compromise.

"Aunt Sharley! Please come out here in front of the house a moment! I want you to see something."

Mrs. Herriott opened the door. Carla was standing on the lawn, in a costume such as Mrs. Herriott had never seen her wear before: a white play suit with a full short skirt, rose-colored linen sandals on her feet. Her light hair was loose and blown with the wind; her face, clear of any make-up, was a little flushed.

"That is my niece," she said, and after a moment turned to glance at Ramon.

Now he was Latin; now he was foreign, and strange to her, with an unholy light in his eyes, a look of bold and joyous surprise.

"She's very beautiful, Mrs. Herriott," he said.

Then Carla saw him and utterly betrayed herself. The charming color fled, she was white as a ghost. She was beyond any doubting frightened. And guilty.

Mrs. Herriott had had no training for drama. But by the time she was sixteen she had learned that there should *never* be an embarrassing silence.

"Carla," she said, "this is Mr. Honess. Mr. Honess, my niece, Miss Pendleton."

That was all she knew how to do, or could do.

CHAPTER SIXTEEN

The young man had *savoir faire*. A little too much of it, perhaps, but she could not help admiring his readiness.

"Miss Pendleton!" he said, going toward her.

She took a step backward, but he advanced; he held out his hand, and when she waveringly offered hers, he raised it, bending his dark head close to it. The poor child stood like a statue, so pale, so rigid.

"Miss Pendleton," he said, "if you should ever come to Cuba—"

Carla said nothing, so Mrs. Herriott felt that she must. "What would happen if Carla went to Cuba?" she asked in a sprightly way.

"There would be riots."

"Well, I—don't expect to go there," said Carla stiffly.

"You wanted to show Mrs. Herriott something?" he said.

"Well... just the—view. The beach."

"It's very nice," he said. "But where I am there's a better—a much better beach. It's a little hotel called the Casino Monte Carlo—rather pathetic, don't you think?"

"I don't know..." Carla said.

Mrs. Herriott stood in the doorway, watching them with a queer detachment. Carla's really very young for her age, she thought. What Silas said about her isn't fair. She isn't really a prig. But she really has very little— manner, for a Pendleton. Well, poor child, if her mother had lived... Or if James had lived, and I hadn't been so short of money, perhaps I could have helped her, taken her around more.

And is this the way those gigolos work? she thought. He's very adroit. He's very... well, I'll admit it. He has quite a good deal of charm. He may be a gigolo, he may be a blackmailer, I don't know. But he has a certain amount of charm. I suppose they have to have that. You can understand— in a way—what poor Madge saw in him.

A car was coming; she looked down the road, and she saw the big square old-fashioned Herriott car. I can't *help* it, she thought. I'll just do the best I can. And if all this cardboard world fell to pieces, this world of lies and masks, of sudden death and emeralds, of grief pushed aside by frantic urgencies, this dread and confusion and humiliation, she would be glad. I'd be glad to go to prison, she thought.

Only not Carla, and not Silas. Let me *think,* she said to God. I need a little time.

Josie got out of the car, with two big paper bags, and Silas followed her, with a load twice as big. Mrs. Herriott could only go on in her own way.

"Mr. Honess," she said, "Mr. and Mrs. Polk."

"How do you do, Mr. Honess," said Silas. "We've been trying to stock up. It's always quite a job in a new place."

It made no difference that he wore a chauffeur's uniform and visored cap and had his arms full of paper bags. Silas could stand before kings. He was the very antithesis of Ramon Honess; he was the fair-skinned, bony Anglo-Saxon against the suave and subtle Latin, but he could hold his own. Only Carla and Josie seemed singularly inept; they looked, Mrs. Herriott thought, like victims.

"I managed to get some of that tea that you like, Mrs. Herriott," said Josie.

"Oh, thank you, Josie," said Mrs. Herriott, who had little liking for any tea.

"Would you like a cup now, Mrs. Herriott?"

"May I stay and have a cup?" asked Ramon.

There was a silence, but before it could become too awkward, Mrs. Herriott said: "We'd be very pleased, Mr. Honess."

"Where would you like it served, Mrs. Herriott?" Josie asked, and she was aggrieved, poor little thing. Naturally. She would have to put all these things away, she would have to get the dinner.

"Oh... I think in the courtyard, Josie," said Mrs. Herriott.

"Patio," said Carla coldly.

I can't go on with this, Mrs. Herriott thought. Not alone.

"Silas," she said, "will you join us?"

"Ten minutes," he said, with his queer tight grin, and followed Josie off to the kitchen.

"I'll have to change, Aunt Sharley," said Carla.

"*Please* don't!" said Ramon. "You're perfect as you are."

The color rose in her cheeks again. "I'm only dressed for the beach," she said haltingly.

"Then will you let me have a party tomorrow on *my* beach?" he said. "Lunch?"

"I don't know," said Carla, and ran off up the stairs.

Mrs. Herriott and Ramon were alone in the patio.

"Mr. Honess," she said, "please don't stay."

He had been looking after Carla with a pleased and lively expression; he turned now to Mrs. Herriott.

"Not for one little cup of tea?" he asked.

"Please," she said. "Please don't stay."

"Whatever you want," he said. "But then will you come to lunch with me tomorrow? All of you?"

"I wish you wouldn't ask us."

"I'm sorry," he said. "Then I won't." He paused a moment, standing before her, deferential and gentle. "I'll go now," he said. "May I telephone you tomorrow morning—to ask if there's any news of my package?"

"Yes," she said. "Yes, certainly."

She stayed where she was, numb with dread, trying to think. The setting sun shone in her eyes; she closed them for a moment.

"Where's the lad?" asked Silas' voice.

"He's gone," she said. "Silas, we're coming to the end. We can't go on."

"What's happening to us?"

"There are some things I didn't tell you," she said. "They didn't seem necessary. But Mrs. de Belleforte had some—property that belonged to Mr. Honess."

"What kind of 'property'?"

"Emeralds," she said.

"Do you believe that?"

"I think I do," she said. "Yes, I do."

"You'd better wait till you hear from Mme de Belleforte."

"Silas," she said, "you know I never shall."

"You still don't believe me?"

"No."

"But you believe the don?" he said. "All that fine story about the missing emeralds and so on?"

"Yes," she said. "I believe that."

"Well, that's just how he makes a living," said Silas. "Women believe him. Nice ladies."

"You talked to my sister, Silas—"

"No, I didn't."

"You talked to—whoever you choose to call her. Silas, if you know about these emeralds, you *must* tell me. They belong to Mr. Honess' mother."

"Oh, Gawd!" said Silas, grinning from ear to ear. "To his mother?"

"Silas, do you know anything about them? Do you know anything about any little package addressed to Mr. Honess?"

"I do not," he said. "You've looked through the bags yourself. There's nothing belonging to Don Ramon. He's a smooth little guy, that's all. Very likely Mme de Belleforte never set eyes on him."

"Silas, he knows."

"Knows what?"

"He knows Madge. He saw her—in the coffin. He knows what Carla's doing."

"Did he say so?"

"No. He doesn't need to."

"Mrs. Herriott," Silas said, "won't you leave this to me? You've left other things to me, and you haven't regretted it. This lad doesn't *know* anything. He's smooth, that's all. He's trying to get money out of you."

"I don't think so," she said steadily.

"Mrs. Herriott," he said, "d'you mean you'd believe him—rather than me?"

She looked at Silas, her friend and ally for ten years.

"Yes," she answered.

He lowered his eyes, with that effect of almost insolent haughtiness; his sunburned face looked pale.

"I never expected to hear that," he said.

She did not try to choose her words; she spoke as she felt.

"I'd trust you with anything I had, Silas. With my life, Silas. But you haven't told me the truth about this. About Madge."

"And now you think I've stolen these emeralds Honess is after?"

She was silent. It's possible, she thought. You might have done that. Because you're utterly reckless, and so sure of yourself, so certain that whatever it is you're doing will come out right. So reckless, and so stubborn. I don't think there's much you wouldn't do to get whatever it is you want.

"You're able to believe I'm a thief?" he asked.

"It's not that...."

"Then what is it?"

"You think—" she said slowly and carefully, "that you can do evil that good may come of it."

There was a long silence between them.

"Then you haven't any use for me any more?" he asked.

"You know better than that," she said sternly. "You know nothing could turn me against you, Silas. No... I've done wrong myself. I've lied, and deceived people, and no good is coming of it. We're in a horrible position, Silas. We can never got out of it without paying for what we've done."

"All right," he said, "I'll pay—when I get the bill. But there's this." He reached into his hip pocket and took out a little automatic. "You know how to use this, I've seen you shoot and you're good. Keep it—"

"I don't want it!"

"Take it, please. Put it in your purse and keep it there. Please."

"Why? Why do you think I'd want a thing like this?"

"I hope you'll never know."

He came to her and opened her purse and dropped the gun into it.

"Silas," she said, uneasy and almost angry, "this is sheer melodrama."

"I should think you'd believe in melodrama by this time," he said. "You're living in one."

"I want to get out of it!"

"Do one more thing for me," he said. "Let Honess have his little party tomorrow, and we'll all go."

"No."

"Just tomorrow," he said. "You've told me to my face you'd believe that damn smooth little crook before me. Give me my chance to show him up."

"Let this end now!" she cried. "It doesn't really matter about Mr. Honess. It's what's happening to us that's so horrible. Let's tell Mr. Quillen the whole thing—and be done with it. I've come to the end of the tether, Silas."

"After tomorrow," he said.

"Do you mean that after tomorrow you'll—let it be my way."

"Yes," he said. "We'll go to Don Ramon's little party tomorrow. And after that, if you want to tell Quillen, all right."

"Silas, what have you got in your mind?" she asked.

"I'm going to settle this thing," he said. "And you're going to win."

"I don't want to win."

"You've got it coming to you," he said. "For years you've been losing out. Losing everything. You've never complained, never blamed anyone else, never let anyone down. Now you're going to get what's coming to you."

"Silas, you don't know what's coming to me. Or to you, Silas, take back this gun. Give up—whatever it is you've set your mind on. I beg you—"

"Leave it to me!" he said vehemently. "Just tomorrow."

She could not move him; she could not even reach him in his stubbornness and recklessness. She turned away and went up the spiral stairway to her room, that airy charming room, got for her God knew how, with whose money. She sat down by the window and looked out at the sea that was gray under a violet sky. All this, she thought—this house, this life, this fantasy—was going to be swept away by some great and unimaginable tide, and she wanted it to be so. It was not fear that she felt, or even anxiety, but a very great sadness. She had come out of her own world into a new and utterly lonely one, where even Carla and Silas were strange to her.

It was growing dark when Josie came knocking at the door.

"Dinner is ready, Mrs. Herriott."

"Oh, yes... all right. I'll come at once, Josie."

She turned on the light, washed, smoothed her hair, powdered her face, and opened the door. Candles were lighted on the table in the patio below; the little flames slanted in the breeze and came erect again, shedding their mild radiance on gay-colored pottery and glittering silver and sparkling glass. There was no one there; it looked, she thought, like a feast for ghosts.

As she started down the stairway, Carla came out of her room, wearing a long pale-blue evening dress and all that make-up again.

"Carla," she said, "there's no use in that any more."

"It's for Josie."

"But Josie saw you this afternoon!"

"I know. But Silas told her Miss Carla had come out for a visit and didn't like it and went home again."

"Carla, it's impossible. It's—preposterous."

"No, it isn't, Aunt Sharley. Josie's as stupid as an owl. She doesn't notice anything. She's too wrapped up in herself and her grievances. She's just not interested in Carla or Aunt Madge or anyone."

"It's a mistake," said Mrs. Herriott. "I hate to see you like that."

"Please don't make things worse for me!" cried Carla. "It was bad enough when that Honess man came out of the house with you. I thought he'd gone. The taxi he came in went away. I suppose he did that on purpose—to trap me."

"No, I don't think he did," said Mrs. Herriott.

She went on down the stairs; she drew back a chair and sat down at the table.

"Aunt Sharley," said Carla, "is anything wrong?"

"I'm tired," said Mrs. Herriott.

"You look—strange," said Carla.

I feel strange, thought Mrs. Herriott. I thought this looked like a feast for ghosts—and I feel like a ghost. Sitting here with the ghost of Madge.

A door opened, and Josie came into the patio, clattering across the tiles, carrying a heavy tray.

"I'm sorry if dinner's a little late, Mrs. Herriott, but it's hard in a new place."

"Yes, of course it is, Josie."

"And it's such a long way here from the kitchen."

"You should have let us eat in the dining room, Josie, and not taken all this trouble."

"Miss Carla said she'd like dinner here. Didn't you—*Miss Carla?*"

The candle flames slanted and straightened; Carla sat motionless in her chair. And the make-up on her face was pitiable now. Josie looked steadily at her for a moment; then she turned to Mrs. Herriott.

"Mrs. Herriott, may I telephone and ask Ferdy to come out tomorrow?"

"Yes, Josie, if you want."

"I'd be glad of his company, Mrs. Herriott. I'd be glad to feel I had *somebody* who doesn't treat me like dirt."

"Josie, you mustn't talk like that. You mustn't think like that."

"It's true! I try.... I work from morning to night. I've tried to help you every way I can. I've tried to save money for you. I've done without everything. I haven't—" She gave a sob. "I haven't one single pretty dress. I haven't even got a—nice pocketbook.... And when there is any money, who gets all the pretty clothes—and gets taken to that hotel—"

"Josie, stop."

"I won't! I won't be made a servant of, while she—"

Mrs. Herriott pushed back her chair and rose.

"You've been doing too much, Josie," she said. "You're overtired. Eat your dinner, Josie, and you'll feel better. Come, Carla."

"But—aren't you going to eat, Mrs. Herriott...?"

"No, thank you, Josie. Not now. Not like this."

"But, Mrs. Herriott, when I cooked it all...? When I worked so hard?"

"No, thank you," Mrs. Herriott said again.

When she reached the top of the stairs, she turned with a bright mechanical smile to Carla, who had followed her.

"Good night, my dear," she said.

She was sorry for the poor child with her bedizenment that was so ludicrously futile now. She was sorry for Josie, too. But she had nothing to say to them or to anyone now. She went into her room and closed the door; she undressed and lay down in the dark. She listened to the sea running up on the sands and tried to think. But she could not; a great apathy weighed upon her. She was waiting.

She fell asleep, and waked with a start. She thought someone had called her.

"Yes?" she said. "Who is it?"

No one answered, but she thought the echo of a voice still stirred the air. She got up and opened her door, and as she crossed the threshold she gasped, for a pool of shining water glistened at her feet.

But she had forgotten where she was. It was not water—it was moonlight streaming down into the patio; it was calm and lovely and silent there. She went barefoot into Carla's room; the girl was breathing gently, lying long and straight in her bed.

No... Mrs. Herriott thought. It isn't tomorrow yet.

CHAPTER SEVENTEEN

"I'm sorry, Mrs. Herriott," Josie said, as soon as Mrs. Herriott came down into the patio in the morning.

Her dark hair was damp and curly at the temples, her earnest little face was flushed, her eyes behind her spectacles were beseeching. "I'm ever so sorry, Mrs. Herriott!" she said,

"Let's not talk about it, Josie," said Mrs. Herriott. "You were overtired."

"I *was* tired, Mrs. Herriott, but that's no excuse for losing my self-control. I don't often do that."

"No, you don't, Josie," Mrs. Herriott agreed, longing to drink her coffee in peace.

"Only, Silas is such a provoking boy," Josie went on. "He's all right—*unless* someone encourages him. But that goes to his head."

This was dangerous ground.

"Well..." Mrs. Herriott said vaguely. She cut a piece of toast into three strips, with an air of intense concentration, hoping and hoping that Josie would go away.

"Silas really is devoted to me," Josie said. "He doesn't mean to be so provoking. It's just that he's so terribly easily flattered."

"Yes, I dare say..." said Mrs. Herriott, more and more vague in her great desire to be let alone.

"When anyone takes too much notice of him—" Josie began but stopped as Carla came out of her room and began descending the spiral stair.

"Good morning, Josie!" said Carla, with almost ominous earnestness.

"Good morning, Miss Carla. I'll bring your breakfast—"

"No, don't bother!" said Carla. "You do too much, Josie."

"Well, I try to do what there is to be done, Miss Carla."

"Don't call me 'Miss' Carla, Josie, please. We've known each other for years and years."

Silly... thought Mrs. Herriott, with a most unusual irritability. Carla's having a fit of remorse now, and it's silly. Why can't she simply be friendly and polite, and keep quiet?

"I'm going to help you with the work this morning, Josie," said Carla.

Stop, you *silly* girl! thought Mrs. Herriott. It's such a mistake to act like this. As if you felt—guilty!

But nothing stopped Carla or Josie; their duet continued.

"Oh, I can manage perfectly well, Miss—Carla. I'm used to it."

"I don't see why you *should*, Josie. I'll do the dishes—"

"I really don't want you to—"

Bah! thought Mrs. Herriott, and rose. "I have some letters to write," she said, and went upstairs.

She made her own bed and tidied the room, so that there would be no need for either of the girls to get in here. She even went so far as to put writing paper and envelopes on the table. If Carla or Josie got in, she was going to pretend to be absorbed in her correspondence. Not that that would stop them, she thought.

It was a warm morning; it was going to be a hot day, she thought. The last day. She had told Silas she would wait this one day more. Wait for what? I don't know, she thought, but tomorrow I'll feel free to telephone to Jeff Quillen—

This is tomorrow, she thought, and stood by the window, looking out over the bright water.

There was that brisk loud knock at the door. Hastily she sat down at the table and took up her fountain pen.

"Come in!" she said.

"Mr. Honess would like to speak to you on the telephone, Mrs. Herriott," said Josie.

"Where is the telephone, Josie?"

"There seems to be only one, Mrs. Herriott, down in the hall near the front door."

Mrs. Herriott descended, and it came into her head that she was perpetually going up and down that spiral stair. It's tiring, she thought.

Ramon's voice spoke, gentle, almost caressing. "Shall I send a car at twelve, Mrs. Herriott?"

"Oh..." she said. "I don't know...."

"Please!" he said. "It's such a perfect day." He paused. "And I don't expect to be here much longer."

A threat, was that? The velvet glove?

"Please!" he said again. "Yourself, and your niece—and the young couple. We'll have lunch on the beach, and I think it will be warm enough for a swim."

"I'll have to ask the others, Mr. Honess."

"It's for you to decide, Mrs. Herriott. They'll all come if you do."

Oh, how persistent, how obstinate everyone is! she thought, with another flare of that unwonted irritation. But I suppose we might as well do one thing as another—and Silas was so set on going....

"Thank you, Mr. Honess," she said. "Twelve o'clock will be very nice."

She went into the kitchen, and there she found Josie washing the dishes and Carla drying them. And it didn't look natural; they did not look like two friends working together; it looked artificial and somehow displeasing. They don't like each other, Mrs. Herriott thought. They never did, and I dare say they never will. It's a mistake. Carla overdoes things.

"Mr. Honess is sending a car for us at twelve," she said. "Tell Silas, will you, please, Josie?"

"I'm here, Mrs. Herriott," he said, from the pantry. "I've been to the town, and I've brought back a couple of bathing suits for you."

"I don't want a bathing suit, Silas."

"You used to be so fond of swimming," he said. "I thought you'd like it now."

He meant to be kind, and she smiled at him.

"We must all be ready at twelve—" she said.

"But, Mrs. Herriott, I don't know if Ferdy'll get here by twelve," said Josie.

"*Ferdy?*" said Silas.

"Yes!" said Josie, with an air of triumph. "Mrs. Herriott said I could ask him."

"Well, you can't," said Silas.

"Well, I have!" said Josie. "I called him long distance a while ago, and he's coming right out."

Silas gave her a narrow sidelong look and strode out of the kitchen, slamming the door behind him. Josie dried her hands and went after him; she did not quite latch the door, and it swung open; their voices were very distinct.

"I told you I wouldn't have Ferdy around," said Silas. "You've got to send him back. You understand that, Josie?"

"I know why you don't want him around," said Josie. "It's because he *knows too much.*"

Mrs. Herriott crossed the kitchen to close that door.

"—and if Sergeant Tucker had ever thought to ask Ferdy any questions," Josie was saying, "he'd have heard some things that would have surprised him."

"You keep quiet," said Silas, as if his jaws were set tight. "Or, by God, I'll—"

Mrs. Herriott opened the door wide and went into the patio. They stood there face to face; she looked at them both with no expression in her face, and went past them, up the spiral stair again. As she passed the chest of drawers in her room she glanced at her image in the mirror and felt a slight surprise. She had changed, in these last days; her features seemed sharper and clearer; her gray eyes seemed almost steely under her fine dark brows. This is me, she thought. This was what had become of Charlotte Pendleton, so mild and amiable, so cherished in her young days. Here she was, in this strange house, in this strange place, waiting for she did not know what. I may be sent to prison, she thought.

Nothing is the way I thought it was, she said to herself. Silas and Josie are not a devoted couple. There's been something smoldering beneath the surface, perhaps for a long time... something I never suspected. Josie has a grievance against Silas. Perhaps she's right. Perhaps he's not kind to her, not faithful to her.

It's Josie's fault, she thought to herself. She was shocked at herself for thinking that, but she did think it. Josie doesn't understand Silas.

And she did understand Silas. Nothing he could do, she thought, would surprise her, not the most gallant exploit, not the most audacious chicanery. It seemed to her that in some way she had always known what he was like. He had driven her car for her steadily and carefully, and still she had always known in her heart that he was capable of driving it into a stone wall or over a cliff.

He had been restrained; more than that, he had been a prisoner, shut into the narrowest and dullest sort of life. And Madge's death had set him free. It had set Carla free, too, in another way; there were new queer little impulses toward generosity and affection stirring in the girl—and a new great hunger and thirst for life. Even Josie had, in some measure, broken her bonds; she was able to speak now, to express the bitter resentment that she must have harbored for a long time.

Mrs. Herriott sat down at the table in her room and began to draw; she drew cats and elephants. They say you can tell a person's character by silly little drawings like this, she thought. Perhaps, but I don't think that's very likely.... It's bad for a fountain pen to draw with it. Well, who cares? There's no one I want to write a letter to; maybe I'll never write another letter.

"The car's here, Mrs. Herriott," said Josie, standing in the doorway. "And, Mrs. Herriott..." she came into the room to the table, "Mrs. Herriott, will you let me have two dollars, please?"

"Why, of course, Josie," said Mrs. Herriott, looking up. Their eyes met; they looked and looked at each other. Josie is ill, Mrs. Herriott thought. She's sick with misery and bitterness. She and Silas must have had a really serious quarrel. And he's not kind to her.

She wanted to say something friendly and kind to this girl who looked so ill, pale, tear-stained, her eyes heavy, her lips tight.

"Things will get better, Josie," she said.

"Mrs. Herriott, I want to leave the money with a note for Ferdy. Silas wants to drive him away. But I won't.... He's my own little brother, only fifteen—"

"Fifteen?" Mrs. Herriott repeated. "I hadn't realized he was so old."

At this rate, she thought, Ferdy won't finish high school until he's twenty. And Josie was in college when she was sixteen. No... Ferdy isn't really very bright. Not a very attractive boy, either. But Josie is devoted to him, and it's not right of Silas to want to keep him away. Because he *knows too much...?* Too much about what...?

"I haven't any money at all, Mrs. Herriott. And I'd like to leave two dollars for Ferdy and a note to say where we've gone. I don't *care* what Silas says."

"Yes, yes," Mrs. Herriott said in haste. "You must try not to mind, Josie." She opened her purse to get out the money, and there was the little automatic. She closed the purse quickly.

A car was standing outside the house, and Silas was there, talking to the chauffeur in uniform. A little pang shot through her, to see how shabby his best gray suit was; yet there was that stiff-necked elegance about him which set him apart from everyone else.

Carla and Josie came out, and they all got into the car.

"Isn't it a lovely day, Aunt Sharley?" said Carla.

"Yes, it's very nice," said Mrs. Herriott briefly. She did not feel like talking; she wanted to think, especially about that automatic. What's it supposed to be *for?* she asked herself impatiently. She did know very well how to use it; she could use a revolver and rifle too. James' idea, that had been. Every woman should know how to defend herself, he had said, and he had been very proud of her skill at the rifle range. Who am I supposed to defend myself against with this thing? she thought.

The two girls kept on trying to talk to her, and she answered them more and more curtly until they gave up and talked to each other. She realized that she was not behaving very nicely, but she did not feel nice; she felt indifferent and remote. She was waiting.

The Hotel Casino Monte Carlo was pleasing and a little touching in its sprightliness—a four-story white stucco building on a little cliff, with a doorman in a plum colored tail coat and white gloves. Ramon was waiting in the lounge for them, and very gay and neat he looked, in a white suit and a corn-flower in his buttonhole. He had engaged a suite for the ladies, where they could put on their bathing suits, and they went up in the elevator.

"I've brought along both the bathing suits, Aunt Sharley," Carla said, with a sort of timidity.

"I think they're just about what you'd like, Mrs. Herriott," said Josie.

Both of them trying to please her, to placate her. And I'm behaving like an old battle-ax *now,* thought Mrs. Herriott with a sigh. The bathing suits were exactly what she would have chosen for herself—dark blue wool, conservative but good. The two girls used the sitting room and gave her the bedroom to herself; she tried the suits and kept one on; she put a white rubber bandana over her dark hair. And an old and forgotten thrill of pleasure came to her. She had been a fine swimmer in her time, and she had loved it above everything else. But it had been a long time, years and years, since she had been in the sea.

The water was cold; she gasped at the first touch of it against her legs. She waded out, waist high, almost breathless from the icy chill; then she began to swim, an old-fashioned side stroke, looking singularly effortless in comparison with the thrashing crawl the others used.

It all came back to her, all the delight, the sense of mastery and strength and ease; she swam and swam through the gentle swell.

"Mrs. Herriott!"

It was Ramon beside her, his wet lashes making his eyes look soft and starry.

"You're rather far out," he said, "and the water's very cold."

"I don't find it so," said Mrs. Herriott, going ahead.

"Won't you turn back now?" he said, after a moment, and glancing at him she saw that his teeth were chattering. "Oh, I'm sorry!" she said, turning back at once. "You shouldn't have come."

"You're my honored guest," he said. "I'm looking after you."

An attractive boy, she thought, a nice boy. Not a swindler. And not a liar. And Silas? His stiff neck made swimming difficult for him; he had come out of the water and was sitting on the beach alone, his hands clasped around his knees, the sun shining on his fair head. He was watching her, and if I needed him, she thought, he'd come to me somehow.

Josie came out of the water, very pretty in a somewhat daring suit, flowered red and white, her midriff bare. Only, after her came Carla in a plain black wool suit, tall, long-legged, and delicate; she shook off her cap and shook her fair hair loose, and she was so much more beautiful, with so much more distinction, that Josie was wholly eclipsed.

The boy from the Casino set up a vast umbrella for them, and then two waiters came with trays, bringing a princely lunch. There was a big glass shaker of cocktails with it. Mrs. Herriott? No, thank you. Miss Pendleton?

"Yes, thanks," said Carla.

It was unusual for her to take a drink, and this was a poor time to begin; Josie refused and Silas refused, and there was only Ramon to keep her company. He raised his glass to her in a silent salute, and she took a sip, looking at him over the rim in a sort of old-fashioned coquetry.

"Do you speak French, Mr. Honess?" asked Josie.

"Oh, more or less," he answered, and she began a conversation in that tongue. She was always different when she spoke French, tenfold more animated, with little gestures; even her dark brows became expressive. Ramon spoke with complete fluency; he responded gallantly to her; they smiled, they laughed.

"I think I'd like another cocktail, please," said Carla.

"It's not a very good idea, in the middle of a hot day," said Mrs. Herriott.

"It won't hurt me, thanks," said Carla.

Like Madge? thought Mrs. Herriott. No! No, it's not. It's only because she doesn't know any better. She doesn't know how to— Well, the word was 'compete.'

"Oh!" cried Josie suddenly. "There's my little brother!"

She got up and ran toward Ferdy, who was coming down the long flight of steps from the Casino to the beach in a heavy penguinlike way, flopping from step to step. His swarthy face was flushed, his black hair was streaked over his forehead; he wore a thick Norfolk suit with clumsy knickerbockers and an old-gentlemanly straw hat with a square crown.

"Ferdy, how ever did you get here?" she said.

"Walked," he said.

"Oh, Ferdy! All that way? Come and sit down, Ferdy. He could take his coat off, couldn't he, Mrs. Herriott? Here's a glass of water, Ferdy."

"I'll send for some lunch for him," said Ramon.

"I got my lunch already," said Ferdy glumly.

He took off his coat, revealing a pink-and-white shirt, strained tight across his chest and soaking wet.

"Do you want to swim, Ferdy?" asked his sister.

"No, I wanna *rest,*" said Ferdy.

He reached behind him for his coat and felt in the pocket. "Letter I found at the house for you, Mrs. Herriott," he said.

"Thank you," she said, taking it from him.

It had been forwarded from the St. Pol; it had a Portuguese stamp and it was addressed in Madge's writing.

Mrs. Herriott could not open it. She looked down at it, and she saw that her hand was shaking. She laid the letter in her lap, and her jaw trembled. It seemed to her that all her body shook with every breath she drew.

No, she said to herself. This is a letter written before.... It's been delayed. Madge is dead. She thought that someone spoke to her, but she did not want to hear; she could not speak. My sister's letter.... My poor sister....

She tore the envelope open and took out its single sheet of thin paper.

DEAREST SHARLEY:
Such a disappointment not to come when I said I would.
It won't be until September now, because—

You don't have to faint. You can't faint. You can't lie down.
Sit up and behave yourself, Charlotte Pendleton.

"Mrs. Herriott!" said Ramon. "You look ill."

"The heat..." she said.

"Let me take you up to the hotel."

"No, thank you. I want to go home," she said.

"Aunt Sharley! What's the matter?"

"*Nothing,*" said Mrs. Herriott, in an unexpectedly loud voice. "I simply want to go home."

She rose and was glad to find Silas at her side. She took his arm, and they went up that interminable flight of steps.

"When you get home," Silas said, "go to your room and stay there."

"Yes," she said. "That's what I want to do."

"Stay there until I get back, will you?"

"Yes," she answered.

Carla had come after them; Carla helped her to dress. "But, Aunt Sharley, dear.... Was it some bad news that upset you?"

"It's only the heat," Mrs. Herriott said. "I'm quite all right. I just want to go home."

"I'm coming with you, darling."

"Carla, no thank you! I'd rather go alone. I'd rather you didn't come."

She was sorry that Carla was worried; she was sorry that she had upset the little party. But she had to be let alone now. She had to be alone to read Madge's letter. She got into a car, and Ramon got in beside her. So you *are* a swindler, she thought.

She was glad that he did not ask her any questions or try to talk. The car went smoothly along. It stopped before her house, and Ramon helped her out.

"Thank you," she said. "Good-by."

"I'll stay here, Mrs. Herriott," he said. "If you want me, I'll be here."

"No, thank you," she said, and went up the spiral stair to her room.

It was a short letter:

There have been all sorts of boring complications, about papers, and so on, and it really would be wiser to wait until September. But I am so long-ing to see you, Sharley; and to talk to you. I'll never forget the old, happy days together, will you?

Mrs. Herriott felt no joy, not even any relief. The impact of this stunned her. She sat down at the table and took up her fountain pen, as if she had to answer the letter immediately. She laid down the pen and looked about the room, almost desperately, in search of something to do. Something to pass the time, she thought, until... until what?

This letter was what Silas had expected, what he had told her to expect. Is it a forgery? she wondered. I was sure I'd know—but I don't. The writ-ing seemed to her entirely like Madge's; the words were what Madge might well have used. Oh, if it were true, and all this no more than a nightmare...!

Now, don't go setting your heart too much on things, Miss Sharley, or you'll be disappointed.... You mustn't expect too much in this world, Sharley, my dear.... I think I'll take a little nap, she said to herself. And she wanted to sleep, to make the time pass. Right or wrong, foolish or not, she was still waiting. The swim had relaxed her; she felt comfortable when she lay down on the bed; she closed her eyes, and it was easy to go to sleep.

She waked quietly and easily. The sky was violet, and she was glad the fiery sun was gone. I'd like a cup of tea, she thought. But not if I have to talk to anyone. I can't.

She put on a fresh dress and with stealthy caution opened her door. Not a sound. She listened outside Carla's door; not a sound in there. If only they haven't come back yet from the beach... she thought. That would be almost too good to be true. She turned back along the gallery toward the stair, and then, casually looking down, she saw Ramon Honess sitting at the table in the patio, smoking a cigarette, perfectly quiet in the gathering dusk. He was looking up at her. He rose.

"Have you been here all this while?" she asked in wonder.

"I went out for a few moments," he said. "To get some tea and sandwiches for us from the hotel."

What are you? she thought, as she came down the spiral stair. A swindler? Blackmailer? Something even worse and more dangerous? Yet she came on with calmness; he drew back a chair for her, and she sat down at the table. He unscrewed a big thermos bottle he had there and poured tea for her into a china cup. He unwrapped a packet of sandwiches done up in waxed paper. She sipped the hot tea and found it fragrant and good.

"It's *just* what I wanted," she said, and added, suddenly remembering her manners, "Thank you, Mr. Honess."

"Nothing could be a greater pleasure than to get you just what you wanted, Mrs. Herriott," he said gravely.

"Thank you," she said again, with the same calmness. "But I must tell you now.... I've just had a letter from my sister, Mme de Belleforte."

"Oh!" he said. "Was that what upset you so? A delayed letter.... It must have been a great shock."

"Not delayed," she said. "My sister's had to postpone her homecoming. She's not coming until September."

He was silent, and in the twilight his dark face looked white.

"May I see the letter, Mrs. Herriott?" he asked.

"Yes," she said, and opened her handbag. There was the little automatic, and she gave a quick frown at the sight of it. Silas asked me to stay in my room until he got back, she thought, and I said I would. But I forgot. Why did he ask me that? Why did he give me this gun? What danger is there? Is it this man?

They were, as far as she knew, alone in the house. Why had he waited like this, sitting here with such strange patience? He held out his hand for the envelope, and she let him have it. Perhaps I ought to be afraid, she thought. But she was not.

"There's something very wrong here, Mrs. Herriott," he said.

"Something very wrong indeed, Mr. Honess."

Now he was cornered. Perhaps he was trying to think up some new invention about those emeralds. Or perhaps he was trying to think of some way to silence her. Perhaps he was dangerous. But she was not in any way afraid.

"Mrs. Herriott," he began, and stopped and turned his head to listen. A car was coming.

Now he's trapped, she thought, and she was not glad.

"Mr. Honess," she said, "you'd better go now. Go out by the side door."

"I'm not going, Mrs. Herriott."

"Don't you realize...?" she said.

Then she heard Josie's voice, calling her frantically.

"Mrs. Herriott! Mrs. Herriott! Silas has gone! Silas has left me. He's *gone!*"

CHAPTER EIGHTEEN

She came running into the patio, followed by her lumbering little brother. "Silas has gone, Mrs. Herriott!"

Automatically, Mrs. Herriott began to take charge. "Sit down, Josie. Try to be quiet, my dear."

"Mrs. Herriott, he's gone! We can't find him!"

"There's nothing serious in that, Josie, at this time of the day."

"Mrs. Herriott, he went with *her...* with Carla."

"That's nonsense," said Mrs. Herriott sternly.

"It isn't! They've run away together!"

"Don't say that again, Josie."

"It's true! It's true! That nasty blond bitch has taken him away from me—"

"Be quiet," said Mrs. Herriott.

"I have my car here, Mrs. Herriott," said Ramon. "Shall I drive you back to the Casino?"

His voice was quiet, and that was balm to her.

"I'd be very glad," she said. "Ferdy, get your sister a glass of water. Now try to tell me what happened."

"He said he'd be back—and we waited and waited, Ferdy and I. We waited and waited—and he didn't come. She's got him! They've gone."

Her voice followed them, piercing and intolerable, as they went out of the house.

"She's very high-strung," Mrs. Herriott remarked, and to make the explanation complete: "French descent, you know. Latin."

She heard him give a quickly stifled laugh, and she remembered that he too was one of those Latins. Well, it didn't matter.

"I don't suppose there's really anything wrong," she said, as the car started.

"Accidents happen, Mrs. Herriott."

"Why do you say that?" she said, troubled by his tone.

"Because it's just as well to be prepared."

"But what do you mean? What are you thinking?"

He was driving steadily, his eyes fixed on the road ahead.

"You've gone through a good deal, Mrs. Herriott," he said. "You've had a very bad time. But you have great courage. If there's any more, you'll have courage for that too."

"What do you *mean?* Why do you think there's—anything more?"

"Mrs. Herriott, do you want me to speak? Do you want to hear...?"

"Yes," she answered without hesitation.

"Your sister's death.... It was very strange."

"My sister isn't dead. She's alive, in Portugal."

"You saw her, Mrs. Herriott."

It came into her head that he was talking like the Devil. A quiet voice in the dusk, trying to destroy all her hope, gently insinuating unspeakable things.

"It was a strange death, Mrs. Herriott."

"It wasn't," she said. "It was a fall."

"The police weren't satisfied, Mrs. Herriott."

"They were. The case is closed."

"They're still not satisfied, Mrs. Herriott."

"Why are you saying things like this?"

"Because I'd like to help you to be ready, in case anything else happens."

"What else?"

"I don't know," he said. "But I'll stand by you, Mrs. Herriott."

But you're a swindler. A liar. *You're* not the one to stand by me. No! Nothing has happened. Very likely Silas and Josie had a quarrel, and he simply walked off. They don't get on as well as I thought they did. Josie's more trying than I realized. And Silas is more—

More what? More reckless, more complicated. A wolf? A silly expression—or maybe it was a little horrible. People used to believe that there were men who could turn into wolves. That was a horrible thing to believe, to think that, in the dusk like this, you might see a wolf loping along close to a wall, going silent and swift about his business, a wolf that wasn't a wolf....

Carla was standing outside the Casino Hotel, tall in her white dress.

"Aunt Sharley!" she cried. "That hateful Josie—"

"Never mind that. Where is Silas, Carla?"

"Aunt Sharley, there's no reason why he should be anywhere, particularly. I mean, this is all nothing but spiteful nonsense made up by Josie. She—"

"I don't want to hear any more of this," said Mrs. Herriott. "Where did Silas go?"

"He just took a stroll along the beach."

"Wait here," said Mrs. Herriott, and went along the path by the side of the little hotel and down the long flight of stone steps to the beach. Honess took her arm; she did not look at him or speak to him.

The tide was full, coming over the sand with a quiet little rush; the sea and the sky were all gray; a light and steady breeze was blowing. There was only a narrow strip of sand left dry now, hard and springy; there was no one in sight.

"I shall look all along the beach," said Mrs. Herriott with an air of defiance.

But in ten minutes they came to the end of the crescent beach where the bank became a cliff of stone jutting out like a wall, with a rickety wooden stair down its face, ending in a landing stage.

"Perhaps at low tide anyone can walk past here," she said.

"Yes, I've done it," Ramon said.

"I don't think the water is deep."

"We can go back to the hotel and along the top of the cliff, Mrs. Herriott."

"I don't want to take the time," she said, "it's growing dark, Mr. Honess."

"Mrs. Herriott, you can't—"

"Don't try to stop me," she said. "Please don't bother me. You told me to be prepared. I am. Please don't bother me."

She stepped into the water that was up to her ankles, piercingly cold. This was the way Silas had gone, and this was the way she was going. She went carefully, feeling her footing, and each wave that receded tugged at her gently. Ramon held her arm again; in a moment the water was up to their knees; her wet skirt clung to her.

Around the corner of the headland was a beach strewn with boulders, desolate and lonely, and Silas was there, lying face down at the edge of the sea, where the waves lapped over him and stirred his hair.

"Help me, Mr. Honess," she said.

He took Silas under the arms and pulled him back on to the beach; he turned him over so that he lay on his back. It seemed to Mrs. Herriott that it was lighter here, with a wild silvery light.

"He's not dead," she said.

"I'm sorry. He is, Mrs. Herriott."

"Go and get a doctor, Mr. Honess. Quickly, please."

"Mrs. Herriott, I'll have to notify the police."

"Whatever you like. Only get a doctor at once."

"Have you a lawyer, Mrs. Herriott?"

She was kneeling on the sand beside Silas; she looked up into Honess' face.

"I don't want a lawyer. Mr. Honess, get a doctor!"

"Tell me your lawyer's name. Please listen to me, Mrs. Herriott. Don't give the police any more information than you can help until you have seen your lawyer."

"Why?" she asked, still kneeling and looking up into his face that she could scarcely see now.

"The police might be too curious about your finding two bodies, Mrs. Herriott," he said. "Two deaths by accident."

She took Silas' wrist to feel his pulse. His long thin hand was lightly closed, and wet and cold; he was holding something. She unclasped his fingers, and she could feel what it was he had held. It was a ring. She took it quickly into her own hand, and she thought, she hoped, that Ramon had not seen what she did.

"Please go for the doctor," she said.

"Your lawyer's name, Mrs. Herriott?"

"It's Quillen," she said. "Jeffrey Quillen. He's in the telephone book."

She kept Silas' cold hand in hers, and she believed now that he was dead.

"You will remember what I said about the police, Mrs. Herriott? Try not to say any more than you can help."

"I'll remember," she said, and waited until he had gone, splashing through the water.

In Silas' vest pocket she found a wallet stuffed with bills and some small objects—another ring, two brooches, some other things. She put them all into her pocketbook and sat quietly beside him holding his hand.

CHAPTER NINETEEN

The two policemen and the doctor who came were very nice. They came down the rickety stairs, with flashlights like glowworms, and they helped her to go up that way. When they reached the top of the cliff, they were unexpectedly close to the little Casino Hotel, brightly lighted now.

They went in by a side door, and the manager took them into his small office.

"But you're very wet, madam," he said. "Let me get the housekeeper—"

"Oh, no, thank you!" said Mrs. Herriott. "I'm as warm as toast."

"Will you let me bring you something to drink? Sherry? Brandy?"

"Whisky, thank you," she said, after a moment's thought. "A double, please."

She had never had such a thing in her life before, only she remembered how Madge had ordered, and she thought it would not hurt her now. She thought nothing could hurt her now. It tasted like fire, so burning that she choked a little.

"Wouldn't you like some water with it, madam?" asked the policeman who had come in with them.

"Oh, thank you," she said. "I didn't know...."

She really had no trouble with the policeman at all, except in explaining Silas.

"He drove my car," she said, "but he was much more than a chauffeur. My husband and I always thought of him as a friend. He did a great many things for us."

"Well, handy man, would I put down?" the policeman asked.

"Oh, no," she said, and thought a moment. "Secretary," she said.

"Are there any relatives to be notified, ma'am?"

"His wife," she said. "She's at my house now. His poor wife...."

"Mrs. Herriott," the doctor asked, "to your knowledge, did Mr. Polk ever suffer from dizziness, faintness, or anything of that sort?"

"No. But some years ago he had a terrible accident. He broke his neck diving."

"Ah! That might account for it," said the doctor. "Some lesion of the spinal cord might account for such a fall."

"He fell?"

"Not much doubt about that," said the doctor. "The wooden railing's been broken up there at the head of those steps. It's a good sixty-foot drop, and he landed on the rocks. Death must have been almost instantaneous."

"I'm glad of that," she said, sipping the whisky. It did not burn her now; she did not bother with the water.

"I'll drive you home, Mrs. Herriott," the doctor said. "I have a closed car. You'll be less likely to catch cold."

I haven't any home, she thought. I don't want to go back there. Or to Carbury. Or anywhere. There is nothing left.

But she thought of Carla and of Josie. There's a lot to be gone through still, she thought. But it seems very—pointless. I don't see how I'll go on without Silas.

Carla and Josie will go on and on, she thought. They'll try to make me listen. Wrangling over Silas... And neither of them could have kept him. That thought surprised her, but she was sure it was true. No, she thought. Neither of them could have managed Silas. They used to say that the first Polks in Carbury were smugglers and wreckers. Maybe Silas was like that. He liked to take chances.

"If you're ready, Mrs. Herriott?" said the doctor.

She finished the whisky, and rose. In a way, she thought, it's a little funny. I've got all that money and those jewels right here in my purse. But nobody'd ever suspect things like that about *me*. Maybe I'd have been adventurous, if circumstances had been different. Of course, James didn't like traveling, and we never went anywhere except to Washington and Boston. I did want to go to the West Indies—the Spanish Main... I did want to do that.

"Mrs. Herriott, if you're ready?" said the doctor.

They went out by the side door again, and the doctor helped her into his coupe.

"This was a great shock for you, Mrs. Herriott," he said.

"Oh, you have to be prepared for things like this," she said.

"That's a fine, courageous attitude, Mrs. Herriott."

Ramon told me I was courageous, she thought. I dare say I am. I seem to be. Of course, in a way, when you've lost everything, you really don't care any more. I can't think of any way to go on. I can't go back to Carbury without Silas. I can't stay here. I haven't any money. Except the money I stole from Silas—that he stole from someone else. He'd laugh at that.

"Here we are, Mrs. Herriott! There's someone here to look after you?"

"No," she said. "I mean, I don't want to be looked after, thank you. If you'll give me—" she looked at him, her gray eyes brilliant, "if you'll give me a good big shot of morphine?"

"Have you ever taken morphine, Mrs. Herriott?"

"No!" she said gaily. "But I'll try anything once."

"Mrs. Herriott, who's here to look after you?"

"My niece," she said. "If you'll give me a good shot of hooch. No. It isn't hooch, is it? Snow? Dope?"

He rang the bell, and Josie opened the door. "Are you Mrs. Herriott's niece?" he asked.

"No," Josie answered. "I'm—"

"Get her niece, please."

"What's *happened?*"

"Get Mrs. Herriott's niece at once," he said, and Josie went away.

"Really," said Mrs. Herriott, "this is monkey business. I can take a nice hot bath and get to bed myself. And then I'll take your pills."

Carla appeared from somewhere, and the doctor said something to her. He took Mrs. Herriott's arm and led her up the spiral stair. It seemed to her that she floated up, lightly and pleasantly.

"Do you know," she said to the doctor, "I've always wanted to go to the Spanish Main...."

"Aunt Sharley!"

"Carla, my dear," said Mrs. Herriott, "you really don't know *anything*. You've never lived at all, and if you don't look out, you never will. Doctor—excuse me, but I didn't catch your name."

"Camberwell."

"Oh!" she said. "There's such a funny old song..." She began to sing:

> *Your old Uncle Bill of Camberwell*
> *Popped off suddenly, it's sad to tell,*
> *Leaving you his little donkey shay—ay—*

"Aunt Sharley!"

"Shut up!" said Mrs. Herriott, for the first time in her life. It gave her great pleasure to say this, but it was, she well knew, altogether wrong. "I'm sorry, my dear," she said to Carla.

Carla was very kind, helping her to get ready for bed, taking off her shoes for her. She took the pins out of Mrs. Herriott's hair, and it fell loose about her shoulders.

"I'll braid it for you, Aunt Sharley."

"Why, no, thank you. It feels nice like this," said Mrs. Herriott. She could not remember ever having gone to bed with her hair loose before.

When she was ready, the doctor came in again. A *nice* doctor, she thought him, slim and trim, with a reddish-brown mustache and hazel eyes.

"You look like a fox," she said.

"I'm not a bit like a fox," he said. "Now, Miss—er... I'd like Mrs. Herriott to take these two capsules now. If she's not sleeping soundly in half an hour, give her one more."

Mrs. Herriott smiled at him faintly. She had the feeling of a traveler arrived at the end of a journey. Everything finished; nothing ahead. You feel light as a feather. Nothing matters.

She felt someone standing near her, and looking at her; she opened her eyes, and it was Carla.

"My dear..." she said. "Carla, my dear...."

The girl looked exhausted, white and hollow-eyed. "I'll get you some coffee, Aunt Sharley—"

"There's no hurry, my dear. Sit down a moment."

She reached for the girl's hand, and Carla sat down on the edge of the bed.

"You ought to have some breakfast, Aunt Sharley. Aunt Sharley, I'm going to look after you. I'm going to be—different.... I'm going to be—like a daughter to you."

She spoke with a dogged determination; her face looked set; she spoke, and she looked, like a Pendleton. And this was life again, and not an end. Mrs. Herriott gave herself one moment more to lie still, and then she sat up and put her arm around Carla. Carla resisted, sitting stiff and straight.

"I'm going to look after you, Aunt Sharley. The doctor said you needed rest and care, and I'm going to see that you get it...."

"I'm rested now, my dear. I'm feeling quite all right—"

"Please let me!" cried Carla, with suppressed vehemence. "I want to look after you—for the rest of my *life.*"

"Well... thank you, my dear..." said Mrs. Herriott, in a panic. "I think I'll get up now, Carla—"

"I'd like to talk to you for just a few minutes, Aunt Sharley, if you feel strong enough."

"Oh, yes!" said Mrs. Herriott.

There would have to be a great deal of talking, endless talking. Let it begin. It would be talk about Silas; she knew that. He would not be allowed to lie in peace. When did you last see him? What did he say? Why is he dead?

"I want to tell you..." said Carla. "I consider myself responsible—about Silas."

"You couldn't be, my dear."

"You know what I'm like," said Carla sternly. "I didn't know myself. But now, when I analyze it.... All that time that I thought I hated Silas, it was simply because he didn't pay any attention to me."

"My dear, there's no need to analyze such things—"

"I'd rather," said Carla. "I want to look things straight in the face."

Well, you wouldn't, if you were my age, thought Mrs. Herriott, with secret rebellion. You'd know there are plenty of things it's just as well not to look straight in the face. And a great many things it's better not to say.

"Silas went there to the top of that cliff—to meet me," said Carla.

"Carla! You haven't told anyone that, have you?"

"What difference does that make?" Carla asked in cold surprise. "I haven't told anyone yet, but that isn't the point. The only important thing is, I'm responsible. If I hadn't said I'd meet him there, this—this wouldn't have happened." Her lip trembled a little. "I knew it was a horrible thing to do. I knew I was making Josie jealous and miserable—and it just seemed—rather exciting. It seemed—rather fascinating, all that making up like poor Aunt Madge, and the new clothes.... And I deceived *you*."

She was close to tears now, thought Mrs. Herriott, still with her arm around the wooden girl, and that would be a good thing.

"I've got to tell you!" cried Carla. "And it will—break your heart...! Aunt Sharley, that letter wasn't from Aunt Madge."

"Never mind, my dear...."

"I *forged* it! Then I got an old envelope from your bureau drawer, and Silas fixed it up."

"You didn't mean to hurt me, my dear."

"How do you know?"

Because Silas would never have meant me any harm. You're young, very young for your years, and you might do thoughtless things, even rather dreadful things, from lack of understanding. But not Silas.

"Silas thought that little by little he could get you used to the idea that— Aunt Madge wasn't coming back. And he thought you ought to have the money she'd brought with her. He wanted to get you comfortably settled, away from Carbury...."

She was crying now, a little.

"But there was something more—he was going to tell me. Only now— he never can.... Yesterday, after you'd left... Ferdy started whining and whining for Silas to take him out in a rowboat, and Silas wouldn't do it. That made Josie angry. She kept on and on—you know the way she does, bringing up all the things she'd done for him and the sacrifices she'd made. She said it was his duty to take Ferdy out, and Silas jumped up and said, 'Come on, Carla! Let's take a little walk.' I *knew* I shouldn't have gone. I knew how Josie must feel, sitting there and, watching us walk off together. Only—all right, I'll admit it. Silas—was sort of fascinating—to me."

She yielded now; she laid her head against Mrs. Herriott's shoulder.

"I'm so sorry!" she cried. "I'm so sorry...! If I hadn't said I'd meet him, he'd never have gone there—in the dark—and fallen.... It's my fault!"

"I'm quite sure it wasn't, my dear."

"He asked me to meet him—in an hour. He said he had something he wanted me to keep for him. He said—he was going to get rid of Josie—"

"Carla! What did he mean by that?"

"I didn't ask him. He was in such a queer mood.... We just walked to the end of the beach, and then I went up to the hotel to dress, and he went back to Josie. I saw him standing there, and she was looking up at him—"

"Carla, is that the doorbell?"

"Yes."

"See who it is, my dear."

"Josie'll go."

"I want to know who it is," said Mrs. Herriott, and Carla dried her eyes and rose and went out onto the gallery. She returned in a moment.

"It's Sergeant Tucker," she said, in a very low voice. "And Dr. Filson."

I knew I hadn't seen the last of Sergeant Tucker, Mrs. Herriott thought, and she was afraid. She got out of bed at once.

"Don't get up, Aunt Sharley. The doctor said—"

"I must," said Mrs. Herriott, and began to dress in very great haste. "Carla, my dear, pay attention to what I'm saying. It's important. You must not tell Sergeant Tucker anything—not anything at all until you've seen Mr. Quillen."

"Aunt Sharley, I'd rather tell the truth—"

"I won't have it!" cried Mrs. Herriott in a voice Carla had never heard before. "You'll have to forget all about your conscience for the time being, and do as I tell you. I'll get the policeman out of the house somehow—on to the little porch. And as soon as I've got him out there, you must come quietly down the stairs and leave the house by the side door."

"Where shall I go, Aunt Sharley?"

"You must take a walk. Not along the road. Some place where he's not likely to find you right away."

"But Aunt Sharley!—"

"Do as I tell you," said Mrs. Herriott, and taking the girl's arm, she pulled her toward her and gave her a kiss on the cheek, almost roughly. "Now wait in here, my dear, until you hear us go out of the house."

She finished her dressing. She did not take the time to make those two smooth rolls of hair over her temples; she bunched it all up in a thick knot at the nape of her neck, and picked up her pocketbook. Mercy, she thought. All that money—and those emeralds.... Well, the only possible thing is to carry it off with a high hand....

She opened her door and stepped out onto the gallery. Sergeant Tucker was standing in the patio, his stomach thrust out, talking to Josie. Dr. Filson was there, too, but at this moment he was superfluous. She looked down over the railing, and Sergeant Tucker raised his pale and heavy-lidded eyes.

"How do you do?" she said.

As she came down the stairs, Dr. Filson advanced to meet her. So kind and good he was.

"Mrs. Herriott," he said, "this is deplorable. I came as soon as I heard, to see if I could be of any assistance. In any way."

"That was *very* nice of you," she said, and she thought, I wish you hadn't come—I wish you'd go away.

"Sergeant Tucker and I met on the train coming out here," he went on. "I'm afraid Sergeant Tucker takes a somewhat cynical view of our fallible human nature...."

He's trying to warn me, she thought. Well, he needn't. I know very well what that policeman is like, and I know why he's here. He thought there was something queer about poor Madge's death, and he thinks there's something queer about Silas's death. Perhaps he's right. I don't know—

and I don't seem to care very much. They're gone.... But I don't want Carla dragged into this. Not until Jeff Quillen comes."

"I believe Sergeant Tucker would like a few moments alone with Josie," said Doctor Filson.

"Mrs. Polk'll have to go along to the station," said Sergeant Tucker. "There's a car waiting for her outside."

"No!" cried Mrs. Herriott. "It's—inhuman! Not now—"

"Mrs. Herriott," said Josie, "I don't care."

How hard it is, to read people's faces! thought Mrs. Herriott. For Josie looked sulky, and nothing more; whatever anguish or terror she felt made no imprint upon her round young face.

"I'll go with Josie," said Dr. Filson.

"Oh do!" said Mrs. Herriott. "Thank you so much, Dr. Filson...."

She and Sergeant Tucker were alone in the patio, not looking at each other.

"Well...?" he said.

"Yes...?" said Mrs. Herriott.

"There are a few little things I'd like to ask you about," he said.

"Very well," she said. "We'll go out on the porch."

"We're all right here," he said.

Her throat contracted a little, and she swallowed.

"I don't care to be questioned in my own house," she said.

She said this extraordinary, this preposterous thing, not haughtily, but quietly, like a Pendleton, and it worked.

"All right," he said, and even held open the door for her. They sat down on the two settlees that faced each other; their knees nearly touched.

"Mrs. Herriott," he said, "if you'd co-operate, it would be a lot better—for all concerned."

"That door..." she said, and rising, opened it and closed it with a slam. She sat down again.

"How can I co-operate?" she asked, in the same Aunt Emma Pendleton way, "when I have no idea what you're doing?"

"Mrs. Herriott," he said, "you knew, all right, that I wasn't satisfied with the Hoff woman's death."

"And why weren't you?"

"It smelt," he said, "and now the whole thing smells worse than ever."

"Don't!" she said. "Please don't talk in that horrible way...."

"I apologize," he said coldly. "If I haven't got the right expressions and—phraseologies, you got to remember I never went to college."

"I never went to college, either," said Mrs. Herriott.

"My schooling ended when I was eighteen years of age," said Sergeant Tucker.

"*Mine* ended when I was *seventeen*," said Mrs. Herriott.

They looked squarely at each other.

"Well," he said, still cold, "if you prefer to put it another way, there was something phony about the Hoff woman's death."

"You mean *you* think so."

"All right. I think so. And if it had been anybody but you living in that house, Captain King would've thought so, too. The woman was okay every way, heart, everything. All right, why would she fall down like that? The medical officer said it had got to be a hard fall or maybe a blow with maybe a sandbag. All right. Who would hit her a crack on the head?"

"You've simply made up your mind, for no reason at all, that it wasn't a fall."

"One reason," he said, "is the law of probability. There was nothing there for her to trip over. The medical officer said she probably must've been running, to fall that hard—if she did fall.... All right. Why was she running?"

"To catch a bus," said Mrs. Herriott.

"All right. There are plenty of people living on Elm Street. Why is it nobody saw or heard a woman running that fast?"

"I have no idea," said Mrs. Herriott.

"So it was decided," he said, "that either she fell, or she got a crack on the head. Very good. In all my years of police work, and all the accidents I've seen, I've never come across anyone yet that just fell down—that hard. For no reason."

"She may have felt faint."

"Well, people don't start running when they feel faint. They kind of collapse. Nope. That falling-down business looked phony to me. And when I hear that Polk was killed by a fall, it's just a little too much. Even Captain King thought it was a little too much. He gave me the green light to come on out here."

"It's entirely different," said Mrs. Herriott. "Silas fell off a cliff—in the dark."

"Couldn't have been pushed off, for instance?"

"I suppose it's possible," said Mrs. Herriott. "But it seems extremely far-fetched."

She heard the side door close softly, and she coughed to cover the sound. She sat there, thin, calm, composed; she was acutely conscious of her untidy hair, but it seemed to her that it would be a mistake, it would show a lack of poise, to touch a single strand.

"When the police here called us up, to get some dope on Polk," Tucker went on, "they told me he was passing himself off as your secretary."

"I told them that," said Mrs. Herriott. "It was the only thing I could think of at the moment to show—how I felt about Silas."

"Well..." said the sergeant, "I wouldn't want to spoil anybody's illusions, but I guess there were a good many things about Silas Polk you never dreamed of."

"You mean about his being a wolf?"

"*What?*" said Tucker.

"I think you heard me, Sergeant Tucker."

"Well, it's a sort of funny word for *you* to use," said Tucker.

"That's what you meant, wasn't it?"

"Yes. That was it."

"I understood Silas very well," she said.

"Ever occur to you that maybe the Hoff woman was coming to meet him? He admitted he used to know her."

"Sergeant Tucker," she said, "even if it was known as a positive fact that she was coming to see Silas, I can't see how it could be of the least importance to the police. Silas was not a murderer."

"Well, it could've been manslaughter."

"He wasn't a slaughterer," she said briefly.

"All right, call it an accident. He gave her a shove."

"Then he wouldn't have gone off and left her there. I can assure you of that, Sergeant Tucker."

"All right. Here's another angle. Polk had a jealous wife."

"You're really not going to make *that* into a theory?" she said. "You're not going to say that Josie ran into the street and hit the poor woman on the head?"

"It's been done," he said. "There's not much a jealous woman won't do."

And suppose Josie tells about Carla? thought Mrs. Herriott. Suppose she gets hysterical and tells all about Carla? They'll lock her up.... No, I'll take the responsibility.

"It's like the Reverend Filson said," Tucker went on. "I'm kind of cynical. I don't like so many people falling down and getting killed. I've got no standing here, of course, out of my own county, but I tipped off the police here to just have a few words with Mrs. Polk."

He rose, and Mrs. Herriott rose too. "How can you?" she asked sternly. "Now—only a few hours after this awful thing?"

"That's the best time to start," he said.

"It's brutal," she said.

"Well, the way I look at it, it's brutal to kill people," he said. "It's my opinion Polk and the Hoff woman were both killed. Call it murder if you like."

The word had no shock now for Mrs. Herriott.

"What are you going to do now?" she asked.

"Me? Nothing. Just mooch around. I've got no authority here. Tell you the truth, Mrs. Herriott, I sort of liked Si Polk and I'd like to get to the bottom of this."

As they stood there a fine black cat came running across the lawn and leaped up on the porch; it looked up at Mrs. Herriott with clear topaz eyes and mewed.

"Kitty, kitty..." she said mechanically. She liked cats. It came closer, and she scratched its hard little head.

"Is Josie—Mrs. Polk being arrested?" she asked.

"Oh, no. Nothing like that. They want to ask her a few questions, that's all. That never killed anyone yet, Mrs. Herriott." He turned. "Any time you're ready to co-operate, Mrs. Herriott," he said, "you could let me know. Now I think I'll go in and see if Mrs. Polk is ready."

He opened the door, and the fine black cat went in with him; it jumped up on the table in the patio and gave a loud imperious cry. Mrs. Herriott was conditioned to giving attention when it was demanded, and she scratched the cat under the chin; it raised its head jerkily, little by little, with an expression of idiot pleasure, eyes closed. But if I tell the truth, she thought, they'll take Carla away.

The door from the kitchen opened, and Dr. Filson and Josie came out.

"Josie is very brave, Mrs. Herriott," he said with grave approval. "Wonderfully so."

He stood aside, and Josie came past him. She was wearing a black dress with a round white collar; she was wan, all her bright color gone; her eyes were heavy behind her spectacles. She looked pathetically young, almost childish.

"Josie, my dear, it's dreadful to make you do this."

"I don't mind, Mrs. Herriott," Josie said. "I'll be glad to answer any questions they ask."

She doesn't mean anything—anything special by that, Mrs. Herriott thought. She couldn't be spiteful *now*. She won't tell them about Carla now—without a word to me. A jealous wife... perhaps. But she stood by Silas and she'll stand by me. She's difficult, sometimes, but she's loyal.

"I shall be with Josie, Mrs. Herriott," said Dr. Filson.

What a good man he is! she thought, and it lightened her heart to see Josie giving a forlorn little smile.

"I don't imagine we'll be very long," he said. "You'll rest, Mrs. Herriott?"

"There's coffee all made, Mrs. Herriott," Josie said. "Now, what's that? A nasty cat!"

"It's a nice cat," said Mrs. Herriott. "Well, Josie, my dear... try not to be too much upset."

"I will, Mrs. Herriott. I'm sorry I didn't have time to make toast for you, but there's nice hot coffee on the stove."

Mrs. Herriott watched them all get into the car driven by a policeman in uniform. She went into the neat kitchen; she put the coffee-pot, milk, sugar, and cup and saucer on a tray, and carried it up into her room. For it was her instinct to get into her own room whenever she could; it made her feel a little protected from the innumerable interruptions of her life. She sat down by the open window, and drank two cups of coffee leisurely. It was the first moment since going to the pier that she had had any feeling of leisure, the first time she had felt able to look quietly and steadily at her situation.

So Sergeant Tucker thinks it's murder, she reflected. Both of them, Madge and Silas. It's hard to believe in things like that, but they happen. In stories, the first question is, who benefits?

The answer to that was very clear. There was one person who most obviously benefited by Madge's death. It was the same person who had been robbed by Silas. It was Ramon Honess.

He was there in Carbury when Madge died. And when Silas died, where was he? I found him here when I waked up, but he admitted he'd gone off in his car to the hotel to get that tea for us. I don't know how long he was gone. But why didn't he take back his ring and other things? Perhaps someone came, and he had to hurry away. But in any case, he'd have all the money Madge left him in her will.

A murderer? That gentle and courteous boy? She tried to picture him, standing on Chestnut Street in the shadow of a tree, waiting for Madge, striking her down when she came. And then, unperturbed, coming to the house and asking for his 'little package.' She tried to picture him pushing Silas off the cliff, standing in the dusk and looking down at the rocky beach, still unperturbed; coming back here with his tea, waiting here until Josie came in, all her frantic alarm; going with Mrs. Herriott and discovering the body, still as unperturbed as he had been when he had seen Madge in her coffin.

She put down the coffee cup, overcome with a dreadful astonishment. On this bright summer morning she felt cold. They'll send him to the chair, she thought, and that will be the end of him. There'll be a trial, and I shall have to give evidence. Alicia Barry's son was excused from jury duty because he didn't believe in capital punishment. Could you be excused from being a witness, if you said that...?

But how could she feel like this, with her sister and her faithful Silas dead? She ought to love justice and hate Ramon. She ought to want to see him punished. Killed. He was not fit to live in the world; he was a murderer. But he's *young,* she thought, and youth, to her, was in itself a plea for mercy. He may have been brought up among the wrong sort of people. Perhaps if someone could make him realize, someone like Dr. Filson, for instance....

Dr. Filson believed that people could be helped, could be saved. If he talked to Ramon...? No. It was too late. The time for talking was long past; the time for retribution had come.

She picked up the tray, to take it down to the kitchen; she opened her door and stepped out onto the gallery. The fine black cat was up on the table crouching, bristling, its ears flat. What's the matter with the poor little animal? she thought. And as she watched, a rope came flashing through the air and caught the beast around the neck, and it was jerked to the floor, and dragged, choking and struggling, across the patio, to the doorway where Ferdy stood.

"Ferdy!" she cried. "What a cruel thing to do! I'm surprised at you. Take that rope off at once!"

For the moment he did not stir; he stood there, in his knickerbockers and tight pink shirt, his face sullen. Then he bent and slipped the noose off the cat's neck, and it went streaking past him out the door.

"Ferdy," she said. "I'm surprised at you."

He looked up at her, and his eyes were black and dull and unfathomable.

"I got no use for cats," he said. "They're treacherous."

"Nonsense!" said Mrs. Herriott. "And, anyhow, even if you don't like them, you mustn't be cruel to any living creature."

"Well, cats are cruel, aren't they?" Ferdy demanded resentfully. "Animals kill each other, don't they? Well, then! Suppose I was out on the plains..." He swung the lariat in a circle, moving his head quick as a cat himself. "I'd bet you I could bring down a buffalo," he said.

The tray slipped from Mrs. Herriott's hands and clattered to the floor.

"Ferdy!

He looked up at her again; their eyes met in a dreadful question and answer. Then she knew, and he saw that she knew, and he came running up the spiral stair.

CHAPTER TWENTY

Now she knew. She knew what had brought Madge down. And Silas. He's a child, she said to herself. I must remember that. He's only a little boy. I must remember that.

He must be dealt with as a child. "Go downstairs again," she said.

"I will not," he said.

"Don't be silly," she said. "I don't like this at all, Ferdy. Give me that rope."

He did not answer or move; he stood at the end of the gallery, watching her.

"This isn't funny, Ferdy," she said. "I'm getting seriously annoyed."

Face to face with him, sure now of that thing beyond belief, she could still speak like this, with dignity, with authority.

"Give me that rope and go downstairs, Ferdy."

He dragged the rope in a circle on the floor, and she thought of Madge, hurrying out to the quiet treelined street. There was nothing there to trip her up, Sergeant Tucker had said. But if a rope had tightened suddenly around her ankles....

"Hey! Where are you going?" he demanded, as she moved.

"I'm going to get something from my room," she said.

He came after her, and she took up her purse from the table.

"Now I want you to go downstairs again," she said.

"Why?" he asked. "What are you going to do?"

"I'm going to stay here," she said.

"You going to tell on me?"

"Well, you behaved very badly about that poor cat," she said.

He wasn't so sure of himself now; he shifted his feet and frowned. "I got no *use* for cats."

"Go downstairs now, Ferdy."

"Well, maybe I don't feel like going downstairs," he said.

She had known Ferdy for a long time and had never made even a suggestion that he had not obeyed instantly. It gave her a feeling of panic when he opposed her now; it was unbearable to have him stand so near her. He's so *little*... she thought. It's unnatural, it's horrible—for him to be so little....

Take hold of yourself, Charlotte Pendleton. This is not a nightmare. This is real. You have to deal with this... with this child.

"You're behaving very badly, Ferdy."

"Well, I got a right to," he said. "Look at how you always treated me and Josie."

"Do you think I haven't treated you well?" she asked.

"*Well?*" he cried with overmastering indignation. "Well? Why, you just make a couple of servants out of the two of us, to do your bidding, that's what *you* do."

"I didn't realize..." said Mrs. Herriott.

"Oh, yes you did!" said Ferdy. "You went around telling people what cheap help you got."

"No..." she said.

"You did so!" he said. "Josie heard you tell people you didn't know how you'd get along without her, because she was so cheap."

"No," Mrs. Herriott said again.

"What's the idea of your saying no?" he shouted. "I guess you think Josie and me are just a couple of fools. Well, you're wrong."

I have that gun here in my pocketbook, Mrs. Herriott thought. But it's no good to me. I couldn't use it. Not against a child. I must think of a way... the right way.... But I don't know—I can't see.... She looked at Ferdy; he was staring down at his rope, a lock of his oily black hair flopping across his forehead.

"You never liked me and Josie," he said. "We knew that, all right. You'd do anything for Silas, but you never liked Josie and me."

No, she thought, I tried to, but I really never did.

"Everybody's been against us!" he cried. "Everybody's got a down on me and Josie. Why, even our own father, that ought to want to help us, what does he do but kick us both out? Why, he's as mean as a skunk, our father is. And look at that Mme de Belleforte! Look how *she* acted. The moment she got in the house, she was after Silas. I heard her, all right. I listened outside the door, before you came upstairs. She was right after him. *Alors, mon ami, il faut que nous—*"

He went on in a sudden stream of French, animated, as Josie was when she used that tongue.

"I don't understand French, Ferdy," said Mrs. Herriott.

"Well, Silas did, all right," said Ferdy. "'Cause Josie taught him. She took all the trouble to teach him, and then he went and cheated on her. Well, you knew that."

"No, I didn't know that."

"You did, too! You got him away from Josie. You left Josie there all alone, and you took him and Carla away to a swell hotel."

Does Josie know? Mrs. Herriott thought. If she does she will try to protect him. What else could she do? If only she'd come back, we could talk it over.

They could, they must talk over what was to be done with this child that was not a child. Some private institution, Mrs. Herriott. Perhaps he could be cured.... But he must be kept somewhere....

Ferdy was moving away toward the stairs, and a great sigh filled her lungs. If she could have even a few minutes without seeing him.... He was going with his head bent, as if in dejection. Where was he going? What unimaginable things were in his mind?

He stopped and faced her again. "You're a bad woman," he said.

"I'm sorry you think that, Ferdy."

"Well, if you're sorry, why don't you give Josie that money?"

"What money?"

"What money?" he repeated, in scornful anger. "The money you took off Silas. Anything Silas had ought to belong to Josie. Not *you*."

"I'll see that Josie is provided for, Ferdy."

"Yes, you will—I don't think! Listen. You give me that money right now, and I'll let you off."

"Let me off?"

"That's what I said. Come on! Give me that money, and I'll let you go."

"We'll wait until Josie comes home, Ferdy."

"We will not! Come on, now! What's in that pocketbook?" She tried to open it, but her fingers were clumsy.

"Never mind about opening it," he said. "Just chuck it over here."

She fumbled at the stiff clasp, and he must have seen her haste and the urgency in her face.

"Stop that!" he cried, in a sudden panic.

She saw him swing the lariat, she saw it spiral upward like a snake; she put up one hand to ward it off, but it came down around her neck. When she tried to pull at it, it tightened.

"Now you stay still," he said, "or I'll pull you right down the stairs."

There she stood, with a noose around her neck.

"Now chuck over that pocketbook," he said.

She got the clasp open then and took out the automatic.

She did not raise it, she did not aim it, but he was frightened.

"Hey! You put that down!" he cried. "Drop that!"

"Take this rope off me, Ferdy," she said.

"I will not!" he said. But he said it uncertainly. He was afraid of her, not only because of the gun she held in her hand but because of what she was.

She had no doubt that he was capable of killing her, but she felt no fear. She felt a great strength rising and rising in her, and she was sure that she would conquer him. Only, this monstrous duel could not be hurried; even with a noose round her neck she must speak with dignity and authority.

"Ferdy," she said, "this can't go on, you know."

"Well, now you'll have a worse down on me than *ever*," he said, afraid to go on, afraid to retreat.

That was what she had to do, to show him a road for retreat.

"This is a very silly game, Ferdy," she said. "I don't like it."

"Game...?" he repeated. And he was wavering.

"I suppose you were playing Indian," she said. "Out on the plains—and got carried away by your game. But now you must stop. You must take this rope—"

She stopped, and they both turned their heads at the sound of a door closing below. Oh, thank God! she cried in her heart. It didn't matter who it was. Anyone would do. There was a brisk loud step in the patio. It's Josie, she thought. Oh, thank God! She'll know how to control him. She's the best....

"Ferdy!" cried Josie. "She's got a gun there! Ferdy, choke her—or something—quick, or she'll shoot!"

For a moment he was motionless. For a moment Mrs. Herriott had her free choice. There was no confusion in her mind, no panic; the choice was entirely clear. She could be jerked down the spiral stair and die, or she could shoot Ferdy and live. I can't shoot that child, she thought. Let it end.

"Quick, Ferdy, you little fool!" cried Josie.

The noose tightened and she was dragged forward; she let the purse and the gun fall and clung to the rail of the gallery. But the pressure around her throat was unendurable; she had to raise her hands and try to tear the rope loose. In a blur she saw Josie's face, looking up eagerly, with parted lips; she was jerked forward.

"Estop!" cried a ringing voice.

Josie gave an ear-splitting scream, and Ferdy dropped the rope and ran down the stairs. Holding to the rail, Mrs. Herriott sank down on the top step.

CHAPTER TWENTY-ONE

She could have done better, she knew that very well. She could have opened her eyes when that rope was loosened, when that woman's voice had asked her how she felt.

She did slip into complete unconsciousness for a time. But when she came back out of that, she could have opened her eyes. When she was lifted up and put on a stretcher, she could have spoken, might even have sat up. Only she did not want to see anything, know anything, feel anything. Nothing confronted her but horror and desolation, and she wanted to stay in darkness a little longer.

Someone raised her head. "Try to swallow this, Mrs. Herriott," said a voice she recognized, Dr. Camberwell's voice. A spoon touched her lips; with her eyes closed she swallowed the contents—delicious pungent sirup. "And another one!" he said cozily, and she gladly swallowed another.

She felt ashamed of herself. The doctor must know I'm only shamming, she thought. Everyone will be disgusted with me. I must make an effort....

She opened her eyes, but there was only a bright blur. "That cat..." she said. "I think we ought to see—if it was hurt."

"Everything will be all right," the doctor said.

Her tongue felt clumsy; she thought she would wait for a while before she talked any more. A tide was rising, gentle and warm, and she floated on it. It was exquisite; it was heavenly. "I'm not asleep," she explained, in case anyone wished to talk to her. She sighed and stretched out, so comfortable, floating gently up and down, so comfortable....

There was a pink-shaded lamp lighted.

"Is it a long time?" she asked, worried.

There was a nice little nurse in white sitting beside the bed. "Oh, no!" she answered, cheerfully. "Only a little while. I'll get you some coffee now, Mrs. Herriott. The doctor said you could have some as soon as you waked up. Mrs. Jones will stay with you till I come back."

She rose and opened the door to another room.

"She's awake now, Mrs. Jones," she said, and a woman came in, a woman a little stout but bearing herself like a queen in a sweeping negligée of black satin, her abundant dark hair beautifully dressed. She was superb; her black eyes were magnificent.

"You are rested," she said, sitting down on the chair by the bed. "That was my own medicine I asked the doctor to give you. I travel always with thees medicine, also many others, and if anyone is ill, I 'ave always the right thing."

"I see...!" said Mrs. Herriott.

"Coffee weel be good for you. My maid 'as made it for you."

"Thank you," said Mrs. Herriott.

She was in a very agreeable room, large, prettily furnished, with three windows where bright chintz curtains were drawn.

"Mrs. Jones...?" she said. "Was it you who came in...?"

"It was I," Mrs. Jones answered gravely. "I 'ad come to pay you a little call. I found the door open. I walked into the patio, and I saw..."

There was no darkness to hide in any longer. The thing that had happened came before her, clear, well lighted, static, a scene frozen in the past.

"Do you know," she asked, "if the police have made—any arrests?"

"I know everysing," said Mrs. Jones. "I 'ave given orders, my dear Mrs. 'Erriott, that you shall not be disturbed until we 'ave 'ad a talk together. I think it is much better if you 'ear all this from me. Yes. The police 'ave arrested your two wicked servants."

"Ferdy—is only a child, only fifteen."

"But that is not always a child, dear Mrs. 'Erriott. At 'ome I know a boy fifteen years old who is already a father."

"Oh," said Mrs. Herriott, a little taken aback.

"He is a wicked little snake," said Mrs. Jones. "It is better if he does not grow any older."

"Sometimes they can cure people like that," said Mrs. Herriott. "It's—I think it's what the psychologists call a delusion of persecution. He thought everyone was against him."

"And why should they not be? He is a very wicked nasty boy. This afternoon his father came, a good decent man. What disgrace for him!"

"I've known them for so long.... Since Ferdy was a little child...."

"It is a terrible thing when someone trusted turns against you," said Mrs. Jones, soberly. "It is a shock, also it is very sad. But that woman servant—!"

"Josie wasn't a servant," said Mrs. Herriott. "She was—like a friend...."

"That is always a trouble," said Mrs. Jones. "I too 'ave done that. I 'ave taken into my 'ouse and wished to train a young girl for something better. And *always* such girls are discontented. You take them out from their low state, but what you give them is never enough. This woman was the same. She escreamed that she did not have enough fine clothes and that you did not allow her to live in some fine 'otel. Also she escreamed against 'er own 'usband. She tells the police that poor Mme de Belleforte ran out into the street to meet 'er 'usband and make love with 'im."

"No...!" said Mrs. Herriott.

"But of course not, dear Mrs. 'Erriott. We know, do we not, that people do not meet in the street to make love. No. I think they were meeting only to talk a little where nobody would 'ear. But that little wicked boy Ferdy 'as already 'eard that they arrange a meeting, listening outside poor Mme de Belleforte's door. 'E tells the police 'e is afraid 'is sister's 'usband will run away with Mme de Belleforte and leave them with no money, no 'ome. 'E says 'e did not mean to kill 'er, but only to pull 'er down and stop 'er. Maybe that is true. I don't know."

"And Josie knew...?"

"They both say no, she did not know until you came out 'ere, and then 'er 'usband told her, so that she would send away that boy. 'Er 'usband knew what this boy 'ad done, from the beginning, but I think the poor man wished to protect 'is wife. Only 'e wished much more to protect *you*. 'E did some bad things, but 'e was always faithful to you."

Mrs. Herriott was silent.

"This woman," Mrs. Jones went on, "tells the police 'er 'usband was wanting to run off with your beautiful niece, and only 'er brother stopped 'em—with that rope."

"That's not true about my niece!"

"But I know it is not true, dear Mrs. 'Erriott. Then I was speaking with your lawyer—"

"Jeff Quillen? Is he here?"

"But certainly 'e is 'ere. It is 'is duty to be 'ere. 'E is employed by you for such duties," said Mrs. Jones.

This was a point of view surprising to Mrs. Herriott. Never had she thought of herself as 'employing' Jeff Quillen. He did send a bill now and then, but it had always seemed to her as if he had paid himself. It was almost as if her money really belonged to him and he paid for things. He gave her advice, but the advice had the force of a command.

"You must forgive me, dear Mrs. 'Erriott, if I 'urt you at all," said Mrs. Jones, and laid her hand over Mrs. Herriott's; a beautiful hand she had, and beautifully kept. "I have told your lawyer it is better if I talk to you first. A woman understands such things. I understand—please believe that I understand 'ow you are feeling about poor Mme de Belleforte."

Mrs. Herriott was silent, savoring that pain again.

"You must forgive me," Mrs. Jones said again, very gently. "We are of an age to know the world, you and I. It is sad—but poor Mme de Belleforte too much liked young men. We know that it is sometimes like that. She gave money—and she gave the jewels that were not 'ers to that man Silas to keep safe for her. I think—from what they tell me—maybe 'e would have kept them safe and given them back to her, only, when 'e saw her dead, 'e thought, 'ere is my chance. 'E wished to do very much for you. Your beautiful niece confessed to me—"

"To—you, Mrs. Jones?"

"People confess very much to me," said Mrs. Jones, with a sort of majestic simplicity. "Even strangers. It is my character to inspire confidence. I know the world very well, I am discreet, also I am practical. Your niece willingly confessed to me that she was going to meet your man Silas. But there was not some illicit amour, dear Mrs. 'Erriott."

"I know *that!*" cried Mrs. Herriott. "Carla is—a very good, fine girl."

"Oh, yes," said Mrs. Jones. "I like 'er very much. But we know, you and I, 'ow it is with a young girl when there is some attractive young man in the 'ousehold. They do not wish to do wrong, but nature is so strong—"

"Excuse me," said Mrs. Herriott, "but my niece isn't—like that."

"Oh, no!" said Mrs. Jones, soothingly. "I believe that. I am quite sure that nothing bad 'ad 'appened yet."

"It *never* would!" said Mrs. Herriott. "Carla's a well-bred, high-principled *good* girl."

"I am sure..." said Mrs. Jones, with a grave inclination of her handsome head.

The nurse came in, with a pot of coffee and a plate of sandwiches on a tray.

"Wait, please!" said Mrs. Jones. She raised the lid of the coffeepot and inhaled the aroma; she delicately examined one of the sandwiches. Then she smiled at the nurse, a brilliant and heart-warming smile. "Everything is right," she said. "You are very nice. Now sit in the other room. Rest. If you wish, smoke my cigarettes."

The nurse went out, and Mrs. Jones poured a cup of coffee.

"It is better that you take it black, after the medicine," she said. "Now, dear Mrs. 'Eerriott, let us finish with all that is disagreeable. Your lawyer is *quite* clever, I think, and most devoted to you. I think you can trust 'im."

"Trust Jeff Quillen? I've known him since I was a girl."

"That is not always a good reason for trusting, dear Mrs. 'Erriott. But I 'ave 'ad much experience with lawyers, and I think this one is clever and true. I am afraid we must believe 'im when 'e says there is a great deal that is most disagreeable ahead."

"Yes..." Mrs. Herriott said.

"He is a little cross, this moment," said Mrs. Jones. "That is because he does not like to think he was deceived—by your niece. But that will pass. 'E thinks there will not be serious trouble for you with the police. 'E is going to tell them that the shock of poor Mme de Belleforte's death a little unsettled your mind."

"You mean he's going to pretend I—wasn't normal?"

"Only for a little while. Only for the police and the court."

"There'll be a trial, of course," said Mrs. Herriott. "And I'll have to give evidence...."

"It will be 'ard, dear Mrs. 'Erriott. We cannot escape from that. But your niece will say she made her deception because she feared to make your mind still more unsettled."

"I don't see any necessity for that," said Mrs. Herriott.

"You must let this clever lawyer arrange all that. And while this goes on, your friends will stand beside you. You 'ave very good friends, dear Mrs. 'Erriott. You 'ave your niece who loves you very much. You 'ave your clever, true lawyer. And you 'ave your good kind clergyman—"

"Is Dr. Filson still here?"

"They are all waiting to see you. Only, I wished to prepare you first. I 'ave invited them all to dinner. It will be served in my sitting room, so that you need only go two steps from your bed, dear Mrs. 'Erriott. It will be a dinner only of persons who love you and wish to 'elp you."

"Mrs. Jones, excuse me, but—who are you?"

"I? But I am Ramon's mother."

"Oh... I didn't know, because of the different name."

"It is the same name. Only in Cuba we pronounce it 'Honess.' The father of my 'usband was a North American, and I 'ave sent my children to school and to college 'ere. Ramon is the youngest of my sons. I 'ave four sons and two daughters, and I am five times a grandmother."

"That must be very nice," said Mrs. Herriott, and after a moment: "The emeralds, Mrs. Jones...?"

"I 'ave them. And I 'ave talked to your lawyer about Mme de Belleforte's will. We 'ave decided to let it stand. It is easier so. Then, when Ramon receives this money, we will return it to you."

"Oh, no!"

"Mrs. 'Erriott, my son cannot take this money. You will understand that Mme de Belleforte a little misunderstood my son. 'E is a very polite boy and *quite* 'andsome, and sometimes a woman of a certain age..." She shrugged her shoulders and raised her dark brows. "That is life," she said. "The money of Mme de Belleforte is yours, Mrs. 'Erriott. There is no question of that. And your lawyer says it will be something really quite good."

"I don't—care about that," said Mrs. Herriott.

"Later, when there is not so much sadness, it will be different," said Mrs. Jones. "Your lawyer will try now that the trial shall be soon. In that case we will wait here."

"Wait?"

"Ramon and I. But if the trial shall be delayed, your lawyer will try to get for you the papers you will need to go with me—"

"Go with you...?"

"To my home. To Cuba."

"You mean—the Spanish Main?"

"Oh, yes! You will like it very much. Cuba is beautiful: *la perla de las Antillas.*"

"Thank you," said Mrs. Herriott. "Thank you very much. It's a very kind idea, but—"

"Mrs. 'Erriott," said Mrs. Jones, "you must bring your beautiful niece. My son already admires 'er—only not so much as *you.*"

"Oh..."

"'E 'as talked to me very much about you. A woman of distinction, 'e called you, and so kind. An angel."

"Oh, really..." murmured Mrs. Herriott.

"An angel," Mrs. Jones repeated. "The first time 'e saw you, 'e thought, a woman of distinction. 'E liked you very much, even then. But the next time... Forgive me if I bring up a sad memory—when 'e went to the funeral.... What is this? 'e asked 'imself." Mrs. Jones gave a glance of flashing amazement; this was her son, questioning himself. "'Ow can this be, and why does Mrs. 'Erriott do this? 'E went then to your 'ouse to see you, and 'e told me that never, never in his life was 'e so touched. You said to 'im: 'Ramon! I protect the honor of my sister, at any cost!'"

Mrs. Herriott found it difficult to recognize herself in this presentation. "Well..." she said.

"It is quite true. And Ramon is disposed to like this young girl brought up under your influence. If they are together for a time, who can tell? He may wish to marry her."

"That's for Carla to decide," said Mrs. Herriott, a little severely.

"Oh, certainly!" Mrs. Jones agreed, with politeness. "But often young girls do not know their own minds. However, we shall see. I should like it if one of my children would marry a North American."

"Mrs. Jones," said Mrs. Herriott, "you're very kind—but it's difficult for me to think about things like this—just now... after what has happened."

"But it is the right moment, dear Mrs. 'Erriott. That is why I introduce these topics. You are a widow. You will be *quite* well off. You are a most distinguished and charming woman. Your friends are 'ere, Mrs. 'Erriott. We wish only to distract you from these terrible things. We will 'ave a good little dinner, and we will drink champagne. We wish to think only of your future, dear Mrs. 'Erriott."

"But I haven't any future!" cried Mrs. Herriott.

"It begins now," said Mrs. Jones. "Come! I will send for my maid. She is a French girl and very clever. She will give you a facial massage, she will arrange your hair—"

"Where am I?" asked Mrs. Herriott.

"In the 'otel Casino Monte Carlo," said Mrs. Jones. "Come, dear Mrs. 'Erriott, or your lawyer and your clergyman will begin to quarrel over you."

"Mrs. Jones, I'm afraid you don't quite understand—"

"I understand perfectly," said Mrs. Jones. "When your niece is settled, dear Mrs. 'Erriott, then it will be time for you to think of yourself. They seem to me to be *quite* eligible, this lawyer and this good clergyman."

"Mrs. Jones, they never dreamed.... They're not...!"

"Dear Mrs. 'Erriott, you will permit my maid to come and dress your 'air?"

THE END

The Matador
By Elisabeth Sanxay Holding

I

Technically Graves was the personnel manager, but we called him "the matador" because it was his job to deal the death blow, to give the fatal thrust. He had, in other words, to do the "firing."

He had developed a beautiful technique, and, like all good workmen, he enjoyed his work. He was really a very kind-hearted fellow. His idea was that it did people any amount of good to be discharged, if it were done in the right way—if, for instance, you told the departing one exactly why he or she was no longer wanted.

It was necessary, he said, to keep the nicest balance between candor and brutality. What you wanted was to destroy conceit without injuring self-respect. He added proudly that all the people whom he had fired remained his firm friends.

I asked him how he knew this, and I refused to believe it a proof of friendliness that these victims had never yet waylaid and assaulted him. He said, however, that he could always tell—that no one could deceive him. I denied that any man could know he had never been deceived. Such a negative statement was impossible to prove.

He brushed all this aside, and continued to explain his technique.

"I never tell a man that we're laying him off because business is bad," he said. "I try to show him what defects in himself make him the kind of man who's always laid off as soon as business drops. And as for those printed slips in a pay envelope—'Your services will not be required after such and such a date'—inhuman, I call *that*. No, sir! I'll call the fellow, or the girl as the case may be into my office and I'll say something like this:

"'Now see here, So-and-So,' I'll say, I'm going to give you the gate; and if you'll listen to me fair-mindedly, it'll be the gate to something a whole lot better.'"

"Always?" I asked.

"Why, yes," said he.

"Of course," I continued, "you've kept a record of the subsequent careers of all the poor devils you've fired, so that you know exactly how much they've benefited by your valediction?"

"Well," said Graves, "well—"

"Of course," I went on, "you keep a card index? You write down the fault for which you discharge the fellow, and you keep track of the length of time it takes him to overcome that fault?"

"Well—"

"What, Graves?" said I sternly, "You make me a positive statement, you tell me it benefits people to be discharged by you, and you have not one fact by which to substantiate your statement. I demand to be shown one of these alleged persons!"

"Well—" he said again.

He was so much perturbed that I hadn't the heart to perturb him further. He was such an honest, artless, enthusiastic fellow, and altogether so likable, that I can't for the life of me explain why it was so natural to worry and badger him; but everybody did. When some especially woeful-looking derelict passed by, some one was sure to call Graves to the window and say something like—

"See here, Graves! Isn't that the shipping clerk you discharged for not keeping his nails manicured?"

Rather gruesomely, we used to read aloud from the newspapers various reports of suicides.

Unknown man found in the river—nothing to identify him but a scrap of paper in his pocket, on which was written "Graves drove me to this."

These fictitious papers varied. Sometimes they said:

And after Graves had turned me down,
What could I do but go and drown?
Graves told me all I didn't oughter,
Despair then drove me to the water.

We kept up a fiction that twelve desperate men were banded together to take vengeance on him, and that their motto was "Give Graves the final discharge." I dare say we were pretty tiresome about it, and sometimes I am afraid we hurt the poor devil more than we intended.

Of course "firing" was not all that Graves had to do. There was also the hiring, but he wasn't nearly so enthusiastic about that—or at least he was warier, for his mistakes in character analysis could be too readily checked up. He pretended that he took every one on trial, and withheld even mental opinions until he had observed the applicant.

That, however, wasn't true. Many and many a time he was tremendously hopeful about some fellow who turned out to be quite worthless. I say "fellow," because he was notably reticent about the girls, and *never* hopeful.

He objected to girls in an office. He said that the principle of the thing was wrong, and so on; but the real reason was that he was afraid of them. They knew this very well. Once he had had a booklet of "Suggestions" printed and circulated among them. He wrote it in a chatty and reasonable style, as for instance:

It isn't a question of morals, but one of tone. We can't have quite the tone I'm sure we should all like to have in this office while some of our young ladies wear peekaboo waists and openwork stockings, and put paint and powder on their faces. In a ballroom these things are all well enough, but—

The next morning he received a visit from the severe and efficient Miss Kelly.

"Mr. Graves," said she, "about your 'Suggestions'—I have been in this office six years, and have never seen a peekaboo waist. I have not observed that openwork hosiery has been worn. My department has asked me to mention this to you, as we feel it an unmerited slight. Incidentally, Mr. Graves," she added, "girls don't as a rule wear waists in a ballroom. *Even* stenographers have *some* knowledge of etiquette!"

The conscientious Graves bought a household periodical, and found no mention of peekaboo blouses and openwork stockings. Unfortunately he was discovered reading this magazine, and he had to explain. He became a little annoyed at hearing so much laughter.

"Oh, shut up!" he exclaimed. "I know I've heard of those things. Read articles about 'em in the newspapers."

"But when?" somebody wished to know. "When did you last cast a glance at a girl, oh, innocent and artless Graves?"

"Well," he said, scowling, "the difference is so small that no one but an idiot would laugh. I might have said 'sheer hosiery' and 'chiffon blouses.'"

Graves talking about chiffon blouses was too much. He regretted those "Suggestions," and made no more. We subscribed to a fashion magazine for him, and by a most pleasing error it came addressed to "Miss F. Graves." This was even better than we had planned.

II

One day Graves came to me with a beaming face.

"You know I don't often express an opinion on an untried worker," he said; "but this time I've made a find. I've got just the sort of girl I want in the office. She's a college graduate; comes of an old Southern family—"

"And her father died, and she was obliged to go out into the world and earn a living," I said.

He was amazed.

"How did you find out about that?" he demanded.

"She hasn't had any experience," I continued, "but ah, what class!"

"Now see here," said Graves. "You've been talking to Miss Clare!"

"I know Miss Clare like my own sister," I told him. "I've met her a thousand times. I've read her in books and seen her in movies—"

"Oh, that!" said Graves. "Well, you're entirely wrong, you chump. She's absolutely original."

"I knew that," said I. "She makes the most wonderful clothes for herself out of old quilts, and she can get up the most delicious little suppers for two for thirty cents—"

He laughed, with that disarming good humor of his.

"Well, I haven't got as far as that yet," he said. "I don't know what she eats or makes her clothes out of, but I can tell you this—she's the neatest, most sensible-looking girl in the place!"

When I saw Miss Clare, I had to admit that in some ways she deviated from the usual type. She was what you might call a tall, willowy blonde. She had fine eyes, and knew it; but she was not kittenish, or pathetic, or appealing. She was doggedly in earnest. I liked her for that.

When I knew her better, I liked her for many other things, too. She was as honest and candid as daylight, and she left her fine old Southern family and her college and all her past glories where they belonged. She was there to work.

I was really sorry when the efficient Miss Kelly spoke about her.

"She's *stupid!*" she told me, with fierce exasperation. "I've told Mr. Graves several times that she doesn't measure up to our standard of efficiency. I don't see why he keeps her on!"

"Beauty in daily life," said I. "It's what Morris recommended. She's an ornament to the office, Miss Kelly. She has artistic value."

"Superfluous ornaments have no value anywhere," said Miss Kelly. "I worked once for an interior decorator, and I learned that. A thing must not only be beautiful in itself, but in harmony with its surroundings, and serving some definite purpose. She isn't and doesn't, and she ought to be scrapped!"

Now not only was Miss Kelly a notably good-looking young woman, and intelligent and alert and sensible, but she was infallible. Graves knew it. He had had other disagreements with her, and had always been worsted. Still, for a time, he defied her in regard to Miss Clare.

"D'you know," he said to me, "I hate like poison to discharge that poor girl! You see, this is her first job, and it'll be hard for her to get another, with only a four weeks' record here."

"Oh, no, Graves," said I. "Not at all! After you've talked to her and pointed out her faults, she—well, she'll get rid of her faults, don't you see? And after that—"

Then Graves declared, with a sort of magnificence:

"She hasn't any *faults,* exactly. It's lack of training that's the trouble. If she could stay on here a little longer, she'd do as well as the others—and better. She has brains!"

"Why can't she stay?" I asked.

"Her output's below the average," he said dismally. "Miss Kelly keeps charts and so on." He scowled. "Miss Kelly's worth her weight in gold, and all that," he said, "but she's pig-headed. I've tried to explain to her that it's actually more efficient to keep and train an employee, even if you have to shift him to another department, than to break in a new one. I've shown her in black and white what the actual cost of this eternal hiring and firing is; but no! She jumps down my throat with a lot of her own figures about what this Miss Clare costs the department every day. Hair-splitting, that's all it is!"

Graves should have been warned, each time he opened his mouth, that what he said would be used against him. Of course this was. Each time he dealt the death blow, we reminded him of the cost of this eternal hiring and firing, and how much more efficient it was, and so on.

Miss Clare was shifted out of Miss Kelly's department into another, which had a human man, young Allen, at its head; but he, too, rebelled.

"She won't do," he said to Graves. "She tries, but she's—well, I don't know just what the trouble is. She's simply not on the job."

"I'll have a talk with her," said Graves. "I'll see if I can find out what's wrong."

III

I saw Miss Clare going into Graves's office, and I felt sorry for him. I shouldn't have enjoyed pointing out her faults to her. She was very young and quite without affectation, but she had a natural and altogether charming dignity about her. You couldn't think of her as an office worker; you were obliged to remember all the time that she was a woman.

She came out after half an hour, looking downcast and grave. She smiled at me, as she passed, with the air of a lady who never neglects her social obligations, but I fancied her lips quivered a trifle.

"Poor girl!" I thought. "She's out of place here. She hasn't the stuff in her for a competitive worker. She'll never get on!"

I was so sympathetic to Graves that he told me the story of the interview.

"The poor girl's worried sick," he said. "It seems she's trying to support her mother, and she's so desperately afraid she won't make good that she can't do her work. She does try, you know, and she's fairly accurate, but she's slow, and she knows it. She said she'd never tried to hurry before, and when she does, she gets nervous." He paused, and frowned a little. "Well," he said, "it's irregular, but I think it'll work. I'm going to let her come half an hour earlier than the other girls and stay an hour later, so that she can finish her share of the work."

"That's hard on her, isn't it?" I asked.

"Not so hard as getting fired," he answered. "She's got a queer point of view about that. She says that if she were discharged, she'd be so discouraged that she'd—I think she said she'd go to pieces."

"Lacks stamina," I observed.

"Well," said Graves, "there's more than one sort of stamina. It takes some grit for a girl brought up as she's been to tackle the job of supporting her-self and her mother, I can tell you!"

I agreed with him, and said so, and he was delighted; but he paid heav-ily for his kind-heartedness. Miss Kelly let the thing go on for one week. Then, on Saturday morning, she appeared before him.

"Mr. Graves," she said, "after due consideration, I have decided that the only course for me is to leave this office. I shall remain, of course, until you have filled my position to your satisfaction."

She knew perfectly well how invaluable, how irreplaceable she was.

"Now, see here, Miss Kelly," said Graves, as man to man. "This wants talk -ing about. Sit down and let's discuss it frankly."

She did sit down, and I thought she looked alarmingly frank.

"Certainly, Mr. Graves," she said very pleasantly.

"Now, then, what's the trouble? Not enough salary?"

"My salary is quite as much as the overhead permits," said she. "In pro-portion to the calculated profits, it is perfectly fair and adequate. No, Mr. Graves—it's a question of prestige and morale."

Graves looked serious.

"My girls are constantly coming to me now with requests to be allowed to finish their work at irregular and unauthorized hours, instead of keep-ing up to the standard output required by my department. They assert that a girl in Mr. Allen's department was allowed to do this, and they had never understood that employment in his department carried any special privi-leges. I went to Mr. Allen about this. I pointed out to him that it affected the morale of my girls to see one of his people favored, but he told me he could do nothing. He said it was not his idea, and—"

"All right!" said Graves, suddenly getting up, with a flushed face and a constrained smile. "I—very likely you're right, Miss Kelly. I'll—I'll make some adjustment that'll suit you."

"Please don't consider suiting *me*," said Miss Kelly. "It's the morale of the office, Mr. Graves."

And she went away like Pallas Athene from a battleground.

I honestly pitied Graves, he was so wretched.

"Well, you know," he said, "she's right. It does upset the routine, and so on; but, hang it all, that girl simply couldn't stand being discharged! She has pluck enough, and all that, but she's sensitive. She's too darned sensi-tive entirely. I wish to Heaven she'd picked out some other office to start in! She's got some fool idea in her head that it's the first job that makes or breaks you. It's no use pointing out her faults to her; she knows 'em. She's trying to overcome them; but she's just naturally slow."

He tried her at filing. Not for long, though; the tumult was too great. He tried her at bookkeeping; but she herself admitted that figures were not her forte.

"There must be *something* that girl can do, or can be taught to do!" he cried in despair. "Everybody has some aptitude, and she's not stupid. She can talk well about books and so on."

"Do you talk to her, Graves?" I asked. "Much?"

"Oh, yes," he answered innocently. "I talk to her a lot. I try to find out what she's adapted for; but I can't, for the life of me. And yet I can't fire her. I simply can't do it. She says no one else would give her the same chance I do; and that's no lie. She wouldn't last a week in any other office!"

"Unless—" said I, and hesitated.

"Unless what?" asked Graves.

"Unless there were another personnel manager as—as conscientious as you."

"Well," said Graves, "it's this way—there's a big responsibility attached to my job. I shouldn't like to think I'd destroyed the self-confidence of a girl like Miss Clare."

"Anything would be better than that," I said.

Graves looked at me with dawning suspicion.

"Well, you're all wrong," he said severely, "if you think there's any—any personal element in this. It's simply that I've got a heavy responsibility—"

"You bet you have!" said I, and left him with that.

IV

The thing began to assume a dramatic aspect. Graves was a haunted man. He was obliged, or he felt himself obliged, to find a place for Miss Clare in our organization, and the task was a hideous one.

He changed. His brisk self-assurance gave place to a harassed air, and he acquired a new and rather touching way of appealing to the rest of us. In fact, we were all deeply concerned about Miss Clare. We would go joyously to Graves, to tell him we thought something had turned up that would suit her. We always phrased it that way; but it never did suit her.

In the final analysis this was Graves's fault, because it was he who had made the office so brutally efficient. To be more frank than modest, it was not so much that Miss Clare was very bad as that the rest of us were so good. She failed to come up to our standard. Graves was the *Frankenstein* who had created this monster, and now he had to suffer for it.

One morning he arrived with a grim and desperate expression.

"An execution?" I asked.

I had become very friendly with Graves during this little complication. He seemed to me less amusing than before, and much more human and engaging.

"Yes," said he. "She's got to go. I've been thinking it over pretty seriously. I'm afraid I've wasted the firm's time and money in this instance; but you don't know how hard—"

"Graves," I said, "you're inconsistent. You'll destroy any number of harmless lives, and boast of it, and then you'll apologize for having been kindly and generous and altogether admirable."

He turned red.

"Oh, get out!" he said, like a small boy, but the sympathy pleased him. "Well, you see, it's—well, she tries hard."

No one denied that. Indeed, the unfortunate Miss Clare looked exhausted and wan from her terrific efforts. She came early in the morning, before there was any work given out, and she was always contriving plans for working through her lunch hour. She was always thwarted in this, however. We were too efficient to allow people not to eat; neither was she allowed to stay after five o'clock.

This day, as on so many others, she was still typing frantically at half past twelve, hoping to escape detection; but Miss Kelly espied her.

"You ought to be out for lunch, Miss Clare," she said, in a human, decent, kindly way. "Run along now. You'll do all the better when you come back."

This was painful to me, because I knew that the poor girl was going to be fired when she came back; but she didn't suspect. She raised her weary, anxious eyes to Miss Kelly's face.

"Please let me stay!" she entreated. "I've fallen behind, and this hour will help me to catch up."

"No, Miss Clare, it won't. You'll be ill, and—" Miss Kelly began.

She was interrupted by the suave and mellow voice of Mr. Reddiman, our great president.

"What's this?" said he. "What's this? One of our young women making herself ill, eh? Working too hard?"

Every newcomer in our office marveled at Mr. Reddiman, and resented him, and was convinced that he had no ability, no force, no possible qualifications for being president of the company; but that never lasted. Mr. Reddiman grew on you little by little until, after a few months, you were willing to admit that you could scarcely have done better yourself.

He had a mild, slow way. He put me in mind of an old gardener pottering about in a greenhouse, when, with his hands clasped behind him, he walked through the various rooms, stopping here and there. He was a notably successful gardener, however. He made the business grow; and—he got things done.

"I'm not working too hard!" said Miss Clare, perilously close to tears. "I don't *want* any lunch. I want to finish these letters."

"No, no, no, no!" said he pleasantly. "That won't do. We can't have that!"

The poor creature was blandly hustled out of the office, well knowing that Miss Kelly would be questioned about her, and that Miss Kelly would answer with complete frankness.

But neither Miss Clare nor any other person could have imagined what actually took place. Personally, while giving due credit to Mr. Reddiman's kind heart, acumen, and wisdom, I am inclined to give still more credit to Miss Clare's eyes; for I assure you that those eyes, when filled with tears and raised to your face, were terribly potent. As I said before, they were blue, but only the advertising department could adequately describe the sort of blue.

Listen to the sequel, and bear in mind that I saw her look up at Mr. Reddiman. I know that if I had been Mr. Reddiman, I, too—

Well, he went in to see Mr. Graves, whom he greatly admired and valued.

"In regard to this—er—Miss Clare," he said. "I hear from Miss Kelly—"

"Yes, I know," Graves answered miserably. "I'm going to discharge her this afternoon."

"You would be doing very wrong," said Mr. Reddiman severely.

Graves was naturally astounded.

"I've done all I can to place her—" he began, but Mr. Reddiman interrupted.

"Graves," said he, "I'm afraid you are just a little inclined to overlook the human element. After all, Graves, what is more valuable in an employee than zeal? A—er—person who works with zeal and loyalty is, to my mind, very much more desirable than one of your efficient, soulless machines. The human element, Graves, the human element! This—er—Miss Clare seems to be most earnest. I learn that she comes early and remains late. To my personal knowledge, she wished to-day to forego her lunch in order to complete her work. I shall not interfere in your province, of course, but I hope—I hope strongly—that you will reconsider your decision."

It was Graves himself who told me about the interview.

"Well," he said, "what could I do? Heaven knows I didn't want to say a word against the poor girl; but in duty to the company I had to tell him what I'd done. He listened, and then he said again that I overlooked the human element. He said that what she needed was encouragement, and that she could start to-morrow morning as *his secretary!*"

"Aren't you pleased?" I asked.

"*Pleased?*" he exclaimed. "I'm—I'm horrified! I'm—it's outrageous! It's cruel! I can't bear to think of it!" He paused. "It's the end of her," he said tragically. "She's about as well fitted to be his secretary as she is to be president of the Chamber of Commerce. It's bound to end in a big row!"

I didn't agree with him.

V

Miss Clare arrived the next morning a little pale and nervous, but wonderfully happy. She was always neat and dainty, but this morning she had a sort of festive air, produced, as well as I can tell you, by little extra ruffles and by magic.

Looking into Mr. Reddiman's private room, and seeing her there, with her fair head bent and her fragile hands so busy, in all her gallant and touching youth, I entertained serious thoughts about the human element. I understood the ancient institution of chivalry. I fancied I knew exactly how knights used to feel about forlorn damsels. It seemed idiotic to estimate a creature as valiant and sweet as she by the number of words she could turn out per minute. Indeed, I forgot all about the economic system for a time, in a long meditation upon a system considerably older.

I rejoiced in her innocent and happy triumph. I delighted in seeing her walk past Miss Kelly and smile at her before entering the august private room.

Graves was decidedly under a cloud now. We were all a little hard on him. We forgot his kindly efforts on her behalf, and remembered only that he had been on the point of discharging one who now worthily occupied an important post.

"You see, Graves, I was right," said Mr. Reddiman.

The rest of us agreed in condemning Graves for a sort of inhuman severity.

Three days passed. Then Graves heard from Mr. Reddiman once more.

"It was naturally a—a tentative arrangement—something in the nature of an experiment," the president said. "I am well satisfied with Miss Clare's zeal and industry, but she lacks experience. I have no doubt she can work up to some superior position; but in the meantime, Graves, wouldn't it be possible to find her some work that carries less responsibility? She's very young, you know."

The implication was that Graves had thrust monstrous responsibilities upon her young shoulders, that he was a sort of *Simon Legree*.

"She's a young woman of education and refinement," Mr. Reddiman continued. "I should imagine it would not be difficult to find a place for her in an organization of this size and scope. I don't mind saying, Graves, that I am very favorably impressed with Miss Clare. Of course, if you're con - vinced that she's not useful—"

"Very well!" said Graves brusquely. "I'll try."

And there he was, with the whole thing to begin over again, and with the wind of public opinion dead against him. I observed him sitting at his desk, with his stubby hair ruffled, his sturdy shoulders hunched, and a look of unassuageable despair upon his not very mobile face. He looked up as I approached.

"Go on!" said he. "Tell me I'm a brute! Of course, I know that what I'm really paid a good salary for is to run a charitable institution here. I know—"

"Look here, Graves!" said I. "I'll try your Miss Clare in my department—"

"She's not my Miss Clare," he returned, with vigor. "She's—" He got up. "I'll tell you what," he said. "She's an albatross! You know the story about the fellow who had one tied round his neck, and couldn't get rid of it."

"That's not very chivalrous," said I.

"Well, I'm not paid to be chivalrous," he said. "I know she's a fine girl—a—a lovely girl; but she's out of place here. She can't do one darned thing well enough to deserve a salary for it. If old Reddiman wants me to start a training school, very well, I'll do it; but if he wants me to keep up the standard of efficiency I've set, then he's got to give me a free hand—that's all!"

"She can start in with me to-morrow," I said rather stiffly.

VI

I had my own ideas about office management. No private room for me! I sat out with all the others, in a little railed off pen. I contended that the moral effect of my being always visible, and always busy, was admirable. Graves, on the contrary, upheld the principle of remaining invisible and popping out suddenly.

I said that my department was a little democracy.

"And you were elected the head of it by popular vote, weren't you?" inquired Graves, with irony. "Bet you wouldn't be willing to put it to the vote now. All bunk! Humbug! You're an autocrat, and so am I!"

I remembered this the next morning, when Miss Clare started to work for me, and I resolved to be a benevolent autocrat. The poor girl had lost her triumphant air. She was crestfallen, anxious, apprehensive.

"I'll let her see that I have confidence in her," I thought.

I gave her some letters to answer herself, without my dictating. They certainly were not letters of importance. In fact, it would make small difference to the business whether they were ever answered or not.

Hypocritically, I told myself I ought to keep an eye on her. As a matter of fact, I couldn't have helped it, because she was the most incredibly lovely creature.

Her concentration was distressing. I felt inclined to tell her that the letters weren't worth all her trouble—that no letters could be. She was very nervous. I saw her put sheet after sheet into the typewriter, only to take it out and crumple it up.

Naturally, she knew our excessive dislike for paper being wasted; and after a while I saw her stealthily stuffing those crumpled sheets into a drawer, where they wouldn't be noticed. Then, suddenly, she straightened her shoulders, gave a despairing glance round the office, pulled all the paper out of the drawer, and put it into the wastebasket. It was a small thing, but it touched me. Whenever I looked at her, and saw that incriminating mass in the basket beside her, in full light of day, I mentally saluted her as an honorable soul.

There had come in the morning mail a letter from a rather doubtful customer, enclosing a check for his last bill and a new order. I felt pretty sure he was ordering a bit more than the traffic would stand, yet he seemed to have substantial backing, and it wouldn't do to risk offending him. It was Saturday, and I had meant to talk the thing over with Mr. Reddiman before putting through the order on Monday, when a telegram came:

Ship goods to-day. Wire, if impossible, and cancel order.

This was very awkward. We were somewhat overstocked just then, and not particularly busy, so that it would have been easy enough to ship the stuff; but I was reluctant to take the responsibility. At the same time I didn't want to cancel an order of that size.

There wasn't much time for thought. I sent for my assistant. I told him to take the check down to the bank it was drawn on and get it cashed. I also suggested his seeing the manager.

"What bank is it?" he asked.

"I don't remember," said I, "but you'll see by the check."

And then I couldn't find the check. It was nearly eleven already, and there wasn't a minute to waste. I turned over every paper on my desk; I made every one else do the same. Check and letter were absolutely gone.

Nothing like this had ever happened before during my regime. I couldn't believe it. Now that it's well in the past, I will admit that perhaps I didn't take it very tranquilly; but, after all, it was not soothing, when I knew some one must be to blame, to have people make idiotic suggestions about my looking in my pocket. Was I in the habit of putting the mail into my pocket?

"The thing's going to be found," said I, "and found now. Empty the wastebaskets, and see if it's been thrown away by mistake."

The office boy appeared to enjoy doing this, but the rest of them failed in loyalty. No one looked worried or distressed.

"It's sure to turn up," said one.

Another almost suggested that such a letter had never existed.

Attracted by the excitement, Miss Kelly appeared, followed by others who had no business to come. How cool and reasonable they all were!

"Mercy!" observed Miss Kelly. "What a quantity of paper thrown away!"

She spoke, of course, of the contents of poor Miss Clare's basket, now turned out upon a newspaper. She approached it, and picked up one or two sheets.

"It seems to me scarcely justifiable to waste a sheet merely for writing 'Dear Bir,'" said she, "or a wrong figure in the date. Errors like that can easily be—is this the missing letter, by any chance?"

It was the letter, and the check as well, torn into fragments.

"Oh, I didn't know!" cried Miss Clare. "I'm so awfully sorry! I must have taken it by accident and torn it up with—with some other things. I'm so sorry!"

But my exasperation was too great to be melted even by tears in those incomparable eyes.

"You ought to be sorry!" I said, and so on.

No use recounting the rest of my bad-tempered outburst. I paid for it later in very genuine regret.

VII

It was probably due to ill temper, but it was attributed to my wonderful business foresight that I did not ship those goods. Mr. Reddiman sent for me on Monday morning and praised my wisdom, good sense, and judgment. That customer was to be dropped.

This praise did not make me happy, but quite the contrary. I knew I didn't deserve it—in this instance, that is. I was already very remorseful on the score of Miss Clare. I remembered things of which I hadn't been aware at the time—her white face, her quivering lip, her wide, tearful eyes. She had gone away, after listening to every word I said, and she had not returned.

It would be hard to describe how startling, how conspicuous, was her absence. I missed her from rooms, from desks, where she had certainly never been. The wan sunshine made phantoms of her bright head in dim corners. Other and very different voices took on fleeting resemblances to hers. Once I saw the neat, spare form of Miss Kelly taking a drink at the water cooler, and she seemed to melt into the gracious outlines of that lost one.

My conscience troubled me. My heart was heavy. Very long was the day; and at the end of it I secured her address and went off to see her.

Never mind the eloquent speech I had prepared, for I never uttered one word of it. Suffice it to say that I intended to offer Miss Clare a permanent position, with no possibility of being fired.

She lived in an apartment house on a side street uptown on the West Side—a street that was just on the border of a slum—a street of woeful and dismal gentility. I rang the bell, blundered down a black, narrow hall, and would have gone upstairs if a voice behind me hadn't murmured:

"Clare?"

Turning, I asserted that a Clare was what I sought, and I was bidden to step through an open door and into a prim little sitting room. It was dismal there, too, but light enough for me to see that I was confronted by a mother out of a book—a gray-haired, delicate little creature with a smile of invincible innocence and good will.

I said that I came from the office to see Miss Clare. Strictly speaking, this was true; but the implication was not, for my business had nothing to do with the office.

"Am sorry ma daughter's not in," said Mrs. Clare, in her slurred Southern accent. "If you'd care to wait, Ah don't think she'll be long."

So I sat down, and was instantly fed with tea and cake.

"Rosemary made the cake," Mrs. Clare explained. "She's wonderful at baking!"

She was; nothing could have been more delectable. Naturally I praised it, and naturally Mrs. Clare rose to the praise like a trout to a fly. There was something very touching in her artless talk about her child, and something still more touching in the picture she created for me of their gracious and gentle life together.

"Ah've never heard a sharp word from Rosemary," she assured me. "Ah don't think you could say the same of many other girls in the same circumstances. There's not only her business career that she's so interested in, but she does almost all of the housekeeping as well. She's a wonderful manager, and so clever with her needle! Ah never saw a girl so handy in the house. Of co'se Ah know a girl with her brains and education is just naturally adapted for business, but—" She stopped, with a smile. "Ah'm an old-fashioned woman, Ah reckon. Ah'm glad Rosemary's going to give it up."

"Going to give up business?" said I, astounded.

"She's been engaged for two years," said she. "That's long enough. Of co'se, dear Denby understood how she felt about proving her ability befo' she settled down, but Ah'm glad it's over. He came up from No'folk yesterday, and he persuaded her to give up her position."

I was suddenly aware that it was late, and that I couldn't wait another minute.

"Ah'm sorry," said she. "Rosemary'll be back sho'tly. She just took Denby to see the Woolworth Building. Ah wish you could have stayed to see Denby."

I said how remarkably sorry I was not to see this Denby, but go I would and did.

As I left the house, I ran into Graves, about to enter.

"Old man," said I, "come along with me. I want to talk to you."

I believe I took his arm. Anyhow, I felt like doing so.

"Graves," I said, "I hope you won't think I've been underhand or treacherous about this. I'd have told you, only that it came on pretty suddenly. I didn't really know until this morning, and then it put everything else out of my head. I acted upon impulse, Graves—upon my word I did! I missed her so much in the office to-day—"

"Yes," said he, with a sigh. "It was pretty bad, wasn't it?"

"And I just hurried off, you know—to call upon her. Graves, old man, it's—in fact, there's nothing doing. She's engaged—she's been engaged for two years to some young—"

"Oh, I knew that," said Graves.

"What?" I cried.

"She told me in the very beginning," said Graves. "Naturally she didn't want it talked about, but she explained it to me. It seems this fellow didn't take her seriously enough. He had plenty of money, but he expected her to settle down there in Norfolk and just be his wife. She didn't say so, but I gathered that he's a domineering sort of young chap. She said that if they started in that way, they'd never be happy. She had to show him that she amounted to something on her own account; and he was impressed when she got a job here with us. She showed me a letter, or a part of a letter, from him about it. He got down from his high horse, I can tell you—said he knew she'd be making a sacrifice to give up her career and marry him, but he'd do his best to make it up to her, and so on."

He paused.

"So you see," he said, "it would have been a very bad thing for her—a very serious thing if she'd been fired. Might have spoiled her whole future life. After she told me that, and appealed to me, why, I had to—don't you see?"

"But, Graves," said I, "didn't you—weren't you—personally—"

"Pshaw!" said Graves, turning red. "D'you know, my boy, I read a story once about a hangman who was a pretty good sort of fellow when he was at home. Ever occur to you that even the matador mayn't be as black as he's painted?"

THE END

Dark Power
By Elisabeth Sanxay Holding

Chapter One
A RESCUE

Once more Di went through the house. Everything was in immaculate order, yet it had somehow the look of a place that had been savagely looted and was now abandoned and forlorn. All the bureau tops were swept bare, all the tables; in every room there were great gaps, where Angelina's flamboyant things had been.

Angelina's own room was simply horrible. Standing in the doorway, Di felt the tears rise in her eyes at the sight of that desolate neatness where only yesterday there had been such wild and joyous disorder.

"I'm tired," she said to herself, to excuse her weakness.

And she had reason to be tired. Angelina's wedding had been like a cyclone, and Di had been whirled along like a leaf in the gale. She had done everything for Angelina; she had seen the caterers and arranged for the wedding breakfast, she had sent out the invitations, had listed the presents and engaged detectives to keep an eye on them. She had stood for hours while Angelina's dresses were fitted upon her, she had packed Angelina's trunks and bags. And she had interviewed the reporters.

There had been plenty of reporters, for Angelina's wedding had been sensational, like everything else she did. The newspapers recalled to their readers the past exploits of the beautiful Angelina Herbert, her marriage at eighteen to Hiram Herbert, a millionaire of sixty, her suit for divorce three years later, charging her husband with artful "mental cruelty," her trip through Borneo all alone—except for a cousin, a secretary, a cameraman and one or two others—her attempt to fly in her own plane to Mexico that had ended in a crash near Asheville.

This second marriage of hers was very satisfactory for newspapers. She had married young Porter Blessington, another millionaire, who had spent six months in prison for assaulting an officer in the discharge of his duties, during a little fracas in a night club. She had gone in her car to meet him as he came out of jail and they were married the next week.

Set down in black and white, these things did not appeal to Di; if she had merely read about her in the newspapers, she would have thought Angelina a pretty objectionable type. But in actual life she had loved her.

"She just forgot," she said to herself.

Just a little oversight on the part of the beautiful Angelina, to go off and leave Di without a penny. She had meant to do something regal, to make a lavish gift, but she had forgotten even to write the promised letter of recommendation that would help in getting another job.

With a sigh, she was closing the door of that desolately neat room, when she caught a glimpse of herself in the mirror of the dressing-table. That image depressed her. She was pretty enough in a way, but it was not a way that anyone noticed; a slender, fair-haired girl with blue eyes and a detached, absentminded air. She had exactly suited Angelina, because she was intelligent and well-bred, and marvelously patient, but there was only one Angelina. Other people would require different qualities in a secretary, more skill in shorthand and typing, a more businesslike presence; other people would dislike her queer, cool little air of reserve. She knew, because before she had come to Angelina a year ago, she had gone about looking for a job.

"I've had more experience now," she thought. "I'm not *quite* such a fool now."

Only, in her heart, she wasn't so sure of that. Would anyone but a hopeless fool be in a situation like this? Another secretary would have reminded Angelina of the salary due her, of the letter of recommendation.

"Perhaps she'll remember and send me a check," thought Di.

In her own room she put on her hat and coat and went downstairs. Her trunk stood there, and her bag, and on the hall-table was a great mass of flowers which had yesterday decorated the drawing-room.

"Connor's late," she thought.

Naturally Connor, Angelina's superb chauffeur, would not put himself out for Di. He was stopping for her as a favor; his term of service was over, and the car was to be put into storage that afternoon. But she had to wait for him, because in her purse there was only one solitary quarter, not enough to get her trunk expressed.

"I'll find *something* to do to-morrow," she told herself.

But though she was resolute enough, she was not too hopeful. So many things had happened to her; she had known so many anxieties and sorrows. Even as a child, care had weighed upon her. Her father had been a clever and remarkably unsuccessful man, and she had had to share his vicissitudes.

"I make a *friend* of you, Di," he often said. "I don't put myself on a pedestal, like the average father. We're friends—pals."

Only, she had been such a very young friend, such a bewildered pal. It had been rather hard to hear about troubles which she could not help or even quite understand. Worst of all, he had sometimes talked to Di about her mother, in a tone of noble generosity.

"She was a fine woman, Di," he would say, "but she never understood me. Well—it was probably my own fault. I never could plead my own cause... I tell you, Di, a good woman can be pretty hard. *Damned* hard, sometimes."

Di had not enjoyed this. Her mother had died when she was four, but she had not forgotten her. And it was then, in those troubled childhood days, that she had developed her aloof reserve. She had learned to listen and to say nothing.

Her father had, apparently, intended never to die. For he had loved his child, in his way, and he would surely not have wanted to leave her without a penny, with no friends, with no preparation for life but a queer, patchy education from various small private schools. But he had died, and here she was.

"Plenty of girls are alone in the world," said Di to herself. "They almost always are, in books... I'll get a job to-morrow, all right."

The bell rang and she opened the door. It was Connor with a cigarette between his lips, sign of his perfect independence.

"Ready?" he asked.

"Yes," said Di. "Can you manage my trunk?"

"Sure!" he said, with lofty good-humor.

It was certainly not very large or very heavy; he got it down the steps and strapped it on behind the car.

"Come on, Miss!" he called.

Di was still in the hall.

"I thought we could just leave these flowers at St. Vincent's Hospital," she said.

"Haven't got time," said Connor.

She was in no position to argue the point just then, so she left the flowers, taking only a small bouquet for herself, and started down the steps. And met a young man running up.

He stopped at the sight of her, and took off his hat.

"Hello!" he said. "Am I too late? Show all over?"

"I don't quite—" she began, puzzled.

"The wedding," he explained. "Angelina's wedding."

"It was yesterday," said Di, looking at him with considerable curiosity. For he had not the appearance of one of those casual, careless people who forget dates or come late. He was a good-looking young fellow, dark, very erect, very neat, and there was about him a remarkable air of cool, composed energy.

"Sorry!" he said. "May I have one of these? Little souvenir...." And stooping, he took a gardenia from the bouquet she carried. For a moment their eyes met; then, with a smile he turned and ran down the steps again and set off along the street at a rapid, easy pace.

"I wonder who *he* was?" thought Di, and forgot him as soon as she got into the car.

She had telephoned that morning to the landlady of the rooming-house where she had spent a horrible month before she had got her job with Angelina, and the landlady had said there was a vacant room she could have, at seven dollars a week. She had highly unpleasant memories of that house, but she did not know where else to go.

"And Mrs. Frick knows me," she thought. "If I went to a strange place, I'd be expected to pay in advance."

The house was downtown in Greenwich Village, but there was nothing Bohemian about it, a dingy old house and very respectable. Mrs. Frick was looking out of the window, and saw Di arrive, in a Rolls-Royce driven by a chauffeur in uniform, and carrying the most expensive sort of flowers.

"Hm..." said Mrs. Frick to herself.

She opened the front door, with a faint, faint smile, and Connor brought in the trunk.

"Top floor!" said Mrs. Frick.

Connor immediately hated her.

"Is zat so?" he said. "Then you better call a couple o' butlers. Good-bye, Miss Leonard!"

The door banged after him.

"Well," said Mrs. Frick. " I haven't got anyone here to take that trunk up all those stairs."

"I'll—find someone," said Di. "Top floor, did you say?"

Mrs. Frick led the way upstairs, three long flights, and opened a door. It was the meanest little room, the chilliest, most depressing little room in the gray light of a February morning.

"I hope I shan't have to stay here long," thought Di.

Mrs. Frick was standing in the doorway.

"There's a clean towel," she said.

"Yes, I see, thank you," said Di, longing to shut the door.

"I told you on the telephone, didn't I?" said Mrs. Frick. "This room is seven dollars a week."

"Yes, you did," said Di.

Mrs. Frick stood there. And, in desperation, Di said what so many other people had said to Mrs. Frick.

"I'm—expecting a check. If you don't mind waiting a few days—"

Mrs. Frick remembered the Rolls-Royce and the chauffeur and was not moved to pity.

"If you'll make a deposit—" she said.

And it was impossible for Di to appeal to her. Her old habit of reserve kept her silent, her sorry experience of life made her expect no kindness and ask for none.

A bell rang downstairs.

"Excuse me a moment!" said Mrs. Frick. "I'll be right back."

As her footsteps died away, Di closed the door quietly, laid the flowers on the bureau and clenched her hands.

"*Think,* you idiot!" she said to herself. "Hurry up! It's your last chance...! I'll tell her she can keep the trunk until I get some money. I couldn't get it away from her, anyhow, without paying someone to move it."

Then Mrs. Frick might want to look in the trunk and would find there some of Angelina's discarded dresses, some photographs, a few books— not a collection likely to appeal to her.

"I'll help with the housework," thought Di. "Make the beds—sweep—anything she wants, until I get a check from Angelina, or a job."

She heard Mrs. Frick coming up the stairs now, and she went out to meet her.

"Mrs. Frick," she began, "I've been—"

"There's a gentleman to see you," said Mrs. Frick. "Your uncle."

"My uncle?"

"That's what he *says*. Your uncle," Mrs. Frick repeated, frigidly.

"But it's a mistake!" said Di.

Mrs. Frick smiled faintly.

"He can't mean me—"

"He asked for Miss Leonard, and I told him," said Mrs. Frick, "that you were just leaving."

"Look here!" said Di.

"I'm sorry," said Mrs. Frick, "but I just remembered I'd promised this room to somebody else. You might try at 280. They sometimes—"

"All right," said Di, briefly, and went past Mrs. Frick, down the stairs. There in the lower hall stood her trunk.

"What can I do with it?" she thought. "If I leave it here, nobody will let me come without paying in advance. And I can't get it moved for a quarter..."

And at that moment she learned a new fact. She saw that shelter was more important than food. If she only had a room, she could have faced hunger with fortitude; it seemed to her that she could even starve without complaining if only she had decent privacy for it.

"There must be places..." she thought, "but I've never heard of them. Perhaps I could ask—a policeman—"

She heard Mrs. Frick coming down behind her, and she moved toward the front door; her hand was on the knob before she remembered that uncle. He was so obviously mistaken that it did not seem worth the trouble to go into the parlor and explain to him that she was the wrong Miss Leonard. She went, only because it meant a little delay in leaving the house.

Opening the door, she found a man in there, a little oddity in a checked suit too large for him, and yellow shoes and a bright tie, a sporting outfit that accorded well with his lean, nutcracker face. He jumped up nimbly and stared at her.

"Well!" he said. "This Diana...? Poor old Harvey's girl...."

She was too much surprised to speak.

"I'm your uncle Peter," he continued. "You'll have heard your father speak of me."

Di colored a little. She had heard her father speak of his family as a unit "the most contemptible, heartless crew that ever breathed"—remarks like that. She had even heard him mention a brother, but not by the name of "Peter"! He had used other names....

The sporting little man sighed.

"Yes..." he said. "Poor Harvey... Well! When we heard that he'd passed away, we wanted to get in touch with you, but we couldn't find you. Only yesterday we saw in the papers all about the wedding of this Mrs. What's-Her-Name—mentioned a secretary—Miss Diana Leonard. That's poor Harvey's girl, says I, so I telephoned the house half an hour ago and I was told you'd just left, to come here. So.../"

He smiled and she smiled back at him.

"I see you've got your hat on," he said. "In a hurry? No? Well, your Aunt Emma—her idea was—perhaps you'd come to us—act as her secretary, with the usual financial arrangement, y'know. Scientific work, y'know."

"Yes, thank you. I *should* like it very much," said Di.

He seemed a little startled by this very prompt acceptance.

"Well!" he said. "That's excellent! Excellent...! Now, when could you come? Next week?"

"I can come—before that," said Di, a little unsteadily.

"Any day that suits you—"

"I can come—to-day," said Di. "I was just leaving here, anyhow, and I hadn't exactly decided where to go. I—"

"Excellent!" he said, with a quick glance at her. "You wouldn't care to come at once, would you? If you would, I could drive you down. Got my li'l' car outside."

"Yes, I *could,*" said Di.

"Excellent," said he. "I'll wait while you pack."

"Everything's packed. I have a bag.... My trunk can wait."

She did not care what happened to the trunk. Let Mrs. Frick throw it down the steps into the street; nothing mattered as long as she could get away from here, could have a roof over her head until she had time to breathe.

"If it's not too big I can take it," he said.

"Here it is—in the hall."

"I can manage that!" said he.

Di took up her bag; then she remembered the flowers.

"Just a moment, please!" she said, and ran up the stairs.

On the first landing she almost collided with Mrs. Frick. With a hasty apology she was about to go on up, when Mrs. Frick stopped her.

"Miss Leonard! You're never going off with that man!"

"Yes, I am," said Di. "He's my uncle."

"You said he couldn't be. You said it was a mistake."

"Well, it wasn't, after all."

"Now, see here!" said Mrs. Frick earnestly. "Don't you do it, Miss Leonard! I'm sorry I was so hasty. You just forget what I said and stay on here."

Di was startled and touched by this tone.

"That's awfully nice of you!" she said. "But, you see, I might not get my check for some time, and I might not find a job, either, for weeks. I was— pretty worried. I only have twenty-five cents—"

"Why didn't you *tell* me that?" cried Mrs. Frick.

"No use bothering you about it," said Di. "And anyhow, it's all right now. I'm going to stay with my Aunt and Uncle—"

"Where?"

"I don't know. I didn't think to ask."

"Don't you go!" said Mrs. Frick. "I don't believe he's your uncle."

"Oh, but he is!" said Di. "He knows all about me and my father.... And why on earth should he pretend to be, if he isn't? I'm not exactly an heiress."

"Don't you go!" repeated Mrs. Frick. "You're young. You don't know what people there are in this world."

"But nobody could possibly have any reason.... He's taking my trunk now. I hear him."

They both looked over the bannisters and saw the sporting little man handling the trunk with surprising ease.

"Oh, dear!" cried Mrs. Frick. "I don't like this! Stay here—"

"I'm awfully sorry, but you see—"

"Then ring me up!" said Mrs. Frick. "Promise to ring me up as soon as you get there, and give me the address."

"I promise!" said Di.

Chapter Two
DI BREAKS A PROMISE

It was a good car, and this uncle was a good driver.

"And I'm afraid I've got soft," thought Di. "Demoralized. For I really don't care much where I'm going if only I don't have to struggle for a while. Or perhaps I'm just tired."

Whatever it was, she was well content to sit back in the little car, to feel the Spring wind in her face, to look at the streets in the bright morning sun.

"Poor Mrs. Frick!" she thought. "So suspicious.... *What* would she have thought of Angelina?"

Her uncle did no talking in the city traffic, but after they were out of that, and headed toward Pelham, he began:

"Your Aunt Emma," he said. "Y'know—very remarkable woman. Very!"

"Is she?" said Di, politely.

"Very!" he assured her. "She's a professor. And a doctor."

"Oh!"

"Psychology," he said. "And so on. It's all too deep for me.... But...." He was silent for a time. "Did your father ever tell you anything about her?"

"I think I remember his mentioning her," said Di, who remembered very well that her father had occasionally mentioned a sister who was, he had said, "hard as nails."

"Too bad!" her uncle continued. "But poor old Harvey couldn't seem to hit it off with the rest of us. Always *was* like that. I hope he never said anything to set you against us?"

"Oh, no!" said Di.

"Well..." he said. "I hope you'll be happy now—with your own people."

He spoke kindly enough, yet, she thought, with a curious lack of warmth. An odd little man altogether; looking at him now in the bright sunlight, she saw that his weather-beaten face was deeply lined with a net of little wrinkles at the corners of his blue eyes.

"Is he old?" she thought. "Or just—battered?" And aloud she asked: "Are you—Father's younger brother?"

"Eh? Yes. Two or three years. Now, I almost hate to ask this—but did you ever hear your father speak of Uncle Rufus?"

"Yes," said Di. "Several times."

"Hm. I'm afraid Harvey didn't care much for the old man."

"I'm afraid he didn't," said Di.

She remembered a letter her father had got from Uncle Rufus, and what he had said about it.

"I simply asked him to make me a little loan," he had cried to his child, "and the damned old skinflint treats me as if I were a beggar!"

He had also spoken of Uncle Rufus quite often as "that damned old hyena."

"Of course," Uncle Peter went on, apologetically, "the old man's got his little weakness.... But he's a very remarkable man. Writes books, and so on. Very remarkable!"

"Is he at your house?"

"Not now. But he'll be coming, for a visit. Y'know, I think you'll like him. You're clever, aren't you? Fond of books and so on?"

"I'm fond of books," said Di, "but I'm afraid I'm not clever at all."

"I bet you are!" he said, and added, sadly. "I'm the fool of the family."

She murmured some polite contradiction, and then, to change the subject:

"It was awfully nice of you to look me up," she said. "I really do appreciate it."

"Oh, rats!" said he, cheerfully, and they both laughed.

The countryside was beautiful that April morning, and the girl's spirits rose and rose. She asked so very little of life, expected so very little; a chance of earning a moderate living, and a morning like this were enough. She was not even especially curious. She was going off bag and baggage, with this man she had never set eyes on before, to a house unknown, unknown people, and she had scarcely asked a question. That was her way. Since childhood, she had had to depend upon her own fortitude, and there was, beneath her half-shy manner, a fine, careless spirit of adventure, an odd little recklessness.

In those days with her father there had been so many disasters.

"I don't know where the money's coming from for the next meal!" he often said.

But it had come. He had often said he was ruined, but somehow they had gone on. And somehow Di, with her patchy education, her one-sided experience, had been able to keep on after she was left alone. No one else had been able to suit the beautiful Angelina, but she had. She had done impossible things; she, who had never had two dollars in her purse, had somehow managed to keep Angelina's chaotic check-book balanced. She, who was so diffident, had been able to talk to the strangest people, to give orders to servants, to confront tradesmen with exorbitant bills.

"I seem to fall on my feet!" she thought. "Look at this! If Uncle Peter hadn't come.... But he *did* come!"

He turned the car now up a road so lovely that she gave a cry of delight. It was a road in the very heart of a wood of birches and pines and oaks; only the pines were dark, the other trees, just budding, were exquisitely delicate against the pure, blue sky. There were no houses, nothing to disturb the sun-dappled peace.

"Nice, isn't it?" said Uncle Peter. "Belongs to me.... One of these days, I'm going to develop it—cut down most of the trees, and put up some nice little houses—what d'you call 'em? That stucco, y'know, with timbers—Elizabethan, isn't it?"

It seemed to Di that "developing" was hardly the word for this place, but she said nothing. They were going up a gentle rise now, and as they rounded a curve, she saw before her a very peculiar house, a large, wooden building, lavishly ornamented with little balconies and gables, a forlorn old place, with uncurtained windows, weather-beaten and in great need of paint.

"It's a nice house," said Uncle Peter. "The Swiss style...."

She glanced at him to see if he were laughing, but he looked melancholy.

"It'll have to come down," he said. "Nobody'll buy a place like that, nowadays."

The road led under a portico before the front door; he jumped out nimbly, and held out his hand to assist Di. Then he ran up the steps and knocked at the door, which was opened almost at once by a dismal little man with red hair.

The interior of the house surprised Di. They entered what was obviously a hotel lounge, furnished with wicker chairs and settees, and with a counter at one end, behind which were pigeon-holes for mail. It was all very neat, and quite empty, no clerk at the desk, not a sound to be heard.

"I didn't know..." she began, but her own voice sounded too loud here. She turned to her uncle and found him whispering to the red-haired man. And she could not help hearing what he said.

"Then *eggs,* you damned fool!"

The red-haired man raised his eyebrows sadly, and went off through a door at the right, and Uncle Peter took up her bag.

"This way!" he said, and began to mount the stairs.

"I suppose they run the hotel," thought Di. "But it doesn't seem very popular. Or perhaps this isn't the season."

At the top of the first flight they came upon the usual hotel corridor, long, narrow, red-carpeted.

"Still," she thought, "it'll be rather nice to be in a hotel. More lively..."

Her uncle had stopped, and now turned toward her, with an anxious frown.

"I don't know..." he said. "Maybe I should.... Your aunt.... Very remarkable woman!"

As he spoke, a door at the end of the corridor opened, and a woman in a surgeon's white overall came out, and behind her, single file, came two children.

"Emma!" said Uncle Peter. "Here she is—"

The woman had stopped, and was looking at him with a sort of steady scorn. Then she turned and pushed the two children gently back into the room they had come out of, closed the door on them, and advanced to Diana.

"So this is Diana!" she said.

She was a sturdy, solid, little gray-haired woman, very erect, and she was smiling pleasantly now. But Di was incapable of answering at that moment. She had caught a glimpse of those children's faces—pasty, yellowish faces, with blank, dull eyes, and loose mouths, hanging open...

"They're idiots!" she thought, appalled.

"I wish I had known Peter was bringing you to-day," Aunt Emma went on. "We could have made some little preparations. Why didn't you telephone, Peter?"

"Never thought of it..." he muttered, apologetically. "Sorry, Emma."

"I'm afraid it's my fault," said Di, making an effort to speak brightly. "I accepted your kind offer so very quickly."

Aunt Emma held out her hand, and Di took it, felt her fingers caught in a strong grasp. This aunt was shorter than herself, a rather dumpy little woman, with a plain enough face, yet there was something unusual about her, an assurance that was curiously impressive. Her blue eyes were fixed upon the girl's face in candid appraisal; she was studying her, with a disconcerting keenness.

"She's looking right through me," thought Di. "She sees that I've got a safety pin instead of a button in the back of my dress, and that I never remember dates."

"See about lunch, Peter," said Aunt Emma.

"I did, Emma," he said. "I spoke to Wren."

"Then show Diana a room," she said. "You'll understand, Diana, that I'm very busy.... Make yourself at home!" And with a pleasant smile she went into the room again and closed the door.

"What does she do?" Diana asked her uncle, in a whisper.

"Too deep for me!" he answered.

"But—those children—?"

"Don't ask me! I don't understand these things."

"But I mean—" she went on, resolutely, "are they any—relation—?"

"Oh, Lord, no!" he said. "Emma's adopted them, that's all."

He opened a door.

"Here's a room," he said, and hurrying on, opened another door. "And here's one—and here's one. Take your choice! They're all pretty much alike."

So they were; bare hotel bedrooms, close and dusty, with stripped beds.

"Well, this one, thank you!" she said, taking the one furthest from that in which those children were.

"Good!" said he, and hurried off down the corridor.

Di looked about her in dismay.

"I almost wish I hadn't come," she thought. "No, I don't! That's silly. It's a wonderful piece of luck for me. And perhaps more people will come—perhaps there are people here already that I haven't seen."

A considerable noise outside brought her into the hall, and she saw Uncle Peter and the red-haired man bringing her trunk up the stairs. With a praiseworthy, but not very effectual, impulse to help, she stepped back into the room and opened the door wide, back against the wall. And as she stood there, out of sight, another door opened.

"What's all this noise?" demanded Aunt Emma's voice, sternly.

"We're getting up the girl's trunk," said Uncle Peter, in his usual apologetic tone.

"Make less noise!" she said. "You disturb me. You shouldn't have brought the girl like this, without warning me."

"But you told me to make her come!"

"Very well. Now hold your tongue," said Aunt Emma, and her door closed again.

The trunk was now carried past Di and set down, and without so much as a glance at her, Uncle Peter hurried off again. Wren, the little red-haired man, stood wiping his hands on his coat.

"I'll make up the bed for you, Miss," he said. "And air the room, while you're down at lunch."

He was such a subdued little man, so shabby, so forlorn in appearance, that Di suddenly gave him her last quarter.

"Thank you, Miss!" he cried. "I—thank you, Miss!"

Pocketing the coin, he stood before her, as if irresolute.

"I'll bring you towels, Miss," he said. "And if there's anything else you want, there's a bell here, Miss. Better ring several times, Miss, in case I'm not within hearing at the moment.... Thank you, Miss."

With his hand on the knob, he added:

"And if you'll excuse me, Miss—I'd advise you to keep your door locked when you're not in the room. Those—little ones is very *mischeevous*. Thank you, Miss!"

He went out, closing the door behind him.

"I certainly shouldn't like those children to get in here," she thought. "I—don't think I like being here, very much."

Then it occurred to her that it would be a matter of considerable difficulty to leave this house now. She had no money for train fare, no money at all.

"Of course if I asked him, Uncle Peter would drive me back to the city, I suppose," she thought. "Only, it would be pretty awkward to say I'd changed my mind. Although they're not very hospitable. 'The girl'—I wonder why they asked me? Out of charity? No, because they couldn't possibly have known how bad things were for me."

The room seemed unbearably close to her; she went to the window and opened it. And there before her were the trees, the dark pines, the old oaks, so close to the house, too close, shutting out all the rest of the world....

Something stirred in her heart, a formless and nameless fear. Wasn't this like a prison?

"What nonsense!" she said to herself. "I'm tired, that's all. It's been a worrying morning. After I've had some lunch—"

There was running water in the room; she washed, and brushed her hair, and then began to unpack her bag.

"There may be other people staying here," she thought. "I hope so. And I must telephone to Mrs. Frick."

She thought of Mrs. Frick with an unreasonable friendliness now. She was impatient to telephone to her.

There was a knock at the door, and opening it, she found Uncle Peter there.

"Lunch, if you're ready," he said.

Since they had reached the house, his manner was undeniably changed; there was a worried, absentminded air about him now.

"I'm ready," she said. "And, by the way, what's the address here, please? I'd like to telephone it to a friend."

"Well..." he said. "You'd better ask your Aunt Emma."

She stared to him in astonishment.

"I mean—" he said. "She doesn't like her work interfered with."

"But that won't interfere with her work, will it?"

"Better ask her!" he said, and stood aside to let her go down the stairs.

As they passed through the lounge, she turned her head to make sure that she had really seen a telephone on the desk, and she was curiously relieved to see that there was one.

At the end of the lounge were sliding doors, pushed a little open now and revealing a big dining-room. And her heart sank at the sight of it. The tables were drawn up against the walls, and the chairs stacked on top of them; near the window was one small table laid with cloth, and at which Aunt Emma was already seated.

"I suppose the season hasn't begun yet," said Di.

"What season?" asked Aunt Emma.

"I mean—don't more people come here, in the Summer?"

"Nobody comes here unless by my invitation," said Aunt Emma. "This isn't a hotel any longer."

"Just—you and Uncle Peter?"

"That's all."

"It's—" said Di, glancing about the big, empty room. "It seems—such a large place."

"It is a large place," said Aunt Emma.

Silence fell. Presently Wren came in, bringing a remarkably meager and unappetizing lunch, a burnt and curdled little omelette, bread and margarine and tea, and one banana each.

Di thought of past lunches, in Angelina's house; she thought of broiled chicken, rice croquettes, mushrooms, crisp salads.

"I'm spoilt!" she thought. "This will do me good."

At least there was plenty of bread; she ate three slices and drank the black bitter tea, and felt better.

"Aunt Emma," she said. "Do you mind if I just telephone this address to a friend?"

"The telephone is disconnected," said Aunt Emma.

Chapter Three
DI MAKES UP HER MIND TO LEAVE

Di was forced to admit that the situation was—uncomfortable. She could not go out anywhere to telephone because she hadn't a penny.

"Well, I can write!" she thought. "There's no such tearing hurry."

And she also made up her mind that she must begin being Aunt Emma's secretary at once, so that she could earn something.

"May I help you this afternoon, Aunt Emma?" she asked.

"We'll see..." said Aunt Emma, with an enigmatic smile. "If you're ready—?"

Di had now eaten everything in sight, and she rose as her aunt pushed back her chair. They went up the stairs together, along the corridor, to the room at the end. Aunt Emma took a key from the pocket of her overall and unlocked the door.

It was a profound relief to the girl that those children were not there. The room looked pleasantly business-like, with a large flat-topped desk, very neat, and a typewriter on a table, and the afternoon sun shining in at the window. Aunt Emma placed a chair before the desk for Di, and seated herself behind the desk, facing her.

"Well!" she said, looking steadily at the girl, "what do you know about cretinism?"

It was remarkably like being at school again, and Di felt the old sensation of defensive resentment.

"Not—very much," she answered.

"How much? What would be your definition of cretinism?"

Di thought very hard.

"Well..." she said. "I think—it has something to do with the—excavations they're making in the island of Crete."

"Good—God!" said Aunt Emma.

She opened the drawer of her desk, took out a cigarette, lit it, and leaning back in her chair, stared at Di.

"A revelation of character," she said. "You're one of those persons who can't say 'I don't know'... Cretinism is a form of idiocy. There are—" She paused, and smoked for a time. "There are," she went on, "a great many varieties of idiocy in this world."

Di grew red.

"The world is largely peopled by idiots," said Aunt Emma. "Of different grades. Most of them attain a development sufficient for the demands of daily life. They can read and write and they can act upon the suggestions of superior minds."

All this time she was steadily regarding Di with a faint smile, and Di began to grow angry.

"I dare say I'm an idiot myself," she said, "but I hope I can be a little useful to you. I can type—"

"Can you read?"

"Read?" Di repeated.

"I mean, are you able to read a book which is not fiction?"

"Yes," said Di.

"Then take this," said Aunt Emma. "It's written by your Uncle Rufus. Kindly read the first chapter and then give me a terse resumé."

Hot and angry, Di took the big volume that was pushed across the desk to her.

Some Observations Upon the Natural Limitations of National Cultures, by Rufus Leonard.

She turned the pages, with a somewhat strained air of intellectual interest.

"I suggest that you begin at the beginning," said Aunt Emma. "The first chapter will do for the present."

"I *won't* lose my temper!" said Di to herself. "She has a perfect right to test me before she takes me as a secretary."

She turned to the first page and began to read. But it was like a nightmare; she had to read sentences over and over, to understand them, and even then, the ideas were hazy to her. And all the time she was aware of Aunt Emma smoking and steadily regarding her. She turned a page.

"One may, for diversion, take a metaphysical view of the problem; one may play with the assumption that the ethos—"

It was no use. She felt that if she had time, and if Aunt Emma were not staring at her, she might manage something, but not in the present circumstances. She closed the book and glanced up, meaning to say that, frankly.

"I see!" said Aunt Emma. "I thought so. No.... You are emotional, instead of intellectual. I do not assert that I can read a physiognomy. I consider that a preposterous claim. But give me fifteen minutes' observation of anyone, of the involuntary gestures, the manner of walking, speaking, and so on, and I will know that person better than his own mother would."

Di essayed an uncertain smile.

"I'm awfully sorry I can't help you," she said. "I hoped—"

"You can help me," said Aunt Emma. "You say you can type. I'll give you some work at once."

"Thank you," said Di.

"I shall be glad to have you here," Aunt Emma proceeded. "Your father and I were never in harmony, but your mother was very agreeable. You're very like her."

Di turned her head away quickly. It was almost intolerable to her to hear that name mentioned. All through her lonely and troubled life she had held as her heart's secret the tenderest image of that mother she could not remember. She had virtually needed something to cling to, some ideal, and she had found it there.

There was a considerable silence; when Aunt Emma spoke again, her voice was grave and kindly.

"You remember her at all?"

"No," said Di, very low.

"Your father, no doubt, often talked to you of her."

"No. Never. He didn't like to talk about—her."

Aunt Emma pushed back her chair, rose, and coming out from behind the desk, laid her hand on the girl's shoulder.

"Work is the panacea," she said. "Now, my dear! Here is a little article of mine which I'd like you to type. 'Basic Fallacies of the Montessori Method.' The main fallacy is this. The Signora Montessori imputes to children a capacity for independent action which is so rare, even in adults, as to be remarkable."

She lit another cigarette.

"The immense majority of human beings have no independence," she said. "The suggestibility of the human race has never yet been fully realized. It is my intention to publish some observations in that field before long... And now, there is the typewriter, and here is paper." With her hand on the door knob, she looked back at Di. "Knock on the door if you want to leave the room," she said. "I shall be conducting experiments in the corridor, and a sudden interruption would be very disagreeable." And she went out, closing the door behind her.

Di stood looking at the closed door.

"I—really don't think I can stay here..." she said to herself.

But how was she to get away, without money? The idea of borrowing from her aunt or her uncle was most distasteful, nor could she think of any decent excuse to make for a sudden departure.

"I was so willing to come," she thought. "I can't rush off and hurt their feelings, when they were kind enough to look me up and ask me here. I've just got to make the best of it."

She uncovered the typewriter, and took up her aunt's neat manuscript; it was easy to read, and she finished a page quickly. Then, as she was putting in a new sheet, she heard footsteps outside the door, shuffling up and down the corridor. There was no sound of voices; nothing but those dragging footsteps.

"It's those children!" she thought, and the room grew stifling to her; it was like a prison. She got up in haste, and opened the window, leaned out, breathing with relief the cool Spring air. Then, beneath her, she heard a voice:

"Hello!"

She leaned further out. Directly beneath her was another window, open, and the voice, which was Uncle Peter's, came from the room inside.

"Hello!" he cried again. "What's the matter, Central? Well, try them again."

"But he's telephoning!" she thought. "Then the telephone *can't* be out of order—"

"Hello!" he said again. "Oh! So you're there...! Now, see here, Miles! Your aunt wants you to come out at once.... What...? I don't care.... No, I can't...! No, I haven't a damned cent.... Oh, pawn your watch—do anything you want, but come out here at once, d'you understand?"

Di drew back into the room.

"That's an idea!" she said to herself. "I'd forgotten that watch."

She remembered now a wrist-watch Angelina had given her, an absurd little thing, no larger than a five-dollar gold piece and not much thicker. It had needed expensive repairs to set it working again, and Di had put it away and not given it another thought, until Uncle Peter's words reminded her that it might at least provide a railway fare back to New York.

"And if I just had the money to go," she thought, "if I felt that I *could* go, then I shouldn't mind staying. It's simply this feeling that I can't get away...."

Very well; but how to convert the watch into money? She thought that over for a time, and then, with a sudden inspiration, began to write a letter.

Dear Mrs. Frick:

Here I am, safe and sound. The address is— Here she left a blank, to fill in later. *"You were so friendly this morning that I feel encouraged to ask you to do me a favor. Enclosed is a little watch. If you could possibly—* She hesitated a moment. Mrs. Frick was probably too respectable for pawnshops— *manage to sell it for me, and send on the money, I should be very much obliged.*

I have already started to work as my aunt's secretary, and I am sure that in a little while everything will be all right. But just at the moment, I am pretty hard up. If you can get me three dollars for the watch, it would be a great help. In spite of her Bohemian upbringing, Di realized that this was an extraordinary letter.

I hope this won't bother you, she added.

Sincerely yours,
DIANA LEONARD

Then she addressed an envelope, put the letter into it, tucked it inside her blouse, and set to work upon her aunt's manuscript with energy.

It was a nice job when she had finished; she was pleased with it. She

sighed and stretched and, leaning back in the chair, with her hands behind
her head, let her thoughts drift. The sun was going down, the sky was
bright and calm.... Angelina and her new husband would be at that inn in
the Berkshires now. They would probably be having tea.

"I'd like tea myself," she mused. "A *very* large club-sandwich—and coffee
éclairs—"

The door opened and Aunt Emma entered.

"Finished?" she said. "That's very nice.... Now, my dear, have you a pretty dress with you? Something light... I'm expecting your cousin for dinner."

"What cousin?" asked Di, startled by the news and by the change in her
aunt's manner, so kindly and solicitous now.

"Your Uncle Peter's son."

"I didn't know he was married."

"You might have known," said Aunt Emma, with a grim smile. "A man
like Peter couldn't help getting married. He's a widower now, though.... I
think you'll like Miles.... Have you a pretty dress?"

"Yes," said Di. "Angelina—Mrs. Herbert—Mrs. Blessington I mean—
gave me lots."

Aunt Emma smiled.

"Run along and put one on," she said. "You'll be glad of someone your
own age to talk to."

"She is nice!" thought Di. "Asking this cousin on my account. Now if only
there's a good dinner!"

She dressed, in a green chiffon frock that suited her very well; she took
pains to look her best, curiously excited at the prospect of meeting this
cousin. Indeed, she was a little surprised by her own emotion.

"Silly!" she thought. "I suppose it's because I haven't any family."

Coming out of her room a little before six, she found Uncle Peter in the
hall, lounging against the wall, smoking a cigar. He still wore his jaunty
checked suit and brown shoes, but he had a quieter necktie, a more subdued air.

"Hello!" he said. "How nice you look!"

"Oh, thanks!" she said. "Uncle Peter, can you lend me a stamp?"

"Haven't such a thing!" he answered. "But if you have any letters to post,
give 'em to me, and I'll look after 'em."

"Thanks! All right!" said Di.

But somehow she did not want to give him her letter to Mrs. Frick.

They went downstairs together, into the lounge. It looked very pleasant
there now, with three shaded lamps glowing. Di seated herself in an armchair, by an artificial palm, and Uncle Peter stood beside her with his
hands in his pockets, whistling under his breath. And an equable illusion
took possession of her. Here she was, in a charming dress, sitting here in
the house of her own people; this cousin was coming; nice, interesting
things would happen.

"I'm an idiot," she thought, "to imagine there's anything—queer here. It's heartless of me to feel this way about those poor little children. No doubt they're getting the best sort of treatment—perhaps they'll be even cured.... No; there's nothing here to be—silly about. It was kind and generous of them to ask me. I'm lucky to be here."

Just then Uncle Peter sighed and stirred, and as she glanced up at him, a singularly disturbing thought came to her. He had been waiting outside her door.... Was he guarding her?

The impulse seized her to find out, to make sure if she really were guarded, not permitted to go about alone in this house. And at the same time she was aware of a great reluctance to make this test. Better not. Better let well enough alone....

She sat very still for a few minutes, then she rose.

"I'll just run up and get my handkerchief," she said.

"I'll send Wren," said Uncle Peter.

"He wouldn't know where to find it."

"You can tell him," said Uncle Peter, cheerfully.

"I'd rather go myself," she said, a little unsteadily.

"I'll hop along with you, then," said Uncle Peter. "These lights have a way of going out, and you'd get lost in this barn of a place."

She turned away her head, so that he might not see her face. A panic fear was rising in her; she wanted to get away; she must get away.

"Don't—*bother!*" she cried, and ran toward the stairs. A bad thing, to run. One hears footsteps running behind, one shrinks from the dreaded touch of a hand on the shoulder.... She fled up the stairs, darted into her room, slammed the door behind her and locked it, turned on the light and sank into a chair, her hand against her racing heart, and her eyes upon the locked door.

She began to grow a little quieter, her breathing less labored; she was ready to reason with herself, when the light went out.

She sprang up, all her fears redoubled. There was a soft knock at the door.

"I won't answer!" she thought. "I won't—I can't...."

She stood motionless in the dark, staring before her. There was another knock.

"Miss!" came a hissing whisper. "It's Wren, Miss."

"What do you want?" she asked, whispering herself.

"I've got an electric torch here for you, Miss. If you'll open the door—"

She did not answer. She thought if *anything happened,* if she called out for help, who in this house would hear or care? Her panic rose to a climax. And then, in an instant, she mastered it; she drew a long breath, and crossing the room, unlocked the door.

The light of a torch shone full in her eyes, dazzling her.

"Excuse me, Miss!" whispered Wren, covering the torch and holding out another one. "I thought.... If you'll excuse me, Miss. I appreciated your kindness to-day. If there's anything I can do for you, Miss...."

By the light of her torch, she could see his pale face, his anxious eyes; she looked and looked at him, but she could not understand him. Was he honest and well-disposed to her, or was he furtive and treacherous?

"If there's anything I can do, Miss—" he repeated.

She decided to take a chance.

"I wish you'd post a letter for me," she said, with a fair attempt at a casual manner. "I haven't any stamps just now, but—"

"Give it to me please, Miss," he said.

"It's not quite ready. If you'll wait—"

"I'd better not, Miss. If you'll leave it were I can get it—"

"How would one address a letter here?" she asked, quickly, infected by his air of haste.

"The Châlet, Miss. East Hazelwood. Just tell me where I'll find it, Miss."

"Under the bureau-scarf," she began, but he had turned away.

"I'll look after it, Miss," he whispered and was gone.

She stood in the doorway, listening. There was nothing to hear; not a sound of any sort; not a light anywhere except the little beam of the torch she held. But her moment of panic was over; she had herself well in hand; a sort of anger filled her. She went along the corridor, and leaning over the bannister, directed her torch toward the lounge below. And the light fell upon Uncle Peter, stretched out in a wicker chair, smoking his cigar.

"Hello!" he cried. "Who's that?"

"Diana," she answered, and began to descend the stairs.

"I suppose that blamed idiot will have the wit to go down in the cellar and change the fuse," he observed. "I don't understand these things, but Wren does. Poor wiring in the house. I warned you!"

"Well, there's no harm done," she said, affably.

She sat down near him in another chair, and waited.

"I've made a fool of myself," she thought. "Rushing upstairs like that and slamming the door. Uncle Peter was only good-natured. The lights *do* go out. And he didn't come after me. He just sat here, smoking. I don't know what's the matter with me—imagining all sorts of things."

"Hark!" said Uncle Peter.

She started nervously.

"I don't hear anything."

"Car coming," he said, and now she heard it too, coming up the drive. What was coming? Who was coming?

There was a step on the veranda, and then an appallingly loud bang on the front door.

"Lend me your torch," said Uncle Peter, and taking it, crossed the room and opened the door. But he let no one in; he stepped outside, closing it behind him.

She was left now in utter darkness. She heard a murmur of voices outside, and she was groping her way across the lounge to the door, when the lights came on. She hurried then, and looked through the uncurtained glass of the door. A car stood out there and the headlights shone along the drive. And she had a glimpse of two men, carrying between them a limp body; then they passed beyond the stream of light, and she could see them no more.

"This is too much..." she thought. "I can't—"

Her knees were shaking; she sat down again. And presently the front door opened and Uncle Peter re-entered, dapper and cheerful.

"Was there an accident?" she cried.

"Accident?" he repeated, staring at her. "No. What made you think that?"

"I thought I saw...."

"Why, it was just a fellow looking for a room," he said. "You know, this place used to be a hotel, and people still come now and then."

Very cheerful and reassuring, Uncle Peter was. But on his cheek and on his shirt-front were two black smudges. Very like coal-dust. Very like the smudge one might get in a cellar. Smudges such as one might get in going down to turn off the current.

"I'm going," she thought. "I'm going to leave here to-morrow, if I have to walk to New York. Perhaps it's all—imagination—but I—don't like to im - agine things like that."

Chapter Four
DI MAKES A PROMISE

No cousin Miles appeared that night. She and Aunt Emma and Uncle Peter sat down to dinner by themselves; a very poor and insufficient dinner, and Wren waited upon them. There was little conversation; Aunt Emma seemed distrait, and directly they had finished she said "goodnight" and went upstairs.

"What about a little game of cards?" asked Uncle Peter. "I'll show you how to play Russian Bank, Diana."

She had nothing to read and no desire to spend the evening shut up in her room, so she accepted willingly. But first she went upstairs, filled in the blank in Mrs. Frick's letter with the address, put the tiny watch into the envelope, sealed it and slipped it under a corner of the bureau-scarf. Then she returned to Uncle Peter. They sat in the lounge and played; they were both cheerful and good-humored. But all the time Di was thinking to herself:

"To-morrow evening, I shan't be here. This is the end."

It was not long before Uncle Peter began to yawn, and to become absent-minded, and when Di said she thought she would go to bed, he sprang up with alacrity.

"I like to get up early," he explained. "Like to get out while the dew is on the grass, this time o' year. Used to ride before breakfast, when I had a horse."

He sighed and she glanced at him, baffled. Was he really a simple and kindly man—or wily and evil?

He made no offer to go upstairs with her, but stood at the foot of the stairs until she had reached the top.

"'Night!" he called. "Sleep well!"

She locked her door and sat down, with the torch handy. What if he had run down in the cellar and turned out the lights? That might have been nothing but rather a childish retaliation because she had run away.

Very well; that might be that. But what about those two men she had caught a glimpse of carrying another between them?

"I don't know!" she cried to herself. "And I don't care! I'm tired of all this! I'm going away."

Then she remembered the letter, and raised the bureau-scarf. It was gone.

"It doesn't matter," she thought. "I don't care what's happened to it."

She undressed then and got into bed, and fell asleep at once; slept profoundly all night. When she awoke the sun was up, shining into the room, it was a clear, gay morning. But she did not feel gay. On the contrary. Whatever dreams she had had were utterly forgotten, yet some faint, sorrowful impression remained.

She got up reluctantly, went to the nearest bathroom for a cold dip, and dressed.

"I don't know what excuse I can possibly make," she thought. "Or how I can get to New York, or what I'll do there. But I'm going. After I've had some breakfast, I'll be able to think of a way."

Pale, unusually serious, she went down the stairs. And there in the lounge she saw a stranger, a tall, fair-haired young man, sitting stretched out in an armchair, and smoking a cigarette. When he caught sight of her, he rose.

"Good God!" he said, staring at her. "You're not this Diana, are you?"

"That's me!" she answered. "Are you Miles?"

He held out his hand, and when she gave him hers, he kept it in a firm clasp.

"I thought you were going to be repulsive," he said. "I mean, they told me to come out here and meet a cousin who was helping Aunt Emma with her damned work. So I thought horn-rimmed spectacles—*you* know—one of these *nice* girls."

She liked him at once; she felt perfectly at home with him. His young face was a little haggard, his blue eyes looked tired, but there was about him a debonair good humor that immediately attracted her.

"When did you get here?" she asked, trying to pull away her hand.

"This morning," he answered and held her hand still tighter.

A silent struggle ensued, in the course of which she freed herself.

"You must have got up pretty early," she observed.

"Doesn't necessarily follow," he said. "Perhaps I just *stayed* up."

She could believe that; there were unmistakable marks of dissipation in his handsome face, and she was sorry.

"You're not a scientist, are you?" he asked.

"Mercy, no!"

"Then what are you, when you're not here?"

"I was a sort of secretary," she answered, "to Mrs. Herbert—"

"Not Angelina?"

"Yes!" she said, eagerly. "Do you know her?"

"I know the fellow she's just married. Porter Blessington."

He knew these people she knew, and they entered upon one of those absurdly inane yet somehow fascinating conversations: "Do you know so-and-so? Oh, and do you know Mrs. This, or Mrs. That?"

His acquaintance was very large, and Di was able to place him pretty well. She had met other young men like him in Angelina's house, well-dressed, good dancers, remarkably good bridge-players, agreeable and amusing fellows, who get plenty of invitations for dinners, dances and week-ends. But who had no austere scruples. She did not conceive any great respect for her cousin Miles, but she liked him, and it was a pleasure even to hear the names of Angelina's friends, to be reminded of those glittering, hurried days.

"Did you ever meet—?" she was beginning when Aunt Emma appeared. She was wearing a spotless white overall, and white shoes and stockings; everything about her was fresh and neat and of a simple dignity. Her plump face, framed by her short gray hair, was rosy and wholesome, and very kindly in its expression this morning.

"Good-morning, Diana!" she said. "Did you sleep well? We'll have breakfast now, Miles—"

"No, thanks!" he said. "I don't feel much like breakfast."

"Go and take a little walk," said she, and led the way to the dining-room, where she rang for Wren.

"She's evidently seen Miles before this morning," thought Di. "Could it—? Oh, I hope not!"

Could it have been Miles who had been carried into the house last night?

"I'm an early riser," said Aunt Emma. "I've had my breakfast, long ago. But I'll sit with you, and have another cup of coffee.... It occurred to me that it might be advisable to talk to you a little about your Uncle Rufus's work. You seemed to find his book—difficult. So I propose to give you an elementary survey."

She lit a cigarette, and leaning back in her chair, began to talk. And then for the first time, Diana began to understand Uncle Peter's description of his sister as a "remarkable woman." All the time the girl was eating, her aunt went on, in her pleasant, assured voice; she never once hesitated for a word, she made of a very dry subject a thing of interest, by her perfect clarity. She had the instinct of the born teacher; she *knew*, without asking, just what needed explaining, what needed emphasizing, just what words to use.

"Now!" she said. "Is it clearer?"

"Much!" said Di, respectfully.

"I suggest," said Aunt Emma, "that you spend the morning looking over your Uncle Rufus's book again. He will appreciate it, if you are able to talk to him intelligently about it."

Di followed her aunt upstairs, with a feeling of remorse. For she did not intend ever to see Uncle Rufus, ever to talk about his boring work, or even to think of it again, once she got away. She took the hateful volume which Aunt Emma handed to her, and sat down alone, at Aunt Emma's desk.

"I shouldn't have let her take all that trouble, explaining," she thought. "The least I can do now is to make an effort. It'll probably do me good."

But she could not keep her mind on the book.

"I need exercise," she thought, "Well, I'll get plenty when I start looking for a job! But I wonder... I wonder if, after all, I hadn't better wait for a day or two, and just see if I get an answer from Mrs. Frick. Then I shouldn't have to borrow any money."

It was Miles who had made this change in her mood. His coming had altered everything; the atmosphere of the house was different now, not lonely and "queer," but cheerful and interesting. She could smile now at her fears of last night. What had happened? Nothing at all!

It was a very, very long morning. Once she opened the door cautiously; the red-carpeted corridor was empty, the sun shining in at the window. She came out, unreasonably nervous, as if she were committing some treachery, and went to her own room. The bed had been made; everything was neat and tranquil. She darted back to Aunt Emma's room, and took up the book once more, with a sigh.

At one o'clock, Uncle Peter knocked at the door.

"Ready for lunch?" he asked.

She was something more than ready; she was very hungry. There had not been one good, solid meal since she had come here. She joined her uncle promptly, and they went toward the stairs. Hearing her aunt's voice below, Di looked down, saw her in the lounge, standing very straight, hands clasped behind her back, a calm, ironic smile on her lips. Before her stood Miles, and the sight of him startled the girl. What was that expression he wore, resentment, shame, bitterness?

"And if you play the fool—" Aunt Emma was saying.

Uncle Peter coughed, and she looked up and saw them. There was no change in her calm, ironic smile, but there was a great change in Miles. As she reached the foot of the stairs, he came toward Di with an eager air of pleasure. And she felt quite sure that the eagerness was forced and insincere.

The lunch was quite as poor as all the other meals she had had here. Aunt Emma was silent, in her somewhat majestic fashion, as if no one here were interesting to her; Uncle Peter was absent-minded, drumming on the table with his fingers. Wren moved about, forlorn and meek as usual. And Miles kept on with that strained cheerfulness. She played up to him as well as she could, because she was sorry for him.

"See here!" he said, abruptly. "Like to take a drive this afternoon, Diana?"

"Oh!" she began, and stopped, glancing toward her aunt. "I'm hoping I can help Aunt Emma—"

"There's nothing of vital importance," said Aunt Emma. "A few hours in the open air will be good for you."

Miles pushed back his chair and rose.

"All right! Get your hat and coat, and I'll bring the car around."

She ran up the stairs, very pleased at the prospect of getting out, and was down again in five minutes. The car was standing before the house, the same car in which Uncle Peter had driven her down.

"You didn't waste any time!" she said.

"I want to get away from this damned house!" he said, vehemently. "Hop in!"

"I'd like to stop somewhere and telephone—"

"All right!" he interrupted. "Get in!"

As soon as she was seated, he started the car with a jerk; before they were out of sight of the house she realized that he was a poor driver, nervous and careless.

"Don't go so fast!" she protested.

He went down the hill and turned the corner in a way that made her gasp.

"I really don't enjoy this!" she said.

"Sorry!" he said, and slowed down a little. "Only, I'm so dam' worried... Lord! You'd think I was a criminal—simply because I'm not much good at business. I'll admit I'm a dud at money-making, but that's no *crime,* is it?"

"Oh, dear!" thought Di. "That's so awfully like poor Father!"

"It's Uncle Rufus's fault," he went on. "He's been hell-bent on making a satisfactory heir out of me. He's made me try all the things that appeal to *him*—wanted me to be a chemist, and then a lawyer—and now it's this business. Never troubled to find out what *I'd* like."

"What would you like to be?" she asked.

"I'll never be anything now—but a failure," said Miles.

Her father had used to talk in that same way, determined to be a failure; taking a sort of bitter pride in it, as if he were revenging himself upon an unworthy universe. And because she had loved her father, in spite of his weaknesses, she made allowances now for Miles.

"I think people can be pretty much what they want," she said.

"All right!" said Miles. "I want to be a millionaire. Now, while I'm young."

"You'll be young for quite a while longer."

"I'm twenty-seven," he said. "And a rotten failure. There's not one living soul who cares a tinker's dam' about me."

"Your father—" she suggested.

"My father's a—grasshopper!" said Miles.

She tried not to laugh, but her lip trembled with suppressed mirth, and presently he laughed himself.

"Well, haven't you noticed it?" he demanded. "The way he jumps around, so busy, doing nothing. He's like the grasshopper in the fable, too; he hasn't put anything away for the Winter."

"I suppose Aunt Emma's the industrious ant," said Di.

"Not she!" said Miles. "Ants work for the good of the whole crowd, and she doesn't give a hoot for anyone or anything but her own affairs."

"I don't know...." Di protested. "Look at those children—"

"I don't want to look at them," said Miles. "I saw them once, five years ago, and that was enough."

"Five years ago! They must have been babies then—"

"No, they weren't. I never know what size kids are supposed to be, but I should think they were six or seven then. Lord! I came in unexpectedly and there they were, at the table, with Aunt Emma. They were imitating her. Every time she'd lift her spoon, they'd do the same, and slobber the soup, or whatever it was, all down their dresses. It was a beastly sight."

"But don't you think it's a fine thing for her to try and help them?"

"No," said Miles. "Naturally I don't. Not when she's so damned heartless to me. If she can get Uncle Rufus's money, I'll never see a penny of it. Only, I don't think she will get it. She may get on very well with idiots, but she doesn't know how to manage a man. You'll see for yourself to-night—"

"To-night?"

"Didn't they tell you he's coming to-night?"

"No," she answered, startled. She remembered that only this morning she had confidently thought she would never see Uncle Rufus. Last evening she had believed to be her last evening in that house. Yet here she was.

Once more the very unpleasant notion assailed her that she was in a net, entangled there by a hundred invisible threads; as long as she was passive, she could feel herself free, but when she tried to move, the threads tightened.

"Miles!" she said, with a sort of haste. "I want to telephone. Stop somewhere, will you?"

"All right!" he said. "On the way back."

He turned up a lane, and stopped the car by the roadside.

"Uncle Rufus comes out every few months," he said, "to see if anyone's improved enough for him to alter his will. At present, everything's to go to some society he belongs to. He's the world's worst. He hasn't a friend on earth. Of course, the idea is, that you'll make a hit with him—"

"I?"

"He liked your mother," said Miles.

Her heart contracted, at the mention of that name.

"Did you ever see my mother, Miles?" she asked.

"When I was a kid. I don't remember very well, but I think she was like you."

A warm sense of kinship filled her; here was one of her own people, her cousin, who had seen her mother. She turned toward him, eagerly. And was disconcerted to see him taking a flask out of his overcoat pocket.

"Have a spot?" he asked.

"No, thanks," she said.

She did not consider herself responsible for the conduct of other people, she had never imagined herself as anyone's guiding star or guardian angel, and it would have seemed to her only offensive and meddlesome to remonstrate with him. But she was sorry, very sorry.

"You ought to make a hit with the old boy," he said. "Or with anyone. You're the prettiest, sweetest girl I ever saw."

"Ah! You don't know me!" said Di. "Let's get along now, Miles, so that I can telephone."

He took a second drink and then caught her hand.

"Diana!" he said. "The first moment I saw you—"

"Please, Miles, don't spoil everything!" she said, in distress.

Then he grew angry and bitter.

"You're like everyone else," he said. "Simply because I don't make money—"

"All right!" said Di. "Let's not argue now. Let's get along—"

Her self-control, her coolness, increased his anger. He accused her of despising him, of having heard and believed false reports of him from Aunt Emma.

"You won't even listen to me!" he said. "You won't even give me a chance!"

"I can't help listening to you," said Di.

She had been through scenes like this before, with her father. He had used to tell her that she was "heartless," "unnatural," "selfish," then, quite suddenly, he would become remorseful, and tell her she was a "little angel."

"Diana!" he cried, "I've talked like a brute to you. Can you forgive me?"

"Of course!" she said. "Just forget about it."

But that tone did not satisfy him. He wanted something more dramatic, and she was quietly determined to keep to a matter-of-fact good humor.

"Diana!" he said. "I'm just about at the end of my tether. Someday you'll know...."

Her father had used to say: "Some day, when I've gone, you'll realize—"

A sorrowful weariness overcame her. She was so tired of this, so sorry for Miles, his weakness, his fatal self-pity. And she felt that she must bear with him, as she had with her father.

"Diana, you don't know what a rotten time I've had!" he said.

And he told her a great many of his latest troubles. He was in debt up to his ears, his creditors were pressing him, he couldn't find a job worth taking; his health was impaired. She listened with kindly patience, but she could think of nothing helpful to say, only:

"I'm awfully sorry, Miles."

At last he talked himself out, and grew sad and resigned. He started the car and turned home; all the way he was respectful, courteous, almost humble in his anxiety to please her, and she responded good-humoredly, but with an effort. She was glad to see a light in an upper window of The Châlet, glad even to get back there.

He stopped the car, and helped her out, as if she were a princess.

"*Sure* you're not angry, dear?" he asked.

In the dusk his face looked very pale, very young and haggard. She could think now that Miles was a tragic figure.

"Very sure!" she said, and gave his hand a friendly squeeze.

It was not until then that she remembered the telephone-call she had wanted to make.

"Well, to-morrow, then!" she thought, with a sigh. "I wonder if Wren has posted that letter? If he has, I might get an answer to-morrow."

She pushed open the front door and entered the lounge; it was dark in there, not with the blackness of night, but filled with twilight shadows; the willow chairs creaked, as if unseen occupants were stirring uneasily. And she did not like this shadowy, rustling place. A crack of light shone through the sliding-doors into the dining-room and she thought she heard someone moving in there.

"I don't see why I shouldn't go and ask Wren if he's posted the letter," she thought. "There's no reason for all this caution and secrecy."

How did she know there wasn't any reason for it? In this dim silence it was easy to believe that there might be many reasons....

"Oh, nonsense!" she said aloud, and crossed to the doors. But they would not open. She pushed at them with all her might, filled with a great desire to get into that lighted room. Behind her in the lounge a chair creaked loudly; too loudly; she heard something like a stifled sigh.

"Wren!" she called.

From the dining-room came a distorted echo of her own voice.

"'En! 'En!"

Shambling steps were coming toward the door, in there. She sprang back, groped for a lamp, and pulled the chain. As the light came on, she gave a shaky sigh of relief. Of course there was no one here....

But as she turned her head, she saw, in a corner, a strange huddled little figure, staring at her.

She stared back, speechless. It was a man with a checked cap pulled far down on his forehead, and wearing an overcoat and muffler. He had drawn up two of the wing-chairs before him, so that his corner was a sort of cage, and there he sat staring at her.

"Who—are you?" she asked, unsteadily.

"You must be Diana," he said. "You're very nervous, it seems to me. I'm your father's uncle. You're very nervous. I don't understand that, and I don't like it. You're young; you look healthy. Why should you be nervous—if you have a good conscience?"

"I'm not nervous," she said, briefly.

"You are," he said. "You were in a panic, trying to open that door."

There was something in his voice and manner which roused in the good-tempered Diana an irritability hitherto unknown to her.

"I suppose I felt that there was someone in here," she said. "It's enough to make anyone nervous."

"No, it's not," said he. "When I was your age, nothing could upset my nerves. That was because I was moderate in eating and drinking, and took plenty of exercise. You smoke yourself silly with cigarettes and ruin your digestion with cocktails and dance all night—"

"I do not!" said Di, indignantly.

"What do you do, then?"

"It's impossible to answer—a question like that."

"Stand nearer the lamp," he commanded. "Well, you don't look like your father. You're like your mother's people. Good, sound stock. Hm.... Like your mother..."

The mention of her mother startled her. Time and again, that name...

"Yes..." he said. "She was a good girl. A kind, good girl. I was fond of her."

She was silent, not able to speak just then.

"She was kind to me," he went on. "Not like the rest of 'em.... Come nearer!"

She approached, stood before him, looking down at him. But, in his corner, with his cap pulled over his brow, she could see little of his face.

"I'm alone," he said. "All alone. I'm old, and I'm rich. Everyone wants me to die, so that they can get my money. There isn't a soul in this house who doesn't want to see me dead."

"Oh, no!" she protested, dismayed.

"It's true, my girl," he said, grimly. "Every one of 'em. I come here, from time to time, always looking to see if I can find one trace of the old family virtues. But I never do. They're like a pack of wolves. I keep on coming, because they're the only living relations I have. But I take my precautions!"

She did not quite understand him.

"I don't—" she began.

"I take my precautions!" he repeated. "I don't trust one of 'em. There isn't one of 'em I'd like to meet on the stairs in the dark, if I had any money in my pocket."

"Oh, don't!" she cried, appalled. "Don't think things like that!"

He chuckled, then grew somber.

"See here, my girl!" he said. "I'm going to stay here a week. You be my ally for this week, and you won't regret it."

"I'm ever so sorry," she said, "but I'm afraid—"

"Yes, you will!" he whispered. "You're your mother's daughter. You won't desert an old man. Not *now*. Not *now*. *Don't you feel it?*"

"Feel—what?" she faltered.

"Death," he said. "It's very near."

Her healthy young instinct revolted against this.

"I certainly don't!" she said, sturdily. "I wish you—"

"But you'll stay?" he persisted, still whispering. "You're young. You can spare one week. You'll be well rewarded. One week, that's all."

She hesitated, doubtful and unhappy. The thought of another week in this house was intolerable, yet still more intolerable was the idea of refusing this miserable, futile old creature.

"Miles said he hadn't a friend in the world," she thought. "That's a horrible thing...."

"Your mother was a kind, good girl—" he said.

"All right, I'll stay," she said, quickly.

Chapter Five
MRS. FRICK'S GENTLEMAN

It was raining the next morning, and as Di awoke, she lay in bed, looking out at the gray sky, depressed and disheartened as she had never been
before in her life.

"Only seven days more!" she told herself. "Perhaps only six—if he counts
yesterday. I can certainly stand it for that long."

And then what? To go back to New York and look for a job, probably an
ill-paid and uncertain one. She couldn't expect to find another Angelina—
and who else would particularly appreciate her amateurish services? She
saw herself going from one job to another, always worried about money,
growing older and lonelier and shabbier....

"What's the matter with me?" she thought, half-frightened by this mood.
"I'm only twenty-three. I needn't begin to despair. Angelina will help me
to find something, when she comes back from her honeymoon."

She found it curiously difficult to believe in Angelina just now; above all
to believe in Angelina's often-expressed friendship for herself.

"She doesn't really care about me," she thought. "If she did, she couldn't
have gone off like that. She's utterly forgotten me by this time. There's no
one but Mrs. Frick. And even she probably won't answer my letter."

She sprang out of bed.

"This won't do," she said to herself. "That's like Miles. I *won't* be sorry for
myself. I never was before. It's this household. They're not very cheery."

She put on a dressing-gown and went down to the nearest bathroom for
a cold plunge. But even that did not restore her usual debonair courage.
The house was so still, there were none of those pleasant early-morning
sounds that one hears in other houses; nothing but the rain driving
against the windows. She imagined the meek and miserable Wren, prepar-
ing a meager breakfast downstairs....

"I haven't had one decent meal since I got here," she thought.

She tried to dismiss that idea, but without success; she could not banish
the memory of the exquisite coffee made by Angelina's French cook, the
hot rolls and fresh butter, grilled shad-roe and bacon, or a bit of sole with
lemon.... On a gray morning like this, there would have been a fire in the
dining-room; Angelina, of course, would have been still asleep, and Di
alone at the table, with a beautiful breakfast before her. And the whole
house filled as usual with that atmosphere of expectation and haste and
gayety; the telephone ringing, the maid—

"Perhaps I'll get a letter from Mrs. Frick this morning," thought Di.

Not only did she want the money, but she wanted a letter, a friendly word from Mrs. Frick, from anyone.

She dressed and went downstairs. The lounge was empty; she went into the dining-room, and saw the one little table covered with a coarse white cloth. She crossed to the swing-door by which she had seen Wren pass in and out, pushed it open, found herself in a pantry, went through that and found the kitchen.

Wren was standing at the sink; above him was a window with a broken pane through which the rain was blowing in; at his feet was a litter of tin cans and papers and potato peelings; the room was altogether the dirtiest, most dismal and repellant she had ever seen.

"Good-morning!" she said.

He jumped violently.

"Good-morning, Miss," he said.

"Did you manage to get a chance to post my letter?" she asked.

"Yes, Miss. The night you gave it to me."

"Then perhaps—" she said. "Has the mail come this morning?"

"Yes, Miss."

"Nothing for me?"

"No, Miss."

"Is there another delivery?"

"Yes, Miss, about four o'clock." He looked at her with an anxious smile. "If you'll wait in the lounge—I'll have your breakfast ready in a moment, Miss."

"Oh, thanks!" she said, and returning to the lounge, walked up and down restlessly. It was not appetizing, to contemplate anything from that kitchen. And no letter.

"It'll come in the four o'clock delivery," she told herself.

Then she noticed that the telephone which had stood on the desk was gone.

"Suppose a letter *had* come and I—didn't get it?" she thought.

It was a mistake to think of things like that; she opened the front door and stepped out on the covered porch, with the instinct to seek in the open air a solace for her vague fears and doubts. From the sodden ground, from the woods, came the fresh, cool fragrance of Spring; the sky was gray, but it was not sad out here. She drew in a deep breath, and began to reason with herself.

"I've promised to stay a week," she thought. "And I've got to stop being so morbid and silly. There's nothing—"

"Breakfast, Miss," said Wren, from the doorway.

She went into the dining-room, and tears came to her eyes at the sight of what he had done. There was a clean cloth on the table, and in the center a vase holding two feeble violets; her napkin was folded fan-shape and standing in a glass; there was a half-orange, carefully cut, in a chipped saucer.

"How nice!" she cried. "How—pretty everything looks! How—nice!"
His dismal face brightened.

"Thank you, Miss!" he said. "It's a pleasure to do anything at all for you,
Miss."

Just as she had finished, Aunt Emma appeared.

"Do you care to work a little this morning?" she asked, dryly.

"Glad to!" said Diana, and they went upstairs together.

"Can you take dictation?" asked Aunt Emma.

"Not in shorthand. But I can manage pretty well in longhand, if you
don't go too fast."

"I shan't go too fast," said Aunt Emma, with a chilly smile.

She was not over-friendly this morning; indeed, the girl perceived in her
something that would have been irritability in one less self-controlled. She
lit a cigarette and began to dictate, slowly, with long pauses. Her subject
was "suggestibility" and her theory was unpleasant. She spoke of the
"average" human being, and Di felt completely average herself. This average human being, said Aunt Emma, does not act from instinct, as is popu-
larly believed.

"His actions," said Aunt Emma, "are almost always the result of suggestion from a superior mind. He will, under the influence of suggestion, act
in a manner directly opposed to his natural instinct. This was very notice-
able during the late War, when the normal instinct of self-preservation
was entirely overcome by the insistent suggestion of the leaders in various
countries."

"But," said Di, "perhaps war's just another instinct. Animals fight—"

"An animal—" said Aunt Emma, "fights to defend itself or to remove a
rival. I have not yet seen an animal fighting for the convenience of another animal. To continue: The profound instinct of woman for maternity is
diverted, and in many cases, perverted, by the suggestion—"

She went on, tranquilly analyzing the utter idiocy and helplessness of
that average human being.

"By a proper use of suggestion," she said, "a superior mind can, with very
little effort, exercise complete dominance over an unlimited number of
average minds."

"Do you mean—" said Di, apologetically, "that you can make other people do things—?"

"I can," said Aunt Emma, "I do."

"Not me!" thought Di.

"Yes!" said Aunt Emma, as if the girl had spoken aloud. "You too."

"Please just try! I do want to see how you do it!"

"My dear child," said Aunt Emma, "naturally it is essential that you
should not know what I want you to do. You must always be persuaded to
imagine that you are acting in your own best interests."

"Have you been making me do things since I've been here?"

"But what should I particularly want you to do?" said Aunt Emma, blandly. "I hadn't considered my words as having any personal applications. They are merely notes, to be worked later into a little article."

Diana said no more, and they worked together until lunch time. No one else appeared at the table but Di and Aunt Emma, but when they had finished, and went into the lounge, Uncle Rufus was coming slowly down the stairs. He was still wearing the checked cap, the overcoat and muffler.

"Good-morning!" said Di. "Are you going out?"

"No!" he said, so sharply as to startle her. "I want to speak to you, when your aunt is out of the way."

Aunt Emma paid no attention to this; she lit a cigarette, and went over to the door and opened it. A current of cool, sweet air blew in, stirring her gray hair.

"The rain is over," she remarked, and stood there, smoking in calm satisfaction, until her cigarette was finished.

"Do you want me to go on, Aunt Emma?" asked Di.

"*I* want you here!" said Uncle Rufus.

"*Je vous en fais cadeau,*" said Aunt Emma, almost gayly, and went up the stairs.

Uncle Rufus settled himself back in his chair.

"Now, see here, my girl!" he began. "Come nearer! There! Now I want you to know that it'll be well worth your while to look after me."

"I wish you wouldn't talk like that!" she protested. "I'll be glad to keep you company, but I don't *want* anything for it."

He leaned forward and stared at her. She had not yet had a good look at his face, and even now she saw only his piercing eyes under bushy eyebrows.

"I can't believe that!" he said.

"Please don't mind my saying it—but don't you think it's a mistake to be so—suspicious?"

He gave a thin, little laugh.

"Suspicious?" he said. "Look here! Put your hand on this cap."

She touched it, and found it stuffed with some sort of wadding. Then he began to unwind his muffler, the length of which surprised her; it went round his neck three times.

"See?" he said.

"But I don't—"

"Hard for anyone to choke me with this on," he said, re-winding the muffler about his neck. "And this cap would considerably deaden the force of a blow on the head."

"Oh! You're mistaken!" she cried. "Nobody—"

"You don't know 'em," said he. "And I do. I always carry a good bit of money with me, in case I should suddenly fall ill. Might not be able to speak—but my money'd speak for me. I shouldn't be carted off to die in a public ward with *that* in my pocket. So far, my loving family here have been considerate because they're hoping I'll change my will and leave 'em something. But if ever they felt *sure* I wouldn't do that, then they'd get rid of me, for the sake of what's in my pocket."

"But if you think such horrible things, why do you come here?"

"I'm old," he said. "I haven't anyone. When I was young, I didn't care. I didn't want anyone. But now I'm old. I need someone!" He caught her sleeve. "I want to trust someone!" he cried. "And I can't! If I could trust *you*—if I thought you'd stand by me—I'd leave it all to you! All that money!"

"But I don't want it, Uncle Rufus," she began, when he collapsed, sank down in his chair as if she had dealt him a cruel blow.

"Don't—want it!" he whispered. "All that money...?"

"I didn't mean to be rude or ungrateful," she said, hastily. "It's very kind of you. I do appreciate it. Only, I mean—you don't have to offer me that. I'll be glad to do what I can for you without—that."

"No," he said. "Nobody gives something for nothing."

"Lots of people do. Haven't you ever met any ordinary people, who were just kind and decent?"

"Nobody's kind and decent," said Uncle Rufus.

She fell silent after that, sitting near him, lost in her own thoughts.

"It's a sort of insanity," she thought, "to feel as he does. How horrible! How pitiful!"

She glanced at him, saw him with his chin sunk on his chest, a grotesque bundle of clothes.

"I wonder why he cares," she reflected. "If I thought the world was like that, I'd be obliged to anyone for putting me out of it."

The loud twittering of a sparrow made her turn to the window; the sun had come out now, warm and bright.

"Wouldn't you like to come out and get some fresh air?" she asked, but he did not answer.

She was longing herself to get out into that gay world, where the rain drops glittered and the sparrows chirped.

"I haven't had any exercise since I came here," she observed, apologetically.

Still he did not answer, and drawing nearer, she stooped and looked at him. Under the shadow of the cap-brim, she saw that his eyes were closed. She opened the front door again and went out on the porch, sat down on the built-in bench there, with a sigh.

"I wonder where Miles is!" she thought. "This would be such a perfect afternoon for a walk. And Uncle Peter—"

"Miss!" whispered a voice behind her, and turning, she saw Wren standing on the grass below the porch.

"Miss!" he said, glancing nervously over his shoulder. "There's a gentleman to see you!"

"A gentleman?"

"Excuse me, Miss, but—" He glanced significantly at the open door.

"Where is he?"

"He's just down the hill, Miss. There's a clearing there, and I thought—perhaps you'd prefer to speak to him there."

"But who is he?" she asked, very much interested.

"He didn't mention his name, Miss. I saw him coming up the hill, and I stepped out, to tell him he was on private property, and he said he was coming to see you, Miss. So I—said I'd fetch you."

"But nobody knows I'm here."

"Excuse me, Miss, but didn't you write a letter?"

Could Mrs. Frick have sent someone, in answer to that letter?

"Excuse me, Miss!" said Wren, in a trembling voice. "Why don't you *go*, Miss? At once?"

She looked at him in surprise, and the thought occurred to her that he was curiously anxious for her to go meet this stranger.

"Lord!" she said to herself, impatiently. "I'm getting as bad as Uncle Rufus. What does it matter who he is or what he wants? It's broad daylight, and I'm capable of looking after myself."

So she rose.

"I'll go and see what he wants," she said. "Thank you, Wren."

She set off in the direction Wren had indicated, round the side of the house to where a faint path began, among the trees. The ground was still sodden, but the sun was warm; she went leisurely, partly because she was happy to be out alone on this sweet Spring day, and partly because she felt half-ashamed of her eagerness to see Mrs. Frick's gentleman. Any message, any contact with the world outside The Châlet was so welcome to her.

Halfway down the hill she perceived the pleasant aroma of a pipe; she went almost noiselessly over the ground carpeted with leaf-mould and pine-needles, and she had a chance to observe the stranger before he saw her.

Only, he wasn't a stranger; she had seen that neat, dark young man somewhere before. She stared at him with a frown. He was sitting on a fallen log, in a little clearing, smoking a pipe, and he was quieter than anyone else she had ever noticed. His lean, sunburnt hands rested on his knees, his swarthy, handsome face was impassive, yet, in his immobility, he was conveying an odd impression of alertness.

"Where have I seen him—?" she thought.

He glanced up then; he could not possibly see her through the trees, yet he was looking directly at her. He rose to his feet and waited, as she came on down the steep hillside.

"Good-afternoon," he said, in a stiff, unsmiling way.

"Good-afternoon," she answered, and waited for him to go on. But he turned away to knock out his pipe.

"Very kind of you to come," he said. "I'm sorry to trouble you, but your man advised me not to go up to the house."

She fancied from his stiff and correct manner, that he disapproved of this, and she answered, with dignity.

"Yes. They're—all resting...."

"I see!" he said, and suddenly his dark face was lighted by a singularly vivid smile.

"I know!" she cried. "I knew I'd seen you! It was outside Angelina's house—Mrs. Herbert's house—the day I left!"

He brought out a card from his pocket and handed it to her.

"Mr. James Fennel."

"You know Angelina, don't you?" she went on, very pleased. "I remember you said—"

"Er—yes," he said.

"Have you heard from her?"

"No," he said, briefly. "I haven't."

"How did she know where I was?"

"I don't suppose she does know," he answered, with an unmistakable air of annoyance.

Di looked at him, startled and a little angry at his manner.

"Then how did you happen to come?" she asked.

"Mrs. Frick sent me—with a note," he said, and from his waistcoat pocket took out an envelope.

"But I don't see—!" she cried, more and more surprised.

The envelope was certainly addressed to herself; she turned it over, as if seeking for mystic information. And he volunteered no information whatever, only stood there, very erect, like a soldier at attention.

"It's very nice of you—" she said, dubiously.

"Oh, not at all!" said he.

There was a considerable silence.

"Well, thank you!" she said. "I won't keep you—"

"Wait a moment, please!" he interrupted. "Mrs. Frick had some idea that things were not altogether pleasant for you here. She—if they're not... There's a train at 5:08."

She could only stare at him.

"If you'd care to take that train," he said. "I'll come up to the house with you, and wait while you pack."

"But—thanks ever so much," she said, "but I've promised my uncle I'd stay the week out."

"Look here!" said Fennel. "You look—rotten. Tell them I've brought an urgent message—"

"I'd be ashamed to do that," she said. "I promised to stay, and I'll have to. But—"

"But you're unhappy here," he said. "And you're worried."

"I am—a little," she admitted. "But I think it's nothing but—nerves. Nothing could possibly happen to me—"

"Don't say that," he interrupted, curtly. "You don't know!"

"But who on earth would want to interfere with me? I haven't a penny and I don't know any secrets. I'm absolutely unimportant."

"You're not!" said Fennel.

She looked at him; their eyes met, and she smiled, her nonchalant and doubtful little smile. Not yet in her life had she been of supreme importance to anyone. People had liked her and had often been kind to her; she had no grudge against the world. But she had never counted for much. Her father no doubt had loved her, and had made her childhood a sorry and anxious time and had died making no provision for her. Angelina had been fond of her and had gone off and forgotten her. She was not even very important to herself; she didn't care much what happened.

She stood where the sun shone on her bare head, still with that little careless smile. But he did not smile at all; he looked at her with a sort of cold anger.

"I've come—" he said, when a sound from above made her turn.

"It's Uncle Rufus!" she cried.

The old man was scrambling down the hill-side, a ridiculous figure in his voluminous overcoat and the cap pulled over his eyes; he slipped and stumbled as he came, and clutched at the trees for support.

Diana ran to help him.

"Uncle Rufus!" she said, "I didn't—"

He struck out at her blindly.

"No!" he cried. "No! You've betrayed me! you're false and lying like the rest—"

"Look here!" interposed Fennel.

"Hold your tongue!" cried the old man. "And get out!"

He stood with his arm about a tree, breathing fast, glaring at them both with savage malignancy.

"I went to sleep," he said to Di, "because I trusted you."

"But I only went out for a moment, Uncle Rufus," she said, so pitying him for his futile and distorted anger, more futile than ever out here, under the Spring sky. "There's no harm done. Let's—"

"I was asleep—and helpless!" he said. "I trusted you—and you ran away. Ran out to meet your sweetheart—like a little servant-wench—"

"Look here!" said Fennel again.

The old man turned on him with a snarl. He tried to speak but no words came. He lifted his arm, as if to hurl a curse, and lurched forward, tottered a few steps, and fell forward on his face. He lay as still as if he were a bundle of rags.

Chapter Six
A DISAPPEARANCE

Fennel went down on his knees, turned the old man over, unbuttoned his overcoat, jacket and waistcoat and felt his heart.

"Is he dead?" asked Diana, in a whisper.

"No..." said Fennel. "But—" He hesitated. "We'd better get him up to the house as soon as possible."

"We can carry him. I'll help you."

"No," said Fennel. "If you'll go on ahead, and see that things are ready for him—and send someone back—"

She set off at once scrambling up the steep hillside, ran across the grass to the house and flung open the front door.

"Wren!" she panted.

There was no answer, and she ran through the dining-room to the kitchen, where she found Wren peeling potatoes.

"There's been—an accident!" she said, breathlessly. "Old Mr. Leonard—down there in the wood. Please go and help to carry him up to the house."

Wren gave her a sidelong glance, like a frightened horse and bolted out of the room. She waited for a moment to get her breath and then hastened up the stairs to tell her aunt. She met Wren coming down.

"I'm going, Miss!" he assured her, anxiously.

At the end of the corridor she saw her aunt come out of her room, and lock the door behind her.

"Uncle Rufus—" the girl began.

"What man was that with you?" Aunt Emma interrupted.

Diana was a little startled.

"Fennel, his name is," she said briefly. "Now what can I do?"

"I'm sure I don't know," said her aunt, and went past her, down the stairs. As Diana followed her, Uncle Peter came tearing down, in his hat and overcoat, and darted out of the door, slamming it behind him.

Aunt Emma went over to the window, and, lighting a cigarette, stood there looking out.

"Can I—get his room ready—or something?" asked Di.

"And how do you propose to get his room 'ready?'" asked her aunt. "It's been swept and dusted and the bed made. Did you contemplate decorating it with flowers?"

"I only wanted to do something—" Di began, reddening a little under that contemptuous tone.

"You've done quite enough, I should say," observed Aunt Emma. "Ah! There they are! Now go and open the door, and look zealous."

Over the top of the hill came Fennel and Wren, carrying the limp figure of the old man between them; they crossed the lawn and entered the lounge.

"Upstairs," said Aunt Emma, exactly as if she were speaking to furniture-movers.

Just then a car shot past the house, and Di saw that Uncle Peter was driving it. Aunt Emma turned away, leisurely extinguished her cigarette, and went upstairs. And Di, feeling entirely superfluous, followed her again.

Fennel and Wren were just laying the old man on his bed.

"Thank you!" said Aunt Emma. "Wren, go down and put on a kettle of water to boil."

Wren sidled out of the room at once, but Fennel stood at the bedside looking down at the old man.

"Mr. Fennel," said Aunt Emma, very amiably, "I don't like to impose on you—but our telephone is out of order, my brother has gone to fetch a doctor, and I'll need Wren here. If you'd be kind enough to go to the drug-store and get a prescription made up—tell them to send it up at once.... It's on your way to the station, so perhaps it's not asking too much—"

"Not at all," said Fennel, briefly.

Aunt Emma sat down and taking a fountain pen and a note-book from her overall pocket, wrote briskly for a moment.

"Now!" she said. "And if you'll be kind enough to take this as quickly as you can.... Diana! You know where the linen-room is? Run and get me four clean towels.... Hurry!"

Di hastened out of the room and along the corridor. But before she reached the linen-room, she heard Fennel coming after her. She stopped.

"Please come again!" she said. "I haven't had time to thank you proper-ly—"

He came close to her.

"See here!" he said. "I'll be waiting for you in that same place in that wood—at nine this evening. I'll wait an hour, and if you don't come, then I'll come here to the house for you."

"Well... no, thanks," she said, surprised. "You see, with Uncle Rufus ill, I can't—"

"Stand out of the way!" said Aunt Emma's voice, so close that she started. "I'll get the towels myself, if you're not going to help me."

"Good afternoon!" said Fennel, curtly, and without another word or glance, went off down the stairs.

Di opened the door of the linen-room and got down the towels from a shelf.

"Now!" said Aunt Emma, "if you're willing to be of any assistance—when there's no male spectator to appreciate it—"

"This isn't the time to answer," thought Di. "I've got to put myself aside when Uncle Rufus is so ill." And aloud: "What can I do?" she asked, cheerfully.

"You can go into my room," said Aunt Emma, "and type the short article that you'll find on the desk there. It must be posted to the Medical Journal to-night."

Then there came to Di a very definite suspicion that her aunt wanted only to get her out of the way. She had sent her brother off in the car, Wren downstairs to the kitchen, Fennel on an errand.... Fear crept up in her heart like an icy tide.

"Good God!" cried Aunt Emma. "Can't you do anything?"

"I'd like to—stay with Uncle Rufus," said Di, in an unsteady voice.

For she had abandoned him once, and then great disaster had happened. And she would not abandon him again. She had promised to stand by him.

For a moment Aunt Emma looked at her, with her blue eyes like ice. Then she laughed.

"Very well!" she said. "And perhaps you'd like to taste any medicine I give him? Come along!"

They re-entered the room where the old man lay on the bed, motionless, still in his grotesque cap pulled down to his ears, and his overcoat.

"Sit down over there, out of the way," said Aunt Emma. "I'm going to get some medicine."

When she had left the room, it seemed to Di that the window might be opened a little. And as she did so, she saw on the drive beneath, Fennel, talking to Wren.

She could hear their words plainly.

"It's for their own good, sir," Wren was saying, earnestly. "There's so much harm they could come to, if they was to get out. I know, sir, it *does* give one a shock to see them looking out of the window like that—but it's for their own good."

"There was a friend of mine, a doctor in Switzerland," said Fennel. "He had some cases like that in his sanitarium. Cretins, aren't they?"

"Yes, sir."

"He kept them out in the air, as much as possible—"

"Did that help them, sir?" Wren interrupted.

"I should think it would help anyone," said Fennel. "But of course he gave them some sort of treatment. Thyroid extract—"

"Thyroid extract, sir? Did that do them good?"

"I believe so. Some of them improved—grew taller, you know, and could talk better. But isn't your Miss Leonard a physician? No doubt she—"

"Would you mind spelling that, if you please, sir? That extract you mentioned?"

Fennel did so, and Wren repeated it after him.

"Do you think it can be bought, sir—?" he began, when Aunt Emma came out of the kitchen door.

"Wren!" she said.

The little man fairly cringed.

"I was just waiting for the kettle to boil, Miss—I—"

"Get in the house," she said, carelessly, and he disappeared at once.

Then she and Fennel looked at each other. Diana waited, with unaccountable dread, for what they would say. But they said nothing. Fennel took off his hat, and with that vivid smile of his, turned away, went off down the hill.

Di closed the window noiselessly, and sat down on a chair at the other side of the room.

"What does it *mean?*" she asked herself. "What does it *mean?*"

For she was absolutely certain that beneath all the things she could see and hear there was something else, some meaning she could not grasp. It was as if she were watching a play in a foreign language; she could see the actors, watch their gestures, their entrances and exits, hear their words, but never seize the significance. She did not even know who was the villain of the piece, or who the hero.

Fennel.... Was he cast for a minor part; had he just "walked on" in this one scene and now was gone, not to appear again? A curious feeling of regret seized her, almost of desolation, because he was gone. She was left alone here with Uncle Rufus; she was his ally, pledged to stand by him, but was he *her* ally? She could believe that there in the wood, in his last conscious moment, he had positively hated her.

She rose, and went over to the bed to look at him. But she turned away hastily; he was so grotesque, so horrible, lying there in his overcoat and cap, his eyes closed, an expression of bitter malice on his sallow old face. She pitied him, that man who had grown old without a friend, she was willing and determined to help him, but she could not feel any affection.

"Is he—very ill?" she wondered. "Dangerously ill? It seems to me that Aunt Emma's doing precious little for him.... But of course I don't know. Perhaps there's nothing that *can* be done. She ought to know. And Mr. Fennel seemed satisfied. If he'd thought there was anything—queer, I don't believe he'd have gone away without a word.... But he wanted to see me this evening.... He certainly wasn't thinking of a lover's tryst. Perhaps he had something to tell me—something I ought to know. It was a mistake to say I wouldn't go. I'm sorry I said I wouldn't."

That reminded her of the letter he had brought from Mrs. Frick, and taking it out of her pocket she tore it open. Folded inside the letter she caught a glimpse of green, and drew out a ten-dollar bill.

Ten dollars! Freedom and independence! She could get away from here, buy a railway ticket, pay a week's rent for a room, and look for a job. And it seemed to her that any job on earth would be joyous and delightful after this. Any job, where she was free to come and go, where there were people to talk to, an ordinary existence. She was about to read the letter when the sound of a car outside sent her to the window again, and she saw Uncle Peter, driving the roadster, and wedged in beside him, two portly, middle-aged men.

Such respectable, such blessedly *ordinary* looking men! The thought of them coming into this house filled her with immense relief. They were coming, and she had ten dollars. At the end of this promised week she would go....

Aunt Emma entered the room.

"They're here!" she said. "Run down and tell Wren to come up at once. We'll have to make the patient a little more presentable for Doctor Coat."

"Oh! Is one of them a doctor?" asked Di, better pleased than ever. Then there couldn't be anything really—queer.

"Don't stop in the lounge to speak to them," said Aunt Emma. "And you'd better not come back, just yet. Wait in the kitchen until I come."

But Di felt that no human power should keep her from speaking to those blessedly ordinary men.

"Why don't you want me to speak to them?" she asked briefly.

Aunt Emma looked at her.

"I suppose," she said, "that you meant to trip in, like a little ingénue in a play, all curls and dimples and they would be enchanted. But in the first place, they're here on business, and they've never heard of you. And in the second place, you're not looking quite your best. You might take a glance in the mirror."

"No, thanks," said Di, turning scarlet.

"Then please send Wren at once."

She went downstairs, and hurried through the lounge without turning her head, traversed the dining room and entered the kitchen. There sat Wren, with his head down on the table, a forlorn little figure.

At the sound of her step, he jumped up.

"Miss Leonard wants you right away," said Di.

"Yes, Miss!" he answered.

Then, glancing nervously over his shoulder, he came nearer to her.

"Miss!" he whispered. "If you'll kindly not mention this..." And he thrust a piece of paper into her hand and hurried out of the room.

With considerable curiosity, she opened the scrap of paper, to see what Wren wanted to say to her.

"Nine o'clock. J. F."

That was not a message from Wren. Putting the paper into her pocket, she crossed the kitchen and opened the door, stood there to enjoy the clear air and to think. The sun was going down. The sky was tranquil; in the trees the birds were chirping their evensong.

"I *will* go!" she thought. "He wouldn't ask me if it wasn't important. He's—trustworthy."

It was so great a comfort to feel that, after all, he hadn't walked off, was not gone; she looked forward with eagerness, with impatience, to seeing him, hearing his cool, unemotional voice. Nothing would confuse him, ever, nothing could deceive him, his quiet dark eyes would see, would judge, would understand

"How idiotic!" she said to herself. "I don't know the man. I never spoke to him before to-day. I don't even know why he brought Mrs. Frick's letter."

It occurred to her that the letter might contain some explanation of Fennel. She felt in her pocket for it. The ten-dollar bill was there, and the note Wren had just given her, but Mrs. Frick's letter was gone.

"I must have dropped it up in Uncle Rufus's room," she thought, very much distressed. "Well, I certainly can't go to look for it now. I'll have to wait."

This was a singularly unpleasing idea, for she was morally certain that Aunt Emma would read the letter if she saw it.

"She'd do anything she wanted to do," thought Di.

Just then she caught sight of a figure breasting the hill, outlined clearly against the pale, clear sky. It was Miles, handsome and debonair and cheerful, carrying under his arm a package wrapped in blue paper. He caught sight of her and waved, and she waved back again.

"Hello, dear!" he said, as he came nearer.

That was an unpromising beginning, but she answered amiably.

"Hello, Miles!"

He came into the kitchen and handed her the package he carried.

"Present for you!" he said.

"Thank you, Miles!" she said. "But first I'd better tell you.... There's bad news. Poor Uncle Rufus—"

"There couldn't be any news bad enough about *him,*" said Miles.

"No, seriously, Miles, he's very ill."

"Stuff! He's always getting 'very ill!'"

"No, but this time.... He came down to that little clearing in the wood after us, and he had some sort of attack. We thought he was dead—"

"Who's 'we'?" asked Miles.

She saw that she had made a mistake, but she was not going to be intimidated by Miles.

"A Mr. Fennel and I—"

"Who's Mr. Fennel?"

"A friend of mine."

"Look here!" said Miles.

And then it began, that scene she dreaded.

"You might have told me there was another fellow, and not let me make a fool of myself, thinking of you all day in the city... bringing you a present."

"Don't be silly!" she said firmly. "You can't imagine that I've lived for twenty-three years and never made any friends. Let's see the present! I love presents!"

But he snatched the box away.

"You needn't be so dam' patronizing!" he said. "I'm not a child."

"You're acting like one," she said. "Oh, Miles! Don't let's quarrel! I'm so—so tired...."

"What about *me?*" he interrupted. "Why, the night I came here, I was so sick I had to be carried into the house."

"Oh, was that you?" she cried, relieved; but added hastily, "I'm awfully sorry you were sick, what was it?"

"You know dam' well!" he said. "They've told you. It was bootleg whisky. It's killing me."

As if in a nightmare, she knew what would come next. He would now go on to say, with considerable profanity, that no one else cared what happened to him, so why should *he* care? Just as her father had used to do, with that same perverse insistence upon his unique unhappiness. That, just as she had never known how to manage her father, she could not now manage Miles. She was not a managing sort of girl: she had no desire to rule, or to influence; she was only ready to help as best she could.

"Miles...?" she said, with that dubious little smile. "Sit down and light a cigarette. It's good for the nerves."

For answer he slammed the box on the floor and set his heel on it, trampled on it until the wrapping and the box inside were burst, and she could see a beautiful assortment of chocolates being mashed. And she, who had in her time endured so much, and with such fortitude, began to cry.

Miles looked at her, astounded. "I didn't mean—"

"No!" she cried. "When you hurt people—you never expect them to *be* hurt...."

"Diana!" he said, really alarmed by her tears. "Diana... I'm sorry... I'll get you another box...."

"It's not *that!*" she said. "It's just everything...."

He came to her side, and took her hand, almost timidly.

"I didn't mean to act like this!" he said, miserably. "I'd been thinking of you all day—and looking forward so to seeing you when I got back. You poor little kid! I meant to be—different. Diana, please give me another chance! *One* more chance! I'll take hold of myself, dear! I have tried to be different since I met you. I haven't touched a drop since that night. Say you'll—"

"Diana!" said Aunt Emma's voice. "Will you be kind enough to cook the dinner?"

Di glanced up, so startled that she forgot the tears still wet on her cheeks.

"Wren will have to sit with your Uncle Rufus," said Aunt Emma. "He won't have anyone else with him; he won't even see Doctor Coat. So I'll have to ask you to help me out. There'll be the Doctor and Mr. Purvis and your Uncle Peter and Miles and you and I—six of us. Just a simple dinner, naturally."

"But I'm awfully sorry—" said Di, "but I'm afraid I don't know—"

"Very well!" said Aunt Emma. "Then, Miles, you and your father will have to cook the best sort of dinner you can. Perhaps Diana will be able to turn on the light in the dining-room and put the chairs at the table."

"She and I will get your dinner," said Miles. "There's nothing Diana can't do, when she puts her mind on it."

Aunt Emma turned, and walked off, erect and composed, and Miles went to Diana and put his arm about her shoulders. She sighed to herself, wondering what new mood this signified, but glancing up, she saw in his face a look that profoundly touched her, a sort of despairing appeal.

"Di," he said, "if I could always be with you.... I—I don't *mean* to be—like I am.... If you loved me—we could go away from this dam' place.... I haven't any money, or any brains, or any character, but if I had you, I'd get them all. If you cared—"

"Miles," she said. "I *do* care. I've liked you ever since I first saw you."

"But not my way," he said.

She did not answer. He bent and kissed the top of her head, and moved away.

"Let's cook?" he suggested.

"You see," Diana explained, "Father and I never exactly did any housekeeping. He liked to eat in restaurants."

"I've never had a home in my life," said Miles. "So between us we might be able to manage something pretty original."

He glanced about him, then, taking the lid of a saucepan, he shoveled up the mess of chocolates and threw it into a pail. He made no more apologies, no more complaints; he only tried to help.

The larder was disconcertingly bare. They found one tin of soup which they diluted lavishly with water; they found a slab of bacon and six eggs, and a large vegetable which baffled them.

"I think it's a turnip," said Di. "Anyhow I'm sure it's a tuber; I'm going to treat it like a potato and peel it and boil it."

"Those bananas—" said Miles. "They seem pretty crude.... Can't we make some tasty little what-not out of them! Mash them?"

His good-humor, his willingness, made the preparation of that dinner the pleasantest hour Di had spent in a long time. She was so immensely glad to laugh again. She forgot, for that hour, all her anxieties, she even forgot poor Uncle Rufus.

"Now!" she said, at last. "I think we've done all the harm we can. If you'll please start setting the table while I dart upstairs and brush my hair. I'll help you when I come down. I shan't be a minute!"

As she hurried out of the brightly-lit kitchen, she looked back over her shoulder, and saw Miles watching her. She smiled at him and went on, her heart warm with a feeling of comradeship and good-will. She went through the dark dining-room, and looked into the lounge. They were all in there, Doctor Coat and Mr. Purvis and Aunt Emma and Uncle Peter, but fortunately they were gathered in a group under a lamp, and the rest of the lounge was fairly dark. She traversed it hastily, keeping close to the desk, and ran up the stairs.

And then, as soon as she reached that upper corridor, her happiness deserted her; she was in another world now, where there was no youth, no laughter, only sordid suspicion and chilly loneliness.

Her conscience reproached her for having forgotten Uncle Rufus. After all, she was staying here only on his account; she had money enough to leave now; nothing kept her but her promise to him.

"I'll just look in and see him," she thought. "And speak to Wren."

She went down the dim corridor to Uncle Rufus's room, and knocked softly at the door. There was no answer and she hesitated to knock louder, for fear of disturbing the old man. She tried the knob and the door opened.

To her surprise, the room was black, and from the open window a current of air blew cold on her face.

"Wren!" she whispered.

There was no answer; no sound at all.

Fear seized her; she stepped back into the hall and closed the door again.

But she knew she must go back. She could not leave the old man there alone in that dark wind-swept room. Once more she opened the door and felt for the switch; she turned it, but no light came.

"Wren!" she whispered again. "Please answer!"

The window-shade flapped in the draft made by the open door. But there was no other sound. She groped her way toward the bed, filled with a thought that turned her blood to ice.

But the bed was empty. She felt over it, from head to foot, and it was empty.

Chapter Seven
THE MONSTROUS NIGHT

Back in her own room, with the light turned on and the door locked, she tried to think coolly.

"Of course, they may just have moved Uncle Rufus into another room," she said to herself. Then suddenly she rebelled.

"No!" she thought. "It's cowardly and contemptible to go on this way, making up explanations for everything, pretending there can't be anything wrong. Suppose there is, and I'm just letting it go on? I ought to make sure. I've got to see Uncle Rufus with my own eyes."

There was a knock at her door.

"See here!" said Aunt Emma. "Will you be good enough to come down to your dinner at once? Doctor Coat and Mr. Purvis are hungry."

"Then I'm sorry for them," said Di, and opened the door. "Aunt Emma," she said, "where's Uncle Rufus? I went to his room, and he wasn't there."

"Nevertheless, he is in his—room," said Aunt Emma. "Perhaps with your customary ineptitude you went to the wrong room. It's not likely that he's gone out for a walk."

"I'd like to see him."

"Unfortunately, he wouldn't like to see you. He never wants to see anyone but Wren in the course of these attacks. To-morrow, when he's better, you can see him. And in the meantime, why not come downstairs and tell Doctor Coat and Mr. Purvis your suspicions? A doctor and a lawyer—you couldn't ask for anything better."

There was something in the older woman's cold insolence, something in her voice, her look, that was beginning to tell heavily upon Di. She resented it, yet in her resentment there was a sort of despair, as if her spirit warned her that she was no match for this woman. In every encounter she was worsted; each time Aunt Emma was able to convince her that she was a fool.

And she felt herself a fool now, as she went downstairs. Her aunt introduced the two strangers to her, Doctor Coat, a courtly old fellow with a white mustache and a handsome face, and a pleasant, rather stupid smile; Mr. Purvis, stout, grave, and a little pompous. Was it likely, if there was anything wrong here, that Aunt Emma would ask them to come? It was utterly impossible to suspect them of anything even mildly irregular.

They all sat down to that atrocious dinner, and though the stout Mr. Purvis looked rueful, neither of them seemed surprised. They were apparently at home here, and accustomed to Aunt Emma's style of living; and they talked, without constraint, of Uncle Rufus.

"Do you think there is any chance of his seeing me to-night, Emma?" asked Mr. Purvis. "If there is, of course I'll wait as late as I can."

"I don't know," she said. "Anyhow, he asked for you, and he knows you're here."

"Poor Rufus!" he said, with a sigh.

"Well," said Doctor Coat, in his comfortable and kindly way, "he's been through a great many of these attacks. And with Emma's splendid care, we'll hope that he'll come through this one. There's really no need for me here. Although, of course, I quite understand how you feel about it, Emma. If anything should happen there'd be criticism.... Yes... quite so.... If he can be persuaded to make a will, he'll feel very much better. Set his house in order... quite so!"

Then he turned to Diana.

"I hear he's taken a great liking to you," he said. "Very nice, I'm sure."

"I don't know," said Di. "I'm afraid—"

"She's almost morbidly self-distrustful," said Aunt Emma, interrupting. "Like her poor mother."

Mr. Purvis and Doctor Coat both looked at Di with a sort of sympathy.

"Come, come!" said the doctor. "Nothing so remarkable in his taking a liking to a charming young lady like you. He was really attached to your mother."

A silence fell.

"I'm going to meet Mr. Fennel at nine o'clock," Di was thinking. "I'm going to tell him every single thing, and get his opinion. I want to know if I'm just a morbid idiot, imagining things, or if there's any reason for being—uneasy. He's an outsider, he'll be unprejudiced."

Mr. Purvis began to talk now, about the League of Nations; he addressed himself entirely to Aunt Emma, and so did Doctor Coat. Occasionally they spoke to Di, amiably enough. Their manner toward Miles was one of distinct disapproval; he was evidently in disgrace. Peter Leonard they quite ignored.

Half-past eight, and they still sat at the table over the demi-tasses of astonishingly strong coffee Di had made. She was growing restless and impatient, looking down at her wrist watch under the table.

"But he said he'd wait an hour," she thought. "There's plenty of time."

She had ceased to listen to the conversation that went on; she was lost in her own confused and displeasing thoughts. And suddenly she had a sort of vision of this scene, as if she were detached and viewing it from a distance. This abandoned hotel in the woods; that black empty room upstairs; those most unfortunate children shut up somewhere; down here this dismantled room with chairs and tables piled against the walls and at this one table, this group. Uncle Peter, incredibly trivial, the "grasshopper" his son had called him; Miles, half-base, half-fine, and wholly reckless; Doctor Coat with his courtly air and his stupid smile; Mr. Purvis with his pompous gravity—and herself.... All fools....? All puppets of that composed, gray-haired woman?

"She wanted me to come here and I came," thought Di. "She wanted me to stay and I'm staying. Is everything I do really what she has planned...?"

It was a singularly disturbing thought. More and more did she long to see Fennel, the outsider who could give her an unprejudiced opinion. She thought of him; how kindly he had spoken to poor Wren, remembered his air of quiet confidence, his steady glance....

"I didn't realize how nice it was of him to come all this way with Mrs. Frick's letter," she thought. "I didn't even thank him...."

Aunt Emma had risen and everyone else rose too, and proceeded toward the lounge. Twenty minutes to nine now.

"Come, Diana!" said Aunt Emma.

"I'll just wash the dishes first—"

"There's no need for that. Wren will come down early to-morrow morning."

"Then I'll just clear the table—"

"No," said Aunt Emma. "Leave everything as it as."

For a moment Diana stood looking at her.

"I ought to take things in my own hands," she thought. "I ought to say I'm going out for a few minutes. She couldn't stop me, before all these people. This is the time. This is the time to speak."

It was curiously difficult to speak, but she did speak.

"I think I'll go out—and get a breath of fresh air," she said.

"Miles will go with you."

This was a battle.

"No, thanks," said Di. "I'd rather go alone."

She was aware that everyone was listening; she was aware that her wish to go out alone surprised them all. But she was desperate. It seemed to her a matter of vital importance that she should conquer, should go out openly and freely.

"I'm sorry," said Aunt Emma, composedly. "But I can't permit it, my dear. This is a very lonely spot. If you object to Miles' conversation, he can walk behind you."

She was beaten. She *could* not say before all these people that she was going out to meet a man—"like a servant wench" Uncle Rufus had said. And what is more, she did not need to tell Aunt Emma that. Aunt Emma knew already.

They all passed into the lounge and sat down; all except Diana.

"I *will* go!" she thought. "And I'll go openly, too."

As she stood by the window, Miles came over to her and offered her a cigarette. She was glad to accept one now, and as she took it, she looked at him, anxiously, half hoping that he might understand, and help her. But his face was white with anger; his glance was filled with anger and bitterness. He knew too, why she wanted to go.

"I'll pop up and see how the invalid's getting on!" said Uncle Peter, brightly, and rising went running up the stairs, two steps at a time.

No one else spoke, a stiff silence had fallen upon the little company. Miles had gone to his seat near the lamp.

Di opened the front door and stepped out, closed the door behind her and began to run toward the hill; she did not stop until she had reached the dark shelter of the trees. As she paused here a moment, she heard someone coming after her, running. She stopped behind a tree and waited.

It was too dark to see, but she was certain that the figure which ran past her was Miles. He went on plunging down the hill-side.

"Suppose he meets Mr. Fennel?" she thought, in alarm. "And tells him I can't come?"

Into her heart came the quiet conviction that Fennel wouldn't believe him, wouldn't believe anyone. He had come to speak to her; he had said he would wait for an hour and then come to the house, and he would do that. She trusted Fennel as she had never yet in her life trusted anyone. Miles would not be able to send him away. Fennel would not go until he had seen her.

The night wind was sharp; hatless and coatless, in her thin dress, she shivered. The pines rustled in the dark and, close to her, a little owl gave its trembling cry.

She waited and listened.

"It must be nine o'clock," she thought. "He's there and Miles will see him. Perhaps he'll pretend to go away, and then come back. Or perhaps he'll insist upon seeing me...."

"Perhaps he didn't go to look for Mr. Fennel at all," she thought. "He may simply have gone to the village—or rushed back to New York in a rage."

She began cautiously to descend the hill, straining her ears to catch any sound. But there was nothing but the rustle of the pines in the wind, and the cry of the little owl. She thought of Uncle Rufus coming down here this afternoon, and she shivered.

At last she was in sight of the clearing and the faint starlight showed it empty. But anyone could be standing in the shadows.... She did not like the thought of Miles, standing there waiting. She remembered his white, angry face....

She waited and waited. If Fennel had pretended to go away, he would come back. Was Miles here, waiting for that?

Her teeth began to chatter with cold.

"Suppose I caught cold?" she thought. "Got ill—in that horrible house?" She felt chilled to the bone already.

"I won't stand this!" she said to herself. "There's no reason why I should-n't see Mr. Fennel or anyone else, if I want to. I won't hide. I won't be—secret. If Miles is there, very well! I'll tell him what I think of him for spying on me."

And she stepped down into the clearing. Was that something stirring among the trees? "Mr. Fennel!" she cried.

No one came, no one answered.

"Mr. Fennel!" she called, again, her voice rising to a high note of fear.

This would not do, panic lay this way. With an effort, she stopped calling, and stood there, waiting. In the faint light of the stars, she could not see the dial of her watch. She did not know how long she had waited or must wait. Only she would endure it for as long as she could, for surely he would come.

She sat down on that fallen log, where she had seen him this afternoon, curled up her feet as best she could under her short skirt, folded her arms about her chest, and kept her vigil; in supreme physical misery, cold and cramped, in dread, in dismay. Sometimes she imagined she heard someone coming, and called his name, but there was never any answer. And at last she began to see that he was not coming.

She would have to go back to that house, to face Aunt Emma, to endure another scene with Miles. And after all she had no friend.

"If I had that ten dollars with me," she thought, "I'd never go back. I'd take a train for New York *now*. There's nothing illegal in not wearing a hat and coat."

But she had left the money in the pocket of her jersey when she had changed her dress before dinner. And there was her promise to Uncle Rufus.

Again she had forgotten Uncle Rufus. She got up, sick at heart, numb with cold, and began to climb the hill. She had promised to stand by him, and she could not leave him there, ill and helpless.

Light was shining from the windows of the lounge; she had no desire to go in there. She went round to the back of the house and quietly opened the kitchen door. The kitchen was dark, but the gas stove was lighted, under a singing kettle; it was blessedly warm. She sat down in a chair near the stove, to wait until this wretched chilliness was gone, before she must pass through the lounge on her way to the stairs.

"He didn't come," she thought. "But I know he meant to come. I know he *will* come soon. He knew there was something wrong. He'll come."

She was weary, almost exhausted; she nearly went to sleep there by the stove. But she heard that footstep. She sat up straight, her heart beating fast. Had he come to the house, as he had said he would? Surely that was someone coming up the back steps....

Then a door opened beside her, the door which led to the cellar, and clearly outlined in the bright light that shone behind him she saw Uncle Peter, pallid, grimy, without a collar, breathing hard, and on his face, a wild terrible look.

She gave a cry, and he leaped forward like a cat. His hand was pressed across her mouth, holding her head against the back of the chair. She struggled but she could not rise, could not make any sound. Then he drew back; she was about to cry out again when his fist shot out and caught her on the point of the jaw and she collapsed unconscious.

■ ■ ■

When she opened her eyes again she was lying on a bed. Her head ached cruelly; she felt deathly sick and giddy. It was utterly dark, she could see nothing, hear nothing; for a few minutes she could not remember.

Then it came back to her.... Uncle Peter, the trivial, the cheerful, the one person in this house she had thought negligible....

She sat up. At first giddiness and the pain in her head forced her back on the pillow again, but the second time she felt better. She put her feet on the floor and still faint and dizzy, stood upright, holding by the head of the bed. She must find out where she was, what this dark prison was.

Her groping hand touched a little table, and a great hope sprang up in her. Moving nearer, she felt the lamp; it was there; she turned the switch and the light came. And with a sob of relief she found herself in her own room.

A little Paradise, it seemed to her, the safest, cosiest place in the world. She looked about her at her own belongings with the delight of one who has made a long and terrible journey and is at last home again.

Then she heard a noise in the corridor outside; a dragging, shuffling sound. She leaned forward in her chair. The wind had risen; that sound could be the branch of a tree brushing her window.... Only it was coming nearer.

She knew now that this room was not safe and snug, but desperately exposed and that there was no corner where she could hide; she was sick and shaken, and defenseless.

Something scratched at her door. And not near the knob, but close to the floor, like an animal. She did not stir.

"Miss!" whispered Wren's voice. "Oh, Miss! For God's sake, let me in!"

She went to the door, but with her hand on the knob, she hesitated.

"What's the matter?" she whispered back.

"Miss! Oh, let me in, quick! For God's sake!" But his voice came from below, as if he were at her feet...

"Miss!" he screamed, suddenly. "Quick!"

She turned the knob. The door was locked.

"Miss!" he screamed again. "For—"

His voice ceased abruptly. She heard nothing at all now.

"Wren!" she called, rattling the knob. "I can't! I can't...!"

Her knees gave way and she sank on the floor by the locked door. Her hand touched something wet, she raised it, stared at it with dilated eyes, saw it red with blood, and fell backward in a faint.

Chapter Eight
THE CANDID EXPLANATION

Sometime later in the night she got up from the floor, took off her shoes and lay down on the bed, wrapped in a blanket. She was shaking with a violent chill, tormented by a racking headache.

All the events of the night had become only part of a vast nightmare. She did not care what happened now, nothing mattered except to get warm. Time had ceased to exist; there was nothing in the world but this physical misery.

After the chill came fever, and a raging thirst. She lay there, crying silently because she so craved for water and could not rise to get it. Her head ached so.... The light hurt her eyes....

"What's the matter, my dear?" asked Aunt Emma's voice beside her.

"I want—a glass of water!" she sobbed.

Her head was raised and a glass held to her lips.

"Another!" she said.

"Swallow these two pills with it."

She did not care what she swallowed, so long as she got the water.

A cold, wet cloth was laid on her throbbing head, the unbearable light was shaded, the tumbled covers straightened. She went to sleep.

■ ■ ■

She waked with a sigh, and stretched herself luxuriously in the cool, smooth bed. The window was open and the sweet air blew in. Turning her head she saw the sky filled with the soft, melting colors of sunset.

"Now!" said Aunt Emma. "A nice cup of broth and a piece of toast."

She had never tasted anything better than that broth, strong and well-flavored, that hot buttered toast without crusts. She still felt weak, but marvelously comfortable now, except for a slight soreness in her jaw.

"I was afraid that last night you were in for a bad time," said Aunt Emma. "You were delirious—quite a temperature."

Di did not answer; but she heard, and she understood; her brain felt extraordinarily lucid. She might have been delirious at some time in the night, but at present she was perfectly clear about everything. She remembered all the things that had actually happened with an odd sort of detachment, as if she were no longer personally concerned.

"I'll just let her go on," she thought. "She'll try to explain away everything by saying I was delirious. All right! Let her!"

She looked up at Aunt Emma with a glance of calm interest.

"Was I?" she asked.

"And no wonder," said Aunt Emma. "You had—a disturbing experience." She sat down in a chair by the window, where the light breeze stirred her gray hair. She looked so rosy, so dignified, so solid....

"If you feel able," she said. "I think we'd better talk this over now."

"I feel all right," said Di.

And so she did; she felt perfectly able to listen to any tale Aunt Emma might choose to invent and to weigh and analyze it.

"It would take a good deal of generosity," Aunt Emma went on, "to forgive your Uncle Peter. I don't expect you to. But I can explain his behavior—if you care to listen."

"Yes, thank you, I should," said Di.

So Aunt Emma was not going to pretend that that blow was part of any delirium.

"Do you object to my smoking?" asked Aunt Emma, with gentlemanly politeness. "Perhaps with the window open, it won't bother you.... No? Thanks!"

She lit a cigarette, and crossed her knees.

"We had a remarkably unpleasant evening," she proceeded, her blue eyes following the smoke. "It's fortunate that Coat and Purvis are such fools. They swallow everything... When you went out, I sent Miles after you, but he couldn't find you. So he did what anyone might expect of him. He went down to the village, and procured a supply of bootleg whisky. I saw, when he got back, that he'd been drinking, but I didn't know he'd brought more of the stuff into the house. He put it in the cellar and every now and then he'd go down and get another drink. Before long, he became very troublesome. Purvis helped me to get him upstairs and into bed. I wanted to lock him into his room, but I couldn't find the key. I was seriously worried, for fear he would molest you. I went to your room to see if you had come in while I was busy with Miles; I knocked and when there was no answer, I opened the door and by the light of my torch I saw that you were lying fully dressed on the bed, apparently asleep. I spoke to you but you didn't answer, and I thought it better to lock your door."

She paused.

"An extremely unpleasant evening..." she continued. "I didn't know where you'd been or what you'd been doing.... I went downstairs again. Coats and Purvis went home in a taxi, and I found your Uncle Peter in the kitchen—almost as bad as Miles. He'd been visiting the cellar.... He was half-frightened and half-boastful. He said he had caught you trying to escape! I'll be quite candid with you. He thinks that Uncle Rufus is going to leave his money to you, and that therefore you're too valuable to lose. I agree with him about your Uncle Rufus. And I am perfectly willing to tell you that, if you do come into his money, I hope you'll give me some of it."

Her candor was astounding; she denied nothing that had happened, made no attempt to disguise her motives.

"I asked you here for that purpose," she said. "Uncle Rufus had been fond of your mother, and I hoped he'd take a fancy to you. And that gratitude, or family feeling, or sentiment, would induce you to give me enough to carry on my work."

Di looked at her aunt in wonder, a little dazed; everything was made so clear, so matter-of-fact.

"But—Wren?" she asked, almost involuntarily.

"Wren?" her aunt repeated. "What about him? Do you know anything about that little rat? For he's disappeared!"

"I don't know..." said Di, with unusual caution. "I thought I heard him call me—"

"When?" asked Aunt Emma. "I'd like very much to know. And it might help the police."

"The *police?*"

"He went off with your Uncle Rufus's watch and money—some six thousand dollars he was carrying in his pockets."

"Oh, I'm sorry!" cried Di.

"He can stand the loss very well—"

"I wasn't thinking of that," said Di. "I'm sorry—for Wren."

"You needn't be," said Aunt Emma, dryly.

There was a moment's silence.

"How is Uncle Rufus?" asked Di.

"Better. He's been asking for you. You can see him to-morrow."

There was another silence.

"I'm not," said Aunt Emma, "extravagant in my personal life." She smiled faintly. "You've probably noticed that my housekeeping is not lavish. But I want—I need money for my work. Your Uncle Rufus is apparently recovering from this attack—but he can't last much longer. I hope that when you see him to-morrow, you'll be as amiable as your very youthful conscience will permit. It may mean more to you than you're able to realize, at your age. But I'm not pretending to think wholly of your welfare. I am thinking of my work."

She lit another cigarette.

"I've told you something about it. I have been making researches in regard to my theory of suggestibility. No one else has yet suspected the suggestibility of the average mind. People talk about the 'herd instinct'! The human herd has long ceased to act instinctively. It will, in fact, act in a manner directly opposed to its instinct. They talk of 'mob psychology.' The only psychology of a mob is that of its leaders. No mob acts spontaneously, but only upon the suggestion of one or more superior minds. A little observation will show you how infinitely more powerful suggestion is than instinct. The instinct of a mother to protect her infant is certainly one of the strongest and most deep-rooted. Yet mothers were willing to throw their infants into the fire of Moloch when it was suggested to them. In times of war, it is suggested to a man that he loves his flag more than his own life, and he acts upon the suggestion."

She was silent for a moment.

"I have been working for nearly six years with those two children you have seen," she said. "In minds of that type one would suppose that mere animal instinct would enormously preponderate. I hope soon to demonstrate that it is not so. My great difficulty has been their propensity to imitate; and to differentiate between what is mere imitation and what is suggested action. They are only too ready to imitate...."

She rose, and tossed her cigarette out of the window.

"I'm afraid I'm inclined to be tedious on this subject," she said, and for the first time Di saw on her face a smile almost appealing. "I must get along now. I have all the cooking and so on to do, now that Wren's decamped. He couldn't have chosen a worse time.... Now, your Uncle Peter will come up and apologize."

"Oh, no, *thanks!*" said Di, hastily. "I'd really rather he didn't."

"He ought to," said Aunt Emma. "He's waiting to do so. I advise you to let him."

"No, thanks, really. I'd hate it."

"Do you hate *him?*" asked Aunt Emma.

"No...." said Di. "I don't hate him...."

"Well!" said Aunt Emma. "I'll be back later, with some dinner for you. You mustn't think of getting up to-day. But by to-morrow you ought to be quite yourself. And after you've seen your Uncle Rufus, the best thing you can do is to go back to New York. You've had a fairly unpleasant visit, I'm afraid. Have you friends in New York, and enough money to carry on for a while?"

"Yes, thank you, Aunt Emma."

"I've brought you some books and magazines, the sort of thing I imagine would interest you. I sent Miles for them."

Then she mounted a chair briskly, and set about fastening an extension cord to the electric light and clamped a reading-lamp to the head of the bed. She put the books and papers on the table and then took up a queer old-fashioned little knitted sack of pink wool.

"Let me put this around your shoulders," she said. "Now!"

There was something touching to Di in these attentions, something she had liked very well in her aunt's blunt sincerity. A sense of profound relief filled her, as if the light of day had been admitted into some dark chamber, and what had seemed horrible was not horrible at all. The shadow of death had passed, Uncle Rufus was getting better and, greatest relief of all, Aunt Emma had herself suggested that she should leave.

Aunt Emma's motives were certainly not disinterested; Uncle Peter had shown himself capable of an astounding brutality; Uncle Rufus was not a lovable uncle. Miles was a distressing problem; Wren had turned out to be a thief; it was not a pleasant household. But she could make allowances now for all of them; she could forgive them their offenses against herself, and pity their sordid failings, because tomorrow she was leaving them and because everything here was explicable now; ugly and depressing, but not sinister, not frightening any longer.

"And Mr. Fennel," she thought. "Something prevented his coming. I *know* I'll hear from him again. Probably to-morrow."

She lay for a time, looking out at the darkening sky, and thinking of Fennel. She felt so certain that she would see him again, so certain he was her friend.

"How nice of him to have come all this way with Mrs. Frick's letter! I wish I hadn't lost it. It might have explained a little about him.... He's different from any other man I've seen. He's...."

It occurred to her that her reverie was becoming a little ridiculous, and reaching up, she turned on the lamp, and picked up a magazine. A footstep in the hall made her glance up, and she saw Miles in the doorway.

"Diana...?" he said.

She thought she had never seen anything more pitiable than his handsome, wasted face, pallid, drawn, hollow-eyed; anything more painful than his strained smile.

"How are you?" he asked.

"Oh, fine, thanks!" she answered, with artificial brightness.

"Anything I can do for you, Diana?"

"Not a thing in the world, thanks, Miles."

He was silent for a moment, and they did not look at each other.

"I thought..." he said. "Wouldn't you like some ice-cream, Diana? I can run down to the village and get it..."

She could not refuse this peace-offering.

"That would be awfully nice," she said, and was distressed by the obviously false cheerfulness of her own voice.

"All right! I'll get it," he said, and was gone.

His haggard, desperate face haunted her; she began to read again, in haste to forget him, for she could do nothing more for Miles.

Presently Aunt Emma appeared with a tray, upon which was a supper immeasurably better than any meal Di had yet had in this house; a broiled lamb chop, a potato baked in its jacket, a salad of lettuce and tomato, a cup of coffee and a slice of sponge cake.

"How nice!" she said, pleased.

Aunt Emma smiled.

"I never cooked before to-day in my life," she observed. "But with Wren gone, I saw it was inevitable. So I sat down and studied the cook-book for an hour, until I'd mastered the general principles of cooking. Then I applied the theory. It's amusing. I was tempted to do superfluous things.

That sponge cake, for instance...." She looked down at it. "I believe it's good," she said. "It's—put it down, child, until you've eaten the chop!"

"I had to try it!" said Di. "It's perfect!"

Aunt Emma was manifestly pleased and so was Diana; there was a charming atmosphere of homely good-will. Aunt Emma making a cake!

Before her footsteps had died away, Miles returned, with the ice-cream in a dish.

"May I come in?" he asked, and when she said yes, he entered and set the dish down on the table.

"Diana..." he said. "I'm—not going to talk any more.... I'll just try to show you.... I—can't expect you—to have any faith in me.... But... but you'll see, Diana...."

His voice was painfully unsteady and he did not look at her.

"If you want anything," he said, "I'll be here—all the time."

She wanted to speak to him, but to save her life she could not think of a word that would sound natural and friendly. Halfway to the door he turned and looked at her, sitting there in the queer little old-fashioned pink jacket, with her fair hair loose. And she could not bear the look on his face. With an anxious, uncertain smile, she held out her hand; he strode back to her, knelt beside her, holding her hand over his eyes.

"Forgive me, Diana!" he whispered. "I'm sorry...."

"Of course!" she said, in a cheerful, matter-of-fact voice. But she nearly wept, looking down at his dark head. From the very first she had felt for Miles this pity, this tenderness, this unreasonable indulgence, that was almost maternal.

"I'm so sorry!" he said, again. "Just give me one more chance!"

"Yes, I will. Miles! Get up! My nice dinner's getting cold—and the ice-cream is melting."

For she felt that if he did not go at once, she would begin to cry over him, and he would certainly misunderstand that. He sprang up, full of contrition.

"See you to-morrow!" she said, brightly, as he left the room, and he smiled at her, comforted.

She sighed profoundly and began her dinner.

"Even when I leave here," she thought, "I shan't be rid of Miles; I'll have to go on seeing him, forever and ever. No one else seems to care a bit for him. And he needs someone to care, so terribly. He's so—doomed...."

But even the doomed Miles could not make her unhappy that evening. She had a quiet, cosy evening, reading, an amiable little chat with Aunt Emma; then she turned out the light and settled herself for sleep, filled with a quiet confident happiness.

"Perhaps he lives at Mrs. Frick's," she thought. "Anyhow, I'll probably hear from him to-morrow...."

And everything was explained now; everything was clear and open. To-morrow she would leave here, and begin a new phase of her life....

■　■　■

She waked with a start, and sat up in bed, her heart racing. She did not know what had awakened her, what had startled her, but there lay upon her the oppression of a forgotten dream.

She turned on the light and looked about the little room. All neat and tranquil here. What was it that she had forgotten...?

Then she remembered. Last night, when she had lain down on the bed, there had been blood on her hand. And now her hand was clean. There had been blood on the carpet, by the door.... She got up and went to the door, and, a little giddy, stooped to examine the carpet. There was surely a faint stain there, as of something that could not be quite scrubbed clean.

If Wren had come to her door, unknown to anyone else, the stain would not be faint, like this. If anyone had washed her hand, and cleaned the carpet, then whoever had done this must know of Wren's coming.

"Perhaps Aunt Emma just didn't want to worry me," she said to herself, with her old instinct to deny what was strange and unpleasant. "I'll ask her in the morning."

She turned out the light, lay down again, and resolutely closed her eyes; immediately she had a vision of Wren crawling along the corridor on his hands and knees, scratching at her door.... "Miss! For God's sake, let me in...!"

She turned on the light again, in haste. When she had spoken of Wren, Aunt Emma had seemed startled, had asked if she had seen him. No.... It *was* queer, it was wrong, that if she had washed the blood from the girl's hand, she should have made no mention of it.

Well, suppose someone else had washed her hand and cleaned the floor? Who else? And if Wren had robbed Uncle Rufus and successfully escaped, what was he doing outside her door, desperately urgent to be admitted?

Everything was not clear and open. With Wren unexplained, all the rest of the explanation was worthless.

"Aunt Emma must have known," she thought. "Nothing goes on here that she doesn't know.... I don't believe poor little Wren's a thief, anyhow. She's just made that up, to explain something.... To explain what...?"

All the old dread and confusion had returned. She took up a book and tried to read, but every sound made her start. It was nearly morning when she dropped asleep.

When she opened her eyes, the sun was shining; her watch had stopped, but she felt sure it was late. She got up at once, washed in cold water, and began to dress. She was immensely relieved to find the ten-dollar bill still in the pocket of her jersey; her way of escape was still open.

"And this time," she thought. "I'm not going to be cautious and tactful. I'm not going to be put off. I'm going to ask Aunt Emma point-blank who cleaned up the carpet."

Her knees were still a little weak and the bruise on her jaw was still sore, but she felt very well, and very resolute.

"I'm sick and tired of all this mystery!" she thought. "I want to know what really happened to Wren."

The lounge was empty, the dining-room was empty, but in the kitchen she found Aunt Emma washing dishes.

"Well!" said Aunt Emma. "You're early! Did you have a good night?"

She looked so fresh and neat and pleasant, in her white overall, so innocently and beneficently employed in this humdrum task, that it was difficult to challenge her.

"Not so very," said Di. "I—got thinking—about Wren."

"About Wren?" Aunt Emma repeated. "Well, I hope we'll soon see that cleared up."

"You see," Di went on, "he came to my door last night.... I couldn't let him in, because the door was locked.... And—blood came under the door.... On the carpet—on my hand...."

Even here, in the kitchen where the morning sun was shining, it was horrible to think of that.

"Ah!" said Aunt Emma. "So that's what it was? I noticed it, naturally. But I didn't know whether you, in your feverish condition had noticed it or not. So I thought I'd say nothing unless you asked me. Wren, was it? He must have hurt himself in some way."

Very composed, very plausible was Aunt Emma. But Di was not satisfied.

"I don't see—" she began.

"Wait a moment!" said Aunt Emma, and opening the back door: "Rogers!" she called.

A stout, clean-shaven man ran up the steps.

"This is Detective Rogers, from the East Hazelwood Police Station. He's come to investigate this robbery, and Wren's disappearance. You must tell him everything you know—while I make you some fresh coffee."

Certainly this cleared Aunt Emma from the last suspicion. She had called in the police herself.

Chapter Nine
"DO NOT LEAVE THIS HOUSE"

"Well..." said Rogers, "it seems you were the last one to hear anything of this man. Now what time did he knock at your door?"

"I don't know," said Di.

"About what time?"

"I haven't any idea what time it was."

"Ten o'clock?"

"I really don't know."

"We'll see if we can't get at it," said Rogers.

He was standing with one foot on the bottom step, and Di stood on the kitchen porch above him, very uneasy at this unexpected examination. There were so many things she did not wish to mention.

"Now, what time did you have dinner?" asked Rogers.

"About quarter to seven."

"And after dinner, what did you do?"

"We went to the lounge."

"How long did you stay there?"

"I—I went out—at nine o'clock for—a little walk."

"How far did you walk?"

"Just to a little clearing, down the hill."

"How long did that take you?"

"Five or ten minutes."

"Then you went back to the house?"

"No. I stayed there for a while."

"How long? Ten minutes?"

"Longer than that."

"Twenty minutes?"

"I—I think it was longer than that. I don't know. I didn't see the time."

"We'll call it half an hour. Thirty minutes then, ten minutes walk each way, that'd bring you back to the house about 9:40. Then what did you do?"

"I was chilly. I sat in the kitchen a little while."

"Ten minutes?"

"I—don't know."

"And after that?"

"I—went to bed."

"You were asleep when Wren knocked at the door?"

"Yes..."

"Well," said Rogers. "I guess we'll have to let the time go. What did Wren say to you?"

"He asked me to let him in."

"What did you answer?"

"I—think I asked him what was the matter?"

"What did he say?"

"He asked again for me to let him in. Then he stopped talking—suddenly."

"Did you hear him walk away?"

"No."

"You say you found blood under the door?"

"Yes."

"What did you do?"

"I—think I fainted."

"When you came to yourself, I suppose you called for help?"

"My aunt was there. I was—rather ill, feverish...."

"I see..." said Rogers. "Now what dealings had you had with Wren?"

"I never had any 'dealings.'"

"Any idea why he came to you?"

"No."

"That afternoon Wren brought you a private message from a man called Fennel?"

"It wasn't a 'private' message. He just told me that Mr. Fennel wanted to see me."

"You met Fennel in the wood?"

"Yes."

"What did you know about Fennel?"

"He brought me a letter from a friend."

"What's the name and address of the friend?"

Reluctantly she gave him Mrs. Frick's address.

"You're personally acquainted with Fennel?"

"I hadn't met him before, but—"

"Can you describe him?"

"Why?" she demanded. "He has nothing to do with this."

"Don't be too sure of that!" said Rogers. "Now, was this Fennel a man of medium height, slender, dark complexion and mustache, nice gentlemanly ways?"

"That description would apply," said Aunt Emma from the doorway.

"That's 'Smoky' all right," said Rogers. "That's just the way he works, too. What they call one of these society burglars."

"He's not a burglar," said Di, briefly. "It's ridiculous—"

"Now, I understand that while you were talking to this Fennel, your uncle came, and there were words."

"He was angry because I'd left him alone. There weren't any 'words,' except his own."

"But just the same he got so excited he had some sort of fit?"

"Attack. Heart attack," said Aunt Emma.

"Attack," said Rogers. "You then went to the house, leaving Fennel alone with your uncle? And Fennel was presently joined by Wren?"

"Yes. But—"

"Did you, at any time subsequent to this, see Fennel and Wren together?"

"I did," said Aunt Emma. "After I'd invented a plausible reason for getting Fennel out of the house, I found him out on the drive, talking to Wren. He went away at once as soon as I appeared."

"Yes," said Rogers. "That's how he works. When he was alone with the old gentleman, he found that money in his pockets. But he was too smart to lift it then. No.... He gets Wren to do the dirty work—"

"That's ridiculous!" cried Di. "Mr. Fennel—"

"He always makes a good impression," said Rogers. "No. He's 'Smoky,' all right. Depend on it! Now, if I can just use your telephone—"

"It's out of order," said Aunt Emma.

"Too bad! Well, I'll just take a look around the house.... Old gentleman able to answer any questions?"

"It's not advisable for him to talk much," said Aunt Emma. "But he's so disturbed about the loss of the money, it may do him good to see that steps are being taken. If you'll be careful to excite him as little as possible."

"Trust me!" said Rogers.

Aunt Emma addressed herself to Di.

"I've just put your breakfast ready in here," she said. "You won't mind eating in the kitchen, my dear? And there's a letter for you, that came this morning. I'll go with Rogers while he questions your Uncle Rufus."

As soon as they were out of sight, Di took the letter from the table, and tore it open.

"Dear Miss Leonard:

"I was very sorry indeed to fail you at our little rendezvous last night. Believe me, it was a great disappointment to me. But circumstances prevented it. Please accept the enclosed as a little mark of my admiration—and my regret that we cannot meet again.

"Yours most sincerely,
"JAMES FENNEL"

She unfolded the enclosed paper, and found in it a fifty-dollar bill.

Her knees trembled under her, and she sank into a chair by the table.

"Oh, no!" she said, half aloud. "Oh, no!"

It seemed to her that she was mortally stricken by this blow, that she could never get over it. Not only the revelation that Fennel was a thief, but the insult of his sending her this money, the tone of his note....

"I liked him," she thought, "I liked him—better than any other man I've ever met."

She poured herself a cup of coffee, cooled it with milk and drank it. And remembered Fennel, his steady dark eyes, his quick, vivid smile....

"It can't be true!" she cried to herself.

Then she thought that perhaps other women had said that of him. "That was the way he worked...." Other credulous women were charmed by that smile, by that quiet, serious, almost stiff manner....

But he had come with a letter from Mrs. Frick.

"If only I hadn't lost that letter!" she thought. "But I'll see Mrs. Frick this afternoon. I'll ask her about him. Perhaps—"

Perhaps he was not a thief. But he had written this insolent note, had sent her money.

"But maybe he didn't realize," she thought. "Maybe he only—wanted to be—kind...." Kind? "My regret that we cannot meet again...."

The profound instinct of her nature was loyalty. She had a quick, and remarkably sound intuition in the reading of character; she saw people's virtues, and forever cherished them; she saw their weaknesses and could excuse them. And she had seen in that man something strong and fine, something which her heart refused to discredit. She was cruelly affronted by his letter, profoundly troubled by the suspicion that Rogers had evoked, but she *could not* dismiss Fennel as utterly worthless.

"I don't understand!" she thought, in despair. "I'll put him out of my mind. I'll forget him. I must forget him."

But she did not. A leaden oppression weighed upon her. That Rogers seemed so confident, so resolute; suppose he found Fennel, arrested him, sent him to prison?

"I'll have to be a witness," she thought. "Against him.... I'll have to admit that I left him alone with Uncle Rufus.... And this letter—"

She jumped up, went to the dining-room door, listened, and when she was sure she was not seen, set fire to the letter and burnt it to ashes in a plate, then threw the ashes out of the window and rinsed the plate.

Now she was finished with Fennel.

She was still trying to eat the excellent breakfast set out for her when her aunt re-entered the room.

"Not very satisfactory," she observed, with a sigh. "Your Uncle Rufus is difficult to handle. And this detective.... Their one idea is to see these men in jail. I don't want Wren in jail. I want him here, in the kitchen. He was very useful to me. As for his theft, it didn't surprise me. Naturally not. I knew he'd been in jail before. Only here, until Uncle Rufus came, there was nothing for him to steal." Again she sighed. "Now there'll be all the stupidity and bother of a trial.... Of course they'll catch Fennel and Wren."

Fennel and Wren bracketed together.

"They may not," said Di.

"Uncle Rufus told this detective that every one of the missing bills was marked, with two crosses in green ink on the corners. That will make it much easier to trace them."

She took a packet of cigarettes from her overall pocket and lit one.

"You'll want to see Uncle Rufus," she said. "And then Miles will drive you in to New York."

Di remembered her promise.

"I think Uncle Rufus expects me to stay..." she said.

"You can ask him," said Aunt Emma. "Now, while we're here, undisturbed, I want to have a little talk with you. It's not going to be very pleasant for either of us, but I'm afraid it can't be avoided."

"It's about Fennel," thought Di, and clasped her hands together under the table.

"I am in need of money," Aunt Emma went on, "desperately in need of money to carry on my work. Neither Peter nor Miles are able—or willing to help me. I have no one else. That is why I am going to tell you—what it would be kinder not to tell you."

Di waited, very pale.

"You know, of course, what your father was like," Aunt Emma went on. "But you can't remember your mother. She was one of the very few persons—she was perhaps the only person who was ever really fond of me. I don't know why. There is nothing natural about affection. Certainly when Harvey was first married, I felt nothing but disgust and annoyance. I knew he couldn't support a wife and I knew he'd ask me to help him. He did. At that time, I had all the money I needed for the rest of my life. I wasn't by any means rich, but my father had left me enough money to live on, so that I could work without troubling about my daily bread. When Harvey came to me for money, I refused him. I had nothing whatever to spare and he knew it.

"Then he sent his wife. She was a pretty girl.... Very pretty, very gallant and honest..." she was silent for a moment.

"Poor little Inez..." she said.

It seemed to Di that this was intolerable, beyond her powers of endurance.

"She came, like you, and offered to help me with my work, for a small salary—any salary... She was quick and intelligent, but pitiably unfit for scientific work. And not strong. She tired easily. I was glad to lend her small sums of money from time to time, but I couldn't let her work for me. I don't know how they managed to live. It must have been hard for her. I have never seen anyone change so.... Then one day she came to me. She was ill then, very ill and desperate. Your father was seriously involved in some discreditable business. I admit that he was more of a fool than a knave; he hadn't realized what he was doing. But that wouldn't have helped him, in court. Inez literally didn't have a penny. She came here, with you.... And I was sorry for her. I helped your father out of his difficulty, and I set them on their feet again. To do this, I had to sell some of my holdings, and my income was cut in half. And I've never had one day free from financial anxiety since then."

She rose.

"That's all," she said. "I have no proofs. It never occurred to me to demand any sort of written acknowledgment from your father. I knew he'd never be able to repay me. If you choose to do so, when you come into Uncle Rufus's money—"

"I'll sign—a note—or something—" said Di, unsteadily.

"It wouldn't be worth the paper it was written on," said Aunt Emma.

"Then I'll give you—my word that if I ever do get any money—"

"Very well!" said Aunt Emma. "I know you mean that—now. But when you've left here, you'll begin to think. 'Why should I believe Aunt Emma. She has no proof. It's very much more agreeable not to believe her.'"

"Then what *can* I do?"

"Nothing," said Aunt Emma. "Except remember. Now you'd better come and see your Uncle Rufus."

Di rose and followed her.

"I wish I'd never been born," she thought.

All her past was clouded with the sorrow of her mother, with disgrace and misery. The present was beyond measure bitter, and lonely; she had no friends, no home, no money, and that letter from Fennel was to her like a personal disgrace.

"There must be something—wrong in me," she thought, "or he wouldn't have dared to do that. He must have been sure I wouldn't show the letter or the money to the police. He must have seen...."

They mounted the stairs and went to Uncle Rufus's room. She remembered that she had believed she found it dark and empty the other evening, but, with so many empty rooms, it would be very easy to make a mistake. It was not empty now, Uncle Rufus lay in the bed, and Uncle Peter sat beside him, sprawled out in a chair. The blind was drawn down, and the room looked singularly gloomy and depressing for a sick room.

Uncle Peter sprang up as they entered.

"Morning!" he said to Di, in a muffled, embarrassed voice. "I hope you're well?"

"Yes, thanks," she answered, curtly enough.

"Uncle Rufus," said Aunt Emma, mildly. "Here's Diana. Do you want to talk to her?"

"No!" said the old man, curtly.

He was, she thought, a remarkably unpleasant object, sitting propped up with pillows, wrapped in a voluminous dressing-gown, and wearing on his head a red Turkish fez with a jaunty black tassel. And the room was so dim, so close, so horribly depressing.... She went nearer to the bed.

"Would you like me to stay here—in the house—?" she asked, in a low voice. "Until you're feeling better, Uncle Rufus?"

"I don't care what you do," he answered, and flounced over on his side, with his back to her.

She waited for a moment and then turned away. Aunt Emma was still in the doorway, with a faint smile on her lips.

"We're not a demonstrative family," she observed. "Now.... Do you want to go at once or wait until after lunch?"

"I'd like to help you—wash the dishes—or something," said Di.

"There's a woman coming from the village to do all that, thanks."

"Then I'll pack now," said Di, and went to her own room.

Locking her door she took the fifty-dollar bill out of her pocket and examined it. On two corners there were tiny crosses made in green ink.

"What shall I do with it?" she thought. "I ought to get it back to Uncle Rufus somehow. It's his...."

She stood looking at it, feeling to the fullest extent all her desolation, her grief, her disappointment. She was going—to what? To no other friend than Mrs. Frick, and going back in immeasurably worse condition than she had left, saddened by the knowledge of her mother's past suffering, worn out by the horrible experiences she had had here, humiliated by her betrayed trust in Fennel, still half-sick from her recent fever, defeated....

Then, suddenly, her spirit rose in arms. She *would not* be defeated and humiliated.

"I've done nothing to be ashamed of!" she said to herself. "I'm going to go back to New York and forget all this. As if it were a nightmare. I have all my life before me. I *won't* be miserable! I won't!"

She opened her trunk briskly and the sight of the dresses that Angelina had given her was balm to her.

"Angelina will come back some day," she thought. "Lord! It's good to remember that there are people like her in the world—happy people, full of life and courage. This house isn't the world. Once I get away, I'll see everything differently. I'm afraid my family isn't very—wholesome."

She looked out of the window, and saw the blue April sky, and her spirits rose and rose.

"Even if Miles is pretty awful, driving in," she thought, "it'll soon be over. To-night—this very night—I'll be at Mrs. Frick's! I'll go out to an Italian restaurant and have a nice little dinner. Perhaps I'll take Mrs. Frick to the movies. It'll be like Heaven, after this!"

She powdered her nose and put on her hat, and the very sight of herself in a hat was a delight. At last she was going. She picked up her bag and turned toward the door.

On the carpet, near the door, was a white square of paper. She stooped and picked it up. There were some words written on it in pencil:

"Do not leave this house. If you go they will kill me. Burn this. For God's sake, do not leave this house."

Chapter Ten
THE FORBIDDEN ROOM

There was no one to turn to, no one to consult, no one to help her.

She read and re-read those words, scrawled on what seemed a scrap torn from a paper bag.

"I think—it's Wren..." she said to herself. "He tried to tell me something before. He's still here..."

She thought of Rogers. If Wren were really in danger...? But Rogers would find him and arrest him, send him to prison. She was not asked to give any assistance, only not to go away, as if only her presence here prevented a crime.

"Aunt Emma wants me to go," she thought.

After all, was it Wren who had written? It might be someone else. Uncle Rufus, perhaps? He had told her plainly enough that he believed his life to be in danger, and had asked her to remain here. Perhaps he had been somehow intimidated, and dared not urge her to stay while those people were in the room.

But whoever had written, and whatever the cause, she could not go until she had discovered the meaning of that note. She took off her hat and almost laughed.

"I can't go," she thought. "I'll *never* be able to leave—"

That was a bad thought to entertain. Never be able to leave? Had she known that the first day she came here? Something had weighed so heavily upon her then.... As if she had known that she could never get away, never get back to the cheerful outside world, that here was the end....

"No!" she said to herself. "I cannot think—things like that. I have no one but myself to depend on now. I've got to keep cool. I've got to be sensible."

She tore the note into fragments, and putting them into the wash-basin, let the water run on them until they were washed down the drain.

What helped her was the thought that some other human creature had appealed to her.

"I've got to find out," she said to herself. "I've got to use my wits."

There was, first of all, the ordeal of telling Aunt Emma that she had changed her mind about going. She discovered then that she was afraid of Aunt Emma; Uncle Peter had been brutal, Uncle Rufus not much better, Miles was dangerously uncertain, yet of all the inmates of this house, Aunt Emma, who had tended her kindly when she was ill, who had brought up her meals, Aunt Emma was the one she feared most.

"But I have the advantage now," she told herself. "Aunt Emma expects to get money from me. She can't afford to antagonize me. I've got to use that advantage."

She opened her door and went out into the corridor. There was no reason why that long red-carpeted hall should seem horrible to her; no reason to think the silence here was sinister.... A door opened behind her, and Aunt Emma came out.

"Ready?" she asked. "If you are, I'll call Miles."

"I've been thinking—" said Di. "While I was dressing I felt—quite miserable.... If you don't mind, I'd like to stay here, in the country, for another day or so, until I feel better."

Aunt Emma made no answer for a time.

"I think you're making a mistake," she said at last. "This house isn't good for you."

A threat, was that?

"The country's so pretty, this time of the year," said Di.

"You're highly nervous and impressionable," Aunt Emma went on. "If I'd realized that before, I'd never have let you come here. There's something about this house...."

She came quickly down the hall, and turned the knob of the door next to Uncle Rufus's room. It opened, she looked at the lock, looked down at the floor, and then closed the door again.

"Let me try your key!" she said, and Di gave it to her.

"No, it doesn't fit," she said. "Very well! If you're going to stay here, let me earnestly warn you against going into that room."

"That sounds like Bluebeard," said Di, with a pretty poor attempt at lightness.

Aunt Emma stood with her back to the door, looking at the girl with a faint smile.

"After Bluebeard was dead," she said, "and the unlucky wives removed, do you think the family ever cared much for that little room?"

Di looked back at her, not understanding, yet uneasy.

"I imagine," Aunt Emma proceeded, "that no one would ever use that room again. Even when the sun shone into it. Even if the castle were pulled down, one stone from the walls of that room, built into some other wall, would bring dreams...."

"Well, but Bluebeard never lived here," said Di, more and more disturbed.

"I believe you went in there once, by mistake, thinking it was Uncle Rufus's room," said Aunt Emma. "Perhaps you felt then that it wasn't—" she paused—"a good room for you to be in," she added, with the grim shadow of a smile. "If you're going to stay here, I warn you, for your own peace of mind. There's nothing there. See!" She flung open the door, and Di saw a neat bare room with the usual hotel furnishings. Aunt Emma closed the door again. "Don't go in there—*if you can help it.*"

"That shouldn't be difficult," said Di, smiling herself.

For she was, to the best of her ability, defying Aunt Emma. She knew she must do this, for the good of her soul. She must not be repressed or dismayed.

"Can I help you with the lunch?" she asked.

Aunt Emma accepted the offer, and they went downstairs together. And all the way, Di was thinking, "Why mustn't I go into that room? And why should I want to?"

She tried to forget that room.

"I've stayed here to find out who wrote me that note," she told herself. "That's the important thing. That's what I must think of."

But she kept on thinking about the room. She remembered going into it that night, finding it empty and dark, with the wind blowing into it. And hadn't she, even then, felt something there, something terrible...?

"No!" she said to herself. "And anyhow, it doesn't matter. That's not the important thing."

She moved about the kitchen, working under Aunt Emma's directions, beating eggs for an omelette, making cocoa for Uncle Rufus.

"Did she mean that something had happened in that room? Well, what of it? Nothing to do with me! I *must* think about that note. I must do something."

With no little effort, she forced herself to return to that subject.

"It must have been written either by Wren or Uncle Rufus. The first thing is, to find out if Uncle Rufus wrote it. If he didn't, then Wren must be somewhere in the house...."

That was not an agreeable thought, that someone was hidden in this house, among all these empty rooms.

"If I find that Uncle Rufus wrote it, I'm going to tell that detective," she thought. "But if it was Wren—I can't. He did all he could for me. I won't help to send him to jail."

"Diana," said Aunt Emma, "will you take this tray up to your Uncle Rufus? Then come down, and we'll have our own lunch."

Di took the tray and went toward the door.

"The back stairs," said Aunt Emma, opening a door. "It saves a good many steps."

Di had not known before of this back stairway leading up from the kitchen. It was dark, with a closed door at the top, and darker still as Aunt Emma closed the kitchen door behind her. And at once, as that door shut, she began thinking again of the forbidden room.

"Oh, how stupid and disgusting of me!" she cried to herself, in a sort of despair. "Exactly like Bluebeard's wife! Just because Aunt Emma said not to go into it.... She probably did that on purpose—one of her horrible psychological experiments.... Perhaps she wants to divert my mind from other things...."

She reached the door at the top and had to set down the tray to open the door.

"If only I can get a word alone with Uncle Rufus.... And I'll look into that room, just to prove to myself...."

She came out into an unfamiliar corridor, that branched off from the main one; this one, too, was lined with closed doors.

"There must be at least twenty-five empty rooms in this floor," she thought. "And I don't know what's upstairs. There's the cellar, too. It's all very well for me to talk about 'searching the house,' but it's not going to be an easy job. Especially without being seen...."

Uncle Rufus's door was closed, and she knocked. There was no answer, and presently she knocked again. The silence alarmed her; she tried the handle, and found the door locked.

"Uncle Rufus!" she called.

A door across the corridor opened and Uncle Peter appeared.

"Ah!" he said, jauntily. "A little refreshment! I can do with that!"

"It's for Uncle Rufus," said Di, indignantly. "His door's locked—"

"I know," said Uncle Peter, with his old apologetic air. "He was asleep, and I just stepped into my own room for a smoke—"

"Please unlock the door!"

"Certainly!" he said. "Certainly!" He took the key from his pocket, put it into the lock and flung open the door.

Uncle Rufus was not asleep; he was sitting bolt upright in the bed in that dark, close room.

"Are you feeling better?" Di asked, stirred to pity and concern for him. He only shook his head.

"Here's some nice hot cocoa," she went on. "Will you let me—?"

"I'll have to feed him," whispered Uncle Peter.

"Let me!" said Di.

"No," protested Uncle Peter. "I understand his ways, y'know." Di went nearer to the bed, but Uncle Peter blocked the way. "Please don't get him worked up!" he whispered.

Di looked over her shoulder at the old man and saw him looking at her sidelong.

"Uncle Rufus!" she cried. "Please just tell me how you feel?"

"Better!" he croaked, in a hoarse voice.

"Is there anything I can do for you?"

"Don't go till I'm better—" he said, in that same hoarse, painful voice.

"I won't!" she said. "Wouldn't you like—?"

"He's hungry," Uncle Peter explained, and at once began feeding him with the cocoa. "When you go down, would you mind telling your Aunt Emma that I'm hungry too? She keeps me shut up here.... Least she can do is to remember my food."

"Uncle Rufus," said Di, looking steadily at the old man. "I'll stay. I'll be here—all the time—if you want anything. I'll come back after lunch and see you."

The room was too dim for her to see his face clearly at that distance, but she hoped that he understood.

"He wrote that note," she thought. "He's afraid. Something horrible is going on."

As she left the room, Uncle Peter closed the door behind her, and she heard the key turn in the lock. The impulse seized her to bang on the door and make him open it again. She could not endure the thought of the old man locked in there, helpless and frightened. And in spite of her previous experience with him, she had no fear of Uncle Peter, only contempt.

"But that wouldn't do any good," she thought. "I'll have to handle this thing better than that. Somehow, I'm going to get away this afternoon and find that detective."

She had almost reached the head of the front stairs when something checked her. That room.... Now was her chance to look at it, to rid herself, once and for all, of this preposterous obsession.

She turned back, she hesitated; she listened.

"Perhaps that's just what Aunt Emma wants," she thought. "For me to go in there. Perhaps there's something—I won't like...."

Better to see it, though, whatever it was; better to go, and be done with it. She went softly past Uncle Rufus's door, to that other door, put her hand on the knob. And again she hesitated.

"Perhaps I'll be sorry..." she said to herself.

But she turned the knob, and opened the door.

Nothing there, surely, to trouble the most timid. Through the window she could see the blue sky, the tree tops, inside, only a dusty neatness. She stepped over the threshold.

Then she felt it. A strange tingling in her veins, a dread, an excitement, that made her heart beat fast. But there was nothing there; nothing at all....

She looked toward the door of the clothes-closet.

"All right!" she said, aloud, and with a sort of rush, went over to it and flung it open. Nothing there but empty shelves and hooks. She closed the door again, and looked about her. Nothing anywhere.

Yet somehow this blankness did not reassure her. Her oppression, her feeling of dread and excitement was increasing; she could not believe there was really nothing here; she felt only that she had not found—what there was to find. She opened the drawers of the bureau; all empty.

And her fear grew. There was something here, something in the very air that stifled her. She hurried to the window, to open it, and stopped there, with her face grown white as chalk.

For printed on the window-sill in neat black letters was a name:

"INEZ"

Her mother's name.... Why was that here?

Ever since she had come into this house, she had been hearing of her mother, had been led back to her vague, childish memories of her. It had always saddened her to think of her mother, and now with that sorrow there was something else, something dark and dreadful. She looked and looked at that name on the window-sill until suddenly she turned and ran out of the room, shutting the door behind her. Tears were running down her cheeks; she was shaken to the soul by an emotion she could not comprehend.

"What is it?" she said to herself. "Oh, what is this...?"

Chapter Eleven
DI GETS ANOTHER LETTER

In her own room she bathed her eyes in cold water, and then went down
by the front stairs to the kitchen. And her heart sank at the sight of Miles
there, slouched in a chair, smoking a cigarette.

"How ill he looks!" she thought, shocked by his pallor, his haggardness.
He glanced up as she entered, without a smile, without a word.

"We'll eat in here," said Aunt Emma. "Get up, Miles, and bring your chair
to the table."

He obeyed, still in silence, still smoking. Aunt Emma set on the table a
savory little ham omelette, fried potatoes and a pot of tea; she seemed very
pleased with her skill in cooking—and with reason—but she had, apparently, no ideas at all about attractive serving. They ate upon the bare table,
from the coarse kitchen china.

Miles did not eat at all; Aunt Emma paid no attention to this; she sat at
the end of the table with a pleased and cheerful expression upon her
healthy face, but Di was troubled.

"Miles, do eat!" she said.

He pushed back his chair and rose.

"I can't," he said. "My head aches...."

"You can drive down to the drug-store," said Aunt Emma, "and get a little prescription filled for me. The fresh air will do you good. Take Diana
with you."

The prospect of a drive with Miles was by no means pleasant, especially
in his present condition.

"Let's walk instead," said Di.

"I can't," said Miles, briefly.

He began walking up and down the kitchen; then abruptly he stopped
beside her chair.

"Di," he said. "*Won't* you come?"

She looked up at him; their eyes met, and she was dismayed by the
anguish she saw.

"All right!" she said, with a sigh. "First let's help Aunt Emma—"

"The woman from the village will be here in half an hour," said Aunt
Emma. "Run along! I don't need you."

Di went upstairs to get her hat and coat, went almost mechanically. Her
mind felt blank, her heart numbed, as if she had exhausted her capacity for
thinking and feeling. Only that sorrow stirred her as she passed the forbidden door, sorrow, formless as a dream.

"I'm tired," she thought. "I don't care very much now—about anything...."

I ought to do something about Uncle Rufus, though."

It was such an effort to think. Again she put on her hat, remembering with a sort of wonder how happy she had been this morning, thinking that at last she was free.

"I can't go," she thought, "until I'm sure that Uncle Rufus is getting proper care. He wants me here.... Something horrible is going on, and I've got to stop it. And I've got a chance now.... I can telephone from the drug-store. To whom?"

She could not think. Somebody must come now to help her. She must tell someone now—but who was there? Uncle Rufus had not a friend on earth and neither had she. There was no possible use in telling Mrs. Frick about this. Then who?

"Doctor Coat? No. He thinks Aunt Emma's a wonderful person. Mr. Purvis? He's a lawyer. If I tell him about the note—about the other things... It's got to be Mr. Purvis. When we go to the drugstore, I'll ring him up. I don't care if Miles hears me."

She came downstairs again, and found Miles waiting outside in the car.

"You'll drive carefully, won't you, Miles?" she asked.

"No," said Miles.

That was not a promising beginning. He started the car with a jerk and went down the hill at a reckless speed, swung round the corner and into the main road.

"Miles!" she cried. "You'll be arrested!"

"I don't care!" he answered.

"Miles! There's a policeman on a motor-cycle—"

That was a lie, but it checked him; he slowed down considerably.

"God!" he said. "I wish I had enough courage to crash into a wall and finish."

"Isn't that just a little inconsiderate?" she said.

"No," said Miles. "You'd be better off dead."

"I suppose I have something to say about that, though."

Now that he was driving more moderately, his wild talk did not very greatly disturb her. She had heard that sort of thing before. Her father, in his bad hours, had used to tell her gloomily it would have been better if she had never been born; he had used to say that life was no more than a curse. Even as a child, her native courage, her wholesome sanity, had rebelled against that, and she rebelled now. It might be that she herself had very little, but life was good. It was beautiful out here, in the Spring sun; there was a place for her in the world, work for her to do, happiness for her, somewhere, and for everyone.

"He's sick," she thought. "In body and mind. And I'm afraid I can't help him. I'm so tired—it's hard to think of anything at all to say."

But it was impossible for her not to try.

"Miles," she said. "Why don't you get a job?"

"What for?"

"You'd be much happier—"

He laughed, a theatrical and bitter laugh.

"You would!" she persisted. "I'm going back to New York presently to look for a job myself. And if you find something to do—we can have nice times together. We can have little dinners together, and go places...."

Even while she was speaking, she didn't believe in it; that cheerful, normal world outside had lost reality for her. But she went on, valiantly.

"We'll have such nice times.... On Saturday afternoons we'll—"

"Di!" he cried. "You don't know...!"

"Yes, I do, Miles. You're—upset now. You're not feeling well. You don't see things as they really are. Why, Miles, think how young you are! Everything still before you—"

"If you knew—what was behind me!"

"It doesn't matter, Miles. If there's anything you're sorry for, or ashamed of—"

"Sorry for!" he cried. "Oh, God!"

"Then look ahead, Miles. Make up your mind that things will be different in the future."

"There's no possible future for me."

In her fatigue and depression, it seemed almost unendurable to be obliged to keep this up. But no one else would bother with Miles, no one else would try to help, and she could see how sorely he was in need of help.

"There is, Miles."

As he turned to look at her, the car swerved a little.

"Diana," he said. "Do you really care what happens to me?"

"Yes," she answered, promptly. "I do."

"Even if I've done something... something...."

"Yes, Miles," she said, steadily.

He turned the car to the side of the road and stopped it.

"Do you care enough—to save my life?"

"Of course," she said, uneasily.

"Then will you marry me?"

"I'm afraid I can't do that, Miles."

"Look here, Diana! I've got a little money—enough for us to get away somewhere.... We'll go to South America, Di. I'll start all over again. I'll be anything you want, Di, I'll do anything you want, Di, Di, my darling! If you're with me, Di, I'll be all right! Di, I *can't* live without you!"

"You don't need to, Miles," she said. He had seized both her hands, and she made no attempt to withdraw them. She had to be careful now, very careful, if she was to help him. "Only, we've got to learn to know each other."

"I won't live without you!" he cried. "I won't try!"

"You're not going to be without me. We're going to see lots of each other—and have such good times together—"

"That won't do," he interrupted. "It's all or nothing. Either you'll marry me and come away with me—or—"

"Nothing of the sort, Miles," she said, almost sternly. "We're going to be the best of friends—"

"Will you marry me?" he demanded.

"Miles, I can't—"

He started the car again, driving not recklessly now, but steadily as if with a purpose.

"This isn't the way to the drug-store," she said.

"No," he said. "It's not. We're going somewhere else."

"Please tell me, Miles!"

He would not answer her; he drove on and on, through a little town, through pleasant roads lined with old trees and comfortable houses, past woods, past fields. His face was set and grim; there was certainly some purpose now in his tormented heart. Time and again she tried to divert him, but he would not answer her. And she grew afraid. Was this to be the end, a sickening crash, perhaps hours of suffering, and then death...?

"Miles!" she entreated. "Please stop! Please tell me where you are going?"

"To hell!" he shouted.

They shot up a hill, and he stopped the car. Beside them was a little bridge over a railway cut.

"There's a train coming now," he said. "When it's in sight, I'm going to jump."

"No, you're not!" she said, but he only laughed.

In despair she looked about her; there was not a living creature in sight, only the empty road, with a wood on one side and the bridge on the other. The distant train whistled.

"I shall try to hold you," she said. "If you—struggle—you may kill me, Miles."

"Then we'll die together," he said.

The sun was shining and the wind blew on this deserted hill-top. Again the train whistled. He got up, and she caught his coat-sleeve, but he was much stronger than she. He got out of the car, and she followed, pulling desperately, to prevent his setting foot on that bridge.

"You shan't!" she cried. "Miles! Miles! If you really do care for me one bit—"

The train was in sight. He tried to wrench himself free, but she flung her arms about him; he tried to push her away, but she twisted her foot round his ankle; he stumbled and fell on his knees. And she pressed down on his shoulders with all her might. The train went by, shaking the little bridge.

She thought then that she was going to faint; she stepped back a pace—and she saw, at her feet a letter that had fallen from his pocket. A letter addressed to herself. She stooped and snatched it up.

"Give that to me!" he cried.

She began to run.

She ran downhill, and she heard his footsteps on the hard road behind her. She ran faster, faster than she would have believed possible, with the strength of desperation. He was close behind her. Nothing about but the empty road.

"Stop!" he shouted.

She ran and ran. Nothing ahead but that straight road, and her strength was beginning to fail her now; her breath was coming in gasps; her laboring heart sent all the blood pounding in her ears. Then at the foot of the hill she saw the level crossing of the railway, and a little hut where the guard sat. He was looking at her now.... Such a long way....

Her second wind came to her now; she quickened her pace; she stumbled and recovered herself, flew down the rest of the hill, to the doorway of the little shelter. She could not speak, only stand there, panting, facing the astonished old man. Then she turned her head; she saw Miles, a few paces distant, standing in the middle of the road. They looked at each other, a strange look, then he turned round and started up the hill again.

"Miles!" she called after him. But she was still breathless, her voice was faint, either he did not hear, or he did not care. She wanted to tell the old man to hurry, to save Miles, but she could not say a word.

"Sit down, Miss!" said the old man, pushing forward his chair.

She pointed after Miles, and half fell into the chair.

"All right!" said the man. "He won't bother you now, Miss. Just take it easy...."

"I'm afraid—" she gasped. "He'll kill...."

Just then she saw his car coming down the hill; he shot past the little shelter, across the tracks and out of sight.

"You young ladies had ought to be more careful who you go out with, these days," said the man. He was a solid, burly old fellow, with kindly eyes, beyond measure reassuring to her.

"But don't you worry any more," he continued. "He's gone and he won't come back, neither. He knows you've got a witness what could prove in a court of law how he was chasing you down the hill—"

"I was only afraid—he'd kill himself," she answered. "He's such a reckless—driver."

The old man obviously did not believe a word of that. He brought her a glass of water, and stood watching her while she drank it.

"Live near here, Miss?" he asked.

"No," she answered. "I.... Perhaps I can get a taxi...."

"Ought to be some along in a few minutes," he said. "Going down to the station, to meet the up train. Next one I see, I'll stop it for you, if it's got a driver I know."

"You're awfully kind," she said.

"Pshaw!" said he.

She sat there in the doorway of the little shelter, with tranquil peace all about her; the railway tracks glinting like silver in the sunshine; she heard a robin singing nearby. And she held that letter tight in her hand. Someone in the world had been interested enough to write to her.... There were kind, ordinary human creatures; there were birds and sunshine....

"If you'll excuse me, I'll just read this letter," she said to the old man. This politeness somewhat surprised him.

"Go right ahead!" he said, and stepped outside.

The envelope had no stamp, and it had been torn open; she took the letter out of it.

"Dear Miss Leonard:

"*I am bringing this along, in case anything prevents me from seeing you this evening.*

"*I think the letter I brought you from Mrs. Frick will have explained me pretty well. I hope you won't think I am a meddlesome ass. But if you get this letter, it will mean that I have not been able to see you this evening, and that will be rather a bad job, because I am going to try every way I know to see you. There are a lot of things that need explaining. I don't want to put them into a letter. I shall try to give this to Wren, to give to you. When you get it, please try to trust me. Clear out of that house the first moment you can. Put on your hat and walk out. Don't say anything to anyone. If anyone comes along with you, go back to the house and try again. But get away. Take the first train back to New York, to Mrs. Frick's. Things are going to happen, and you must be out of the way.* This is important.

"*I hope you will believe that ever since I saw you with those flowers I have been, and I always will be,*

"*Faithfully and respectfully your friend,*
"JAMES FENNEL"

It was as if she heard him speaking, in his blunt and somewhat masterful way, as if she could see his face, unexpressive, except when that vivid smile crossed it. He, a professional thief?

"I never really believed it!" she thought. "I knew...! I knew...!"

She could have wept, with delight, with relief. He was her friend. He would come back—

"But what happened to him that night?" she thought. And the greatest fear she had ever known in her life seized her. Why had he not been able to see her?—"That will be rather a bad job, because I am going to try every way I know to see you."—She had gone out, to meet him; she had waited.... What had happened to him?

Now she remembered what Miles had said, his words that hinted at some desperate remorse. She had not paid much heed to them at the time; she had thought he referred to his drinking, to Heaven knows what episodes in his unhappy wasted life. She had not tried at all to account for his intention to kill himself; it had seemed so in keeping with his unstable, reckless nature. But now she could believe that there was something in his heart he could not endure. He had had Fennel's letter in his pocket....

"Here's a cab, Miss," said the old man. "And a driver I know, and can vouch for. Nice, steady young man."

She rose and managed to smile.

"You've been so nice—" she said. "Some day I'm coming back—to thank you. Only to-day—I'm—tired."

"That's right!" he said, seriously. "All upset. Well, you remember if you want a witness to these goings-on, here's Joe Archer, that seen it all."

She came out of the little shelter and found the taxi waiting. She glanced at the driver, a squat, swarthy young Italian, then she got in.

"Where to, lady?" he asked.

She looked at him, dazed; she needed time to think. Should she go back to Mrs. Frick's at once? Not back to The Châlet. Not there again....

"First I'd like to go somewhere to telephone, please," she said to the driver, and as the cab started, she took out her vanity-case, to see how she looked after all this. Angelina had given her that case.

"Oh, if only I could reach her!" she thought.

She had a vision of Angelina arriving at The Châlet, dashing up in a racing car, or arriving by airplane, sweeping in like a whirlwind, facing Aunt Emma with her sublime assurance..... "What do you people think you're doing? Lord! What an awful old house! We'll have a doctor and a nurse for that poor old man. Where's Fennel? I'm going to look for him. I want to talk to that detective."

Angelina wouldn't care whether or not it was her business to interfere, or whether anyone wanted her. She would simply take possession of everything and everyone.

"Child, you're simply exhausted! Go and lie down this instant, you poor little angel, and I'll come up and have tea with you in your room."

She had said that so often; she had been, for all her sensational exploits, so strong, so confident, and, for all her carelessness, so generous and kind.

But it was not possible to reach her; the itinerary of her honeymoon was a secret.

"There never seems to be anyone but Mrs. Frick," thought Di.

The driver stopped at a little stationer's and she got out to telephone. It seemed a little impossible, that she could really communicate freely with the outside world; she half expected that there would be no answer to her call, or that someone would stop her.

But the usual routine went forward and she actually heard Mrs. Frick's voice; not very amiable.

"Well?"

"It's Diana Leonard—"

"Miss Leonard!" cried Mrs. Frick. "Merciful Powers! I've been so worried and anxious about you. Especially not hearing a single word from that Mr. Fennel. Where are you now? Are you coming back to-night?"

"What about Mr. Fennel?" asked Di.

"Why, he promised to come right straight back here after he'd seen you, and tell me all about things. And he never did. I rang up the Ritz, where he's living, and they said he hadn't come back. I didn't know if I ought to take any steps, but I thought I'd better not. Of course he has lots of friends. If anything was wrong, *they'd* know. But tell me, dearie, when are you coming back here?"

"I—don't exactly know," said Di. "But very soon, Mrs. Frick."

"But are you all right, dearie?" asked Mrs. Frick. "It seems to me your voice sounds sort of queer."

"Perfectly all right, thanks."

"Did you get the letter I sent by Mr. Fennel?"

There was a moment's pause.

"Yes, thanks. He gave it to me," said Di.

"I wish you'd tell me whatever has happened to Mr. Fennel."

"I'm—going to try to find out," said Di.

For she had made up her mind that she must go back to The Châlet at once.

Chapter Twelve
"YOU ARE LIKE HER"

She had come to this decision rapidly, but quite deliberately.

"No one there would do me any real harm," she thought. "They can't afford to, because they're hoping to get Uncle Rufus's money through me. Aunt Emma was going to make Uncle Peter apologize. She'll see that he doesn't do anything like that again. And if Miles comes back, she'll keep him in order. I've got to go back, and find out what's happened to Mr. Fennel."

She was perfectly sure that something had happened to Fennel, and that Miles was responsible for it; she was profoundly alarmed and troubled, yet in her heart there was still that unshakable confidence in Fennel. She could not imagine him defeated by Miles. He might have been deceived, sent away with some false message from herself; he might even have been taken by surprise, have been hurt, temporarily put out of the way. But if he had been deceived, he would soon find it out; if he had been hurt, he would recover. He would come back; she knew it.

Her chief motive was loyalty. Fennel had come entirely on her account; any misadventure that had befallen him was due to his wish to help her. And now she would help him.

"I can't very well go to the police," she thought. "I haven't any evidence that anything's happened. And Aunt Emma would know how to make things look all right. She called in that detective herself.... I wish I'd kept that other letter—the one with the money in it. It was a forgery, of course. Who did it? Miles? Is that what he's so wretched about?"

It was so difficult to evaluate Miles's emotions. He was capable of being overcome with remorse for something pardonable, and equally capable of feeling not the least regret for some horrible act. His rudderless spirit knew no measure, no proportion; he did not know what he wanted or where he was going.

"If anyone had ever cared for him," she thought, "had ever taken any trouble over him, he might have been—a decent man."

And that, in a way, was her requiem for Miles. She had pitied him and had done what she could for him, and now she had finished with him.

The sun was beginning to set; another day was ending, and still she was not free. Going back there again....

"If you'll drive to the East Hazlewood Station," she told the chauffeur, "someone there can tell you how to reach a house called 'The Châlet.'"

It seemed to her a surprisingly long drive.

"But of course Miles came so terribly fast," she thought. "And perhaps he came a shorter way, too. Now I must make up my mind what to do."

She leaned back in the cab and shut her eyes, but, instead of the clearly defined plan she wanted, trivial and aimless little thoughts drifted through her mind.

"Paying for this taxi is going to make an awful hole in my ten dollars," she thought. "But Mrs. Frick's turned so amiable.... He remembered that day he saw me on the steps of Angelina's house.... He must be a friend of hers.... He must have plenty of friends. He couldn't just disappear.... But some people do... I've read in the newspapers...."

She opened her eyes and sat up straight.

"I know that he came that night. I must find out why I didn't see him. What happened to him? Miles knows. And almost certainly Aunt Emma knows. But if she won't tell me, if I can't find out anything, I shall have to go to the police."

She tried to marshal in her mind the facts she had to lay before the police. That letter that had fallen from Miles's pocket? That, combined with the fact that Fennel had disappeared, ought to be enough. But suppose he hadn't really disappeared, but had only gone somewhere about his own affairs? It was possible that Fennel had left that letter for her, had given it to Wren, and Miles had got hold of it. That might be his only offense, the purloining of a letter. His remorse, his wild talk, might so easily be without foundation. Suppose after all that nothing had happened to Fennel?

But there was that other letter she had had, signed with his name, enclosing the marked fifty-dollar bill. She was sure that letter was a forgery, done for the purpose of discrediting Fennel. Perhaps the whole story of the robbery was sheer fabrication, with Wren and Fennel the victims.

"I don't know!" she cried to herself. "I can't think it out. There are so many little things—that don't seem to fit together.... Only there's something horribly wrong.... And Mr. Fennel came that night, and I didn't see him."

She realized with dismay that she was not thinking clearly. She was worn out, almost exhausted by her terrible struggle with Miles, coming close upon the heels of so many other shocking and inexplicable things.

"If I could wait and rest—before I went back..." she thought. "Maybe it's simply idiotic to go back. But it seems to me now the only decent thing to do. Mr. Fennel came on my account. I ought at least to try to find out what happened. And now, of course, it's very different. I was—almost a prisoner before, but I've got out, and I'll take care not to be trapped again."

They were going up the hill now, along the woodland road. The sun was gone, the sky was drained of color; here among the trees there was a somber twilight. The Châlet was a house easy to get into, but not so easy to leave.

"I'll see to that!" she thought, and leaning forward, spoke to the driver.

"Please wait for me," she said. "And if I don't come out in half an hour, please go to the door and ask for me."

He turned round to look at her, and in the gathering dusk his swarthy face had, she thought, a strange, secret look.

"No!" she said to herself. "That's ridiculous...." And aloud: "Please—don't go away without me," she said. "No matter what anyone says.... Even if someone comes out and pays you and says I'm not coming. I—I *am* coming...." She stopped, ashamed and half-frightened by the tremor in her voice, the unmistakable note of appeal. "You see," she said, "I've—left my bag there.... I—they they'd like me to stay longer—but I can't.... So if you'll please wait...."

"Why don't yez leave me go and ask for yer bag?" he asked.

The kindness in his voice nearly unnerved her. "Thanks ever so much, but I've—got to—go in."

"I'll wait," he said. "And if they won't leave yez come out, will I tell some friends of yours?"

"Yes!" she cried. "I'll give you an address—if you have a pencil."

He stopped the cab, halfway up the hill and not yet in sight of the house, and on a bit of paper she wrote Mrs. Frick's address.

"If you'll please let her know...."

Putting the paper in his pocket, he turned away again.

"Well..." he said. "Maybe they got a right to keep your bag, but they got no right to keep *you*. That's agin the law."

"Oh—" she began, and stopped. Evidently he thought this was an affair of unpaid board; better let him go on thinking that.

"I'll wait, aw' right," he added. "Don't you worry!"

But she did worry! As they turned the corner, and she saw the house again, so desolate, and bleak, such a fear swept over her that for a moment she was paralyzed.

"I can't!" she said, half aloud.

"What?" asked the driver.

"Nothing," she said, and tried to reason with herself.

There was nothing really to be afraid of; the cab would be waiting for her and the driver had Mrs. Frick's address. And even without that no one would want to hurt her, for only through her could they get Uncle Rufus's money.

"I'll tell Aunt Emma the whole thing," she thought. "How Miles acted and about Mr. Fennel's letter. I'll tell her that if she doesn't let me know at once what happened to Mr. Fennel, she needn't expect me to help her out with any money ever. I've got the upper hand. I *must* remember that."

Light was shining from the windows of the lounge. But all the other dark rooms....

"I have the upper hand!" she said to herself. "Perhaps I'm the only person who can find out what happened to Mr. Fennel. Perhaps they've done something—horrible...."

It was very easy to believe that, when she stood again in the shadow of that house.

"And Uncle Rufus!" she thought, with a shock. "I promised not to leave him!"

She stopped outside the door, appalled. How was it possible that she had forgotten that? For a moment, despair seized her. Then she began to think sanely and lucidly.

"I'll stand by him. I won't desert him. But I will not—I *cannot* live in that house. I must see him and explain it. There must be some sort of hotel in the village. I'll stay there, and come to see him every day until he's well enough to leave. I'll beg him to insist upon having a nurse for the nights. I'll do it all quite openly. I have the upper hand. I will not be cowardly. I will not be underhand and secret. I have the upper hand."

She glanced back at the cab that stood square and solid in the driveway, its lights shining out clearly. Then she opened the door and entered the lounge.

"Ah!" said a bland voice, and Mr. Purvis rose from his chair. "Miss Diana.... We've been waiting for you!"

In her condition of nervous fatigue she was ready to believe even the respectable Mr. Purvis a sinister figure.

"Waiting for me?" she repeated.

"Sit down!" he said. "Yes.... Yes.... It is your uncle's wish that you should be informed.... Yes.... Your uncle sent for me again this afternoon, my dear young lady, and he has at last made his will.... He wishes you to know— 'So that she will stay here with me'—those were his words. He is leaving you practically his entire estate of seven hundred thousand dollars."

His pleased smile died on his lips.

"Are you ill?" he cried.

"No," she said, faintly. "Only, naturally... I... I want to see Uncle Rufus, please."

"Quite natural and proper!" said Mr. Purvis. "Perhaps I was somewhat too abrupt.... And mind you, I don't by any means intend to suggest that your uncle's condition is worse. By no means! In fact—" He smiled almost archly, "it's a curious thing, but well attested—that very often a patient takes a turn for the better after making a will. There's no cause for im - mediate alarm, my dear young lady. Doctor Coat assures me...."

"May I see him, please?" asked Di. "Uncle Rufus, I mean."

Because, before anything else, she must see that old man who had, in spite of his malice and unkindness, trusted her and so greatly rewarded her; she must assure him that she would return to-morrow morning; that she would look after him and protect him.

"I don't know..." said Purvis. "Your aunt and Doctor Coat are with him now. They may not think it advisable—"

"I'll just go up and see," said Di. And all the way up the stairs she said to herself: "I have the upper hand. I'll *insist* upon seeing him. And I'll say what I want to say. I'll see him alone. Aunt Emma wouldn't dare refuse, with Doctor Coat there."

As she reached the top of the stairs, she was startled to hear her aunt laugh, a low, cheerful chuckle, answered by another laugh, a man's. It seemed to her that this sound came from the corridor that branched off from the main one, and she went very quietly in that direction.

There they were, Aunt Emma and Doctor Coat; Doctor Coat leaning against the wall with his hands in his pockets, Aunt Emma standing facing him, smoking, looking up at him with a glance that was coquettish and gay.

"And what did you do then, Emma?" Doctor Coat was asking, with evident admiration.

"I told him that for every remark like that, the price of the article would increase one hundred dollars," said she.

Di turned away, astounded by this new aspect of Aunt Emma.

"But now's my chance!" she thought, hastening to Uncle Rufus's room.

The door was open, and Uncle Peter was sitting in there, half asleep. But at the sight of her he came wide awake in an instant.

"Hello!" he said, jauntily.

She looked past him, to the bed where the old man lay.

"Uncle Rufus!" she said.

"Come here!" he answered, in a voice so hoarse and faint she could scarcely hear it. She went toward the bed, but Uncle Peter sprang up and barred the way.

"Look here!" said Di. "I won't have this! Uncle Rufus wants to speak to me—and if you won't let him, I'm going to tell Doctor Coat and Mr. Purvis."

The room was lighted only by a small lamp with a green shade; outside that bright circle it was in darkness. Uncle Peter's face was little more than a pale blur, the old man on the bed was lost in the shadows.

"Stand out of the way, please!" she said.

"No!" said Uncle Peter.

"And what's this?" asked Aunt Emma's voice from the doorway, where she had appeared, with Doctor Coat.

At the sound of her voice, the old man on the bed half-raised himself.

"Don't go..." he said, in that hoarse, extinguished voice. "They'll kill me. Stay...."

He sank back, turned his head, still wearing the grotesque fez, to the wall, with the covers drawn up to his chin. Diana faced Doctor Coat.

"Did you hear?" she asked.

"Most unfortunate...!" he murmured.

She was indignant at so weak a word. She stepped out into the hall, where she could speak without Uncle Rufus hearing.

"Don't you see—?" she demanded, in a sort of despair.

"He doesn't 'see,'" Aunt Emma interrupted, and, addressing Doctor Coat: "I must warn you, Matthew, that Diana takes this all very seriously. I believe she's convinced that we're all engaged in a conspiracy—to murder Uncle Rufus Leonard."

"Come, come, Emma!" said Doctor Coat, shocked. "I'm sure she thinks nothing of the sort." He glanced at Di, and smiled; no doubt he meant it for a benign, and reassuring smile, but it was not; it was nervous, apprehensive. "The important point," he went on, "is that Rufus doesn't believe in this—this conspiracy himself. He's been expressing these—unpleasant suspicions for years, yet he never stopped coming here. And only this afternoon, when I suggested moving him to a hospital, he refused. That is pretty conclusive proof that this is not a genuine delusion.

"Now, the most marked characteristic of the genuine delusion, such as can be observed in the paranoiac, for instance, is not the irrationality of the fixed idea, but the tenacity with which the patient clings to it. I emphatically deny that Rufus shows any symptoms of a genuine delusion. These—suspicions are simple willful assertions, made with the clear intention of annoying, as opposed to the perfectly involuntary belief of a paranoiac. I am willing at any time to testify to the fact that Rufus is of sound mind. A little crochety, perhaps, but as sane as you or me. He—"

"It's no use, Matthew!" Aunt Emma interrupted. "I'd like a word with her, if you'll excuse me. Come here, please!"

Di followed her into the next room; not until the door was closed behind them did she realize what room this was. It was almost in darkness; through the window she could see the pines black as ink against the pallid sky.

"I should like to prevent you from making any more of a fool of yourself than is necessary," said Aunt Emma. "Are you able to realize that if you persist in taking this notion of your Uncle Rufus's seriously you are tending to invalidate his will?"

"I don't care!" said Di. "I can't—I won't—see him—like this. He's— frightened."

"My God!" said Aunt Emma, with a sigh. "Very well! I'll admit that he's frightened. And that he had a genuine delusion. It's a well-defined case. He has the paranoiac delusion of persecution. Technically, he's insane. Like your father."

"My father!" cried Di.

"Like your father," Aunt Emma repeated. "*He* believed he was persecuted. He—"

"He wasn't insane!" cried Di. "That's not—"

"The stock is tainted," Aunt Emma went on, tranquilly. "You must have observed it. Peter's a high-grade moron. Rufus is a paranoiac. Miles, just at present, is a borderline case. But alcoholism will very shortly send him over the line. A somewhat difficult household to deal with."

Di was silent for a moment.

"My father—" she began, in an unsteady, defiant voice.

"Naturally," Aunt Emma interrupted, "you want to deny that he was unbalanced. It's a quite instinctive reaction with you to deny anything that's unpleasant to you. It's time you faced facts with a little courage. This inclination of yours to build fantasies is dangerous. It was just that refusal to accept reality that destroyed your unfortunate mother."

"Don't—*talk* about her!" said Di.

"I think," said Aunt Emma, slowly, "that she'd be glad if I were to tell you now. It's time.... I've kept it from you, until now, because you are so remarkably ill-adapted to hear any unpleasant truths. But now... Here, in this room..."

In this room? Where her mother's name was printed on the window-sill....

"I don't—want to hear..." she said.

"But you're going to hear," said Aunt Emma. "It was in this room that I last saw her alive. She came here, to me, in a lamentable condition. She had found out for herself what your father was. She realized that he could never make a living for her, and her own health was too much impaired for her to contemplate any sort of work. I was fond of Inez, but I had seen from the beginning that she was pitiably maladjusted. Like you, she was incapable of facing reality. Like you, she believed that she 'needed' things that do not exist. She demanded a love and loyalty from other people which is never given. She wanted to be 'happy.' You are like her."

Her voice stopped; the dark room was silent. Then in a moment she went on:

"She was in despair because she couldn't 'do anything' for you. She was perfectly convinced that she had been born for the express purpose of 'doing' things for other people. And because her ill-health made that impossible...."

Her strong fingers closed upon the girl's arm.

"Come here!" she said, and led her to the window. "She wrote her name, here, on the sill. It is too dark for you to see it, but her name is here. You see those three pines, standing together? That is where she died."

Diana could only look, with dilated eyes, at those three black trees.

"Here, from this spot where you are standing," said Aunt Emma, "she threw herself out of the window. Because she could not face life as it is."

Her grasp on the girl's arm relaxed.

"Now perhaps you understand," she said, "why I warned you against this room."

"No..." said Diana.

"You're like her," said Aunt Emma. "Too much—like her."

Chapter Thirteen
A WILL IS MADE

Diana remained silent, motionless, infinitely withdrawn from the woman beside her. A measureless sorrow weighed upon her, something beyond the natural grief and pity she must feel at hearing the story of her mother's death. This was bleak, hopeless woe; it was as if she, too, had come to the end of all dear and pleasant things: before her lay the garden, somber, in the dusk; behind her the empty room, haunted by that poor spirit....

"Am I—like that?" she thought. "Not able to face life as it really is...? I've managed to get on—without very much, but I've always thought there was something better round the next corner.... And suppose there isn't? Suppose there's never going to be any more for me—than this?"

Aunt Emma had said the stock was tainted. Was she, too, tainted with some fatal instability, some moral weakness that would leave her always friendless, poor, a failure? She had nothing—and from him who hath not, even that which he hath should be taken....

All the anxieties, the bewildered distress of her childhood, came back upon her now; her school-days, when she had been sent to one little private school after another, always trying to adjust herself, always aware that disastrous changes might come at any moment, never knowing that feeling of security and permanence so vital to a child. And as a young girl, there had been no dances, no pretty clothes, no good times; she had had to be her father's "pal," he had taken her with him where he wanted to go, had lived as it suited him.

Only those months with Angelina had been happy, in spite of the strange and varied duties. She had loved Angelina; she had been alive there, energetic, alert, gaining every day in self-confidence.

But evidently Angelina had not cared at all about her; she had gone off and forgotten Di.

"I don't think anyone could ever care much for me," she thought.

"Now!" said Aunt Emma's voice, startling her in her bitter reverie. "Don't stay in here any longer, Diana."

Di did not answer or move.

"Come!" said Aunt Emma. "For a suggestible mind, the scene of a tragedy is not wholesome. In a room like this: But never mind! Now that I have explained, I think you'll keep your ideas about Uncle Rufus to yourself. He's not legally competent to make a will—but it would be extremely difficult to prove that. There would be only your word against Doctor Coat and Purvis and myself and others. And the word of a hysterical person isn't worth much. No.... He's done as he wanted to do with his money, and it's to your benefit. You need money more than an ordinary person would. You're not capable of earning your own living. You're hysterical and unstable, badly educated and trained."

Di listened to this without protest. Perhaps it was true.... She thought of her mother, who had stood here, where she herself was standing; her mother who had found life too hard, and had put an end to it. Perhaps it had been dark, twilight, as it was now, and when she had died out there, under the pines, perhaps she had seen a sky like this, soft, merciful, with one silver star.... And then had closed her eyes, and drifted away into peace.... Death was beautiful and blessed, and life was so hard.... To close her own eyes and die—like her mother... She raised her eyes to the sky, and sighed....

Then, suddenly and sharply, something awoke in her; something that had brought her gallantly through all her young life. She straightened her shoulders, and sighed again, a long sigh, as if she were waking from a dream.

After all, it didn't matter whether life were hard or not, whether it were lonely and anxious.

"I don't have to be happy," she thought. "I've just got to do the best I can. I'm not down and out yet!"

There was a knock at the door.

"Emma!" said Uncle Peter's voice, apologetically. "There's a taxi-driver here, asking for 'a young lady.' Shall I pay him—?"

"No!" said Di. "He won't go, anyhow. I told him to wait."

"Very well!" said Aunt Emma. "Then you'd better go."

She crossed the room, and opened the door, and Di followed her.

"Please wait a moment, Aunt Emma!" she said. "I want to speak to you."

"Peter, tell the driver she'll be down in a few moments," said Aunt Emma. "Now!"

The door was open and the dim light in the corridor shone into the room. She heard Uncle Peter running down the stairs.

"Well?" asked Aunt Emma.

For a moment Di was silent, struggling with a too rapid flow of thoughts. As if that terrible depression had been actually a dream, she felt a little dazed. It was difficult to come back; to remember all at once....

But she knew now that the blackest hour of her life had passed, and that she had conquered some nameless, formless horror.

"I want to ask you—" she said, "where Mr. Fennel is."

"I'm sorry I can't tell you," Aunt Emma answered. "But no doubt the police will find him before very long."

"No. I don't believe that," said Di, briefly. "Something's happened to him."

"Is this a presentiment?" inquired Aunt Emma. "People of your type are very fond of presentiments and strange, occult feelings. Do you 'just *know*' that something's happened to Fennel?"

"It's not very occult," said Di. "I've got some pretty definite information."

"Then take it to the police," said Aunt Emma. "You'd better do that, anyhow. You'll feel easier. Tell the police that we've murdered Fennel. And Wren, too, isn't it? And that we are now engaged in murdering Uncle Rufus. And any others you feel worried about."

Diana reflected for a moment.

"She let that detective come and search the house. She's not afraid of the police. She feels sure that they can't find out. And what can I really tell them? There's no proof of any crime—anything having happened to Mr. Fennel. Only that letter, and that could be explained. I'm the only one who can find out. I have the upper hand. This is my chance. The taxi is waiting outside."

She chose her words with care.

"Aunt Emma," she said, "if I'm to have Uncle Rufus's money, and you want to share it, I'll have to know about Mr. Fennel."

"You've already promised me a share," said Aunt Emma. "But no doubt you are always able to find satisfactory justification for breaking your word."

Her cool contempt was having its usual effect, sapping the girl's self-confidence, making her feel weak, petty, contemptible.

"All right!" she said to herself, "I don't care! I'm going to see this through, anyhow." And aloud:

"I'll make a bargain with you," she said.

"I'm afraid," said Aunt Emma, "that making a bargain with you is rather uncertain."

"Then you *could* make a bargain?" said Di, quickly. "You *do* know what's happened to him?"

"That's quite intelligent!" said Aunt Emma, in a tone of pleased surprise. "You must be considerably interested in this man, to wake up so."

"I am," said Di.

"And what bargain do you propose?"

"If you'll tell me where he is and what happened to him, I'll sign some sort of paper, giving you a certain sum."

"Unfortunately you haven't a penny."

"When I get it."

"I'm sorry," said Aunt Emma, "but I'm afraid that won't quite do. A very short time ago you were moved by an impulse of gratitude to offer me a share of any money you might get. This gratitude has apparently evaporated now. You are now, as far as I can see, actuated by an infatuation for this man you scarcely know. If this infatuation should—not be requited, you would resent giving me anything. And you would no doubt find excellent reasons for repudiating this 'paper' you are always speaking of. I suppose that idea comes from your father. Probably he signed a good many 'papers' in his time."

"Very likely," said Di. "But I don't quite see..." She paused a moment, then she went on, deliberately. "You said you asked me here so that Uncle Rufus would take a liking to me and leave me his money. But if you can't trust my word, and it's no good signing a paper, how did you expect to get any of it?"

"Really," said Aunt Emma, "you have more intelligence than I gave you credit for."

"I'm just beginning to think..." said Di, half to herself.

It seemed to her of vital importance that she should think, that she should remain quiet and cool, unmoved by the elder woman's scorn, unconfused by the darkness gathering about her. She had no one but herself to depend upon now.

"I'd like to know," she said.

"I had," said Aunt Emma, "three well-considered plans for obtaining a share of that money. One of them has failed. But one of the other two will succeed."

"What is it?"

Aunt Emma did not answer, and looking at her, Di saw by the dim light an expression that horrified her. For those blue eyes were regarding her with a monstrous sort of pity, as one might look at the last struggles of a trapped animal.

"What are—your plans?" she asked.

"We'll leave that for the present," said Aunt Emma; "and discuss this bargain of yours. You wish to know what happened to Fennel. And I'm not at all disposed to tell you. He was a very unwelcome intruder. What's more, if I do tell you, I have no sort of guarantee that you won't go off and never communicate with me again."

"If you won't tell me," said Di, "I'm sure to do that."

"Perhaps it's better so," said Aunt Emma.

Di paid no attention to this fencing.

"What do you want me to agree to?" she asked.

"Whatever you agree to will have to be in public," said Aunt Emma. "Purvis is a lawyer—"

"But you don't want me to go to him and promise to pay you anything?"

"That would be somewhat crude," said Aunt Emma. "Even Purvis would find that peculiar. After all, it's really your affair, to find some way of satisfying my not unreasonable demands without arousing suspicion. I am certainly entitled to some of that money. From any point of view. I am a nearer relation than you of Rufus Leonard. I should use the money in an excellent cause. And it is due to me alone that you are going to get it. I can't make you give me anything, and, apparently, the sole claim I have upon you is my knowledge of this Fennel's whereabouts. Naturally, I shall not relinquish my one advantage without excellent security."

"What do you suggest?"

"It's for you to suggest," said Aunt Emma. "I can think of nothing, except that you might make a will in my favor—"

"A—will? But—"

"Oh, I see the drawbacks to that perfectly well!" said Aunt Emma, with a frown. "In the first place, your Uncle Rufus may live for another five years. And in the second place, there's nothing to prevent you from making another will to-morrow. The only value would be, that you would be making a public declaration of your no doubt excellent intentions. If you were to declare, in the presence of Purvis and Coat that gratitude impelled you to assign me a share of your legacy, you'd hesitate, after that, to refuse me a loan, when you inherit. It's a very poor plan—for me. I hope you can think of a better one."

"I could tell Mr. Purvis that you'd lent money to my parents, and that I considered it my duty—"

"No, thanks!" said Aunt Emma. "That puts me in a very unpleasant light."

Di was silent, thinking this over in her own characteristic way. She was not cautious, not patient; she wanted to learn about Fennel in a hurry, and be gone. She was certain now that he had been sent away by some chicanery. An attempt had been made to discredit him in her eyes, and probably something had been done to make her seem contemptible to him. And she wanted to find him, and explain.

A new thought struck her, a thought that frightened her. Was it likely that Aunt Emma would willingly let her meet Fennel, to compare notes? He was not likely to let matters rest.... No. Aunt Emma must somehow feel herself quite safe from any future interference on the part of Fennel. And what could make her feel safe?

"You *promise* to tell me where he is?" she asked.

"If I don't," said Aunt Emma, "you can very easily destroy any paper you've signed, if my information doesn't suit you."

"That's true," thought Di. "Suppose I do make a will.... She can't very well be planning to murder me. In the first place, as she said, Uncle Rufus is still alive, that Mr. Purvis and Doctor Coat are here, and the driver's waiting. Even if she tells me a lie, there's no harm done. I'll get away at once, and find some of his friends. And if she's lied, I'll destroy the will—make another.... No... I don't see what possible harm it can do, to agree to that now. I want to hear what she has to say about Mr. Fennel."

She glanced up.

"All right!" she said. "I'll make a will. And you promise to tell me, as soon as I've done that?"

"I promise. But it's going to be very awkward for me. Purvis may refuse to draw up a will for you. And if he makes any objections, if he appeals to me, I shall certainly uphold him. I don't intend to appear in the light of a blackmailer, I assure you. You'll have to make your impulse plausible. And you'll have to assure him that I know nothing about it."

"All right!" said Di, again.

"And even when you've done that," said Aunt Emma, "the will won't be worth the paper it's written on. I'm obliged to trust you to deal honorably with me. I'm going to give you information that you can use against me. I admit that there was a certain amount of misrepresentation involved in getting Fennel away. I can count only upon whatever sense of honor you have to prevent any further trouble for me. And also upon your disinclination for a family scandal."

"Misrepresentation..." What had Fennel been told to make him go away?

"I must know," she thought; and aloud: "I'll see Mr. Purvis now—"

"I doubt if you can manage him," said Aunt Emma. But Di, for all her honesty, her carelessness, was not without subtlety. She made up her mind to "manage" Purvis, and to manage quickly. And she did remarkably well. She found Purvis in the lounge, reading, and she went up to him with an air of urgency.

"Mr. Purvis!" she said. "I've got to go back to New York at once, and I don't want to leave this house until I've made a will."

"A will! But my dear young lady—!"

"Please let me!" she said. "Aunt Emma's my nearest relation. And she asked me here when it meant—a lot to me. I'd like to feel that if anything should happen to me—a train accident, or anything—"

"But my dear young lady, at the present time.... Your Uncle Rufus is—is improving—"

"I know," she said. "But you never can tell what might happen. And I'd like to feel, before I go away, that I'd done that."

He began to argue. But Di maintained her attitude of an illogical and impulsive young creature, and that seemed to him perfectly natural. What is more, as the heiress of Rufus Leonard, she had a new importance to him.

And she was assisted by an interruption. There was a knock at the door, and when she ran to open it, the taxi-driver spoke.

"Everything aw' right?" he asked.

"Please keep on waiting!" she said, very low. "Don't go away, please. And if I'm not out in half an hour, please knock again and insist on speaking to me."

"Aw' right!" said he, in a reassuring whisper, and closing the door she turned to Purvis.

"My taxi's waiting!" she said, plaintively. "Please let me just dash off a will, leaving half the money to Aunt Emma. Even if it seems silly—I'd *like* to do it."

Mr. Purvis, like almost everyone else, was rendered nervous by the thought of a taxi-meter steadily ticking up a charge. He urged her to wait, to come to his office the next day and discuss the matter, but he was infected now with her sense of haste.

"I will come to your office," she said. "This is just temporary—just to make my mind easy before I go. Please help me! That meter must be running up terribly!"

Very reluctantly he yielded, and took out his fountain pen.

"Just please say that half of anything I get is to go to Aunt Emma—"

"And the rest—?"

"Oh... I don't know.... To—Mrs. Frick."

"Who is Mrs. Frick?"

"Oh, what does it matter!"

"It does matter," said Purvis. "You don't realize what you're doing in the least. Who is this Mrs. Frick?"

"Oh, don't bother about her. Just say—my heirs and assigns—or whatever they are."

He argued again, and she became more and more obstinate.

"Well!" she said, with a sigh. "If you won't, then I'll have to find some sort of lawyer in the village, on my way to the train. I'm sure I have a legal right to make a will when I want."

"Yes," he said, shocked and distressed. "If you insist upon this—this most irregular and unreasonable proceeding. Your aunt—"

"Please don't tell her!" said Di. "Now!"

He drew up for her a brief will, leaving half of any estate of which she might be possessed to her aunt Emma Leonard, and the remainder to her legal heirs and assigns.

"I'll read it to you—"

"No, thanks, I'm sure it's all right. I'm in such a hurry—"

"I insist upon your reading it," he said, sternly. "You cannot sign a document you have not read."

So she read it, or pretended to read it.

"Now," he said. "We must have two witnesses. I'll get Doctor Coat and your Uncle Peter. And remember, young lady, you are coming to my office tomorrow, to discuss the matter."

As he began to mount the stairs, Di went to the window and looked out, the taxi stood there, its lights shining on the drive.

"Thank God for that taxi-driver!" she thought. "I'm not—cut off."

In a few minutes Mr. Purvis descended again, followed by Uncle Peter, very jaunty, and Doctor Coat.

"State in the presence of these witnesses the nature of the document you are signing," said Mr. Purvis, frigidly.

"This is my last will and testament," said Di.

And as she spoke those words aloud, she began to realize what she was doing. As she took the pen in her hand, it seemed to her that she was about to sign her own death-warrant.

Chapter Fourteen
MILES CONFESSES

Doctor Coat signed, in a neat, small hand, and Uncle Peter added a scrawling, infantile signature.

"Will you keep it for me, please?" she said to Purvis. "Thank you all very much.... Now, I'll just run up to say good-bye...."

She ran up the stairs, and found Aunt Emma in the upper corridor.

"It's done," she said. "Signed and witnessed. Now please tell me—"

"Coat's coming up!" said Aunt Emma. "I don't care to be found talking alone to you just now. Go down in the kitchen and ask Miles. He'll tell you all you want to know."

"I don't want—"

"Then you'll have to wait," said Aunt Emma, and turning on her heel, walked into Uncle Rufus's room just as Doctor Coat's benevolent and stupid face appeared at the head of the stairs.

"I can't wait!" thought Di. "I mustn't be so cowardly about Miles. He can't make any trouble here, with Doctor Coat and Mr. Purvis in the house— and that driver out there. I'll go and ask him anyhow. And if he's—impossible, I'll insist upon Aunt Emma telling me at once. She can't get out of it. I can threaten to tell Mr. Purvis to tear up the will."

But she dreaded the thought of seeing Miles again.

"On the borderline," Aunt Emma had said, and alcoholism would soon send him across it. Was that true? Her father "technically insane," Uncle Rufus a paranoiac, Uncle Peter mentally deficient... all of them...? And she herself?

"I won't think about that now," she said to herself.

But she had thought of it, and the horrible shadow would not leave her. She went down the stairs and into the lounge, where Purvis and Uncle Peter stood talking together; she went past them without a word and into the dining-room that was in complete darkness.

"My last will and testament...."

"What have I done?" she asked herself, stopping halfway across the room. "I wish... I hadn't...."

But even here, through the window, she could see the lights of the waiting taxi, her link with the world outside. She went on, resolutely, pushed open the swing-door, went through the pantry and into the kitchen.

Miles was sitting on the edge of the table, smoking. He glanced at her as she entered, but he did not speak or move. He was white as chalk, and on his handsome, wasted face was a queer, blank look.

"Miles!" she said, in as matter-of-fact a way as she could manage.

But he did not answer.

"Miles," she said again. "Please tell me what happened to Mr. Fennel—"

He sprang to his feet, stood looking at her with dilated eyes.

"Aunt Emma said you'd tell me—" she went on, unsteadily.

Still he did not speak; she looked at him, and was appalled by the expression on his face.

Then suddenly anger flamed up in her.

"Miles!" she cried. "Stop—staring like that! Miles! Can't you talk like a human being...? I—I'm sick and tired of all this.... Where's Mr. Fennel?"

"He's in hell!" shouted Miles.

She caught him by the arm and tried to shake him.

"Tell me!" she said. "I *will* know!"

"You'll never see *him* again," said Miles, with a laugh.

That laugh brought her to her senses. This was not the way to handle Miles. Her hand dropped from his arm; she drew a long breath and began, in a friendly, easy tone.

"Please tell me all about it, Miles. Aunt Emma told me to come and ask you."

"I can't!" he groaned.

"Yes, you can, Miles!"

He flung himself into a chair, and covered his eyes with his arm, a childish and pitiable gesture.

"Oh, Di!" he said. "Oh, Di!"

She laid her hand on his shoulder.

"Come on, Miles!" she said, encouragingly.

Evidently he was filled with remorse for whatever part he had played in this affair, and she was sorry for him. But no doubt he was exaggerating as usual; she would have to sift out the truth from his words.

"I didn't think—I *could* do *that*," he said, still with his eyes covered. "I didn't mean to.... But it was because I love you so.... She promised to help me. She said you'd marry me. And you would have loved me, if he hadn't come. You liked me at first. If he hadn't come...."

He let his arm fall, and looked up at her, with a sort of anguished bewilderment.

"That night when we cooked the dinner together, Di.... That was the happiest hour I ever had in my life.... Then when you went upstairs to dress, she told me she'd heard you promise to meet that fellow at nine o'clock, in the clearing.... She said I could stop it. She told me she'd keep you in the house as long as possible, and I could meet him. I was to tell him that you and I were secretly married and ask him to lend us enough money to get away, and ask him to clear out for a few days—for your sake—so that no one could question him. She said that would disgust him with the whole show, and that if he thought *you* were mixed up in everything he'd simply drop it—anyhow, until you'd had a chance to get away.... But when she couldn't keep you in the house—when you ran out like that, Di, I—couldn't stand it. To see you, hell-bent on meeting another man.... I went after you. I only meant to stop you.... But I missed you, in the dark. I couldn't find you.... I went to the clearing, and I saw him standing there... He had heard me coming.... I found I had Uncle Rufus's loaded stick in my hand. I don't remember taking it. I swear I had no idea of—of *that*—when I left the house.... But when I saw him.... Di, I didn't mean to do that! I swear I didn't!"

Her hand had fallen from his shoulder; she was leaning against the table, looking and looking at him.

"What—was it—that you did?" she asked.

"I only struck once, Di I swear it...! And then I heard someone coming down the hillside, and I dragged him back, among the trees. It was you...! Oh, God, Di! You called him! You sat down there—and waited for him—you called him again.... And he was lying there, not ten yards from you... all the time..."

She stood as if frozen with horror. He was still speaking, but she could not hear.

"Lying there..." she thought. "When I called to him.... Dead—*murdered*...."

Suddenly she caught Miles's sleeve.

"Miles!" she said. "No.... Miles, perhaps it's not true.... Miles, you're not—*sure...?*"

"I wish to God I wasn't!" he said. "After you'd gone, I tried.... But he—was gone...."

"Gone?" she echoed, catching at any straw. "You mean disappeared?"

"No!" he said. "Disappeared...? No. He lay there. I didn't know what to do with—it... I thought—I'd go mad.... I dragged him along—and pushed him into the old quarry... And later.... I went back again—and called him...." His hand covered hers that lay on his sleeve. "That's why I wanted to kill myself," he said. "But now—I don't care. They're sure to find him. I don't care. I'm ready—to go."

"No, Miles—" she protested, almost mechanically.

"I am, Di," he said. "I'll be glad to finish."

He rose, stood looking down at the ground, with a look somber and austere.

"She's told me, often enough, that I'm not to be trusted. And it's true. I've never done anything but harm. I never could. I'm ready for the police, whenever they come...."

"Aunt Emma will help you," she said, with the same mechanical kindness.

"She doesn't know what I've done. I'm not going to tell her. She'd get me out of it. There'd be more lies and lies and lies.... And there's nothing ahead for me, Di. I've been thinking over—everything. My whole life.... I've always done what she wanted. She was the only one who did anything for me. My father never had any money. She sent me to school and to college. I suppose she was good to me. But she always told me what a weak, good-fornothing devil I was.... It didn't help much.... But she was right.... Di, there in the wood, something—happened to me—something sprang up inside me... I'm not fit to live.",

There was no instinct for revenge in the girl, no impulse to retaliate. The death of this wasted, broken boy could in no way compensate for the life he had taken; it could give her no possible satisfaction to see him punished. But she could not pity him. Not now. She was thinking of Fennel.

It seemed to her the greatest misfortune possible that she was never to know him better, never to see him again. It seemed to her as if the vital, the significant part of her own life had ended with him.

"He came to meet me," she thought. "If it hadn't been for me, he would be alive now."

Miles was still talking, but she did not listen. Nothing mattered at all now; there was no object, no motive left. She could not care what she did, or what happened to her. She wanted to get away, alone and think.

"Well.... Good-by, Miles!" she said, with a polite little smile.

She was not even aware that she had interrupted him in the middle of a speech.

"Di..." he cried. "Where are you going?"

"I'm just going back to New York, Miles. I'm—tired."

"You're going to *leave* me, Di?"

"Miles," she said, with a sort of despair. "I've got to go. I—can't stand any more." As she turned away, the swing-door was pushed open, and Mr. Purvis entered.

"This taxi-driver insists upon speaking to you," he said, severely.

"I'll come—" she answered, and followed him into the lounge, where she found the driver standing with his back to the door.

"I'm coming," she told him, with that same polite little smile, and went toward the door.

"But—your bag?" he said.

"I don't care. I'll send for it later," she said.

"My dear young lady!" protested Purvis. "Surely you're going to say good-by to your uncle?"

Again she had forgotten Uncle Rufus. She was very reluctant to leave him like this, yet it seemed to her certain that if she went up those stairs, she would not easily come down again. She had her chance now to get away and she must take it.

"I'm coming back very soon," she said, and, indifferent to Purvis's shocked face, she followed the driver out of that accursed house. The Spring night was cool and fresh, she drew a deep breath.

"When I've had time to think," she said to herself, "I'll find some way to get him away from there. But I can't think just now."

The driver opened the door of the cab; she had her foot on the step, when a window on the floor above was opened and Doctor Coat's voice called, in a tone of severe indignation:

"Miss Diana! One moment, if you please! Your uncle wishes to speak to you for a moment!"

She began to cry. Fatigued and miserable tears, like a child.

"I—can't!" she called back.

But Doctor Coat had closed the window and retired, and she knew she had to go.

"Well, shall I keep on waiting?" asked the driver.

"Yes," she said, and once more entered that house. After all, Doctor Coat was upstairs, Mr. Purvis was in the lounge, the driver was waiting. Nothing could happen to her. And in any case, she could not refuse to hear what the old man had to say.

Once more she mounted those stairs to the dimly-lit corridor above, and went to Uncle Rufus's room.

But Doctor Coat was not there; the room was empty except for the old man lying on the bed with his face to the wall in the almost dark room. She went over to the bed.

"Uncle Rufus!" she said, softly.

He turned his head; she had a glimpse of something in his eyes that made her cry out. Then a hand pressed over her mouth, her wrists were caught behind her back. She struggled in vain, her wrists were tied, and her ankles; the hand over her mouth was supplanted in a flash by a handkerchief; she was jerked backward, someone lifted her feet, someone else her head.

It was Aunt Emma who held her bound ankles. She looked straight into those blue eyes. Then she was carried into the next room, laid on the bed; she saw Aunt Emma and Uncle Peter go out; she heard the key turn in the lock.

"The driver won't go away," she thought. "I must keep my head. I mustn't...."

She felt the world slipping away from her, there was a roaring in her head, a swirling blackness before her eyes. It seemed to her that the handkerchief over her mouth was smothering her; she tried to raise her bound hands, and fainted.

■ ■ ■

Mrs. Frick.... Someone was speaking of Mrs. Frick. She tried to call out, and realized that she was gagged. It was Aunt Emma speaking in the corridor outside.

"No. I don't know who this Mrs. Frick is. But if—she's a friend of the poor child's...."

"Well, then..." said Mr. Purvis's voice. "I'd better tell that chauffeur, eh? Tell him to communicate with this Mrs. Frick? Apparently she gave him the address."

"Yes," said Aunt Emma, with a sigh. "He'd better advise Mrs. Frick to come out here to-morrow and see the poor child. It's a little beyond me. I've knocked and knocked on her door, but she refuses to answer."

Doctor Coat's voice intervened.

"You don't think, Emma...? We ought to—er—force an entrance?"

"No..." said Aunt Emma, with hesitation. "I'm afraid that would make her worse... An hysterical condition like hers is only intensified by attention. It seems to me, Matthew, that if she's let alone, she'll come to her senses more quickly. But if you advise—"

"No," he said. "No, I agree with you, Emma. No.... Most unfortunate...."

"I noticed," said Purvis's voice, "that she was distraught. As to that fantastic idea of making a will..."

"I'm sorry you humored her," said Aunt Emma gravely.

"Yes," said Doctor Coat, in the same grave tone. "A mistake, Purvis. She has this notion that she's responsible for her uncle's illness.... Of course, in a way, she is. If she hadn't run off like that to meet this man...."

"Fortunately," said Aunt Emma, "Rufus seems to be doing very well. But it's quite possible, of course, that he may take a turn for the worse. And if he should, I'm afraid it would completely unbalance her.... She'd believe she had practically killed him. I can only hope that this Mrs. Frick will take her away."

"You don't consider her... er—?" said Doctor Coat.

"Insane?" said Aunt Emma. "Not at all. She is uneducated, impressionable, childish. But no more insane than nine people out of ten. Her father encouraged her to believe in her own importance. She's capable of the most irrational actions, due to her faulty training and her lack of reasoning ability.... If I had time and opportunity, I believe I could do a good deal with her. She's attracted to me—as you've noticed. But I have my hands full, just now. I shall be glad if this friend, this Mrs. Frick—will come and take her away to-morrow."

"Well!" said Purvis. "We'd better be going now, Emma. You'll let us know, of course, if poor Rufus is worse...? I'll explain to the driver then, that he's to notify Mrs. Frick, as she told him to do.... Very unfortunate."

"Yes," Aunt Emma agreed. "But to-morrow morning when she finds her uncle improved, she may be more reasonable. Good-night, Matthew! Good-night, Sam!"

In desperation, in a passion of helpless anger, Di had struggled to call out, to make any sort of sound that would attract their attention. And, as she heard their answered "Good-night, Emma!" she deliberately rolled off the bed on to the floor, with a thud that made her dizzy.

"What's that?" asked Purvis.

"The children," said Aunt Emma. "They're in that room."

The faint squeaking of someone's shoes died away. For a few minutes there was absolute silence. Then Di heard voices below, in the driveway; the engine started, the door of the cab slammed, the tires crunched over the gravel. They were gone.

She had thought that nothing mattered, that she did not care what happened. But it was not so. Every valiant and healthy impulse of her soul rose in revolt against this ignominy, this defeat. She lay still, gathering her strength.

"Everything's come out just as she wanted it," she thought. "I've made my will. I've played into her hands perfectly.... Now she thinks she'll get rid of me. She has some plan all made, of course.... Well, it won't succeed! I'll do something. I'll find some way...."

She had read stories and seen pictures of people who escaped from bonds like hers, who freed themselves from more urgent dangers than this. And she tried; she tried to narrow one hand so that it would slip out of the bandage that held her wrists; tried to move her ankles. But she had never realized before how it hurt to have one's hands tied behind the back, or the pain of a gag. And worse than anything were the tides of panic fear that threatened her again and again, in this utter helplessness. She could not make a sound; she could not even sit up; her struggles had no other effect than to leave her panting, desperate, with a cold sweat on her forehead. She lay quiet again, in the dark room.

And then an appalling thought struck her.

If Aunt Emma were to profit by that will, not only must she herself die, but Uncle Rufus must die first. That will had condemned him to death, as surely as if she had sent a bullet through his head; perhaps even at this moment—

She remembered the utter terror she had seen in his eyes. First Fennel, and then this forlorn and helpless old man, both to die because she had made fatal errors....

She strained her ears, to catch any sound from that next room, and once more that panic desperation assailed her; she tugged wildly at her bonds, made strange stifled sounds that frightened her.

She did not know whether hours or minutes went by. There were periods when she was scarcely conscious, and other times when she reflected, with a cool, impersonal lucidity.

"If Aunt Emma's going to let Mrs. Frick come out here to-morrow, that means that she'll be ready for her. She couldn't possibly afford to let me talk to Mrs. Frick. She can't afford to let me go—after this. She doesn't mean to let me go.... There's no one to help me. She can make Miles think and act as she pleases. Mr. Fennel's—gone.... Wren's gone. Mr. Purvis and Doctor Coat will believe what she tells them. The taxi-driver's doing just what I told him to do—notifying Mrs. Frick. I've got to help myself."

But how?

"I don't know," she said to herself. "But I won't give up. I shan't struggle any more. I'll save my strength. I'll try not to think of what's happened...."

She made a gallant effort to remember poems she had learnt in school, to fill her mind with fine and beautiful thoughts. But while she repeated lines to herself, horrible images came into her mind: Uncle Rufus in his terror, Fennel at the bottom of that old quarry. Fennel, above all. She could see him so clearly, could recall the tones of his voice, his vivid smile.

The door opened, and a sturdy white figure stood before her, outlined against the dim light in the hall. She paused a moment, and then entering the room, screwed a bulb into the electric light socket and turned on the switch, closed and locked the door, and kneeling beside the girl, untied her hands.

Di gave a smothered scream of pain as her arms dropped to her sides and the blood began to circulate. Aunt Emma untied the twisted handkerchief that had cut so cruelly into the corners of her mouth, and that done, sat down on the edge of the bed.

"My God!" she said, with a sigh.

Her face looked drawn with weariness, its fresh color vanished; she sat staring at the ground.

"Miles has told me," she said. "What folly! What criminal folly! All my plans ruined...."

Di sat down in a chair, and tried with numb, clumsy fingers to untie her ankles.

"Everything ruined...!" Aunt Emma went on. "And I'm dragged, against my will, into a dangerous and repugnant course.... I never forsaw this...." She sighed again. "It's too late now," she said. "I'm sorry."

"Uncle Rufus—?" asked Di, with dry, stiff lips.

"He doesn't really matter," said Aunt Emma. "It's you I'm thinking of. It's you I'm sorry for."

Her ankles freed, Di looked up, into that tired, middle-aged face, framed in gray hair. This could not be a criminal, a monster of duplicity and evil....

"Then—if you're sorry—" she began.

"I've never disliked you," Aunt Emma went on, indifferent to her words. "I hoped at first that you'd marry Miles. That was my first plan. That would have kept the money in my control. And it would have been a very good thing for him. But that failed. And now that you know what he's done... That's the end, of course."

"What—do you mean?" asked Di.

"Why, that you can't live," said Aunt Emma, sighing again. "And I'm sorry."

"Do you mean," asked Di, "that you're going to try to murder me?"

"There's nothing else I can do," said Aunt Emma.

They both spoke in ordinary, normal tones, sitting in that commonplace hotel bedroom, filled with the garish light of the unshaded bulb.

"You can't expect not to be found out," said Di. "Mrs. Frick will make inquiries. Even Doctor Coat and Mr. Purvis will ask questions."

"I think I've planned it pretty well," said Aunt Emma. "But I didn't come here out of mere wanton cruelty—to gloat over you, and so on. I'm really very sorry. Only, it's a question of my safety, the opportunity to go on with my work, against your life; and naturally.... The idea of killing you is horrible to me. And no doubt to you, also," she added, politely. "I thought—I hope you'll take the way I shall suggest. It is as your mother did. It will look quite natural to outsiders. Coat and Purvis believe that you were filled with remorse for your uncle's condition. They'll see that when you heard of his death—"

"His death...?"

"You committed suicide," Aunt Emma went on. "I give you my word to make it as easy as possible for you. The ground out there slopes down pretty sharply. The chances are that it will be a fatal fall. But if it isn't, if you're injured and in pain, I'll attend to you immediately. I'll see that you don't suffer at all."

"And if I don't do that?"

"Well, you'll have to go out of that window," said Aunt Emma. "If you won't do it voluntarily there'll have to be a very unpleasant struggle." She rose. "Think it over!" she said. "Think of your mother in this room. She found that life wasn't worth living. And it isn't for you, either. You're ineffectual, incompetent. You're of no value to anyone. There's nothing ahead of you but a lifetime of poorly paid work."

She unscrewed the bulb and put it in her pocket. Di made a rush for the door, but it shut in her face, and the key turned outside.

Chapter Fifteen
A WHITE FIGURE

She was free to move about now; to call for help if she wished; she was left quite undisturbed to make what plans she could for her escape.

And she could make none. It occurred to her to knock on the wall of Uncle Rufus's room, but she decided against it. It would either frighten the old man still more, or wake in him hopes that she saw no way to realize. Or perhaps he could no longer hear anything....

She would have done anything possible to help him, but she could think of nothing. There had been, in that talk with her aunt, something that robbed her of the last hope. Her death had been arranged in so cool and matter-of-fact a way; she herself was so utterly negligible; there was nothing in her aunt to which she could appeal.

If this were to be her last hour, she meant it to be a good one, undaunted by fear and weakness. She faced her danger with courage and dignity. She thought of all the happy moments she had had, of all the people who had been kind to her, with a regret that was almost impersonal. It seemed to her that the past was already immeasurably remote. She thought, above all, of Fennel.

Then her mind turned to her childhood, and she tried to remember her mother. Here, in this room, her mother had battled with despair and anguish, and had lost. The room seemed filled with that tragic presence. In the darkness, the daughter tried to recapture some childish memory of that face, that voice; she wanted to feel near to her mother. She wanted to understand how her mother could, of her own free will, have left her child.

Was it because, after all, life was not worth living?

"If she could come back, just for a moment," she thought. "If she could tell me why she wanted to die—and what she found—on the other side.... How could she bear to leave me?"

Aunt Emma had said that some strange and disturbing thing lingered here.... If only she could pierce the veil, could come closer to that presence....

"Mother..." she said, half-aloud.

She had no one else to love. It seemed to her that if her mother would draw near to her, and she could go—with her.... It would be good to go....

Why not? Why wait for a horrible and futile struggle? Did not the very walls of this room whisper to her—"Life is cruel, and death is peace"— Why not go to her mother...?

She rose, and crossed the room to the open window. Here, on this very spot, her mother had last stood.... Out there—

An awful fear choked her; her heart seemed to stop. For there, at the foot of the dark pines, lay a white figure.

"Mother!" she said, inaudibly.

Her mother had come back, to show her the way. One instant, and she could lie there too—

"Miss Leonard!" said a voice behind her.

She turned, to see a figure standing there in the dark. Another ghost.... She opened her mouth to scream, but no sound came.

"Steady!" said the voice. "Steady, dear girl!" His arm was about her shoulders, and she clutched his coat frantically.

"How can you come!" she whispered. "You were dead, too."

"Never was less so," he answered. "But come now. Let's get away."

"How—could you come?"

"I found the kitchen door open, and I saw the back stairs, and came up them. I didn't know where you'd be, or whether I'd be—welcome. But I saw this door locked, with the key outside. Didn't want to knock, you see, so I walked in."

"He said—he killed you."

"His mistake, whoever he was. I was knocked out for a while. Then I found myself lying in a quarry, and I got up and came out. I went to a doctor—but I only told him I'd been in an accident. I haven't told the police or anyone. I wanted to see you first. I'd have come before, but—I was a little—bothered by that whack I got. Now let's clear out."

"No! We can't leave Uncle Rufus without—"

"Uncle Rufus!" he repeated. "But look here! You needn't worry about *him.*"

"I do! You don't know—"

"I know one thing," he said. "The poor old fellow was dead when we carried him in—"

"No! He's—there—in the next room...."

"He's dead," said Fennel. "I'm sorry if I'm—blunt, but—"

"Come and see!" she cried. "If it's not too late."

"Wait a minute! I—you see, I don't exactly understand what's going on here. And I'm sure you don't. That's why I didn't call in any outside help. I wanted to know first how much you're—involved in this."

"I don't know exactly what you mean."

"I mean," he said, "have you promised to conceal anything—given any sort of help—done anything that could get you in trouble with the law?"

"I—don't know," she said, doubtfully. "I don't think I have."

"Good!" he said, "Then we don't care how much of a row we raise, do we?"

"But if I had—?" she asked.

"Then I'd have had to get you away quietly."

"But did you think I might have done something—wrong?"

"No," he said, "Nothing wrong, and nothing silly. But you might have made a mistake. And there's something going on here. When we carried the poor old fellow in, I saw that he was dead. But your aunt behaved as if he were alive. That's why I wanted to see you that evening. I wanted to tell you, and get you out of the way before the big break. Now it's too late. Now you'll have to be mixed up in it."

"I did do one thing. I made a will. You see, Uncle Rufus had left his money to me, and I made a will leaving half of it to Aunt Emma."

"How did she work that?"

Di hesitated a moment.

"I wanted to find out what had happened to you. We made a bargain—"

"I see!" he said, and was silent for a moment. Then he took his arm from about her shoulders and moved away a little.

Everything he did was right, every action, every word of his was perfectly clear to her; she knew how he felt about things; she knew that he understood her. His quiet acceptance of the situation had steadied her, made her feel resolute and safe.

"The trouble is," he said, "that there are three men here, and my wrist's broken—"

"Oh!" she cried.

"It'll mend. But we'll have to manage carefully. Somehow we ought to get a look at the man in the next room. I want you to be able to swear that he's not your uncle.... I'll just take a cautious survey."

He went over to the door, but he did not open it. She came to his side.

"I *was* a fool!" he said. "When I unlocked the door, I left the key there. And now we're locked in."

For a moment they were silent.

"What about the window?" he said. "You were looking out when I came in—"

"Oh, it was horrible!" she cried. "I thought I saw something.... I was nervous...."

They went together to the window—and it was still there, that white figure.

"Do you—see it?" she whispered.

"Yes," he said.

"I thought—it was my mother. She died like that. She—fell from this very window....."

He reached for her hand and held it.

"No way to get out of here," he said. "Can you shoot?"

"Shoot?"

"I have an automatic, but I can't do much with my left hand."

"I never even saw one, except in the movies," she said. "And I'm afraid— I *couldn't* shoot anyone—even if I knew how."

"Of course you couldn't," he said. "I was only thinking of shooting the lock, so that we could get out."

"I'll try it."

"I'm afraid it would—"

Something fell past them, something like a great white bird and struck the ground with a terrible thud, and did not move.

And from the next room came a scream.

"My child! You've killed my child...! Let me go...! My child...."

"It's Wren!" cried Di.

"Stand here!" said Fennel. "You can see the white doorknob. Stand close—there. Aim just below the knob. Pull the trigger."

The noise dazed her. And in the next room that wild voice was still shouting; some article of furniture was overturned with a crash.

"Try again!" said Fennel's quiet voice beside her. "Not so high."

Again a stab of flame and the crash of the shot, and the splintering of wood.

"Too low!" said Fennel. "Now! This time you'll do it."

She aimed with desperate care, tried to steady her shaking hand. Her finger was on the trigger, when there came a yell from the next room.

"Help! Help! Murder!"

The shot went wild.

"Last bullet," said Fennel. "Never mind, dear. You've splintered the wood. I'll see if I can kick through that panel."

"Help!" yelled that voice.

"We're coming, Wren!" she called, with all her strength.

Fennel gave the door a well-directed kick; a second. Then another shot sounded, there was a cracking, tearing sound, and Fennel collapsed on the floor.

"What happened?" she cried. "Oh, what's the *matter?*"

"Stand away from that door!" he shouted.

But she was on her knees beside him. She spoke to him, but he did not answer. All noise had ceased in the next room, all noise everywhere had ceased; there was a silence that seemed to ring in her ears.

"James!" she said.

"Yes?" he answered, in his ordinary, composed voice.

"What's happened to you?"

"I got a bullet in the leg," he said. "Through the door."

She was passionately determined to be as quiet, as cool as he; she *must not* disappoint him.

"What can I do for you?" she asked.

For answer he laid his head back against her shoulder, and she began to stroke his forehead.

Outside the pines stirred in the breeze, and far away a dog barked and a motor horn sounded.

"I must get him to a doctor," she thought.

They were locked in this room. And God knows who or what was in the corridor outside. Even if she could get out, how was she to leave him alone in this horrible house while she went for help? He might be bleeding to death, dying here, now, with his head against her shoulder. No one knew they were here. No one would come.

"James," she said, "can you move?"

"I—can," he answered, "but—I don't care much about moving—just now...."

"I'll bring the chair for you to lean against," she said. "I want to look around."

She pushed the chair so that he was propped up against it, and then she stood behind, in the dark, and tried to think. Other people had escaped from situations like this.... She could not make a rope of sheets, to lower herself from the window, for there was only a mattress on the bed.

"If I threw out the mattress," she thought, "and then jumped.... If I missed it, if I hurt myself, he'd be worse off than ever. Perhaps I can kick the door panel in..."

She had an unconquerable aversion to making any more noise. But it must be tried. She had started forward, when a sound outside made her jump. Was it possible...? She went to the window; her glance fell indifferently upon the two white figures that lay there; she strained her ears to catch that sound again.

No doubt about it; a car was coming up the hill.

"This way, please!" she called. "*Please* come here! Please come here! This way! I need help! Please—!"

Her light young voice seemed to float off on the breeze; there was no answer. Now she could see the glare of the headlights as the car turned the corner.

"Please come here!" she cried, desperately. "This way!"

"My darling child!" called back a strong, beautiful voice. "What *are* you doing?"

"Angelina!" she cried. "Don't go away!"

The car had stopped and Angelina sprang out, and ran along the path. She stopped suddenly, and bent over the white figure lying there.

"What's this?" she cried.

"Angelina! Get in somehow—"

A man had got out of the car, and stood beside Angelina, looking up at the window.

"Come in!" cried Di, in a fury of impatience. "There's someone hurt here. I'm locked in. Hurry up!"

They both disappeared round the corner of the house, and for a long time she heard nothing.

"James!" she said. "Could anything happen to them...?"

"Nothing can happen to Angelina," he said.

Then she heard voices outside, Angelina's voice. The key turned in the lock, the door was flung open, the light of an electric torch shone in her face.

"James is hurt," she said, in a quiet, dignified voice.

And that was the end of her strength.

Chapter Sixteen
"IT'S OVER"

She opened her eyes to look into the face of Doctor Coat, who was bending over her. She stared up at him in wonder; he gazed back at her with an expression so unutterably woebegone that her heart sank.

"James...?" she asked.

"The young man? Doing very nicely," he answered. "And how are *you* feeling now?"

She forgot to answer him. She was looking about the shabby little old-fashioned room where she lay on a sofa; the chairs ranged against the walls, the ancient magazines upon the center table, evidently Doctor Coat's waiting-room. Then at last she was really out of that house....

"What happened?" she asked.

But Doctor Coat turned away his head.

"Oh, please tell me!" she cried, alarmed, and, as he turned back to her, she saw tears in his eyes.

"I have known Emma since she was a child," he said. "I can scarcely grasp this... I... find this... very hard... to credit...."

She was sorry for him, but, in her anxiety, she could not spare him.

"Please tell me about Wren!" she said.

"Now, my dear Miss Diana!" he said, with a pitiable attempt at professional cheerfulness, "put off your questions until you've had a good rest. Tomorrow—"

"I can't wait—a minute! It'll make me much worse, not to know. Is Wren—?"

"It's horrible!" he cried. "Unbelievable! A holocaust...."

He began to pace up and down his shabby, brightly lit little room, intolerably stirred, filled with bewilderment and grief.

"Three dead!" he said.

"Who? Oh, if you'd just please tell me! Can't you see...?"

"Yes, I can," he said. "Only, it's so difficult.... I haven't quite grasped it yet.... They sent a chauffeur for me, and I went.... I hadn't been warned in any way. I thought of course it was Emma who had sent for me.... I went to Rufus's room—and I found Wren there, dying from the effect of a murderous assault made upon him; he said by Peter Leonard.... By Peter Leonard.... Even then I didn't understand. I looked about the room for Emma and there was no one present but this chauffeur in uniform. He heard Wren's last statement...

"No one will ever believe us—Purvis and me. In court—we shall appear—either fools—or knaves.... But it isn't hard to deceive people who

are utterly unsuspicious. No doubt I am very much to blame. I never examined the patient. I saw him only in a darkened room, heavily muffled. But
he had always had that peculiar habit of muffling himself. If there was
anything strange about his voice or manner, I attributed it to his illness....
I—I *couldn't* have suspected that Rufus was dead, buried in the cellar, with
no more ceremony than a dog, and that the man I had seen in his place
was Wren. It's the sort of thing that—doesn't occur to anyone.... He had
had similar attacks and Emma understood the treatment of them....

"When Emma told me he wanted to make a will in your favor, I was
pleased. I was always fond of your mother—"

"Did you know how she died?" the girl interrupted.

"Why, yes, my dear. Typhoid."

"What makes you think that?"

He looked at her in surprise.

"I saw her the week before—the end. She was in the hospital then, and
on the road to recovery, we all believed. Then she had a relapse—Don't
cry! Don't cry, my dear!"

He drew a chair up beside the sofa, and sitting down, patted her shoulder.

"Don't cry!" he said. "It was a very happy end. She always had the greatest confidence in your father. She was sure he was going to make a fortune
for you. A happy life, my dear, and a happy death."

She could not stop weeping; tears were streaming down her face; she
groped for a handkerchief, and he gave her one of his own.

"You're *sure?*" she asked.

"Absolutely! Come, come!"

"Just don't pay any attention to *this,*" she said. "Go on telling me...."

"I've sent for Purvis," he went on. "It will be a terrible blow for him....
Rufus, or the man we thought was Rufus, was apparently too weak to talk.
Purvis drew up the will in the form Emma said he wanted. He had not
enough strength to sign his name, but he made his mark which we both
witnessed.... How could we suspect anything wrong? Emma did not benefit in any way; she was not even mentioned in the will. And later on,
when you insisted upon making a will in her favor, we saw nothing amiss.
We thought you were grateful to her, and perhaps a little—overwrought....
Why did you make that will?"

"I'll tell you later. Please go on!"

"Wren was able to tell us only the main facts of this—this imposture.
Emma had forced him into it by threatening to send his child to an institution. He said he agreed.... He had rebelled against helping to bury poor
Rufus, and in the end had had a physical encounter with Peter in which
Peter had badly wounded his foot with a spade. I saw that wound... Emma
told him that if he would impersonate Rufus for a few days, until the will
was made, he would then pretend to recover and could start to return to

Rufus's place in New York, and could disappear on the way. He believed her—then, and he had been promised a large reward. He had planned to take his child to some doctor he had heard of in Switzerland. But he was well aware that his life was in danger. He felt that as long as you were in the house, they would not dare to make away with him. He had the highest opinion of your courage and intelligence—the greatest faith in your kindness. The fact that he was making a will in your favor was a great comfort to him. They had told him that he would be allowed to leave today. A number of persons, yourself and Purvis and I among them, would have seen him take the train to New York, with his cap and muffler and so on. Then in the waiting-room at the Grand Central, he would have removed the disguise. And in order that nothing should happen to you, when you got this money, he had written you a letter, explaining everything. He was very anxious that you should enjoy this fortune. But unluckily, Emma found that letter....

"I don't know whether in any case he would have been allowed to leave the house. I—am afraid not. I am afraid that I should have signed a death certificate without any proper examination.... And looking back upon it now, I think.... But that's too horrible!"

"You mean I was to die, too?"

"She told Purvis and myself that you were brooding over your responsibility for your uncle's attack of illness, and that she found you had suicidal tendencies.... I *cannot* credit this...! I have known Emma since she was a child...."

"She's gone?"

"She and Peter."

"But Miles?"

"We found Miles—dead—in the dining-room. He had shot himself."

"Oh," she cried. "If he'd only known!"

"Known what?"

"He thought that he had done some—committed a dreadful crime—but he hadn't. If I could have told him!"

"His troubles are over, my dear," said Coat, and was silent for a moment. Then he went on:

"Perhaps the most shocking part of this whole terrible affair—to me—was the part played by those unfortunate children... I have never particularly interested myself in mental cases, and I took it for granted that Emma was giving them the best possible treatment. She was not. She had made no effort whatever to ameliorate their condition. She used them, in the most callous and unethical way, for her experiments. I don't mean that they were physically ill-used. Simply, she took advantage of their misfortune for her own ends. She withheld any treatment that might have helped them. Wren told me this. I don't know how he came to suspect it—"

"One of the children was his?"

"Yes. Emma had come across the child, and had offered to adopt it and give it proper care and treatment. And the wretched man had acted as an unpaid servant for years, in the belief that he was benefitting his child. Your friend did a very beautiful thing."

"What friend—did what?"

"Mrs. Blessington. He wished to see the body of his child. And found it was not his child, but the other one. And Mrs. Blessington made him a solemn promise that she would look after his daughter, would take her to the best specialists, would do everything humanly possible. It was the greatest possible comfort to him in his last moments."

"That's like her," said Di. "And the other poor little thing was dead?"

"That disaster is inexplicable to me. Near where the child fell, we found a peculiar object, a sort of dummy in a white dress.... Fennel thinks that the child saw this from the upper window, and in some way was influenced by the suggestion. But I don't know.... Perhaps at the inquest...."

He rose hastily, and crossed the room, stood by the window with his back to her.

"I can't tell you—" he said, unsteadily, "how sorry I am that you will have to be dragged into this—horrible thing. The innocent to suffer for the guilty... But there is no escape for you—or for any of us. The publicity will be merciless.... I only hope to Heaven that Emma will not be found and brought back. I—should find it—very painful to appear as a witness—against my old friend.... As it is, we shall come out badly, Purvis and I...."

She lay still, thinking of that. It was not over; she had not escaped. Every detail of this monstrous crime, every smallest action of her own, would be made public. She would be an important witness in an incredibly sensational case, she would be examined, cross-examined, re-examined, all her words would be printed in the newspapers, she would have to endure the most hateful and shameful publicity. All her life, people would remember—"Yes—the one who was mixed up in that murder case." It seemed to her that, when she had crossed the threshold of that house, she had left normal, cheerful life behind her forever. That shadow could never lift.

"And now—how are you feeling?" asked Doctor Coat. "The effects of such a shock—"

To his surprise, she rose to her feet.

"I feel perfectly all right," she answered. "What ought I to do? Tell the police?"

"Fennel has looked after that."

"I've dragged *him* into it," she thought. "He's not only been wounded—twice—but he'll have to be a witness, too."

She tried to consider what to do now. In the circumstances, it wouldn't be fair to go to Mrs. Frick's. Reporters would come, and the police.... Hadn't she read of "material witnesses being kept in prison"? She didn't care. If she were not in prison, what could she do? It would be impossible to get a job now.... She would be a notorious character. She might even be suspected of complicity.

"Mrs. Blessington waited to take you back to New York," Doctor Coat continued, "but I said I feared you couldn't stand the journey. However, you seem so much better than I expected—shall I call her in?"

"She's here?"

"Waiting in the next room. I should be glad to see you go with her. A very kind and generous woman...."

He opened the door into another room, and Angelina hastened in; she was pale, but radiant as usual.

"My dearest Di!" she cried. "Put some powder on your precious nose and let's get going!"

"Will I be allowed to go? I mean—the police—?"

"My dear, James can do *anything* with the police."

"Did you know him well, Angelina?"

"But my dear! He's my *brother!* You *must* have heard me talking about 'Jammy.' He's a marvelous person. He's written books, my dear, about reptiles. And he's just come back from a trip up the Amazon, looking for boa-constrictors and things. The police will eat out of his hand. And of course they're frightfully impressed with Porter's money. I made a statement!" she added, with relish. "I'll be in the newspapers tomorrow morning—with one of my photographs. We told them you were *much* too ill to be questioned to-night, but they'll be around early tomorrow morning. So come along and get a good night's rest."

"Come—where?"

"My dear, some fearful woman told Jammy that you left my house without a penny, and then I remembered.... And both Jammy and Porter went for me. I admit that I was a vile beast. But why didn't you remind me, darling?"

She put her arm about the girl and kissed her.

"I'm going to make up for it, every way I know!" she said. "Porter and I are going to give you the most *peerless* wedding-present—"

"I'm not thinking of getting married," said Di, with a faint smile.

"Oh, James told me!" said Angelina. "He wants the engagement announced before the trial."

"Angelina! No!"

"My dear, you must! Think how romantic—in the newspapers."

"Angelina, you can't see anything—romantic—in this terrible affair—"

"Darling," said Angelina, earnestly, "you haven't done anything awful, have you?"

"No. But think of the publicity—"

"Well, what of it?"

"Don't you realize how—disgraceful and—"

"My dear—chump," said Angelina, "you can't be disgraced by things that other people have done. You're trying to act like these people in French novels, when everybody has to commit suicide and break off their engagements because some member of the family has 'disgraced the name.' It *will* be trying and painful for you, but you are no more disgraced than if you'd been in a shipwreck. And you've got James and Porter and me to stand by you."

"Angelina, you don't understand—"

Then for the first time, Di could realize that Angelina was Fennel's sister. Across her radiant dark face came a look very like him, cool, steadfast and grave.

"Di," she said. "You've come to the crisis. You've been through fear and suffering and horror. And you've come through with courage and honesty. James told me. He thinks there never was anyone like you. Now look!"

She drew the girl to the window, and pulled aside the doctor's prim little curtains. The moon was going down behind a hill, the sky was still bright with the soft radiance; the Spring night was alive with exquisite promise.

"It's an awfully big world," said Angelina. "And it's so beautiful. You're just coming out of a horrible black hole. And now you've got to forget. It's all over. Now you've got to go forward."

"She's right, my dear!" said Doctor Coat's voice behind them.

"And now come on!" said Angelina, quickly dropping her serious air. "James is in the darlingest little hospital here, and we'll come out to see him to-morrow. Porter's waiting in the car. We're going to drive back to New York now—and eat. You look hideously thin. Come on, Di! It's over! We're all sorry for the terrible things that have happened—but they're done. James will be all right in a week or so. And you're going to be *happy*. Come on, Di!"

THE END

43070621R00157

Made in the USA
Middletown, DE
29 April 2017